The stranger called Springer spoke to them. "You see, there is nobody else. You saw the girl, you saw the eels. You are the only ones who truly believe. You were brought together by design, rather than by accident. Your destiny was laid out for you this morning. You have to find the beast, and find it quickly. You have to destroy it."

"What if we refuse? What if we don't want to have anything to do with it?"

Springer slowly shook his head. "You have no choice whatever, my dear sir. Because if you fail to find the beast, then the beast will almost certainly find you."

NIGHT WARRIORS

Look for all these TOR books by Graham Masterton

CONDOR
DEATH TRANCE
IKON
NIGHT WARRIORS
THE PARIAH
PICTURE OF EVIL
SACRIFICE
TENGU
WELLS OF HELL

NIGHT WARRIORS

GRAHAM MASTERTON

A TOM DOHERTY ASSOCIATES BOOK

NIGHT WARRIORS

Copyright © 1987 by Graham Masterton

Reprinted by arrangement with Wiescka Masterton

First printing: January 1987

A TOR Book

Published by Tom Doherty Associates, Inc.
49 West 24 Street
New York, N.Y. 10010

ISBN: 0-812-52185-4
CAN. ED.: 0-812-52186-2

Printed in the United States of America

0 9 8 7 6 5 4 3 2 1

For Tom and Barbara Doherty,
who never forget that tors are peaks, and
that peaks are there to be climbed.

"For one thousand years, Devils shall live in the dreams of men and hold dominion over the dark realms of the night. But then shall come a company whose name shall be the Night Warriors, and it shall be charged unto them to banish the Devils and to rid the darkness of all evil influences forever. And those who are Night Warriors shall be secret, and their names shall not be known. Nevertheless they shall be counted as the greatest heroes of any age, and they will be remembered in the chronicles of Ashapola for all eternity."

—*The Great Book of Darkness*, Chapter IX. Published by the Camden Society, 1844.

1

They approached the body on the beach as if their meeting had been preordained. Henry was the first to reach it and he hunkered down beside it but wouldn't touch it, while Gil and Susan walked cautiously closer and then stood silently watching, their bare toes half buried in the sand.

"No doubt that she's dead," Henry said in his clear, lecture-room voice. He brushed back his white windblown hair.

"I thought it was a dog at first," Gil said. "You know, an Afghan or something."

Henry stood up. "I guess we'd better call the police. There's nothing *we* can do."

Susan kept her arms folded close across her T-shirt and shivered.

Henry said, "Would you and this young man like to go call the police? I'll stay here and make sure nobody disturbs it." He hesitated, looked down at the body and then corrected himself by saying, "*Her.*"

Susan nodded and she and Gil jogged away across the beach. Henry remained where he was, his hands clasped behind his back, tall and stooped in the silvery mist of the early morning. Almost unseen, the gray Pacific roared in protest as the moon tugged it inch by inch from the shore, and seagulls shrieked like anxious women as they swooped for fish. It was April but it was chilly and the sea mist would probably envelop the coastline for most of the day.

Henry hadn't yet been to bed. He had been sitting in the study of his beach house all night, under the light from his brass-shaded lamp, working on his article for *Philosophy Today*: "The Concept of Life After Death," by Professor Henry Watkins. He had been writing in thumb-cramping longhand and rewarding himself after the completion of every page with a large vodka and tomato juice, and so at six o'clock he had taken a walk along the beach not only to clear his mind of ten centuries of philosophical morbidness but also to disperse the cumulative effects of twelve large Bloody Marys.

And here she was, lying dead on the sand, a naked young woman. Stark and direct proof that everything he had been writing all night was pretentious nonsense. He felt as if he had been almost fated to find her, as if stern gods had directed his footsteps this way to show him in the most jarring way possible just how ridiculous his theories were. Nobody can ridicule the living quite as effectively as the dead.

She was lying facedown, her bare skin covered in fine gray grit. Her long, blonde hair was ribboned with seaweed and fanned out on the beach like a mermaid's. One hand seemed to be clutching at the sand as if she had been trying to stop herself from being dragged out to sea again, as if to be drowned twice was more than she could endure. Her body was so white that in the pearly gray mist it was almost luminous.

Henry walked around her. Alone, he felt suddenly so sad for her that he found his throat was tightening and the sea wind was bringing tears to his eyes. Perhaps he was drunk, but she could have been any one of his philosophy students, she was so young. Although her face was hidden, she couldn't have been more than nineteen or twenty years old. She had a long, well-shaped back and wide-flared hips. There was a fine silver chain around her left ankle, the only jewelry she wore. The white, blue-veined curve of one half-exposed breast showed the kind of figure most men would turn around to look at twice.

The sea foamed briefly around her outstretched foot and then retreated, as if it sourly decided it had done enough.

Henry thrust his fists into the pockets of his fawn-colored windbreaker and deliberately turned away toward the cliffs. He had never had children of his own. His four-year marriage to a marine biologist from the Scripps Institute had been barren in every conceivable sense. He had learned to drink during that marriage, and he had also learned to be alone. Now he taught philosophy to successive waves of cheerful young men and women and occasionally played chess with his next-door neighbor, and that was sufficient to make him feel fulfilled. At least it was sufficient to stop him from taking two bottles of sleeping pills before going to bed with a copy of *Thus Spake Zarathustra*.

His students at UCLA San Diego called him Bing because of his faint resemblance to Bing Crosby. He had grown his hair long in an attempt to look more like Timothy Leary than Bing Crosby but the nickname had stuck.

After five minutes or so, Gil and Susan came back down the concrete ramp that led up to the parking lot and half-jogged, half-walked across the sloping beach.

"The police are on their way," Gil said breathlessly.

"Thank you," Henry acknowledged.

Susan said, "I never before saw anybody dead."

"She was young too," Henry remarked. "Nineteen, twenty."

They waited, uncomfortable and fidgety. There was no sound of a police siren yet. The sea kept on snarling and the seagulls fluttered silently against the wind.

Gil said flatly, "I was just jogging, you know? I really thought it was a dog at first."

Susan couldn't take her eyes from the body, from the fanned-out hair, the clutching hand and the shoulders sparkling with grit.

Gil was one of those young Southern California men who defy immediate classification. He could have been a student, an automobile mechanic, a bartender or anything at all. He was thin, tanned, with a narrow, serious face and a prominent, freckly nose. His hair was thick and dark, and now it was mussed up into a fright wig by the wind. He wore a navy-blue sweatshirt with "Crucial" stenciled on it in white, and chopped-off denim shorts.

Susan had all the hallmarks of the spoiled-but-rebellious daughter of a middle-class family. Her fair hair was cut short in spikes and she wore a white Italian-style T-shirt with red and green lightning flashes on it, and tight white-satin running shorts. She was plump-faced but pretty. Henry could see that in two or three years some very striking features would emerge from that teenage roundness. Her blue eyes were already large and dreamy-lidded like the eyes of those girls in the romance comics.

"I guess the police will want us to make statements," said Henry.

Now they could hear the *whip-whip-whip-whooo* of a distant police siren, followed by the wailing of an ambulance.

"What can we say?" asked Susan. "We simply found her here, that's all."

"That's all we have to say," Henry reassured her.

The police car drove down the ramp onto the beach and drew up only fifteen feet away. It was hotly pursued by an ambulance from the county coroner's office. Henry, Gil and Susan waited in silence as three detectives climbed out of the police car and two medics noisily dragged a folding stretcher from the back of the ambulance. A second police car arrived, slewing across the sand, and two uniformed officers hastily emerged.

The detectives came over and looked down at the body, their hands on their hips. Two of them were big-bellied and white, Tweedledum and Tweedledee; the third was as lean as an adolescent wolf, a dark-eyed Hispanic with a drooping black mustache and a cinnamon-colored three-piece suit that looked as if it had been chosen by his wife at Sears.

"Lieutenant Ortega," he announced himself. "These are Detectives Morris and Warburg."

"Henry Watkins," said Henry.

"And these young people?"

"We haven't had time to introduce ourselves."

"You don't know them?"

"This is the first time we ever met. I guess we all caught sight of the body at the same moment."

"Your name, please?" Lieutenant Ortega asked Gil.

"Gilbert Miller."

"And yours, young lady?"

"Susan Sczaniecka."

Lieutenant Ortega said over his shoulder, "You get those names?"

Detective Warburg replied, "No, sir."

Lieutenant Ortega let out a short, testy breath and went across to inspect the body. He stared at it for a long time and then walked around it, peering at it closely, bending down, not touching it.

"Any of you people know this girl's identity?" he asked.

"No," they replied. Henry felt strangely guilty that he didn't, but he supposed everybody felt the same when they were interviewed by the police.

"Looks like a straightforward drowning to me," said Detective Morris, clearing his throat as if he were about to give a recitation. "Kind of early in the year but the pattern's familiar. Skinny-dipping off Cardiff Beach, too much to drink, and there's a pretty sharp undertow there once you get out a ways. You get pulled out to sea, it's cold in April, you die of hypothermia in less than ten minutes, that's if you can swim. Then the tide brings you down here." He checked his watch. "Right on time, I'd say."

Lieutenant Ortega stood up. "You people were down on the shoreline exceptionally early," he said, waving his finger from Susan to Gil to Henry.

"I was jogging," Gil said. "I hurt my leg in a motorcycle accident last December. I have to jog a couple of hours each day to exercise it. Early morning is the only free time I get."

Lieutenant Ortega raised his eyebrows at Henry.

"I, um . . . I was working on a magazine article all night," Henry explained. "I live right up there . . . the cottage with the white-painted balcony. I finished around five-thirty, then decided to take a walk." He hoped Lieutenant Ortega couldn't smell his breath.

Lieutenant Ortega turned to Susan. "How about you?" he asked. "Exceptionally early to be down on the beach, wouldn't you say?"

Susan said, "Guess it is."

"So what were you doing here so early?"

"Walking, that's all. Thinking."

"You had a spat with your parents?"

"My parents are dead. I live with my grandparents."

"You had a spat with them?"

"I just went for a walk, that's all."

Lieutenant Ortega worried something out from between his front teeth with his thumbnail. Then he sucked at his teeth and said, "Okay. I want you all to make statements to my officers here, full statements. How you found this dead person, everything."

"Straightforward drowning," Detective Morris repeated.

At that moment two more cars arrived on the beach: a dilapidated Buick Regal and an olive-drab station wagon from the coroner's department.

"Ah, the photographer," said Lieutenant Ortega, rubbing his hands. "And the medical examiner too, remarkably prompt for a change."

The photographer was a dour young man with a monklike tonsure and a repetitive sniff. He began work right away, laying out measurement markers and then photographing the young woman's body from all sides. The medical examiner, a short, bullnecked man in a loud black-and-white houndstooth sportcoat, whistled tunelessly while he waited for the photographer to finish.

"Straightforward drowning, what do you think?" Detective Morris asked him.

The medical examiner stared at him. "Do *you* want to do the postmortem, or are you going to leave it to me?"

Detective Morris gave him a hesitant grin. "No, sir, you go right ahead."

"Can we turn her over now?" asked Lieutenant Ortega. "I'd like to see what she looks like."

The medical examiner didn't answer him but carefully brushed away the sand from the dead girl's shoulders and ran his hands down the length of her bare back. He stood up straight, frowned and then looked out along the beach.

"Do any of you know this beach well?" he asked thoughtfully.

"Yes, sir," said Detective Morris. "I've lived here just about all my life."

"Have you attended drownings here before?"

"Five or six."

"Can you recall how far up the beach those other five or six bodies were discovered?"

Detective Morris looked puzzled. "On the waterline, I guess, just like this one."

"Take a look at that washed-up weed and that other debris," the medical examiner told him. "See where it lies? Most of it's lighter than a body and far less bulky, yet it's way down the beach by comparison."

Lieutenant Ortega came forward and looked down at the body uneasily. "So what do you infer from that?" he asked.

"I don't know, I'm just making an observation," the medical examiner replied.

"You observe that the body is lying farther up the beach than the seaweed and the logs and the other trash?"

"That's correct."

Lieutenant Ortega sucked at his teeth again. "You observe that the body is lying farther up the beach than the seaweed and the other trash, and from this observation you conclude that the girl was not drowned at all but that she died in some other way and was left on the beach, either by accident or with the deliberate intention of making it appear as if she had drowned?"

"You said it, not me," replied the medical examiner, palpating the dead girl's right leg and noting his finger marks. He motioned and one of the gum-chewing medics brought him his medical case and opened it for him. He rummaged around inside it until he found his thermometer, which he lubricated and then unceremoniously inserted into the body's anus. "If she's been floating around in the ocean all night, the probability is that her body temperature will be far lower than if she's been lying on the beach. That will depend on when she died of course, but this beach is pretty well crowded right up until sundown, isn't that true?"

"Yes, sir," Detective Morris agreed. "Sometimes well after sundown too, when the kids have cookouts."

The medical examiner waited patiently for the girl's body temperature to take effect on the thermometer. Meanwhile he looked up at Henry, Gil and Susan and asked, "Who are these people? Gawkers or what?"

"These people found the body," said Lieutenant Ortega.

The medical examiner asked Henry, "Ever see anybody dead on this beach before?"

Henry shook his head.

"Fine way to start the day, finding a body," the medical examiner remarked as casually as if he were discussing the weather. He withdrew the thermometer carefully and frowned at it. "Sixty-one degrees."

"And what does that mean?" asked Lieutenant Ortega.

"It means that the temperature inside the body is sixty-one degrees," said the medical examiner.

"But what do you conclude?"

"Conclude? I don't conclude anything. It's up to you to make the conclusions. But you could take into consideration the fact that the air temperature here is something like fifty-five or fifty-six degrees and that the ocean temperature is something like forty-two to forty-eight degrees."

"So if the body had been floating in the water all night, her body temperature would have been lower than sixty-one degrees?" said Lieutenant Ortega.

"Possibly," the medical examiner replied.

Lieutenant Ortega let out another of his short, testy breaths. "All right," he said. "Now can we turn her over?"

The medical examiner stood up and fastidiously brushed the sand from the knees of his pants. As he did so, the two medics came forward and positioned themselves on either side of the body. Henry, watching, was gripped by an irrational feeling of dread and he had the strongest urge to turn and look the other way. Somehow, however, he found that he couldn't, that he had to watch. Otherwise the girl on the beach would remain faceless forever and when he dreamed about her at night, which he inevitably would, he would see nothing but that mermaid hair tangled with weed and that long, pale back.

"Be careful," the medical examiner instructed the medics. "I don't want any extra bruising."

He came over and stood next to Henry, Gil and Susan. "You didn't touch her or try to move her?"

Henry shook his head. "I don't think I would have had the nerve."

Susan ventured, "Do you suppose that somebody might have killed her? I mean, on purpose?"

The medical examiner pulled a face. "Girls of this age are always susceptible to being killed either on purpose or accidentally, or else through carelessness. Pretty girls especially. They have more power than they know. Their youth and their looks give them power. The trouble is, they never know how to use it. Not safely anyway."

With exaggerated care the two medics eased the girl's body out of the sand and rolled her onto her back. Her arm fell against the wet beach with a slapping sound and one of the medics gasped, "Jesus Christ!"

Henry stared but at first he couldn't understand what he was staring at. The medical examiner moved forward at once and stood over the body, his face disassembled into no recognizable expression. Fear? Horror? Fascination? The two medics took a step back, one of them holding his hand over his mouth and looking watery-eyed. Lieutenant Ortega had been standing with his back to the body, talking to

Morris and Warburg, but then Warburg nudged him and he turned around and saw what the girl really looked like.

Her face was almost beautiful in spite of the fact that it was swollen by the sea. A classic blonde with classic American bone structure, the sort of girl who could easily have found herself an acting part in *Matt Houston* or *Magnum, P.I.*, or even *Dynasty*. Wide-shouldered, large-breasted, but beneath her rib cage the horror began. Henry, suddenly understanding what he was looking at, whispered, "Oh, God," and Susan buried her face in her hands.

The girl's abdomen had been completely ripped out from her ribs to her pelvis, and inside her abdominal cavity scores of silvery-black eels were writhing, a tumultuous nest of slithering creatures twining and untwining themselves, blindly feeding on what was left of the girl's softer organs.

Gil turned away, buckled at the knees, crouched on the sand and retched. The policemen stared in alarm and helplessness, and the photographer even crossed himself. For minutes on end there was nothing any of them could do but stare at the knotted tangle of eels and the pale, emotionless face of the girl.

The medical examiner turned to Lieutenant Ortega with wide eyes. "Ever see anything like that, ever?"

Lieutenant Ortega shook his head abruptly.

"Me neither," said the medical examiner. Then he turned to the medics and said, "Get rid of those things."

The medics looked unhappily down at the body. "You mean . . . ?"

"Whatever they are. Those eels. Those snakes. Get them out of there."

One of the medics picked up a stick from the beach and approached the body gingerly. He leaned forward and prodded the eels with the tip of it. Immediately the eels wriggled and twisted even more furiously and the medic jumped back with a high-pitched "*aah!*" of irrepressible disgust.

The medical examiner impatiently took the stick from him and circled around the body himself. While everybody watched him with flesh-crawling apprehension, he prodded the eels two or three times and each time they boiled in the dead girl's stomach with the same slippery fury. Suddenly, however, the medical examiner managed to hook the end of the stick underneath one of them and flip it out onto the beach.

The eel was almost three feet long and had a flat, chisel-shaped head and tiny blind eyes. It flapped and writhed on the surface for a while, then burrowed its head into the sand and disappeared. Almost immediately the remaining eels poured out of the girl's pelvis and scattered in all directions, burying themselves deep into the sand.

"Catch one!" the medical examiner shouted urgently.

One of the uniformed policemen snatched at the tail of the last eel to disappear and tugged at it furiously.

"Give me a hand, for chrissake!" he gasped to his partner, who came hurrying across and gripped the eel's body nearer to the sand, and between them, cursing and grunting, they gradually managed to drag the creature backward out of the hole it had been burrowing for itself.

As soon as its head was clear, though, the eel lashed, looped and twisted wildly in the air. Henry saw its teeth flicker. Then it wriggled like a whip and caught one of the policemen in the face, clamping its jaws over his upper lip and part of his nose. The policeman shrieked and snatched at the eel's head, trying to prize its jaws apart. Henry watched in horror as the man danced around on the sand, the silvery-black eel clamped to his face like a carnival nose. Bright-red blood began to sprinkle all around them.

Lieutenant Ortega dodged forward and seized the officer from behind, tripping him so they both fell heavily to the ground. The policeman was screaming wildly and thrashing his legs. Lieutenant Ortega reached around to the officer's face and clutched the eel behind its chisel-shaped head, squeezing the gills closed so the creature would be unable to breathe. Then he held up his free hand and yelled, "Knife, for God's sake!"

The medical examiner hurriedly dug into his pockets and came up with a single-bladed clasp knife. Lieutenant Ortega snatched it from him and then cut into the welter of blood in front of the policeman's face. The man screamed again and again while Lieutenant Ortega sawed through the eel's body. The eel's blood spurted out dark, like bile, and splattered Ortega's hands and arms. Its tail lashed furiously from side to side until the last moment, when Ortega cut its spinal column and flung its body across the sand. The headless body lay twitching and jerking and the medics cautiously stepped away from it.

The medical examiner knelt down and examined the policeman closely. The man was shivering and trembling, and Lieutenant Ortega was trying to soothe him. The eel's severed head was still gripping the man's face and when the medical examiner quickly dabbed away the blood with cotton and distilled water, he could see that the creature's teeth had already detached half of the nostrils and most of his upper lip. The eel's jaw muscles showed no signs of relaxing and it was plain that any attempt to pull its head away would make the injury more severe than it already was.

Henry came up and although he was trembling, he said as steadily as he could, "You know what they used to do in Viet Nam to get the leeches off them?"

"That's right," said the medical examiner. "They used to burn them off with lighted cigarettes. Does anyone here have a cigarette?"

They looked at each other. In the end, Detective Warburg said, "Nobody smokes, sir."

"Jesus," said the medical examiner. "Southern California."

"Perhaps a cigarette lighter from one of the cars," Henry suggested.

Detective Morris jogged off to the nearest car and came

back with a glowing cigarette lighter held up in his hand. He gave it to the medical examiner, who immediately touched it against the eel's raw neck.

There was a sharp sizzle, a sickly odor of burning, but then the eel's jaws clamped convulsively and bit away the whole of the policeman's upper lip and nostrils, dropping onto the ground in a sudden spurt of blood. The man let out a tight, choked shriek, his upper teeth hideously exposed, and Lieutenant Ortega had to wrestle him down against the sand.

"Plasma!" the medical examiner shouted. "And you!" he ordered the injured man's partner, "take that head and cut the damn thing in half, and get your buddy's face out of its mouth!"

It took the medics less than five minutes to bandage the policeman's face and set him up on a plasma drip. While they worked, the other officer took a pair of bolt cutters out of the trunk of the patrol car and nudged the eel's head around on the sand so he could position it between the blades. He tried twice to cut it in half but each time the head slipped out. Then Gil came forward and rested the head against the toe of his shoe so it wouldn't roll away. There was a sharp, crisp crunch and the eel's skull was chopped apart. The medical examiner stooped down and extracted the bloody rag of flesh the creature had wrenched off the policeman's face.

"I want that bastard in a plastic bag," he told Detective Morris. "Head, tail and anything else you can find."

Lieutenant Ortega looked at his watch. "It's almost seven. Let's get this beach cordoned off. Warburg, call for some backup. I want a digging detail. If those eels killed that girl, I want them dug out and destroyed. I want the coast guard alerted too. They'll probably want to put up a temporary ban on swimming. Morris, you go along with the M.E. I want the fastest postmortem in the history of the world."

"Is there anything we can do?" Henry asked.

Lieutenant Ortega stared at Henry as if he had never seen him before. "You? Oh, you can go home. Give your name and address to Detective Morris here, he'll come and talk to you later. And please don't leave the area, not until you've made your statement. And please don't talk to the newspapers or the television. This is one of those situations that cause panic, you understand me? I'd rather we kept the whole thing quiet just for now."

Henry said to Gil and Susan, "That's it. I guess we can leave."

Susan was very pale. "I think I'm going to faint," she said.

"Sit down for a moment," Henry told her. "Put your head between your knees."

While they waited for Susan to recover, Henry looked across the beach at the body of the girl. From where he was crouching next to Susan, he was unable to see the gaping cavity of her stomach and the girl could have been lying serene and naked in the mist, waiting for the sun to break through. She was really quite beautiful, Henry thought, and somehow that made her death seem even more horrifying.

"I'm all right now," Susan said. She tried to get up and Gil gave her his arm.

Henry was watching the medics lift the girl's body off the beach and zipper it into a body bag. Against the mist, the figures looked like an oriental shadow play. "I never saw anything like that in my life," he said. "Those eels—did you ever see anything like that? And I used to be married to a marine biologist."

They walked up the beach together. When they reached the boardwalk, Henry suggested, "Come and have a drink. That's my cottage right over there. I expect you could use something to settle your nerves."

"I think I want to get home, thank you," Susan said. She glanced back at the beach, her eyes staring with repressed hysteria.

Gil asked her gently, "Where do you live? I could take you."

"Do you have a car?"

"Sure, that Mustang convertible right across the street."

"Okay then. Thank you."

They walked off together, leaving Henry standing alone. After a while he shrugged and walked the sixty yards back to his cottage, unlocking the door with the key he always kept on a loop of string around his wrist. He went through to the living room, opened the glass-fronted cocktail cabinet and poured himself a large vodka, straight up, no ice.

He coughed as the vodka burned its way down his throat. Then he filled his glass again and walked over to the wide sliding doors that led to the balcony. He could see the police cars from here, with their flashing lights, and Lieutenant Ortega in his cinnamon-colored suit. Farther down the beach, toward Del Mar, two uniformed policemen were already dragging trestles marked "Police Line—Do Not Cross" over the beach.

Henry watched the police activity for almost twenty minutes. Then he went back into the cottage, sat down on the white-painted bamboo sofa and stared at himself in the shiny glass door of the stereo cabinet on the opposite side of the room.

Life after death? The only life in that poor girl had been those wriggling eels, and what kind of life did they represent?

He thought about the morning's events, and all he could see was a series of frightening still pictures. The girl's hand clutching the beach. The silver chain on her ankle. The whiteness of her back. Then the eels in their complicated Chinese-puzzle pattern. And the severed head of that single captured eel, gripping the policeman's face like an ancient symbol of evil persistence.

He finished his third glass of vodka and then tilted across to the cocktail cabinet to drain the bottle into his glass.

"*Stolichnaya*," he pronounced with what he liked to think was a thick Russian accent. Then, "*Zadrovya.*"

With inebriated care he went to the bookshelf under the window at the end of the room and ran his finger along the spines of the marine books his less-than-dear departed wife had left behind. At last he came across a large illustrated volume entitled *Anguilliformes: Migration and Life Cycles of Common Eels*. He tugged it out, took it over to the coffee table and opened it.

It was the quotation on the opening page that caught his attention first: "The eel was eaten in olden times because it was thought to give exceptional potency. In certain parts of ancient Scandinavia, shoals of eels were described by a single mystical word that meant 'sperm of the Devil.'"

Henry was about to take another drink but he paused and read the quotation again. Then he looked toward the balcony, out toward the beach beyond, and frowned.

— 2 —

Gil and Susan said little as they drove back to Del Mar Heights Road, where Susan lived. Gil glanced across at her from time to time and he could see that she was still shocked. He was queasy himself, thinking about those eels writhing silvery-black in that woman's white body and that policeman's face half bitten off.

When Susan said, "Here—here it is," Gil turned the shiny yellow Mustang up the steeply angled concrete driveway and cut the motor. He hopped out of the car without opening the door and went around to let Susan out.

"This your grandparents' place?" he asked. It was a small, Mexican-style house with a balcony overlooking the garden and rows of pink-painted arches. Three lizards watched them from the clay-tiled roof, blinking in prehistoric small-mindedness. Outside the back door there were six or seven recently watered azaleas in terra-cotta pots, and white-painted wicker rocking chairs.

"Thank you for driving me home," Susan said. "I felt really nauseous."

"You're welcome," Gil told her. He nodded and smiled but made no move to get back into the car.

Susan glanced behind her. "I'd invite you in but . . . well, my grandparents are kind of old-fashioned. They'd want to know everything about what happened, you know, and right now I just don't feel like talking about it."

Gil scuffed his trainers on the concrete driveway. "You're going to want to talk about it sooner or later. You're going to have to."

She stood with her hand on the wrought-iron balcony rail, looking at him with one of those distinctively teenage expressions—bored, curious, go-on-show-me—her eyes in shadow. They could hear a vacuum cleaner ruminating from room to room inside the house and a television turned up

17

loud so that whoever was using the vacuum cleaner could listen to *Josie and the Pussycats*.

"Could I call by later?" Gil asked.

"Well, I don't know," Susan answered. She turned toward the house. "I mean, no offense or anything, but I really want to forget it."

"I'll tell you what," Gil suggested. "I'll leave you my number and if you want to talk about it, you can call me. Or even if you *don't* want to talk about it, I don't mind."

Susan thought for a moment and then said, "Okay. But I have to go in now."

"Do you have a pencil?"

She picked up a piece of chalk from the flower bed. "I'll write it with this."

"Okay, then. It's seven five five, nine eight five eight."

"Where's that?"

"Solana Beach, on The Boardwalk. My father owns the Mini-Market."

"Oh, really? Okay then."

At that moment Susan's grandmother came out of the house, a small, porky woman with strawberry-sherbet hair done up in curlers and wearing a strawberry-colored track suit.

"Susan?" she said querulously. "You came back quick."

"Oh, Gil here gave me a lift."

"Gil?" demanded her grandmother, lifting up the gold-framed glasses she wore suspended around her neck on a long gilded chain.

"Gil Miller, ma'am," Gil said, giving her a wave. "Nice to meet you."

"Have I seen you before?" Susan's grandmother wanted to know.

"Could be, ma'am. My father owns the Mini-Market down at Solana Beach. Sometimes I serve behind the deli counter."

Susan's grandmother lowered her glasses and allowed her face to subside into a soft puddle of disapproval. "Susan's dating a medical student from Scripps," she told Gil. "A fine boy with a fine career in front of him. Irish."

Gil said, "Well, ma'am, that's excellent," even though he could see that Susan was desperately embarrassed. He waved his hand again, an odd Howdy-Doody kind of wave that he hadn't meant to use at all, and then he swung back into the car and started the engine.

"Grandma," Susan protested under her breath. Then she called out, "Thanks for the ride, Gil."

"Yeah. You're welcome," he said and backed down the driveway.

Susan watched him turn around in the road, all screaming torque and squealing tires, and roar off back toward the beach. Then she followed her grandmother into the house, making sure the screen door banged noisily behind her. In the kitchen her grandfather looked up from his *San Diego Tribune* and said, "Your friend Daffy's here."

"Yes, and I was ashamed to let her into your room," her grandmother admonished her. "The mess! I never saw anything like it. You have drawers for your clothes, don't you, and shelves for your books?"

"Oh, Grandma, I can't keep everything immaculate the way you do."

"It's a state of mind," her grandmother told her. "If your mind is tidy, your house is tidy. Goodness knows what Daffy thinks of you."

"Daffy thinks I'm very neat. You should see her room. World War Eight isn't in it."

Her grandmother hovered by the doorway. Susan, sensing she was torn between going back to her vacuum cleaning and broaching the subject of Gil Miller, went over to the refrigerator and poured herself a large glass of Mountain Spring water, topping it with ice cubes. She drank almost the whole glass without taking a breath.

"That boy," said her grandmother. "You won't be seeing him again, will you?"

"Is there any reason I shouldn't?"

"Well, what will Carl say?"

"Grandma, it's none of Carl's goddamned business."

"Suzie," put in her grandfather, taking off his half-glasses, "in this house we don't use words like that."

"Well, it's none of Carl's blank-censored business then. Grandma, we're not even dating."

"You should be. He's a very well-mannered young man."

"I know but I don't happen to like him. And anyway, he's not Irish, he's Armenian."

"His mother is half Irish."

Susan closed her eyes and leaned against the refrigerator, and her grandmother knew there was no point in nagging anymore. Her grandfather shrugged and smiled. "She'll find somebody nice, don't worry about it. The whole planet is wall to wall with eligible young men."

"It's these boys from the beach, that's all," Susan's grandmother complained. "These surfers. One day some surfer is going to make her pregnant and then what? It's a responsibility, bringing up your own daughter's child. Sometimes I think it's too much."

Susan opened her eyes. "Grandma," she said, "I am not going to get pregnant by any surfer."

Her grandmother shook her head and went off to finish her vacuum cleaning. Every morning she vacuum-cleaned for at least two hours and watched television at the same time. Those were her two principal obsessions in life: cleaning the house and watching TV.

Susan's grandfather held out his hand and hooked his arm around Susan's waist.

"You'll find somebody, you wait and see. You're young yet, you haven't even finished your education."

"Grampa, I'm not actually panicking to get married," Susan told him. Unannounced, unwanted, a vision of the dead girl on the beach suddenly flashed in front of her eyes. White breasts coated in grit. Squirming eels. She pulled herself away from her grandfather, went to the sink to rinse out her glass and stood there for a moment to steady herself.

"You all right?" her grandfather asked.

"Sure, I'm all right."

"You look like you're upset. Your mother used to look like that when she was upset. Kind of chalky, know what I mean? Wasn't anything to do with that boy, was it?"

"It's not morning sickness if that's what you're trying to suggest."

"Well, I wasn't," said her grandfather, offended.

He glanced toward the hallway, where Susan's grandmother was vacuum-cleaning in surge after surge of roaring decibels, and then he stood up, came over to the sink and laid his hand on Susan's shoulder. He was short and tubby like Susan's grandmother, but unlike her grandmother, he was quite content to look his age, which was sixty-six. His bald head was varnished like a candy apple from hours of sitting out in his rocking chair and watching the bouncy golden schoolgirls go by.

"Your grandma means well," he told her in a low voice.

Susan nodded. "Yes, I know."

"She's only trying to keep you from making a mistake."

"Yes, I know."

He didn't know what else to say. He fiddled with the cuff of his droopy gray cardigan. Then he shrugged, went and sat down and picked up his paper again, although he kept his eyes on Susan. The newspaper headlines warned of more earth tremors, mainly centered in Tijuana.

Susan went across the hall to her bedroom. Her grandmother looked up from her vacuum cleaning with a hurt, impatient expression but Susan tried to ignore her. It wasn't *her* fault that she had to live here and just as soon as she could, she was going to move out. She briefly glimpsed the dead girl's face again and somehow it became tangled up with her mother's face, crushed and lopsided after the accident. She opened her bedroom door with the flat of her hand.

Daffy was sprawled across Susan's bed, her legs kicked up, engrossed in *Cosmopolitan*.

"Oh, hi, Suze. You're early. Did you read this thing about the sponge?"

Susan went straight across to her dresser and brushed her hair before the mirror. Her grandfather had been right: She did look chalky.

Daffy turned over and said, "It says here that it's only seventy percent safe."

Susan frowned at herself in the mirror. "What is?"

"The sponge, deaf ears. Can you imagine that? Seventy percent. That means for every hundred times you make love, you get pregnant thirty times. My God, I'll have ninety children before I'm eighteen."

Susan found that she was crying. Silently but bitterly, so that the tears ran down her cheeks and dripped around the sides of her mouth. Daffy didn't notice at first and went on reading, but then Susan let out a high-pitched sob.

Daffy jumped off the bed. "Suze, what's the matter? What's happened?" Outside the door, the vacuum cleaner was still roaring and banging at the baseboards. "It's not *her* again, is it?"

Susan shook her head, dragged two tissues out of the box on her dresser and noisily blew her nose. Then she dragged out another one and wiped her eyes. "I don't know what it is. It's probably nothing, just my period."

"I was going to ask if you wanted to come to my house. We're having a barbecue and some of the kids from Escondido are coming over."

"I don't know. I feel kind of weird."

"Weird? Why?"

"It's . . . I don't know, it's something that happened down on the beach. I'm trying not to think about it but it won't go away."

She sat down on the edge of the bed and Daffy sat down beside her. "Well?" Daffy asked with incandescent curiosity.

Susan dabbed at her eyes again. "I'm not sure I can tell you."

"Was it a boy? You weren't raped, were you? You definitely look like you could have been raped."

"It wasn't anything like that."

"Then what, for Christ's sake?"

Outside the door, the vacuum cleaner suddenly whined to a stop. There was silence, even the television had been turned off, and both girls listened in case Susan's grandmother had heard Daffy take the name of the Lord in vain. Susan's grandmother prayed in front of the television every Sunday morning with Dr. Howard C. Estep, who sternly disapproved of anyone taking the name of the Lord in vain.

Susan whispered, "I saw a body, a dead body."

"You're kidding!"

"No, I am not kidding. It was a girl, she was drowned or something. The police were there, and the ambulance and everything."

"Oh, my God," Daffy said, shocked and sympathetic but still desperate to hear all the details. "You must have been absolutely paralyzed! I mean, what was she like? I never saw a dead body."

"Daffy," Susan said in an uncontrolled voice, "she had *eels* in her stomach, where her stomach was supposed to be, and they were eating her."

Daffy stared in shock. "Eels! You're kidding! Oh, my God, that's absolutely disgusting! What did you do? Were you sick?"

Susan couldn't speak. She kept seeing those eels twisting and wriggling underneath the dead girl's rib cage. She clasped her hands over her eyes and forced herself to cry, her chest heaving, her throat clenched, trying to wrench out of herself all the fright and the horror, trying to exorcize all the nightmares she knew would come crowding in on her come nightfall.

She had dreamed for months of her mother's distorted face; she knew she would dream about the girl on the beach forever.

Daffy put her arms around Susan and held her close,

shushing her, rocking her gently back and forth as if she were a small child. In the hallway, the vacuum cleaner started up again and began to harvest the dust next to the living-room door. Although Daffy was younger than Susan by four months and two days, she was much more mature. She was a tall, skinny, brown-skinned girl with masses of curly brunette hair and one of those pouting, provocative mouths that every senior in high school dreamed of kissing. She had wanted to write to Hugh Hefner and offer herself as Playmate of the Month but her mother, although she was broad-minded, had said no. Her mother had brought up Daffy on her own. Daffy's father had gone to work on the oil pipeline in Alaska and had never quite managed to come back and so Daffy's mother was generally not in favor of the male exploitation of women. She had brought up Daffy to be pretty and suspicious and worldly wise, not to take rides from strangers and to take the pill.

Susan stopped crying as suddenly as she had begun and sat quietly in Daffy's arms, looking around the room.

"Are you okay now?" Daffy asked.

"I guess. I wasn't really crying. It was just thinking about it. That poor girl, you know, all gnawed away by eels. And one of the eels bit a cop too, right in the face."

"What were they, some kind of man-eating eels? What do they call them, moray eels? There was one in that movie. You know that movie with Nick Nolte? Anyway, it bit some guy's head off. Don't you think Jerry looks like Nick Nolte, if he had a mustache, I mean?"

Susan stood up and mechanically took off her T-shirt and her running shorts so that she was naked except for her socks. She dropped her shirt and shorts onto the floor next to yesterday's skirt and a copy of *Rolling Stone*, which she had been cutting up for pictures of Bruce Springsteen, and her badminton racquet, and her broken hair-dryer, and the sleeve of her new Eurythmics' album.

"Are you sure you're okay?" Daffy asked worriedly.

Susan nodded. Her eyes were still reddened and watery.

"I just want to go take a shower. Then we'll go over to your place."

Daffy waited while Susan went to the bathroom. She paced up and down for a while, nudging with her sneakers at discarded clothes and dismembered magazines. Then she went to the window and looked out into the yard, a small paved area with flower beds and a stone fountain that rarely worked. It was a hot, clear day, and lizards were poised in the shadows of the undergrowth.

From here it was possible to see a small part of the street and Daffy's attention was caught by a young man in a black sportcoat and white tennis slacks sitting on the wall outside the house, smoking a cigarette. He looked as if he were waiting for somebody because every now and then he lifted his wrist and Daffy could see a spark of reflected light from the face of his watch. His eyes were masked with impenetrably dark sunglasses.

She watched him for almost five minutes. Cars passed on both sides of the street but nobody stopped for him, and it occurred to Daffy that he wasn't watching for any particular car either. He remained where he was, never turning his head, smoking and occasionally checking the time.

She turned away from the window and suddenly realized that Susan had stayed in the shower for a long time. She walked through to the hallway, where Susan's grandmother was now burnishing her collection of brass figurines of Mexican dancers, and down to the bathroom.

"Is Susan going to your barbecue?" Susan's grandmother asked, busily flapping her duster.

"She said she would," Daffy replied. She hesitated by the bathroom door and then knocked. "Susan? Are you okay?"

"She's taking a shower," Susan's grandmother said testily. "Of course I've just cleaned up the bathroom. Now what am I going to get, soap all over the tiles and hair in the drainpipe? Not to mention wet towels all over the floor. She really has to be the messiest girl ever."

"Susan?" Daffy repeated.

"Go on in," said Susan's grandmother. "She probably can't hear you because of the water."

Daffy opened the door and peered into the bathroom. The shower was clattering loudly and the room was clouded with steam.

"Susan?" she called again and stepped inside. For some reason she began to feel frightened and she suddenly thought of the story Susan had told her. The dead girl eaten by eels, the policeman whose face had been half bitten off. The glass door of the shower stall was obscured with steam, although Daffy thought she could make out a pink shape on the other side of it that must be Susan.

Her throat was constricted with alarm. Slowly she approached the shower and knocked tentatively at the glass. "Susan? Suze? Are you okay?"

At that moment there was a hair-raising moan, and Daffy jumped away from the shower and whispered, "Oh, Jesus." But then the moan was followed by an anguished, suppressed sobbing, and Daffy slid back the shower door to find Susan crouched in a huddle, her legs drawn up, her hands clutched over her head, shivering and weeping with delayed shock.

Daffy turned off the faucet, reached over to the towel rack and dragged a large bath towel from it, which she wrapped around Susan's shoulders.

"Susan, come on, you're upset, that's all. Susan, it's Daffy. Come on, baby, let's get you out of here."

Susan numbly and shakily allowed Daffy to lift her and half-carry her out of the bathroom. They encountered Susan's grandmother as they came down the hallway, and for a split second her grandmother was going to protest about Susan's wet feet on the carpet, but then she saw how white Susan was, and how distressed, and how determined the challenge was on Daffy's face.

"What on earth's the matter?"

"She fainted, that's all. Her period." For some reason

Daffy was reluctant to tell Susan's grandmother about the body on the beach. Between them they helped Susan into her bedroom and quickly dried her off. Susan's grandmother searched through the untidy heaps of clothes in the drawers until she found a striped nightshirt, which Daffy pulled over Susan's head.

"Maybe I ought to call Dr. Emanuel," Susan's grandmother said anxiously.

Susan opened her eyes. Her fragmented thoughts were beginning to slide back into place again, like the film of a car-bomb explosion being played slowly in reverse. She found that she could focus once more and that sounds coagulated into words. She recognized Daffy sitting on the end of the bed and smiling at her. She recognized her grandmother peering at her from a safe distance through her gold-framed glasses, as if worried that whatever Susan was suffering from might be contagious.

"Did I faint?" Susan asked, with a dry mouth. "I thought I was someplace else."

Daffy squeezed her hand. "You're okay now. You'll live. But you gave me a scare, I can tell you. Would you like some coffee?"

Susan nodded. "That would be great."

Her grandmother said, "I'll fix it," pleased to have something to do that didn't involve actual nursing. She fretted endlessly about her own ailments but was totally squeamish when other people were sick. She wobbled off to the kitchen in her bright-pink track suit, leaving the door open.

Daffy told Susan, "Get under the blanket. You need to keep warm."

Susan said, "I'm okay now. Really."

"It must have been shock, you know, from seeing that body."

Susan shook her head. Her hair was tangled and wet. "It was kind of like shock but there was something else too. I don't know how to describe it. I thought I could hear somebody's voice, loud and echoing. Then I was traveling very fast. It was like I was in a helicopter or something, speeding over the surface of the sea. It went so fast I couldn't keep my balance and I fell down. The next thing I knew, I was back here with you."

"Shock," Daffy pronounced. "Now, will you keep warm? The Pink Panther's going to be bringing you some coffee in a second."

It took Susan a little over a half-hour to stop shivering. Then she dressed slowly, in a green T-shirt and white pedal-pushers, and combed out her hair.

"You're sure you're going to be okay?" Daffy kept asking her. "I mean, you don't have to come to the barbecue if you don't want to. I won't be offended."

"Daffy, I *want* to come. I'm not an invalid."

"You just take good care of yourself," her grandmother instructed.

"Yes, you take good care," her grandfather echoed.

They left the house and walked down the sloping driveway in the hot mid-morning sunshine. Daffy lived a ten-minute walk away in one of the new houses on Jimmy Durante Boulevard. Usually she borrowed her mother's Seville to drive around in but this morning her mother had gone to her beautician in La Jolla to have her hair jacked up another inch, as Daffy put it.

They had almost reached the intersection with the main road when a man's clear voice behind them said, "Pardon me, are you Susan Sczaniecka?"

The girls turned around. Daffy saw it was the man who had been sitting on the wall outside Susan's grandparents' house. He was tall—taller than Daffy had thought—with dark, wavy hair. He took off his sunglasses and both girls had to admit to themselves that he was undeniably good-looking. Thin-faced, brown-eyed, with one of those slightly amused expressions that can make most young girls feel both excited and at ease.

"Didn't I see you sitting on the wall?" Daffy asked in a

tone that meant the man ought to establish his credentials before either she or Susan would start talking to him.

"Sure you did. I was waiting for you to come out."

"Why didn't you call at the door?" asked Susan.

"I didn't want to disturb your grandparents, that's all. You know what they're like."

Susan frowned. "Sure I know what they're like. But how do *you* know what they're like?"

"It's my job. I'm a newspaper reporter. Here—here's my card. Paul Springer, *San Diego Tribune*."

"You're really a reporter?" Daffy asked, squinting at the card.

"Sure. Why else do you think I've been staking out Susan's grandparents' house?"

"To rape us?" Daffy suggested.

"You don't have to sound so hopeful," grinned Paul.

Susan handed back the card. "Is this about what happened on the beach this morning?"

Paul gave her a reserved glance. "Kind of. That's part of it."

"How did you know about that? The police said they were keeping it out of the media."

Paul continued smiling and shook his head. "If the police had their way, everything would be kept out of the media. Except successful drug busts of course, and police baseball-team scores."

"I don't really have anything to say about it," Susan told him. "I didn't see any more than anybody else did."

"It was pretty horrifying, wasn't it?" Paul asked.

Daffy butted in. "My friend here doesn't actually want to talk about it, you know? She was very sick this morning because of what happened. So, you know, do you mind? We're on our way home and we'd just like to get on with it."

But Susan said, "Come on, Daffy, it's okay. He's not bothering me."

"May I walk along?" asked Paul.

They continued north along Camino del Mar, between the rustling yuccas, waving occasionally to friends hanging out beside the bars and hotels and stores along the strip. One group was gathered around a VW Beetle that had just been sprayed in ruby metallic flake and decorated with airbrushed pictures of surfers and Western heroes. There was a strong scent of marijuana in the air, mingled with piña-colada suntan lotion.

Paul seemed straight enough, yet Susan felt there was something strange about him, something almost unreal. When he spoke, she felt she could anticipate everything he was going to say, and in a peculiar way she felt that she had met him before, although she couldn't remember where. It didn't seem to be necessary to get to know him; they talked from the very beginning as if they were longtime acquaintances.

"I've been assigned by the *Tribune* to write a series of feature articles on young people," Paul said. "Each of the articles is supposed to cover a different aspect of the way young people think and react. I guess you might call it a kind of psychoanalysis of youth. Well, it sounds like pretty corny stuff but I think that if it's written and researched properly, it doesn't have to be corny. In fact, I think it could be really enlightening."

"You want to write about *me*?" asked Susan, more curious than flattered.

"Well—to come straight to the point—one of the articles has to do with death and how young people cope with it."

"How do you mean?" Susan asked.

"I mean, how do young people come to terms with losing somebody they love? Their parents maybe, like you did—"

"How did you know that?"

"I'm sorry. I thought I recognized your name when the police passed me the list of witnesses to what happened down there on the beach. I looked you up in the morgue. Your parents were killed in a car crash, weren't they, over at Lake Hodges?"

Susan nodded. "I didn't realize I was quite so famous," she said, not without a touch of bitterness, although she knew Paul hadn't meant to upset her.

"The thing is," Paul continued, "you not only lost your parents, but today you saw a complete stranger lying dead on the beach. It would be interesting to compare your reaction to each of these events. The death of someone you loved and the death of someone you didn't even know. I'd like to know how you really felt then and how you feel now."

"Isn't that pretty ghoulish?" Daffy demanded.

"Well, maybe it is," Paul admitted, "and if Susan doesn't want to have anything to do with it, that's as far as it goes. But death is a part of life and there isn't any point in trying to hide from it. I think that other young people—if they read about Susan and how she's handled those trage-dies—well, they may find it easier to cope with their own experiences of death."

Daffy pulled a face. "Sounds like bull to me, if you'll pardon my French."

But Susan said, "I don't know. Maybe we could talk about it some more."

"Maybe this evening?" Paul asked. "Supposing I buy you dinner, on the *Trib*."

"Okay then. Where?"

"You know Bully's North? I'll meet you there at seven."

Susan thought about it and then nodded yes. "Okay. The only thing is, I have to be home at nine-thirty. That's the house rule."

"I know," said Paul.

Daffy was frowning ferociously with her "for-Christ's-sake-be-careful" face. But Susan, without knowing why, felt safe with Paul, and reassured. She didn't even think to ask him how he could possibly have known she had to be home by half past nine.

"I left my car at the Oceanside Hotel," Paul said. "I'll catch you later, okay?"

He crossed the street and made his way back along Camino del Mar toward the Oceanside. Susan watched him go while Daffy waited a little way farther down the sidewalk, an exaggeratedly skeptical expression on her face.

"What a bull artist," she said.

"I don't think so," Susan said, ignoring the special face Daffy had put on for her.

"You don't mean to say you fell for all that baloney about death and stuff? My God, Suze, he wants your body, that's all."

"Don't be ridiculous. He doesn't even know me."

"Oh, no? Well, he knows your name, and he knows that your parents died in a car accident, and he knows that you were down on the beach this morning, and he knows that you live with your grandparents, and he knows what time you're supposed to be home, and he also seems to know that your favorite restaurant is Bully's North. Now, if he's telling the truth, he got your name from the cops only about an hour ago. How did he find out all *that* in just one hour?"

Susan looked toward the ocean, glittering between the buildings on the opposite side of the road like smashed diamonds. "I don't know," she said.

"Well, don't you *care?* I think it's scary."

"No," said Susan, and in her own mind she was quite sure of this. "It's not scary. But something's going to happen. Something's going to change. I can feel it."

"Burr-rurr-other," Daffy said, shaking her head. "The lightning bolt of true love has struck you straight in the brain."

"No," Susan said emphatically. "It's more important than love."

3

Gil swerved his Mustang into the parking lot across the street from his father's Mini-Market and gunned the engine before switching it off. He sat where he was for a moment, thinking, and then hopped out and crossed over Highway 101, jingling his car keys.

The Mini-Market was wedged between the Mandarin Coast Chinese Restaurant and Freddy's Instant Print Service. It was the kind of store that sold everything from ice cream to cans of Chef Boy-ar-dee Spaghetti Bolognese to shoelaces to golfing hats to get-well cards. It had a wonderful aroma to it, an aroma of feta cheese, Hungarian salami, penny candy and Superman comics. Gil's father was a qualified engineer and could have brought down four times as much money designing hydraulic controls for locomotives, but he had dreamed about owning a store like the Mini-Market ever since he was a kid and he wouldn't have lived out his life in any other way.

Gil's mother said he must have had a deprived childhood, to want to run a general store, but she knew how happy he was and that made her happy too. She stocked the shelves, kept the store clean and even made quiches for the deli counter. Along the strip Gil's father and mother were known as the "M&Ms"—Mr. and Mrs. Miller.

Gil's father was standing behind the checkout packing a week's groceries for old Mrs. Van Buren, who lived on the other side of the Santa Fe railroad tracks. He was tall and big-boned like Gil, with wiry gray hair and one of those husky-looking outdoor faces like Lloyd Bridges'. He wore a blue-striped apron with his name sewed on the pocket: "Phil."

"Hi, Dad," Gil said.

"How're you doing?" his father asked. "You're back early."

"I didn't feel like swimming, that's all."

"They closed off the beach, somebody told me," Phil said. "Did you want the barbecue-flavored beans, Mrs. Van Buren, or the vegetarian?"

"Yeah, I think somebody drowned or something," Gil remarked.

"There were ambulances and police cars coming from all directions," Phil said, reaching down for another paper sack and opening it out.

"I heard that it was a girl," put in Mrs. Van Buren. "Some girl, drowned on the beach. Nude, that's what I heard."

"Taking dope, if you ask me," said Phil. "They take dope, they swim, and they think they can swim all the way to Japan."

"I guess we were just as crazy in my day," said Mrs. Van Buren. "In those days, of course, it was bootleg liquor. We used to drive up and down the Pacific Highway in a De Soto CK Six, high as kites on McNamara's home-brewed whiskey, and see how far we could get without putting our hands on the steering wheel. First person to grab for the wheel was a chicken."

Phil laughed. "Why now, Mrs. Van Buren, I didn't know you were a juvenile delinquent."

"You show me a juvenile who isn't," said Mrs. Van Buren, "and I'll show you a juvenile who's never going to get anywhere in life."

"I don't know about that," Gil said. "This girl got only as far as the beach."

Phil glanced across at his son questioningly. Gil was conscious that he had sounded as if he had known the girl, or seen her. He deliberately changed the subject by rubbing his hands briskly and asking, "Want me to slice up some ham, Dad?"

"Sure thing, and maybe some of that Italian salami too."

Gil walked between the shelves of groceries to the back

of the store, where the glass-fronted deli counter was. He went around it, ducking his head to avoid the plastic cloves of garlic that hung from the ceiling, and through to the stockroom, where there was a washbasin and a mirror. He washed and dried his hands thoroughly. In the mirror his face looked detached and expressionless, like the face of somebody who has just witnessed a hideous death and a frightening accident.

Back at the counter, he hefted up a large Maryland ham covered in golden bread crumbs and positioned it on the slicer. He switched on the motor and began to slide the slicer back and forth, heaping up a pink stack of aromatic ham. His father had finished with Mrs. Van Buren and came around to the back of the shop, wiping his hands on his apron.

"By the way," he said, "some girl came by asking for you."

"Some girl? It wasn't Gina Chappell, was it?"

"I don't know. I don't know what Gina Chappell looks like."

"Blonde, gappy teeth, small tits."

His father grunted in amusement. "No, this wasn't Gina Chappell. This one was tall and dark, and I have to say that she had very big—" He left the word unspoken but held out his hands as if he were comparing the weight of two large cantaloupes.

Gil switched off the slicer and lifted the stacked ham with a spatula. "Don't know who *that* could have been."

"She seemed quite anxious to see you. She said she'd have a cup of coffee down at the bookstore and then come back."

Gil smiled at his father and switched the slicer on again. "Maybe it's my lucky day. For the first time in my life, a beautiful girl has come chasing me."

"She's probably an officer of the court trying to serve you with a summons for all those parking tickets of yours."

"Don't shatter my illusions, Dad."

Phil watched his son for a moment or two and then said, "Are you okay?"

Gil glanced up. "Okay? Why shouldn't I be okay?"

"I don't know. You look kind of worried about something."

"Worried?"

"Well, I don't know. You look like something's preying on your mind."

Gil shook his head. "Nothing I can think of."

But his father didn't seem satisfied. He stayed silent a while longer and then said, "It's not like you to miss out on your swim."

"I jogged. The jogging was enough."

"Your leg isn't hurting?"

"My leg is fine. What is this, the third degree? You're going to beat a confession out of me with a Hungarian salami?"

Phil laughed again but without much amusement. "I know you. I know you better than you know yourself. That's because you're like me. And when I'm worried about something, I behave just like you do. I laugh, but all the time it's false. And that's how you're laughing. I knew something was wrong the moment you walked in the store."

"God protect me from an understanding father," Gil said. "Do you think that's enough ham? There're about three and a half pounds there, in half-pound batches."

"That's enough. You can always slice more later."

Gil's mother came in carrying two cartons of Cocoa-Puffs from the storeroom at the back. "Oh, Gil, I'm glad you're here. You can stack these on the shelf for me."

Gil took the cartons and carried them around to the cereal display. His mother followed him and stood beside him. She was a small woman, still handsome at forty-four. Phil said she reminded him of a statue, a Greek statue, not the one without the arms but the other one with the classic face and figure. She was smiling as she watched Gil cut open the cartons and take out the boxes of cereal.

"Who's the girl?" she asked.

"You mean the girl who came around looking for me?"

"There's another girl?"

"Well, Dad told me about her but I don't know who she is."

"She's very pretty," said Fay Miller, looking at her son closely to see if he was telling the truth.

"That's what Dad said."

"And you really expect us to believe you don't know who she is?"

Gil slapped his hand over his heart. "Mom, believe me, I wish I did."

About ten minutes later, Gil's friend Bradley came in. Bradley's father ran a fishing-tackle store in Encinitas, a few miles up the coast. Bradley was lanky and humorous and almost invariably wore Hawaiian-style beach shirts and Bermuda shorts. He and Gil had been classmates in grade school, and although Bradley was now studying to be a computer programmer while Gil was taking business studies, they saw each other almost every weekend and all through their summer vacations, going fishing, swimming and telling each other absurd jokes.

Bradley lifted the new issue of *Hustler* off the revolving magazine rack and appreciatively leafed through it. Gil's father had made sure that his general store had an adult-magazine rack. He derived benign amusement out of watching teenage boys pluck up enough panicky courage to buy themselves a copy of *Chic* or *Penthouse*, paying for it red-faced and then rushing out of the store. The adult-magazine rack was part of a general store's mystery and excitement, along with the strange bottles of Japanese cooking ingredients, the lurid candies and the peculiar kitchen gadgets.

"How're you doing, Bradley?" asked Gil. He took a quarter from a small ginger-haired boy who had been carefully counting out eight licorice whips and gave him a penny in change.

"Oh, bored pretty much," Bradley replied. "Did you hear about what happened at the beach?"

"Yeah, I heard."

"They've still got it cordoned off. Jellyfish warning, that's what they're saying now."

"Oh, yeah?"

Bradley opened up *Hustler*'s center spread. He was silent for a long time. Then he said, "Do you know something? It isn't fair. It just damn well isn't fair. Some guy got paid for taking this picture. *Paid*, can you imagine that? And I couldn't get to see a girl like that with her legs wide open if I crawled all the way to Mount Palomar and back pushing a rat's turd with the end of my nose."

"Well, that explains it," Gil told him. "Girls like that don't really go for boys who push rat's turds up and down mountains with the ends of their noses. Didn't anybody tell you that? Your social-science teacher?"

Bradley swatted at Gil with the rolled-up magazine.

"Hey, you take care of that," warned Gil. "Some jerk-off is going to want to buy it."

"I'd buy it myself but I just couldn't stand the unfairness."

Gil shook his head and said, "You're a real dope sometimes, Bradley. I hate to think of what the inside of your brain is like."

"Listen, I have to tell you this joke," said Bradley. "What do you get if you let an elephant walk across your living room?"

"For God's sake, Bradley, I don't want to know about that."

"No, come on, what do you get if you let an elephant walk across your living room?"

Gil sighed in exaggerated exasperation. "I don't know, Bradley. What *do* you get if you let an elephant walk across your living room?"

"You get a thick pile on your carpet."

Gil said, "I should throw you out of here right on your

head, you know that?" But then he turned around and there she was, standing in the doorway with the sunlight shining brightly behind her so he had to narrow his eyes to make out what she looked like. Bradley turned around, too, and was suddenly silent.

Gil's father had been right. She was tall, almost as tall as Gil, and dark-haired. Her hair was brushed, clean and shining, and it reached down over her shoulders. Her eyes were wide and her lashes extravagantly long; her mouth was slightly parted as if she were about to say something or as if she were about to kiss somebody. She wore a tight white T-shirt that clung to her overfull breasts, and it was obvious from the way the tint of her nipples showed through the cotton knit that she was wearing no bra. She wore white rolled-up shorts and white sandals, and that was all.

"Gil Miller?" she asked.

Bradley whispered, "My wish has been granted. Did she say Bradley Donahue?"

Gil looked the girl up and down, trying to be steady, trying to be cool, but with an extraordinary tightness around his heart.

"That's—" he began in a choked falsetto. Then, much deeper, "That's me."

The girl stepped into the store and smiled at him. "My name's Paulette Springer. I hope you don't mind my surprising you like this."

"Well, uh, no," said Gil, wiping his hands on his denim shorts. "No, no. My folks told me you called by earlier. I'm just sorry I wasn't here."

"I know. You had to take Susan Sczaniecka home. But that's all right. I had a cup of coffee at the secondhand bookstore. That's quite a place, isn't it? I bought a book called *De Sortilegio*."

Gil glanced at Bradley, but all Bradley could do was to look baffled.

Paulette came closer. Gil couldn't help noticing the tantalizing sway of breasts underneath her T-shirt. Close up, he could smell her perfume, which was like sweet peas, roses and something else altogether, something subtle and arousing and barely perceptible, like the smell of a warm, clean body.

"I was hoping you could help me," she said.

"Well, sure," Gil told her. "Anything, you name it."

"I'm writing an article for *San Diego* magazine about the different things that get washed up on the beaches."

"Oh, yeah?" Gil's heart still felt tight; in fact, it felt tighter than ever now.

"I know it sounds silly," she went on, "but actually it's going to make a pretty interesting piece. You'd be amazed at what gets washed up. I mean apart from whales and driftwood and things like that. There's an old man who lives about a mile north of here who's furnished his whole cottage with chairs and tables and beds that were washed up right on the beach."

Gil drummed his fingers on the top of the cash register. "That's pretty interesting. The only thing is, what does it have to do with me?"

"Well," Paulette smiled, her eyes sparkling at him, "you go down to the beach every morning, don't you? You have to jog because of your leg."

"That's right," Gil agreed. "It's part of the therapy. But I still don't see—"

She lifted a finger to silence him. He didn't know why, but he was silent. She said, "You're almost always the very first person down on the beach, aren't you? Sometimes you're down there at daylight. So if anything was washed up during the night, anything at all, you'd be the first person to find it."

Gil looked at her closely. Then he looked away, jammed his hands into the back pockets of his chopped-off jeans and made one of those faces that means, "Hey, hold up a minute. What exactly is going down here?" Paulette watched him, her soft smile never wavering, and Bradley watched Paulette. His face was saying, "It isn't fair. The nearest living thing I've even seen to a *Hustler* center spread walks right into my life and wants to talk to Gil, not me."

Gil said at last, "Have you been talking to anybody?"

"I don't know what you mean."

"Have you been talking to Susan Sczaniecka? Or to that old guy who lives along the beach?"

"Who's Susan Sczaniecka when she's at home?" Bradley wanted to know.

Paulette didn't answer Gil's questions but said in the simplest of voices, "You've found one or two interesting things washed up on the beach, haven't you?"

"I found a case full of Johnny Walker once. My dad made me hand it over to the coast guard. I expect they drank it. I'm pretty damn sure they drank it."

"And then of course you found what you found today." Paulette's mouth may have been smiling but the expression in her eyes was serious.

"You talked to Lieutenant Ortega?" asked Gil.

"Gil," Paulette coaxed him, "all I want to do is to write my article. You don't have to be mentioned by name. All you have to do is to describe what happened to you, how you felt about it."

There was no doubt that Paulette was almost irresistibly attractive. If Gil had seen her in a crowd of girls, he would have picked her out at once. She was exactly the type of girl who turned him on. Long brunette hair, sooty-lashed eyes and the kind of figure that just had to be felt to be believed. She was standing even closer now so that her breasts were almost touching his arm and he could see the tiny green flecks in the irises of her eyes.

The tip of her tongue ran lightly across her lower lip. Gil melted inside, into white-hot liquid boy. He was confused by Paulette and irritated by how much she knew about him. She even frightened him a little. But he knew that whatever she suggested, he wouldn't be able to refuse because a girl who looked like this would probably never walk into the

Mini-Market again, not in a grillion years, and what a dope he would be if he chased her away.

Who cared what she knew? Who cared what she wanted? His throat was dry, his shorts were uncomfortably tight, and she was so goddamned *nice*, as well as sexy, as well as beautiful, and if she went to the secondhand bookstore and bought books with names like *Day Sortie Ledgey*, she was intelligent too.

"What exactly do I have to do?" Gil asked cautiously.

"You have to answer some questions, that's all," Paulette told him. "There's nothing to it."

"Questions about . . . what I found on the beach?"

"Umh-humh."

"You really want to know about that?"

There was a look in her eyes that warned him not to ask her any more, not in front of Bradley at least.

"We can't very well discuss it here," she said. "Why don't you meet me this evening? We could talk over dinner."

"Sure, if that's what you want. Sure." He tried to sound offhanded.

"Okay then," said Paulette. "Meet me at seven at Bully's North. You know Bully's North?"

"Well, yes, but I can't afford dinner there."

"That's okay," Paulette smiled. "The magazine will pay for the meal. Expense account."

Just then Phil Miller came up to the front of the store. He nodded to Paulette and then said to Gil, "Aren't you going to introduce me?"

"I'm sorry, Dad. This is Paulette Springer from *San Diego* magazine. She wants to write an article about some of the things people find on the beach. Paulette, this is my dad."

They shook hands. "Good to know you, Mr. Miller," said Paulette. "How's your insurance problem?"

"Oh, I guess we'll get the money eventually," said Phil. "The insurance company's been arguing that a brownout doesn't constitute a blackout and so none of our freezer food was covered, but our lawyer seems pretty hopeful about it."

He suddenly stopped himself and frowned at her. "How do you know about that?" he asked.

She smiled at him, half-knowingly, half-provocatively. "Word gets around," she said, winking.

"Word gets around about two hundred seventy-five dollars' worth of spoiled pizzas?"

Paulette wouldn't say more but gave Gil's hand a squeeze and told him, "I'll see you later. Don't be late. Bully's North at seven."

"I'll be there," Gil promised.

They watched her walk out of the store and the way she moved in her tight white shorts. Bradley whispered reverentially, "No panties, did you see that? Not a pantie crease in sight." He stared wide-eyed at Gil, clenched his fists and said, "God! I could hit myself in the face with a brick."

"It might do you some good," Phil said.

Gil just stood behind the cash register, staring at the open door of the Mini-Market as if he couldn't believe his visitor had actually been real.

Phil said, "You're seeing her tonight?"

Gil nodded. "She's buying me dinner."

Phil laid his arm around his son's shoulders. "You know something?" he said. "There do seem to be times when you can fall on your feet." He glanced behind him but Gil's mother was still in the stockroom. "Just make sure, you know, that you take all the necessary precautions. She might be a lovely young lady but I don't know her well enough yet to entrust her with my first grandchild."

Bradley wrenched his golfing hat down over his head. "Precautions! What are you doing to me? I could hit myself in the face with two bricks."

Phil laughed and gave Bradley a playful punch in the stomach. Bradley coughed, spluttered and pretended to expire.

"Listen," said Phil, "I'll do you a favor. You can have that *Hustler* at a fifty-percent discount."

"While he goes out with Miss Super Bosom, Nineteen Eighty-six? Are you kidding?"

Gil served behind the deli counter until lunchtime. Then he made himself a roast-beef and onion submarine and took off for San Pasqual Valley, out by the San Diego Wild Animal Park, where his friend Santos Ramona lived. Santos had briefly attended the same business college as Gil, but after two semesters, his father had been hospitalized with emphysema and Santos had been obliged to give up his education and work in the San Pasqual vineyards to support the family. Bradley was fun but Santos was the man to see if you felt serious or reflective. Santos had sampled peyote and yage, the mind-expanding drugs taken by the Jivaro Indians, and claimed that he could see the future.

Gil ate the roast-beef submarine as he drove one-handed along the winding road that led up from Solana Beach to Rancho Santa Fe. Beyond the quiet retirement community of Rancho Santa Fe, with its whitewashed houses and neat streets, the road ribboned out into more mountainous country around the edge of Lake Hodges and then into the San Pasqual Valley. Hot and sheltered, with slopes of dry, tawny soil, the San Pasqual Valley was ideal for growing grapes. The vines stood hand in hand on the hillsides, their green leaves fluttering in the afternoon breeze like tattered shirts.

Santos Ramona's house was set close by the road in a steep, sloping hollow so deep that the clay-tiled roof was almost on the same level as the pavement. Gil drove the Mustang down the dusty gradient into Santos' front yard, where five or six chickens scattered around his wheels. Santos himself was out back, a wrench in one hand and a can of Mexican beer in the other, staring without much optimism at a battered John Deere tractor and occasionally wiping the sweat from his forehead with the back of his arm.

Gil brought the Mustang to a halt and a cloud of sandy-colored dust drifted away through the eucalyptus trees that shaded the back of the Ramona property. Gil jumped out and walked over to stand next to Santos, joining him in staring at the tractor.

"What's wrong?" he asked.

"You've been eating onions," Santos remarked.

"So what? What's wrong with the tractor?"

"Won't go."

"Do you know what's wrong with it?"

Santos swallowed beer and spat into the dust. "If I knew what's wrong with it, I'd fix it."

"Maybe the fuel line."

"Maybe the fuel line what?"

"Well, maybe it's clogged. That happens with tractors, working in dirty conditions."

Santos stared at the machine for a moment longer, then let the wrench drop to the ground with a clank. "Come inside," he said. "Do you feel like a beer? Where have you been for so long? These past two months, I hardly seen you."

They walked into the house. It was shadier inside but not much cooler. In the blue-and-yellow tiled kitchen, Santos' mother was making *empenadas*, occasionally flicking away flies with the fringe of her black, embroidered shawl.

"How're you doing, Mrs. Ramona?" Gil asked.

"Phoof, don't ask me," Mrs. Ramona replied. Her face was thin and wrinkled, and her eyes were as black and glittering as two beetles. "My husband is still sick, you know; the winery is cutting its work force; who knows what will happen?"

Santos went to the refrigerator and took out two more beers. He lobbed one across the kitchen to Gil, who caught it left-handed.

"Come through," said Santos and they walked through to Santos' bedroom. Santos kicked the door shut behind them and suddenly Gil felt peaceful and quiet and very enclosed.

To look at Santos, it was almost impossible to guess that he had a room like this. He was short and pudgy, and his shirt was always hanging out of his jeans. He had one of those Mexican faces that reminded Gil of a Mayan mask, flat like a pancake, and featureless. His black hair was combed into a nineteen-fifties' crest at the front and duck-tailed at the back. He spat a lot by way of punctuation.

His room, however, was almost monastic. It was white-painted and cool. The bed was neatly draped with a plain, light-blue cover. There was a pale-oak armoire with brass hinges and a shelf with half a dozen books on it, each in Spanish and each concerned with mysticism. On the wall between the two shuttered windows there was a large gilt-and-enamel crucifix set with red-glass rubies and pieces of mirror. The Christ that hung on it was like a pink-painted doll with an almost ludicrously agonized expression on its face.

"Well, what worry brings you here?" Santos asked, prizing off his sweaty loafers and sitting cross-legged on the bed. He tugged the ring pull of his beer can and sucked at the opening before the contents could foam out.

"Does it have to be a worry? Maybe I just felt like shooting the breeze with my old friend Santos."

"You sound more like a bad cowboy movie every time you come here. What's the matter? You're forgetting those times we had, those bottles of wine we drank, those things we talked about?"

Gil shook his head. He hadn't opened his beer yet. He pressed the ice-cold can against his chest. "It's because of those things we talked about that I came this afternoon."

"Which things in particular?"

"Magic. You know, people who can work magic. Shamans, medicine men, people like that. People who can make themselves invisible and people who know everything about you even though they've never met you before."

"Oh, yeah?" asked Santos. He seemed unimpressed but Gil could tell that he was interested.

Gil said simply, "I went out jogging on the beach this morning. I found a dead body. Well, me and this girl and this old professor-type guy, we found it together. It was a girl, a naked girl, and she was way up on the sand, way beyond the weed line."

Carefully, with little embellishment, he told Santos about the girl's body and the eels, and about what had happened to the policeman. Then he told him about Paulette Springer, especially how Paulette Springer seemed to know so much about him.

"Do you know something?" he said. "I've been thinking about this on the way out here. She's *exactly* my type. Can you believe that? The more I think about her, the more it hits me. She's my dream girl, my fantasy girl come true. I love her face and I love her body and I love the way she dresses. I love the way she talked and I love the way she laughed. Jesus, I'd marry her tomorrow. I'd marry her this evening."

Santos listened carefully. Then he reached into his pocket and took out a key. He unlocked his armoire and from one of the shelves near the top he brought down a tin box with a plaid pattern printed on it. Originally it had contained Genuine Scottish Petticoat Tails. Santos opened it and inspected its contents: about a half-ounce of marijuana, a packet of cigarette papers and some shag tobacco.

"We should smoke," he said. "Then maybe we can find out what's going down here."

"I'm not sure I want to."

"I can't help you if you don't," Santos told him matter-of-factly.

Gil glanced up at the crucifix and then said, "Okay. But I'm not getting totally stoned. I want to get back and meet this girl this evening."

"You'll get back," Santos assured him.

Gil watched silently as Santos rolled a joint. Then Santos

closed the tin box and reached into his shirt pocket for matches. He lit up unhurriedly and blew smoke across the room. "This is good stuff. I got it from Benès. You remember Benès, who used to come down to the college sometimes?"

"Sure," Gil said. He waited while Santos drew in a deep, sharp breath of marijuana. Then he said, "You must miss college pretty bad."

Santos shrugged, his mouth leaking smoke. "What's to miss? Look what I got here. A tractor that won't go, a mother who never stops complaining, grape vines, heat, dust and fucking chickens."

He passed over the joint. Gil hesitated and then inhaled, dragging the pungent smoke deep into his lungs. He closed his eyes and waited before slowly allowing the smoke to roll out. He took another drag and then passed the joint back to Santos.

Gradually, as they smoked, the room seemed to Gil to open out, to expand. Before he knew it, the tiny adobe cell was like a vast cathedral, echoing and empty. He could see Santos, but Santos appeared to be far away and shrunken, as if he were nothing more than a half-developed embryo with a checkered shirt and a pompadour.

Santos said slowly and loudly, "You have to tell me what she said . . . exactly what she said."

Gil tried to think of Paulette. For a moment he couldn't assemble a picture of her in his mind but then he forced himself to remember the first moment he had seen her, standing against the sunlight that irradiated the street outside the Mini-Market door. In a blurry voice, he told Santos, "She said . . . Gil Miller. She spoke my name."

"Then what did she say?"

"She said . . . I'm sorry to surprise you . . . she said, I've had a cup of coffee and I've bought a book. She told me the name of the book. She seemed to think I would know what it meant, like it was a secret message or something."

49

"What was the name of the book?" asked Santos. His voice sounded distant and metallic.

"It was foreign, I didn't understand it. I can't remember it now. *Day* something."

"Remember," Santos urged him. "It could be important."

Gil closed his eyes and tried to recall the name of the book. Day something. *Day after Day. Day for Night. Day of the Triffids.*

He heard a voice, different from Santos' voice, and he opened his eyes again. He was startled to see that the floor of the room was bright blue and swirled with streaks of white that looked like horsetail clouds. One second he was sitting still, the next second he was traveling over the floor at what seemed like sixty or seventy miles an hour, the clouds flashing past beneath him. The voice said, *"Remember nothing. Remember nothing."* And then he was hurtling faster, even though he was still sitting with his legs crossed.

There was a flash of ultimate speed before the opposite wall of Santos' room came rocketing toward him and hit him in the face. He was conscious of falling, of tilting sideways. Then he looked around and he was lying on the tiles and there was blood splashed everywhere. Santos was kneeling beside him, staring at him in fright.

"Hey, you're not dead?" Santos asked anxiously. His high seemed to have vaporized.

Gil touched his nose and his forehead. His fingers came away bloody and his head pounded.

"What happened?" he croaked.

"What happened? I wish I knew. One minute we were sitting here talking, the next minute you jumped up like a fucking space shuttle and banged your face straight into the wall."

"Did you hear anything?" Gil asked, gripping the edge of the bed and sitting up.

"Hear anything? Like what?"

"Like a voice, another voice. Not yours and not mine."

"I didn't hear anything like that but what I did hear was quite enough."

Gil tugged out his handkerchief and dabbed at his nose. He hoped his face wasn't going to be bruised for this evening's date.

"What did you hear? You mean you heard something from me?"

"Sure, you said the name of the book."

"Well, Day something was all I could remember," Gil told him.

"No, no, you said the name. And believe me, that's all I needed to hear. *De Sortilegio*."

"Hey, that was it!" Gil responded. "*De Sortilegio*. That was the book she bought."

Santos shook his head. "No way did she buy *De Sortilegio* at any secondhand bookstore in Solana Beach. You were right, she was giving you a message. Pity you were too dumb to understand it."

"Well, what is it then, this *De Sortilegio*? Sounds like some kind of Italian cookbook."

Santos said, "*De Sortilegio* was written by some guy called Paul Grilland in fifteen-something. It's a famous book if you're into mysticism, magic and that kind of stuff. You don't find it in any secondhand bookstore though. No way, José. It's rare, and what's more, it's all in Latin because it's so dirty."

"What are you trying to say? That this Paulette was trying to talk dirty to me in Latin?"

"Are you kidding? *De Sortilegio* is dirty only because it explains how the Devil, who happens to be a spirit, can have physical sex with mortal women. I mean it tells you how he uses living ectoplasm to provide himself with a viable dick."

Battered and sore as he was, Gil was still a little bit high. He kept a straight face as long as he could but then he burst out laughing and rolled onto the bed.

"Oh, God, Santos, you had me fooled with that one! Oh,

God, I can't stand it! A viable dick! Oh, God, that's the funniest thing I ever heard!"

But as Gil laughed and pounded his fists on the bed, Santos remained unsmiling. He waited for Gil to finish and kept his eyes fastened on the crucifix that hung on the wall. He closed his eyes for a moment and prayed, and then he crossed himself twice.

Gil abruptly stopped laughing and stared at him, his forehead marked with a glaring crimson bruise, his upper lip caked with dried blood. "What are you doing?" he asked in a hollow-sounding voice.

"I am praying for my own protection," Santos said.

Gil turned toward the crucifix and then back toward Santos. "Protection from what?" he demanded. "Come on, tell me, protection from what?"

4

Henry was asleep on the couch when Lieutenant Ortega stopped by. At first he thought the persistent buzzing of the doorbell was a large mosquito and he flapped at the air several times to get rid of it. Then he opened his eyes and saw the sunlight and the half-empty bottle of vodka on the table next to Andrea's book on eels, and he was jolted back to reality like a man arriving at the lobby of a cheap hotel in a badly serviced elevator.

He opened the door. Lieutenant Ortega was standing on the concrete doorstep, neat and smart in his cinnamon-colored suit and his cinnamon-colored necktie, his hands clasped behind his back.

"Eighty-two already," he smiled, inspecting Henry's outdoor thermometer. "Looks like we're in for a hot afternoon."

Henry smeared his hand over his face, trying to reassemble his features. The older he got, and the drunker he got, the larger his face seemed to spread and the less disciplined its component parts seemed to become.

"You'd, uh," he said, gesturing behind him, "better come in."

Lieutenant Ortega walked past him into the living room. His suit may have looked cheap but his after-shave was Giorgio of Beverly Hills. He stood in the center of the room, carefully tugging his cuffs and looking around. Henry closed the door. He was almost certain the detective had immediately taken note of the vodka bottle and the book on eels.

"What happened this morning on the beach, that was very distressing," said Lieutenant Ortega. His Latin accent was soft but distinctive.

"It was not only distressing, it was *unnatural*," Henry

52

said. He walked across the room, tucking in his shirttails, and collected the bottle of vodka. He tightened the cap and put the bottle back in the cabinet.

"I will be talking later to the young people who were with you," said the lieutenant, "but I thought that first of all I would like to discuss the matter with you. You are, after all, a man of learning, are you not?"

Henry shrugged and sniffed. "Learning, yes. Wisdom, only possibly."

Lieutenant Ortega leaned over and peered at the book on eels. Henry had been reading about their dietary habits. He watched the lieutenant for a moment and then volunteered, "There doesn't seem to be any record of eels attacking a human being *en masse* the way those eels did."

"Well, it's something of a mystery," Lieutenant Ortega admitted. "We still have the beach cordoned off and we have asked the people from Scripps to come along and dig out the remaining eels for us. Then perhaps we can find out how to deal with them."

"It could be a serious problem, couldn't it, killer eels just before the vacation season?"

Lieutenant Ortega smiled distantly. "I don't think we have a *Jaws* situation on our hands, Professor Watkins. This is probably an isolated tragedy. Some deep-sea eels that were brought close to shore by the current. We've been having some unusual tides here lately, and you know for yourself how uncharacteristic the weather has been."

"What does your medical examiner think?" asked Henry. "He seemed like a pretty opinionated kind of guy."

"Oh, him, John Belli. Don't take too much notice of him. He would run the whole investigation single-handed if we allowed him to. He watches too much *Quincy* on television. He's good, yes, I have to confess; but he sometimes fails to see the whole picture. How and when somebody died is usually not half as important as *why*."

Henry asked, "What do you think I can do for you? Would you like some coffee?"

Lieutenant Ortega nodded. "Yes, some coffee would be appreciated. Black, please."

Henry went through to the kitchen, which was an untidy jumble of washed-up dishes that hadn't yet been put away, cups, glasses, boxes of cereal and sprawled-out newspaper sections. He rinsed out the coffeepot, filled it with water and unfolded a fresh filter paper.

"Mocha. You like mocha, Lieutenant?"

"Perhaps you should call me Salvador," said the lieutenant, who had followed him into the kitchen. "I'm not much of a stickler for formality."

"Salvador, okay. My name's Henry. Well, you know that."

They shook hands. Henry looked around and said, "Excuse the mess. I was working all night. The place doesn't usually stay too tidy when I'm working."

"You were thinking about the eels this morning then?" asked Salvador.

"Yes, I was thinking about the eels."

"And what line of thinking were you pursuing? Is it possible for you to tell me that?"

"Well," frowned Henry, "it struck me that the eels were unusually aggressive. I mean, although the eel that attacked your officer was only trying to defend itself, it was particularly fierce and it was unusual that when its head was cut off, instead of its jaw muscles *relaxing* as they would have done under normal circumstances, they actually *tightened*. So here we have a creature that not only attacks but goes on attacking even after it has been mortally injured. You don't get that very often in nature, that kind of, well, ferocity."

"Go on," said Salvador, watching him with steady, dark-brown eyes.

"If you try to work out what must have happened to the girl," Henry said, "you end up with pretty much the same pattern of blind aggression."

"What do you mean?" Salvador asked.

"Well, she couldn't have been in the water all that long, could she? She wasn't swollen up or anything like that. I'm not an expert by any means, but I can remember the body of a fisherman they dragged out of the harbor at San Diego two or three days ago and he was bloated up like a blimp. Maybe your medical examiner will prove me wrong but I wouldn't have thought she was floating around for more than a few hours."

Salvador said, "You're right. Mr. Belli's first opinion was that she hadn't been immersed for longer than two or three hours, possibly less."

"Fine. Then that bears out my theory. It says in this book on eels that they have been known to devour the flesh of drowned bodies when those bodies are trapped on the seabed and well-decayed. But apart from an occasional attack by moray eels, they hardly ever go for living people swimming in the water, or even for bodies floating on the surface. What these eels did to that girl was completely outside the normal feeding pattern of marine teleosts. They attacked her either when she was alive or when she was freshly dead and still floating around. It wasn't as if her body was down on the seabed for a while, where the eels could have gotten at her, and then bobbed up and floated into shore later."

The last of the water dribbled through the filter and into the coffeepot. Henry found two clean blue mugs and filled them to the brim. Then he led the way back into the living room and sat down on the couch. Salvador sat facing him, clasping his mug in both hands.

"I have to say that I subscribe to the idea that she didn't float into shore but was dragged," Salvador said. "You remember what Mr. Belli pointed out—that her body was lying higher on the beach than the rest of the flotsam."

Henry thought about that. "There were no footprints though, were there?" he asked. "If somebody had dragged her up beyond the tide line, there would have been footprints. But the sand was completely smooth."

"Ah, yes," said Salvador. "But the sea *did* reach up that far at the very turn of the tide and so any prints would have been washed away. I personally believe, however, that she was dragged, footprints or not, because the water that far up the slope of the beach would have been much too shallow for her body to float."

Henry sipped a little coffee, then stood up, went over to the drinks cabinet and took out the bottle of vodka. He poured a large dose into his mug without offering any to Salvador. Salvador said nothing. He was used to drunks, both civilian and police. Who was he to criticize those people who couldn't manage to get through the day without being half-blinded?

Henry asked, "So what does that leave you with? A naked girl, her stomach eaten by eels, lying in a place where somebody must have dragged her?"

"That's right," Salvador said. "And a million questions, such as who dragged her, if anybody? Her murderer, if she was murdered, or a would-be rescuer who then decided she was beyond saving and left her where she was? Also, was she killed or knocked unconscious or perhaps drugged before she went into the water? Mr. Belli will be able to tell us this. What's more, did the eels attack her before or after she was dead? Were the eels themselves responsible for her death or were they simply predators on a body that had already expired? Then we still don't know who she is, where she came from or why nobody has reported her missing."

Henry was silent. He finished his coffee in three large gulps, although it was still scalding hot. "Best cure for a hangover I know," he said at length.

Salvador said, "Perhaps I shouldn't trouble you with this matter. Perhaps it would be better if I went."

"I don't have any answers of any kind," Henry said. "My questions are the same as yours." He paused for a moment and then said, "What are you going to do if you can't find out any more?"

"All cases of homicide have some kind of handle on them somewhere," said Salvador. "It is simply a question of groping for it and recognizing it when you have found it."

Henry nodded. Then he looked away and stared out the window at the beach and the ceaselessly grumbling ocean.

"I must go," said Salvador. "But it has been interesting to talk to you. I was fairly sure that as an educated man you would apply your mind to what has happened. I would very much appreciate it if you would continue to think this tragedy through and call me if you happen to think of anything new. Every problem is more susceptible to solution by two minds rather than one."

"I'm afraid I'm a philosopher, not a detective," said Henry.

"This tragedy may have something to do with philosophy," Salvador replied. "To a greater or lesser extent, most man-made tragedies do. At least the ones I have to deal with."

"What kind of detective talks like that?" Henry asked with a sharp glance.

Salvador buttoned up his coat and smiled. "The kind of detective who is tired enough to search not just for causes, but for reasons."

"Well," Henry said, "I'm not sure there *are* any reasons. You know what Kierkegaard said, that there are only two ways. One is to suffer and the other is to become a professor of the fact that somebody else has suffered. Believe me, be a professor."

Salvador Ortega left. Henry stood by the window holding the slats of the venetian blind apart and watching him drive away in his bright-green Datsun. He wasn't sure why, but the detective had disturbed him deeply. Perhaps it was because he had been unable to do what Henry expected the police to do: come up with a rational explanation for an irrational event. He expected his police to be factual to the point of pigheadedness. He wanted them to insist that everything was normal. Violent, yes. Frightening, yes. But *normal*.

What Salvador had said about every homicide having a handle, it was obvious to Henry that the lieutenant didn't have very much faith in being able to find one, not in this case. There was too much weirdness, too little evidence. And then there were the eels.

After he poured himself a large vodka, he went back to the book and leafed through it again. Page after page of staring, shining eels. Then he came across a reference to hagfish, any of the marine fishes of the family Myxinidae, order Cyclostamata, class Agnatha. Hagfish *look* like eels, he read, having no lateral fins and a slight median fin at the end, but unlike eels they attack other fish, such as haddock or cod, and cling to them, rasping away their victims' flesh with their tooth-studded tongues. All they leave of their prey is the skeleton. When they are not hunting for food, they bury themselves in the mud on the ocean floor.

He read the paragraph twice. Then he swallowed more vodka, lifted his telephone and punched out the number of the Scripps Institute of Oceanography at La Jolla.

"Mrs. Andrea Caulfield," he requested when the switchboard answered.

"May I ask who's calling her?"

"Jacques Cousteau."

"Could you hold on for a moment, please, Mr. Cousteau?"

After a long wait, Andrea's extension was picked up and her brusque, mannish voice said, "Yes, Henry, what do you want now?"

"Andrea, how are you doing?"

"Don't ask, Henry. You don't really want to know and I don't really want to tell you. What do you want?"

"Andrea, it's to do with fish," Henry explained, trying to sound both apologetic and desperately in need of expert advice.

"What kind of fish?" Andrea demanded. "The only kind of fish you were ever interested in was baked flounder."

"No, no, Andrea, this is different. This is eels."

"Eels?" she asked suspiciously.

"Well, I came across an eel on the beach this morning. It must have been washed up by the tide. I tried to pick it up but it bit me. I mean, I washed the bite out with antiseptic and everything but I was wondering what kind of an eel might do that. I mean, if it's dangerous, maybe I ought to warn the coast guard about it."

Andrea said, "You're lying, Henry."

"What are you talking about? All I want to know is what kind of an eel this could be."

"You and the county police department and just about every newspaper and television reporter for two hundred miles around. Come on, Henry, I know all about it. Three of my colleagues are down at the beach now, trying to dig the eels out of the sand. The remains of one of the eels are being sent up here this morning so we can examine them."

"And?" asked Henry because it didn't sound to him as if Andrea had finished.

"And I'm expressly forbidden to discuss any of this with anybody, including my ex-husband, until the police give me permission."

"Come on, Andrea. The police themselves have been here this morning talking about it. They want every scrap of assistance they can get."

"They won't get much from you, will they? Maybe the regurgitated thoughts of Bertrand Russell, God help them."

"Andrea," said Henry, trying hard to be patient, "I looked up eels in that Kaiser and Cohen book you left behind and it mentioned hagfish. It occurred to me that since these eels are so vicious, they might not be eels at all, but hagfish."

"Yes?" asked Andrea. "And what else?"

"Well, that's it. It just occurred to me, that's all."

"I see. All right then, thank you."

"But what do you think?" Henry persisted.

"I think you'd better stick to what you're good at, which is drinking and thinking in that order. Hagfish, for your information, have four sets of tentacles around their heads that they use for gripping their prey. Although I haven't yet had the opportunity to see it for myself, I know for a fact that the eel the police are asking us to examine has no such tentacles."

"All the same, it could be some kind of mutation."

"Henry, for God's sake! You don't know anything about it. Now put the phone down, there's a good boy, and pour yourself another Vodka Collins and then philosophize."

"Philosophy isn't a theory, it's an activity," Henry retaliated.

"Ludwig Wittgenstein," Andrea countered. "You used to cite that quote every time you cut classes to play golf."

"I've given up golf."

"Well, that's a pity," said Andrea. "You were always a great deal better at golf than you were at philosophy."

"Andrea," said Henry, "will you do me a favor? Will you call me if you and your colleagues find out what kind of creature that eel happens to be and let me know? You know you can trust me."

Andrea drew a long, impatient breath. "I'll consider it. I do owe you for letting me have the Volkswagen, I suppose."

"Is that what our relationship has come down to?" Henry asked. "A trade-off?"

"All relationships are trade-offs," said Andrea. "If you'd understood that from the start, maybe our marriage would have worked better."

Henry was about to reply but managed to keep his sudden surge of hostility to himself. *Just repeat after me: We weren't suited. That's all. There was no animosity between us. We never threw crockery, we never blasphemed. She was into oceans and I was into vodka, and that was all there was to it.*

"Andrea," he said, "maybe we should have dinner together sometime."

"Sure," she replied. "And maybe we shouldn't."

He put down the phone, sat back in his leather-upholstered captain's chair and rocked from side to side. He pictured that girl on the beach, her hair fanned out and her hand clutching the sand. Somebody's daughter, somebody's friend, somebody's lover. But what events had led her to Del Mar and death? And why?

He was about to pick up his drink again when he caught sight of a man standing outside his cottage beside the wooden railings that separated the promenade from the beach below, smoking a pipe. There was something about the man that attracted Henry's attention. He was elderly, with white curls protruding from under his yachting cap, and he sported a bushy white mustache. He seemed at peace with himself; his hands were thrust into the pockets of his mid-length coat and he was puffing at his pipe and staring out to sea. But there was more than that. He had some indescribably reliable look about him, as if he were a man of considerable certainty and confidence.

Henry didn't know how he could tell that the man was reliable, but somehow he just knew he was.

The man seemed to be in no hurry to continue his walk along the promenade but remained outside Henry's cottage contentedly smoking. Henry watched him for a long time and then at last felt impelled to go outside and speak to him. He found his door keys, shuffled into his sandals and walked around the side of the cottage into the steady breeze that blew from the sea.

The man remained where he was, smoking, hands in pockets, staring out at the foaming breakers. Henry walked up to him and said, "It's a fine day, wouldn't you say?"

The man took his pipe out of his mouth, licked his lips and looked Henry up and down. It suddenly occurred to Henry that the man might think he was a faggot making a proposition. The man himself might be a faggot and then what was Henry going to do? Say, "Pardon me. On second thought, it's a terrible day," and rush off?

But the man smiled and said, "Well, Henry Watkins. I've been waiting for you to come out and say hello."

"Do I know you?" Henry asked, perplexed.

"You do and you don't. I used to attend your evening classes in modern philosophy, the ones you held up at Encinitas. You probably don't remember me now; my name's Springer. But I remember you. In fact, there's hardly a day goes by that I don't think about you."

Henry said, "I'm sorry. I have a terrible memory for faces. Springer, did you say?"

The man held out his hand. "Paul Springer. You can call me Paul if you want to. I was one of your keenest students, I have to tell you."

They shook hands. Then Paul Springer said, "Maybe we could walk a little. I always find it refreshing, walking along here. Do you have time? We could talk a little too."

"I'm, uh, free for most of the day," Henry said.

"Well, that's good to hear," smiled Paul. "Everybody should take their leisure regularly and take their leisure seriously. Do you know who taught me that?"

Henry shook his head. "I'm sorry, I don't."

"You should, Professor, because you did. You said it in class and you even wrote it down. Remember that essay you wrote for *Time* magazine, April, nineteen seventy-eight? 'The Philosophy of Leisure.' That was a good essay, that. I tore it out and stuck it on the back of my galley door."

"You're a yachtsman?" asked Henry.

"A kind of a yachtsman. You could say that. Yes."

"You live around here?"

Paul sucked at his pipe for a moment, his eyes looking amused, and then said, "Kind of. You could say that. Yes."

"Was there anything in particular you wanted to talk about?" asked Henry. Although the day was sunny, and even hot in the shelter of the cottages, the wind that blew off the shining back of the ocean was cool and Henry was beginning to feel like having another vodka to give him warmth, and maybe courage too.

The man reached a break in the railings, where steep wooden steps went down to the sand, and stood there for a moment, watching the coast guard and the police as they systematically searched the distant beach with long, pointed sticks, probing for eels.

"Somebody told me you were the first to find the body," Paul remarked.

Henry said "Yes" in a voice suddenly hoarse. He cleared his throat and added, "How did you know about that?"

"Oh, it's in all the papers."

"How can it be? None of the papers has talked to me yet. The police said they wanted to keep it quiet in case of a panic."

"Panic?" Paul smiled. "I don't think people are capable of panic these days. Panic is the response of untutored masses to the sudden threat of deadly danger. These days everybody knows what to do about the sudden threat of deadly danger; they've seen it time again on television. *Earthquake, The Towering Inferno, The Poseidon Adventure.* The women should scream without stopping and the men should get hold of a gun and shoot indiscriminately in all directions. So whenever danger threatens, that's exactly what people do. At least that's what naturally hysterical people do. The rest of them do what they've always done, which is to sit and stare and wait for further instructions."

They walked a little farther along and then Paul said, "You don't think the girl died from natural causes? She didn't drown is what I'm trying to suggest."

Henry said, "I don't know. I wish I did. The police are still waiting for the medical examiner's report."

"Was she beautiful?"

Henry stopped, stared at Paul and frowned. "Yes," he said. "As a matter of fact, she was."

"Do you know something?" said Paul, abruptly changing the subject. "There was something you said in class that

I could never quite understand. I mean I understood it but I could never quite grasp the wider implications of it."

"What was that?" asked Henry. For some reason, in spite of the stranger's offhandedness, there was something about him that Henry found friendly and comfortable. He seemed like the kind of fellow who could easily become a close companion, sharing an evening drink, talking about philosophy and listening to Rossini overtures. The kind of fellow who asked for nothing except your opinion and your liquor.

Paul puffed furiously at his pipe for a moment and then said, "You talked about the world being the sum total of our vital possibilities."

"That's right. I was quoting Ortega y Gasset."

"Well," Paul said, "I have all sorts of thoughts about that." He looked around as if he had heard somebody call his name and was trying to locate the voice. "But you know, this isn't really the time or the place, is it?" He looked back at Henry. "To discuss philosophy, I mean. One should have a good meal, a bottle of wine and a pleasant atmosphere. That's when philosophy really becomes fun, don't you think? Your mind can take flight. But not out here in the middle of the day with the ocean interrupting and all these damn joggers."

Henry said wryly, "It's a few years since *my* mind took flight, I can tell you."

"Perhaps it's time it did then," Paul suggested. "Listen, I know this sounds impudent. You may not like the look of me at all. You may think I'm a bore or some kind of tedious eccentric. But I would very much like to talk about Ortega y Gasset a little more. You were so clear when you brought up his philosophies in class!"

Flattered, Henry said, "Well then, what do you suggest?"

"Perhaps I could buy you dinner this evening. Do you know Bully's North? The prime ribs are excellent and the bar's well up to standard."

"Sure I know Bully's North."

"Could you meet me there this evening at seven, say?"

Henry thought about it and then nodded. "Okay." The idea of spending an evening eating, drinking and talking about philosophy seemed irresistibly warm and attractive, and Paul Springer had just the kind of voice he liked to listen to and just the kind of face that appealed to him. Oddly, Paul Springer reminded him of his father. It was a look about the eyes, keen and kindly. "Okay," he repeated. "I'll see you at seven."

Paul Springer walked away. When he reached the first footpath that led from the promenade up toward Camino del Mar, he stopped and waved. Henry waved back and then turned and walked slowly north again. The wind blew sand across the pathway with a soft, sizzling sound, and above his head the gulls kept turning and turning. He remembered that someone had once said that gulls are the lost souls of people drowned at sea and that they search forever for the loved ones they left behind. That's why their cries sound so sad.

Henry had almost reached the short flight of concrete steps that ran up alongside his cottage when he saw a girl walking toward him. She was wearing a colorless cotton shawl draped over her head so it was impossible to see her face. She passed by Henry so close that he could have touched her without reaching out. It struck him as peculiar that she was wet. Even her shawl was wet and clung to her shoulders. He looked down and saw that she had left wet footprints on the sidewalk.

He slowly raised his head and focused on the beach. The sun was glaring off the sea now and he had to shield his forehead with his hand. The beach was still closed; there were police trestles at every access point, and lifeguards driving back and forth in Jeeps to keep people away. He could see a knot of policemen, and a group of men in T-shirts and jeans who were probably the marine biologists from Scripps. He saw a cinnamon-colored suit and recognized Salvador Ortega.

But if the beach was closed and there was no swimming, how had that girl gotten herself wet?

Henry turned and a sensation like two hundred twenty volts of electricity prickled down his body from his scalp to the soles of his feet. The girl was gone but her wet footprints led all the way down to the pathway where Paul Springer had left him.

There had been something familiar about that girl, something about the whiteness of her skin, something about the fine, gritty sand that had stuck to her calves and her ankles. And something more. A fine silver chain around her ankle.

Henry began to jog back along the promenade. The wind was gradually drying the girl's footsteps so they looked like nothing more than question marks printed on the tarmac. Henry jogged faster and reached the corner of the footpath out of breath.

He looked up toward Camino del Mar. In the distance, at the head of the footpath, he could see Paul Springer. He recognized him by his sailor's cap and his white hair. But there was no sign of the girl even though her footprints turned around here and made their way uphill. There were two dilapidated cars parked by the side of the footpath, a '76 Caprice and a bronze Firebird with oxidized paint. On the other side there were fences made of corrugated iron and concrete slabs painted white, spiky grass and trailing vines, and a stunted row of shabby-looking yuccas. A white bullterrier that had been gnawing at an old beef bone pricked up its ears and stared at Henry balefully.

Paul Springer had disappeared from sight now. Henry stayed where he was for a moment and then began walking slowly back to the cottage. There was no sign of the girl's footprints and he was beginning to think he must have hallucinated.

He reached the cottage, unlocked the front door and went straight to the bottle of vodka. He poured himself half a glassful, draining the bottle and dropping it noisily into the metal wastepaper basket with the picture of galleons on it. He walked over to the window and stared up and down the promenade. When he drank, he found that he was shivering.

He left his drink on the table and went through to the kitchen. Perhaps he needed something to eat. All this drinking without eating, it was bound to give rise to hallucinations. He rummaged through the refrigerator, through half-finished packs of longhorn cheddar, leftover chicken legs, prepacked salads turning brown at the edges, strawberry yogurts that had been "best before" the last time he had gone to the theater. He found a reasonably fresh pack of Oscar Mayer's bologna, made a sandwich laden with French's mustard and added a large pickle to eat on the side.

He came out of the kitchen arguing silently with himself about whether hallucinations were fractionally less troubling than indigestion. Then he looked up and said, "*Aah!*"

The girl was standing by the window. This time she had let her shawl fall down to her shoulders and he could see her face clearly. He stayed where he was, with his sandwich and his pickle, staring at her. Her wet hair clung to her head. One side of her face was marked with sand.

"*Are you afraid?*" she asked in a light, transparent voice.

He cleared his throat. "I think so," he said. He was. His heart was running up and down inside his rib cage and he could hear himself panting.

The girl took a step forward. Behind her, the sun came out and diffused her outline, and Henry found it difficult to see her face. "Are you real?" he asked.

"*Real?*" she whispered. "*I am as real as you want me to be. Or as imaginary.*"

"Was it you on the beach this morning?"

"*In a way,*" she said.

Henry put down his sandwich and pickle on a side table. "You know what I'm thinking?" he asked her. "I'm thinking I'm drunk and that I'm hallucinating."

"*I know what you're thinking,*" the girl said softly.

She came nearer. She seemed to be able to approach him without moving her legs. Her eyes were strangely blank, like the eyes of a mannequin in a store window. It was as if she were talking to him without being aware of him. He remembered that look in Andrea's eyes during the last few months of their marriage.

"What does this mean?" Henry asked her.

"*I don't understand.*"

"Well, does it mean that you're still alive? Does it mean that you're a ghost? Or does it mean that I'm going mad?"

She smiled. She had such a beautiful, sad smile. It looked to Henry like the kind of smile that might have touched the lips of Annabel Lee or Lenore or any of Edgar Allan Poe's limpid loves in the kingdom by the sea.

"*I am your own creation,*" she said and touched him, although he felt no touch. "*I am here to remind you of what you must do. Springer will see to it.*"

"You know Springer?" Henry asked, baffled.

The girl lifted her shawl over her head. It came up in a curious snaking way, like a film being run in reverse. She said as softly as before, "*I know Springer now.*"

"You scare me," he said.

She smiled that smile. "*Then you are only scaring yourself.*"

"But you said you were here to remind me of what to do."

"*I am, and you will know it when Springer mentions it.*"

Henry didn't know what else to say. The girl moved toward the door, still smiling at him. Then she opened the door and even though he could have sworn later that she opened it no more than an inch, she disappeared out of it as quickly as smoke disappears when it is blown by a sudden draft.

Henry looked over toward the window, toward his large glass of vodka.

"Something's happening," he said to himself. Then, "I'm frightened." Then after a pause, "God help me."

5

In spite of the heat of the day, the sea fog closed in early that afternoon along the north beaches of San Diego County and by six-thirty the world was prematurely gloomy and almost unbearably humid. Cars traveled slowly along Camino del Mar with their lights on, an endless procession rolling through the fog. Speed restrictions were in force on Interstate-5 and the coast guard advised small boats to stay tied up in the harbor until the fog lifted.

Susan was feeling better, almost light-headed. She took a shower and put on her white low-waisted dress with the red, yellow and green dots on it and blow-dried her hair while she watched *CHiPs* on her portable television.

Her grandmother knocked on her bedroom door and came in before Susan could invite her. She stood watching her granddaughter for three or four minutes, waiting until Susan switched off her hair dryer, and then said, "You wouldn't be going out tonight if it was up to me."

"Grandma, I'm absolutely fine now," said Susan, tweaking her hair with styling gel to give it that ragged look. "I was just feeling faint this morning, that's all. I'm not sick or anything."

"Well, make sure you're not too late. I'm responsible for you—you just remember that. If anything happens to you, it's me who has to answer for it." She paused to pick up Susan's discarded T-shirt, grunting with the effort of it. Then she said, "This man too, I'd like to know more about him. Picking you up in the street like that."

"Grandma," Susan sighed with concentrated seventeen-year-old impatience, "he works for the *San Diego Tribune*. He's the nicest person ever, and we're only going to Bully's North for something to eat. I promise, promise, cross my heart and hope my eyes will drop out, that I will be back by nine-thirty, alive and well and unraped."

"You don't have to talk like that," her grandmother protested.

"I'm sorry," Susan said, primping up her hair and pouting at herself in the mirror. "But I *can* look after myself. I'm not a child anymore."

"If only you knew," her grandmother told her.

"Grandma, I can drive a car, I can almost vote, I can almost get married without consent."

Her grandmother looked resigned. "All right, go. Your mother was the same. You're a good girl, Susan. I know that. Untidy as all get out, but good. Well, at least I hope so."

The phone rang. She heard her grandfather answer it. He said, "Yes, okay," three times and then put the phone down.

"Who was that?" Susan asked. Most of the phone calls were for her.

"Your friend Daffy. She said not to forget to call her when you get back from dinner tonight and tell her all about it."

"Fwoof, did she think I wouldn't?"

Her grandmother came closer and watched her put the finishing touches to her lipstick. "Are you going to have your picture in the *Tribune*?" she wanted to know.

Gil had been up in his bedroom for almost an hour, shaving, combing his hair and trying to make up his mind whether he was going to dress up suave and elegant or go for the Rambo look. He dressed and undressed four times— each time becoming increasingly bad-tempered—until at last he settled on a pair of dove-gray cotton slacks, a short-sleeved white shirt and a charcoal-gray, Italian-cut coat. He sprayed on Signoricci eau de toilette and accidentally squirted himself in the left eye so that when he came downstairs, he was holding a wadded-up handkerchief to his face.

"You're crying already," his father teased him. "You haven't even said hello to her yet, let alone good-bye." His mother shushed him and asked Gil, "What did you do?"

Gil said, "After-shave," and blinked furiously. "Is it bloodshot?" he asked his parents.

"Bloodshot? You look like the teenage son of Dracula," said Phil Miller cheerfully.

"Oh, you *don't*," said Fay. "Your eye looks a little watery, that's all. Did you splash some cold water in it?"

"It's okay," Gil told her, waving her away. "I'll get over it."

"I'll unlock the door for you," Phil offered.

They walked together through the darkened store. Phil put his arm around his son's shoulder and said, "Have a good time. But, you know, don't forget about the precautions if it comes to that."

"Okay, Dad."

Phil unlocked the store door, top and bottom, and let his son out into the street. He stood on the sidewalk for a while, his hands on his hips, inhaling the fog. "Be careful how you drive, won't you? This stuff looks like it's getting thicker."

"Yes, Dad."

"And don't drive drunk, you understand me? If you have too many beers, get somebody to drive you home, or call me. I'd rather be wakened by you telling me you can't drive than by some cop telling me you're dead."

"I got you, Dad."

Gil jogged across the street to the parking lot, where his Mustang was waiting. He folded back the sheet of blue plastic he used to cover the seats and then vaulted into the car. He started up the engine, switched on the lights and pulled out of the cinder-surfaced parking lot in a long, slithering skid. He blasted the two-tone horn, waved to his father and then disappeared into the fog in the direction of Del Mar.

Phil watched him go and shook his head. Kids. But he knew that Gil wasn't crazy, not like some of the boys who hung around the beach. Some of those kids would surf when they were high and ride their motorbikes right off the road and onto the sand, even when families were sunbathing there. Some of them would speed all the way along Camino del Mar, which was intersected by over a dozen side streets, and run every stop sign from Jimmy Durante Boulevard to Carmel Valley Road. Five boys had been killed last year in head-on collisions.

Phil went back into the store, closed the door and locked it.

Henry was already walking along Camino del Mar toward the restaurant. He wore a gray turtleneck sweater that made him look grayer than ever and a black-and-white houndstooth coat. His head was thumping and his tongue felt as if it were lying curled up in his mouth, as hairy as a Persian cat. He was carrying a copy of *The Revolt of the Masses* by Ortega y Gasset, with the spine missing, and also a copy of his own pamphlet, *The Necessary Evil*.

His hallucination this afternoon had badly shaken him even though he was now convinced it had been due to too many glasses of undiluted vodka. He had almost decided not to meet Paul Springer but to call up the restaurant and make some Byzantine excuse. However, by five o'clock he had begun to feel a little more composed and the more he thought about meeting Paul Springer again, the more the idea appealed to him. He was also vain enough to want to hear what somebody else thought about *The Necessary Evil*, which he had always considered one of his best works.

He had walked along the beach promenade partly to see if the beach was still cordoned off and partly (he had to admit it) to see if the wet-footed girl was anywhere around. The police lines around the beach were marked by flashing amber beacons; they winked through the fog like hopeless messages. There was scarcely any wind and the surf sounded flat and clattering as the tide came in. He was passed by two gasping joggers and a rotund woman walking her weimaraner, but there was no sign of the girl.

I am your own creation, she had told him. *If you are scared, you are only scaring yourself.*

He walked up one of the narrow, sloping side streets to Camino del Mar. In a house close to the top of the street, a man and a woman were shouting at each other in Spanish. In the house next to them, a television was blaring out *Galeria Nocturna.* When he reached the corner, Henry dropped a quarter into the newspaper-vending machine and bought a copy of the *Tribune.* He shook it open with one hand and read the headlines.

"North Beaches Closed by Jellyfish Threat" was the headline. Henry skimmed through the front-page story and recognized it for the cover-up that it blatantly was. Lieutenant Salvador Ortega must have been working overtime, he concluded.

The story read, "Police and coast-guard today cordoned off several miles of north-county beaches from La Jolla to San Elijo Lagoon after the body of a young woman was washed up at Del Mar, apparently having been stung to death by jellyfish. The young woman, who is believed to have been swimming alone, has not yet been identified. Police say she was a blonde and that she wore a silver chain around her left ankle. Lt. Salvador T. Ortega, in charge of investigating the death, warned that there could be 'dozens more' jellyfish swarming off the beaches. He has called in marine biologists from the Scripps Institute to assist in identifying the deadly creatures. They could be 'sea wasps,' scientific name *chironex fleckeri,* usually found off the coast of Australia but possible migrants to Southern California waters. Sea wasps can kill a human being in eight minutes. Bathers and surfers were warned this afternoon that—"

Henry folded the paper and tossed it into a trash can without breaking his stride. So Salvador had successfully managed to persuade the media that the beaches had been closed off because of jellyfish. Well, he supposed Salvador was not to blame. Jellyfish were at least explicable. There was nothing explicable about those eels.

As he reached the entrance to Bully's North, he was surprised to see Gil's yellow Mustang turn into the entrance, and then as he reached the doorway, he saw Susan Sczaniecka arrive in her dotted white dress.

He waited by the doorway without opening it. A middle-aged couple pushed past him, the woman frowning at him for being in the way. From inside the restaurant he heard laughter and the clinking of glasses. A man came out, stood next to him and said loudly to his companion, "We can lease for half that. Why do you want to buy when we can lease?" Above his head, green neon flashed the name "Bully's North."

Susan Sczaniecka came up the steps toward the doorway and it was obvious that she didn't recognize Henry. She must have been very shocked this morning down on the beach. Probably all that she could remember with any clarity were the body and the eels.

Just as she passed by him, Henry said, "Susan?"

She stared at him. Her face was blank. Then she suddenly realized who he was. "Oh, hi!" she said breathlessly. "I didn't recognize you! Well, you look so much more dressed up now. Listen, I have to thank you for being so kind to me this morning. I thought I was going to pass out. In fact, I *did* pass out when I got home. *Zonk!*"

"You look fine now," he told her.

"Well, thank you. I have a date."

"So do I," said Henry. "That's why I waited for you. And look—" he pointed across the front lot, where Gil was taking his parking check from the carhop. "Our friend has a date here too."

Susan turned to look at Gil and then she turned back and stared at Henry. "Can this be *coincidence?*" she asked in a soft, alarmed whisper. "I mean, all three of us meeting on the beach this morning and now coming here?"

Gil came up, stopped and stared at them, just as they were staring at him. "Well," he said, "I sure didn't expect to find you two here."

"And we sure didn't expect to find you here either," Susan told him.

"Well . . . as a matter of fact, I was invited here," said Gil.

"Me too," said Susan.

"And me," added Henry.

"This is really weird," Gil exclaimed. "I never saw either of you before today and yet here you both are, waiting for me. You're sure this isn't some kind of practical joke?"

"If it is, we're not playing it," Henry said. "We're just as much victims of it as you are."

"Who invited you?" asked Susan. "I was asked to come here by a newspaper reporter from the *Tribune*."

"It was a girl who asked me," Gil said. "She said she was writing an article for *San Diego* magazine."

Henry lifted up his philosophy books. "That settles it. It must be nothing more than an incredible coincidence. The fellow I'm supposed to be meeting was one of my evening-class students when I was teaching up at Encinitas."

Gil shook his head. "Some coincidence, huh? I mean, the three of us meeting on the beach and now meeting here."

Henry turned and peered past the restaurant doorway. "I hope nothing's wrong," he remarked.

"Wrong?" asked Susan. "What do you mean?"

"I hope that what we saw on the beach wasn't something we weren't supposed to see."

"In what way?" asked Gil.

"Well, just suppose that girl wasn't drowned by accident. Just suppose those eels didn't drift in to shore on a freak current or whatever it was the police were trying to suggest. Just suppose those eels were actually bred as killers . . . deliberately bred to attack swimmers or divers or anybody going into the water. You have your Scripps Institute just down the road here and you have your naval base at San Diego. Suppose the Scripps people have been working on a government project to supply the navy with man-eating eels. And just suppose we saw the result and now we've all been invited here to be dealt with. You know, like Karen Silkwood.''

"Boy, do you have an imagination," Gil whistled. Then he laughed and said, "Are you serious or are you just trying to scare us?''

Henry said a little too pompously, "I'm a philosopher, Gil. I'm trained to use my mind. I'm trained to hypothesize, to think problems out from every conceivable angle. All I'm saying is that the idea of specially trained eels is a conceivable angle.''

"But Karen Silkwood was killed," said Susan worriedly.

"This is nothing *like* Karen Silkwood," Gil protested. "We don't have any evidence at all. It's just a theory, right? And if I know anything about theories, the real explanation is really uninteresting. That's one thing you learn about life, that the explanation for just about everything is really uninteresting.''

"So cynical, so young," smiled Henry, but not patronizingly. He agreed with Gil almost one hundred percent. In his experience, the wildest phenomena always seemed to have the most mundane solutions. Like Bridey Murphy, or the *Mary Celeste*. He nodded back toward the restaurant door and said, "All we have to decide for ourselves is, are we in any kind of personal danger here?''

"I can't see how we could be," said Gil. "I mean, this girl from *San Diego* wasn't threatening in any way you could possibly think of. Just the opposite.''

"Well, you may be right," said Henry. "My philosophy student wasn't exactly your stereotype of a hit man.''

Susan said, "I vote we go in and see what happens. Nothing ventured, you know.''

Henry thought about it and shrugged. "Come on then.''

Inside Bully's North it was noisy, dark and crowded. The television was tuned to the Padres, playing at home, and people were smoking, laughing and drinking beer. They walked the length of the cocktail bar and approached the young blow-dried maitre d', who was answering the telephone and handing out menus at the same time.

After a moment the maitre d' hung up the phone, grinned and said, "Good evening. Can I help you folks? Table for three?"

"Well, we're not together as a matter of fact," Henry said. "Each of us is meeting somebody." He turned to Susan and asked, "What is the name of your *Tribune* reporter?"

"Springer," Susan told the maitre d'. "Mr. Paul Springer."

Henry looked at Gil with a shocked expression. "That's the name of my philosophy student," he said in bewilderment.

"And the girl from *San Diego,* her name's Paulette Springer," said Gil.

The maitre d' stared at them as if they were playing some kind of lunatic game. "You're not together, each of you is meeting somebody, and each of those somebodies happens to have the same name?"

"It appears so," said Henry in a tight, constricted voice.

The maitre d' skimmed down the list of names on his clipboard. Halfway down, his PaperMate came to a stop. "Here it is, Springer. Table nine." The PaperMate continued down to the bottom of the page and the maitre d' shook his head. "Only one Springer, I'm sorry."

Susan glanced at Henry anxiously. "What you said outside. You don't think that—?"

"I don't know," said Henry. "I think we'd all better stay together and see which Springer we've got here. Mine, yours or Gil's."

The maitre d' whipped out three menus. "You all want to go to the same table?" he asked.

"If there's only one table booked in the name of Springer, I don't think we have a lot of choice," said Henry.

The maitre d' led them between the crowded tables, where diners were laughing, drinking wine and tucking into ribs and cracked crab. At the very back of the restaurant, beside a frondy coconut palm in a wicker basket, was table nine, and sitting there was a single figure in a black Homburg-style hat and a black three-piece suit. The brim of the hat was lowered so that as they came across the restaurant, they were unable to see the figure's face. But Henry immediately noticed the hands, which were spread flat on the salmon-colored tablecloth. They were very white, the same hue as blanched almonds, and very long-fingered.

"Here you go then," said the maitre d', dragging out three chairs. "Mr. Springer? One of these people is a guest of yours. Well, I don't know. Maybe they all are."

Henry, Susan and Gil stood around the table apprehensively as the figure slowly raised its face toward them, in the way a white-petaled flower raises its face to the sun. "Yes," said the figure, quietly but distinctly. "They all are."

Henry was transfixed. The figure's face was pale, smooth and androgynous, like the almond-shaped face of a portrait by Modigliani. Yet despite its smoothness and its sexlessness, it was quite clearly Paul Springer, the same Paul Springer he had met outside his cottage on the shore. It was not so much the detail of the face that carried the man's character as the personality it projected. The difference between the man he had met on the beach and this man was the difference between a highly finished portrait and a deft but accurate sketch.

Gil slowly sat down. To Gil, the figure was Paulette. A severely dressed Paulette, with her hair pulled back from her face, yet indisputably the same girl who had visited the Mini-Market and asked him for dinner. He understood that she was different, although he would have found it difficult to say exactly how. Her eyes were still the same, her cheekbones were still the same, her mouth was just as tempting as before. She attracted him just as much, yet she was something else now, apart from Paulette. She wasn't less than she had been before, but more.

Susan said shyly, "Hello." Because for her, too, the figure was the same Paul Springer she had met outside her grandmother's house. A changed Paul Springer, certainly— more mysterious, more remote, less chatty—but the same presence, the same personality. The same calm and penetrating eyes.

"Please, all of you, sit down," said Springer. "You're confused, I understand that; and you're concerned for your safety. But I hope I can set your minds at rest and that you will forgive me for playing a few little tricks on you."

Henry dragged out a chair and sat down. Susan hesitated for a moment and then perched herself on the edge of the chair next to him.

"You're one and the same person," said Henry, his voice thick and off balance. "You're three people rolled up into one. Not all the same sex either. Now how do you do that? How come I think you're my old philosophy student, Gil here thinks you're a lady journalist and Susan believes you work for the *Tribune*?"

Springer removed his, or her, hat. His blond hair had been razored short and combed straight back. The style was completely neutral, completely sexless, just like his clothes. He laid his hat on the table and rested his long, pale hands on either side of the brim.

"Let me put it this way," he said. "It was necessary for me to appear to each of you in a guise you would find irresistible. Each of you had a severe shock this morning when you came across that girl's body. None of you were in the mood for going out to dinner with a complete stranger. Because of that, I considered it more effective to use my particular facility for appearing—how shall I put it?—all things to all men. And women of course," he added, nodding to Susan.

Gil said sharply, "All right then. Just exactly what kind of scam is this? You've got us here. Now what?"

Susan stood up. "I'm going home. I don't like this one bit."

Springer raised a hand, palm outward. He lifted it toward Susan's face and it was almost as if he had a mirror hidden in it because Susan found herself staring at it as though mesmerized. She hesitated and then sat down again. Henry laid a hand on her arm and asked, "What's the matter, Susan? Are you all right?" but she only nodded and whispered, "I'm all right," and touched her fingers to her forehead.

"What did you do to her?" Henry demanded. "What was that, hypnotic suggestion?"

"Nothing of the kind," Springer said gently. "I simply assured her that there was no need for her to be afraid. There is equally no need for you to be afraid either."

A waiter came up and asked them what they would like to drink. Henry ordered a large vodka, Gil asked for a beer, Susan wanted a fruit punch. Springer said, "The driest white wine you can find."

Gil asked, "Are you a woman or a man or what?"

The waiter heard that and turned to stare at Springer curiously. Springer waited until the man had gone to fill their order and then said quietly, "I am neither. I am an agent of sorts. A messenger. I am neither man nor woman, flesh nor spirit. I am not even 'I' in the sense that you would normally understand it."

"So what are you?" Henry asked. "If you're not either of the Paul Springers and not Paulette Springer, and not a man and not a woman, and not flesh and not spirit, what in heaven's name *are* you?"

"Are you hungry?" asked Springer.

"Not exactly," said Henry. "Gil, how about you?"

Gil shook his head. "I couldn't eat if you held a gun to my head."

Susan said, "Me neither."

"All right then," said Springer. "Let us all take a walk somewhere quiet where we can talk. I have one or two things to show you. Things that will startle you perhaps, but things you will find most fascinating."

Susan had been watching Springer closely. Just as the waiter brought their drinks, she asked, "May I touch you? I mean, may I touch your hand?"

Springer turned his eyes toward her without moving his head. "Why do you ask?"

"I don't know. There's something about you that makes me want to touch you, that's all."

Springer moved his left hand across the table and rested it on the tablecloth in front of her. "Go ahead."

Gingerly Susan reached out until her fingertips were only a quarter of an inch from the back of Springer's hand.

"Don't be afraid," he encouraged her.

Susan stroked his knuckle. There was no outward evidence of the touch, no visible sparks, but she felt as if she had brushed a bare terminal fizzing with electricity. The sensation was shocking but curiously pleasant too. She stared at Springer, gazed into his eyes, and Springer said, "Touch me again. Lay your hand right on top of mine and hold it there."

Susan turned to Henry and Gil but they said nothing. Slowly, tentatively, she laid her hand fully on top of Springer's hand and stared into his eyes again, waiting and watching for something to happen.

For a moment, nothing did happen. Then suddenly Susan felt as if she had been plucked out of her chair and hurled at enormous velocity across the restaurant, through the doors, which slammed open before her and slammed shut behind her, then through another set of doors, and another, and another. At the end of the rows of doors— She took her hand away. She stopped. She was still at the table, still sitting with Henry and Gil and the extraordinary person called Springer.

"What happened?" she asked. "I felt like I was flying. Flying through all these double doors that opened and closed to let me through. I could actually hear them banging!"

Henry lifted his glass and swallowed a large mouthful of

neat vodka without taking his eyes off Springer and without offering any kind of toast. "You're a hypnotist," he told Springer. "I don't know what you've been trying to do to us and I don't think I'll be very enthralled when I find out, but I for one would like some kind of coherent explanation for this evening's little get-together or I'm finishing off this drink and going home."

"Finish your drink and come with me," said Springer.

"Where do you have in mind?" asked Henry. "Mugger's Cove? Or Dope's Leap?"

Springer shook his head. "I will not harm you. I think you are conscious of that already. There *is* harm around us; you *are* threatened, but not by me."

"Then by whom?"

Springer finished his wine and raised his hand toward the waiter. The man turned toward them but as soon as he caught sight of Springer, he turned away. "Come along," Springer said. He stood up and helped Susan from her chair.

"Aren't you going to pay?" Gil asked.

Springer shook his head. "I have no money. But there is no question of theft. They will find when they check their inventory that they are missing nothing, no wine, no beer, not even a measure of Smirnoff."

Henry looked at Springer interrogatively but kept his questions to himself. He preferred to hold back and see how this confrontation with Springer turned out. But there was no doubt that it was deeply disturbing. He kept his eye on the waiter and the maitre d' as the four of them walked toward the exit making no attempt to pay for their drinks. Nobody noticed them. They might have been invisible. Henry passed only inches from the maitre d' and the man didn't even turn to bid him good night or ask why they were leaving only five minutes after they had arrived.

Gil said, "This is weird with a capital W."

Susan said, "It's as if they can't even see us." She paused for a moment, went over to the bar and peered into the face of a leather-jacketed man who was sitting alone drinking

Piña Coladas. She stared directly into his eyes, first from about a foot away, then closer and closer until her nose was almost touching his. He remained completely motionless, unblinking, as if he couldn't see her. But just as Susan was about to turn away and rejoin the others, the man unexpectedly kissed her on the tip of her nose and laughed.

"You want a kiss, sugar, you have only to ask."

Susan, red-faced and furious, stalked out of the restaurant in front of Henry and Gil and wouldn't even look at Springer. Henry and Gil chuckled, and even Springer seemed to allow himself a neutral smile.

"We are not invisible, I regret," Springer said. "We have simply failed to make an impression on the memories of the staff."

They left the restaurant. Susan was sulking but she didn't want to go home yet, especially if the others were staying. Springer beckoned and they followed him along Camino del Mar to the block just before the Bennett Coast Hotel. The night was still foggy and humid, although a light wind was getting up. In the middle of the block, between the Cord Realty offices and the Eleganza Fashion Boutique, there stood a three-story, stucco-fronted house, its shutters tilting from corroded hinges, its pink paint stained black with damp, its front yard densely overgrown with wild bougainvillea, its railings broken and rusty. It was a house that spoke silently but eloquently of neglect, decay and lost lives.

"In here?" asked Gil, wrinkling his nose in distaste. "Come on, man, this has to be a put-on. Either that or the most creative mugging I ever heard of."

"Follow me," Springer said and walked up the weedy concrete path. He unlocked the front door and hesitantly they followed him inside. The door silently closed behind them. Springer crossed the hallway, found the light switch and flicked it on.

The interior of the house was completely bare: no furniture, no carpets, only naked light bulbs dangling from the ceiling. At one time it must have been a house of considerable elegance. The mahogany staircase curved down to the hallway in a graceful sweep and the doors were of solid oak, with detailed beading. Despite the decrepitude of the outside, the inside rooms seemed dry and clean, as if they had been freshly swept. Their footsteps clattered on the bare boards and their voices echoed as if the house were already occupied by furtive spirits. There was a strong and curious smell of laurel.

"We have to go upstairs," said Springer. Without hesitation he led the way up the staircase, one long-fingered hand trailing on the banister. Henry, who came close behind him, noticed that his shoes were more like moccasins that street shoes, made of black leather all in one piece.

They crossed the upstairs landing and on the opposite side Springer opened a door that led into a large room with French windows at one end. These windows were as black as ink now but during the day they must have offered a wide view of the gardens behind the house and beyond, possibly as far as the shore. Henry, Gil and Susan could see themselves reflected in the glass, the anxious occupants of a strange and empty room.

The walls of the room had been painted turquoise many years earlier. There were still rectangular marks where pictures had once hung and scars on the plaster where light fixtures had been removed from either side of the fireplace. Springer closed the door and turned to face his guests, his straw-colored eyes as pale as the dry white wine he had been drinking.

Henry said, "All right. Here we are. Now are you going to tell us why you brought us here?"

"This house is built at one of the nine hundred key locations in America," said Springer. When he saw that they didn't understand him, he explained, "There are nine hundred places in the continental United States where the power may be tapped, and this is one of them."

"Power?" asked Henry suspiciously.

"The power that created me and, ultimately, the power that created you," said Springer. He pointed up toward the ceiling.

"Are we talking about the power of God?" Gil asked. "Is that what we're talking about?"

Springer smiled. His hand made a brushing motion in the air as if he were stroking a soft, invisible animal. "You may call it the power of God if you wish, but that is to suppose that it is wholly good. That is the popular human conception of God, a divine being without fault or weakness. The reality is rather different, as most realities are. The reality is that there is a power capable of being turned against those who rob and murder and corrupt the lives of the young, but this power is only *relatively* good. It would not be effective if it were wholly good—good without compromise—because no war can be fought on terms of totality. Extremism in the name of whatever cause is the most destructive of all human characteristics. It is equally the most destructive of all spiritual characteristics. No, my friends, this power is wise, and this power is terrible, and this power is hugely creative, but this power is not perfect."

Henry asked with undisguised skepticism, "Does the power have a name?"

Springer nodded. "The power is called Ashapola, after the ancient word that means 'avenger of great wrongs.'"

Susan, in a thin, quiet voice, asked, "Are you trying to tell us that Ashapola is God?"

"God is whatever you want him to be," Springer explained. "But the true power of creation is not 'God' or 'Buddha' or 'Gitche Manitou'; it is Ashapola, who embraces all of these deities and more. It was Ashapola who made man in his own image, with all of his own strengths and his own weaknesses. Unlike the deity you worship as God, who is forever punishing his children for failing to be perfect, Ashapola recognizes their imperfections as his own and teaches them instead to overcome them, to use their weaknesses as strengths."

Henry thoughtfully rubbed his chin. "Well," he said, "I

think I've heard just about everything I need to hear. In my opinion, Mr. Springer, you're cracked. You're welcome to your own religion, your own point of view. This is a free country. But I regularly turn the Mormons away from my door, as well as the Seventh Day Adventists; and while you've found a novel way of claiming my attention, I'm afraid that Ashapola doesn't impress me any more than Moroni or Boroni. I'm going now, and I expect these two young people will want to come with me.''

He took a step toward the door, just one step, and it was then that Springer lifted his right arm into the air and the room began to darken, until Henry could see little but the glistening of Springer's eyes and the whiteness of his upraised hand. There was a soft, crackling sound like a fire burning, or cellophane being crumpled, and the atmosphere inside the room grew dense with the smell of laurel.

Gil said, "Jesus Christ, Henry, what's that?" and Susan drew in her breath sharply.

In the center of the room, a tall, transparent figure had suddenly appeared, indeterminate at first but quickly growing clearer. Henry stared in horror. The crackling sound grew louder until it sounded like radio interference, and then louder still, so they could scarely hear themselves think.

The figure was white, and naked. It was the figure of a young girl, her back toward them. Her blonde hair fanned out in the air as if she were floating in water rather than standing in the center of a room. Springer stepped away from her but his hand was still raised and his face bore an expression of intense concentration.

"Springer! Do you hear me, Springer!" Henry bellowed. "We've had enough of these tricks, you understand me? We're going! Now stop this nonsense and put on the lights!"

Springer ignored him. Instead, he made a twisting gesture with his left hand and the figure of the girl began to slowly turn around.

"Springer, what the hell is going on here?" Henry roared. The crackling noise was louder than ever.

The girl gradually turned to face them. As before, she was beautiful. This time her eyes were open and she was staring at them with an expression so sad and hurt that Henry was completely silenced. Gil reached out jerkily and gripped Henry's left shoulder—out of fear, out of a need for companionship, out of the plain fact that he didn't know what to do and all he could hope for was that Henry might somehow be able to guide them out of the room, away from Springer and away from the girl who was staring at them so pitifully even though she was dead.

The girl's hair undulated in the air. Her features seemed to change and shift as if viewed through water. She opened and closed her mouth several times, giving Susan the impression that she wanted to say something, that she was trying to appeal for help.

"This is how it happened . . ." Springer's voice began. "This is what she was like in the beginning. Look at her closely . . . see how beautiful she was."

In spite of their fear, they looked at the girl intently. Her face was beautifully structured, the face of a fashion model. Her breasts were large white globes patterned with traceries of blue veins and nippled with palest pink. Her waist was slim, uncreased; she had obviously never had a baby. Her thighs were slim and well-shaped. She wore a thin silver chain around her left ankle.

"We know nothing about her—not even her name—but she is the first," said Springer. "Watch what happened to her."

Gradually the girl's expression altered. She gave a smile, a little distant but still a smile. She held out her arms and although they could see nobody there, she appeared to be holding and kissing somebody, an invisible lover. Her thighs rubbed together rhythmically in a slowly quickening erotic rhythm and she kissed the air in front of her more fiercely now, using her tongue, and her teeth.

Then she opened her mouth wide and began licking at the

empty air in a lewd and suggestive way. Her tongue ran down some invisible length before her lips stretched wide to contain something pendulous, which she lightly thrummed with the tip of her tongue. While she was doing this, she squeezed her breasts with her hands until the nipples rose so hard they jutted between her fingers.

Now she arched her head back and let her hands slide down her stomach and between her thighs. She opened herself with her fingers, just a little at first, revealing pink, glistening folds; but as she kissed and kissed again, she stretched herself open wider with each kiss.

Then something extraordinary happened. She seemed to be penetrated by something invisible but huge, and she was stretched even further to accommodate it. She squeezed her eyes tight with pain and opened her mouth in a silent scream, but the remarkable thing was that there was nothing there, at least nothing anyone else could see. The girl began to buck her hips back and forth, holding her arms out with her hands clenched as if she were tightly gripping the back of a furious assailant. Her thighs were wide apart now, and she was opened up beyond anything Henry had ever imagined.

The girl's bucking movements reached a frenzied crescendo. She shuddered, twisted, and was abruptly flooded with viscous white fluid that coursed down her thighs. Then she closed her eyes, crossed her hands over her breasts and for a long time was motionless, as if she were sleeping.

"Time passes . . . days pass," said Springer's voice. The light in the room flickered on and off, swiveling as it did so from one side of the room to the other. Henry suddenly realized they were watching a living diary: a record of passing days, with the sun rising in the east and setting in the west, over and over again in double time, like a speeded-up movie.

Almost imperceptibly the girl's stomach began to swell. She woke and slept, woke and slept. Her stomach grew larger until it was the size of a woman three- or four-months pregnant. It was then that it began to show movement. Not the uneven bumping movement of a baby's arms and legs but an extraordinary twitching, writhing movement.

The girl's eyes opened. They registered pain. Her stomach began to knot and ripple; she clenched her teeth in agony and screamed. The days poured past, sun rising, sun setting. Her stomach heaved and churned, her eyes bulged. She opened her mouth in a long shriek that never seemed to end. Henry, Gil and Susan could hear nothing but they could see that the pain she was suffering was intolerable.

Then there was a strong, convulsive jerk in the girl's stomach, a localized movement near her navel. Suddenly her skin rose in a narrow, chisel-shaped protrusion, dark gray like a cancer. But this wasn't cancer. The dark gray was the head of an eel visible through her skin. And then the skin burst open and a vivid streak of blood slid down her stomach and the waggling head of an eel appeared, staring out at the daylight from yellow, slitted eyes, its scales slicked with blood.

"Do you want more?" asked Springer. "Do you want to see everything?"

"Stop it!" Henry roared. And as quickly as she had materialized, the girl disappeared. The lights in the room abruptly brightened and everything was back the way it had been.

Susan screamed at Springer, "You're sick! Do you know that? You're sick!" She was shaking and tears had streaked her eye makeup.

Gil stepped toward Springer and demanded, "What are you, some kind of pervert or something? Somebody who gets kicks out of—what was that?—some kind of Three-D snuff movie or something?"

But Henry held Gil's arm, restraining him. "Whatever we feel about Mr. Springer, Gil, I don't think we ought to misjudge him. What he just showed us was disgusting but it was also true. It was a playback of what happened to the girl we found on the beach. I don't know how it was done but I expect Mr. Springer can explain it to us."

"A small but comprehensive sample of DNA taken from

the girl's brain was quite sufficient to help me re-create her memories," said Springer without emotion.

"It sounds as if the Lord thy God is a scientific god," Henry commented, not altogether kindly.

"Science is only the human discovery of everything Ashapola created," retorted Springer. "I call it DNA because that is the name by which you will recognize it. Ashapola calls it something else altogether."

Henry said, "I read something interesting in my ex-wife's book on eels. It said that in ancient Scandinavia, eels were sometimes referred to as the 'sperm of the Devil.'"

Springer nodded, almost with relief. "What you saw— those images—they were an exact re-creation of what happened to that girl in the last few months of her life. In late February of this year she had intercourse, as you so graphically saw. As the year progressed, she became increasingly gravid, but not with child. At least not with *human* child. Whatever she had intercourse with, she was impregnated with creatures that appeared to be eels. Eventually they killed her. How she got into the sea, I don't yet know. But I suspect she may have been dumped there in order to make her death seem less suspicious."

Susan whispered, "You don't know what . . . what it was that had sex with her?"

Springer shook his head. "Henry referred to the Devil. But the opponents of Ashapola take on many different forms, some of which you would identify as animals, some as men. This girl's memory has been blotted out—by shock perhaps, or by the deliberate intervention of the creature that had sex with her, or by a version of the same technique I used in the restaurant to avoid being remembered by the waiters. Whichever it was, she remembers the sexual act but cannot remember what it was that had sex with her— human, animal or something else altogether."

Henry saw that Susan was still trembling with disbelief and disgust. He put an arm around her shoulders and held her close. He looked at Springer defiantly.

"Very well. You've shown us what happened to the girl on the beach. You've told us that she was . . . well, that she had sex with something. We've seen the consequences. I think I can speak for all of us and say that we believe you, although I must question the necessity of your showing it to us so graphically, especially to Susan."

"And?" Springer asked, bland-faced. "What is your point?"

"I have no point except that we believe you and that we wish to leave now."

"I second that," put in Gil. "There might have been some reason for that little picture show, but what it was sure beats me."

Springer laid one hand flat across the other and carefully examined his fingernails. "The reason for it was simply this, my friends. It was necessary for me to make you believe me, and I know that none of what I have been telling you is easy to accept. I am not only asking you to believe in Ashapola, I am asking you to understand that it is desperately urgent that the beast that impregnated this girl be found."

"Not by us, Charlie," Gil told him sardonically.

Springer raised his eyes. "Yes, my friends, by you. You see, there is nobody else. You saw the girl, you saw the eels. You are the only ones who truly believe. You were brought together by the will of Ashapola, believe me. By design rather than by accident. Your destiny was laid out for you this morning when you found the girl lying on the sand. You have to find the beast and find it quickly. You have to destroy it."

Henry's lower lip wouldn't stop quivering but he managed to ask, "What if we refuse? What if we just go about our business and refuse? What if we don't want to have anything to do with it?"

Springer slowly shook his head. "You have no choice, my dear sir . . . because if you fail to find the beast, the beast will almost certainly find you."

6

Nancy's eleven-year-old Cutlass had almost reached the turnoff at La Jolla Drive when the steering stiffened, the brakes went mushy and the oil warning light blinked on. The car rolled slower and slower, and it was only by wrenching the steering wheel violently to the right that she managed to maneuver the vehicle off the freeway. It stopped and she applied the parking brake. She said, *"Shit."*

It had been the crummy evening to end all crummy evenings. Now she was stranded on the northbound freeway at eight o'clock in the evening, dressed up in her best blue-linen suit and her matching blue shoes, angry, frustrated and unhappy.

It had been her second date with John Bream, who worked beside her in the creative department at Sutton & Ramirez, the second-largest advertising agency in San Diego. John was advertising's answer to Richard Gere. At least that was what Nancy had thought at first. He was athletic, argumentative, highly creative and sullenly handsome, and when he had asked her out two weeks ago, she had spent half a week's salary on a new silk dress from Capriccio and three hours at Young Attitude having her bright-red hair cut and styled.

Their first date had been wonderful. A Korean dinner at the Seoul House, disco dancing and then a drive out to the shore to watch the surf. They had kissed and John had told her how attractive she was: "You're the most sparkling, vivacious girl I ever met, bar none."

Tonight though, when she had arrived at his apartment in the Old Town, he hadn't made a dinner reservation and he hadn't planned on dancing. He had been wearing a bright-green terry bathrobe and what he must have thought was a seductive smile. When she had protested, he had lost his temper. "Do you know how much money I've spent on you already? And now you're telling me you're not going to come across because it's against your principles? Jesus, you women! Some feminist revolution! You're independent only when it happens to suit you!"

His crudeness had appalled her. She had read letters from readers in *Cosmopolitan* about men who expected sex in direct repayment for money invested on dinners but she herself had never encountered it before—at least not so blatantly. She had turned around and left. He had shouted obscenities at her down the stairs. "You tight-assed bitch!"

She twisted the key again and again in the Cutlass's ignition. The starter motor whinnied until it began to sound like a regurgitating horse, and at last it refused to do anything but click. Her previous boyfriend, an overbearing know-it-all named Ned, had warned her several times that her alternator was on the fritz. She climbed out of the car and stood glaring at the hood as if expecting the motor to start up out of sheer embarrassment.

Although it was summer, there was a cool wind blowing up here where the freeway cleaved between the grassy hills of La Jolla Village. The sky was the color of pasqueflowers, blue fading into violet, and southern swallows soared high above her head. Oh, well, she thought wryly, at least they aren't vultures.

Traffic whizzed past, orange parking lights glowing smugly, interiors dark and private, and even though she raised the Cutlass's hood and switched on the emergency flashers, nobody stopped. There had been too many rapes and muggings on the freeway lately. Too many motorists had stopped to assist a stranded lady, only to find themselves attacked by two or three hoodlums jumping out of the bushes.

Nancy began to feel shivery and she rubbed her arms to keep herself warm. It was almost dark now and she was beginning to think she would have to leave the car and walk all the way to La Jolla Village to find a taxi to take her home.

She reached into the car for her pocketbook and was just about to lock the door when a white Lincoln slowed down and pulled off the road only twenty yards ahead. It waited with its engine running and its brake lights flaring bright, indicating that the driver was holding the car in gear. Nancy hesitated for a moment and then began to walk toward the Lincoln, ducking her head a little to see what kind of person was sitting inside.

She drew level with the passenger door and the driver put down the window. She looked in, her hand shading her eyes from the glare of the traffic. White-leather upholstery, expensive. The driver was wearing a black-leather designer jacket and black pants. His face was thin, hollow-cheeked and swarthy, almost Mexican. His eyes sparkled white in the darkness.

"Having trouble?" he asked. Nancy could hear the soft tones of hymn singing on the car tape deck. *O Jesu, I have promised.* Perhaps he was a priest, she thought to herself. But what kind of priest wears a black-leather designer jacket and drives around in a white late-model Lincoln?

"My car died," she said anxiously. "The battery's dead, I guess. Anyway, it won't start."

"Where are you headed?"

"La Jolla. Right at the top of Prospect Street."

"Is that far?"

"If you take the next turnoff, it's about two miles toward the ocean."

"Can I offer you a ride?"

Nancy bit her lip. She remembered her friend Carole, who had accepted a ride home from a Thanksgiving party in Leucadia last November and had been robbed and raped by three teenage boys. She remembered a girl from the office, Linda, who had been attacked in Balboa Park in broad daylight and almost killed. Just because this man was good-looking, well-dressed and driving an expensive car didn't mean anything. Sex criminals came in every color, every size and every conceivable variety.

The man waited patiently while Nancy tried to make up her mind. At last she said, "Okay. Thank you. That's very kind of you."

He released the automatic lock and Nancy opened the passenger door and climbed in. Before he started off, he looked at her appraisingly and said, "You're a pretty girl. You ought to be careful out on the freeway."

Nancy tried to smile. "I was scared at first that nobody was going to stop. Then I was scared that somebody might."

The man glanced in the rearview mirror and then took the Lincoln out into the traffic. "You're not scared of me, are you?"

"Do I have any reason to be?" Nancy asked.

"I don't think so. But you can never tell, can you, what evil lurks in the hearts of men?" He paused, steering the car with one hand. Then he added, "Only the Shadow knows, ho-ho-ho."

"That dates you," Nancy said. "My father used to know all those radio catch phrases."

"Like 'Nobody home, I hope, I hope, I hope,'" the man suggested.

"That's right! How did you know that?"

"That was Elmer Blurt, out of *Al Pearce and His Gang*."

Nancy shook her head in amusement. "You know, I never met anybody who knew all those catch phrases except for my father."

The man looked in the mirror again. "I should turn off here?"

"That's right. Where it says La Jolla Village Drive."

He piloted the Lincoln off the freeway and up the La Jolla exit ramp. At the top of the ramp he took a left and headed uphill toward La Jolla.

"I should introduce myself," he said. "My name's Ronald DeVries."

"I'm Nancy Busch."

"You might have gathered that I don't live around here," Ronald said. "As a matter of fact, I just came up from Mexico. I was living in San Hipolito for quite some time."

"I don't know San Hipolito," Nancy confessed. "Is it a nice place?"

Ronald lifted a hand as if to say "San Hipolito? What can I tell you?"

"You didn't like it too much, then?"

"It's okay if you don't have to stay there. I had to."

"I love La Jolla," Nancy told him. "I've lived here for eleven years now. It's much more commercialized than it used to be but it still has charm. You can sit right out on the rocks in the winter when nobody else is around and you might just as well be the only person in the whole world."

"You'll have to direct me," Ronald said as they reached the top of La Jolla Drive.

"A left here. A left."

Ronald said, as he turned the corner with exaggerated care, "You look like you were going out someplace tonight."

"I was. I had a slight disagreement with my boyfriend. Well, ex-boyfriend from now on."

"That's too bad," Ronald said and lapsed into silence.

Nancy asked, "Are you a priest or anything like that?"

"A priest?" he laughed.

"Well, those are hymns, aren't they, on your tape deck?"

Ronald reached over and switched off the tape. "It was something I was just listening to, passing the time."

"Are you going far?"

"I was planning on getting to Santa Barbara."

"That's a long drive. I hope I haven't delayed you."

Ronald overtook a toiling cement truck and then pulled over to the inside lane again to let a red Porsche blare past. "As a matter of fact, I was thinking of giving up on Santa Barbara and inviting you out for dinner."

Nancy shook her head vigorously. "Oh, no, I can't

expect you to do that, not after giving me a ride. Besides, I have to arrange for somebody to get my car. I don't want to wind up with no wheels and no engine."

"Listen," Ronald said, "call the emergency service and arrange for them to get your car. They won't need your keys. Then come out to dinner with me."

"I'm sorry, Ronald," Nancy told him. "That's real generous of you, I mean it. But I hardly know you, and I'm not sure that I feel in the mood for dinner anymore."

Ronald turned the Lincoln into Prospect Street without Nancy directing him and then parked on the slope outside her house.

"How did you know I lived here?" she asked in amazement.

"You told me. Right at the top of Prospect Street, that's what you said. Now, how about dinner? I've really gone cold on the idea of driving all the way to Santa Barbara and I'm going to have to eat somewhere."

"But you're right *here,* right outside the exact house."

"Coincidence," Ronald told her offhandedly. Then, "Come on, Nancy, how about it? A friendly *diner à deux,* no strings attached, no complications. All I'm looking for is company. I hate to eat alone."

"Well . . . all right," Nancy capitulated. "But I'm going to have to call the tow truck first. Do you want to come inside?"

"I'll wait in the car if you want me to."

"Of course not. Come along in."

The house in which Nancy lived was large and secluded. It had been built in 1936 out of red brick, although it was difficult to see much of the brickwork now because of the thickly overhanging ivy. Fifteen years ago the owner of the house had gone back East and ordered that the property be divided into apartments for long-term leasing. Nancy had sublet the second-floor apartment at the back of the house from an oceanologist who had been sent to work in Kyoto for four years.

She opened the door and led the way inside. The hallway was gloomy and smelled of lavender furniture polish and Chinese cooking. Opposite the stairs there was a grandfather clock that ticked with infinite weariness and whose half-seen pendulum always reminded Nancy of something by Edgar Allan Poe.

She climbed the stairs, Ronald following her. "Do you know who to call to pick up your car?" he asked, as she unlocked her apartment door.

"Don't worry, it's happened before," she told him, switching on the lights. Ronald came in and looked around the living room with approval. It was sparsely but tastefully furnished with plain modern furniture, glass-topped tables, Italian lamps with necks like futuristic giraffes, and Indian blankets on the walls. While Nancy went to the phone, he walked over to the window and drew back the plain woven drapes.

"You have an excellent view of the neighbors," he observed. "Are those two having a fight over there? They look like they're shouting."

There was an oil painting on the wall beside the telephone. It was a nude, and it was obviously Nancy. Ronald came closer and made a deliberate play of comparing the portrait and the model, turning his head from one to the other as if he were watching tennis. The likeness was unmistakable: the pale-skinned, slightly squarish face with the short, straight nose and the sudden splash of freckles; the bright-red hair; the tall, angular figure with small but well-rounded breasts.

Nancy watched him as he made his comparison, the phone still held to her ear.

"One of my boyfriends was an art student," she commented.

"He was good," Ronald acknowledged.

She looked around at the portrait. "You're the first man who's ever said that. Usually they say they prefer the original. You know, flattery. Jealousy too, that some other man has seen me nude. My girl friends don't like it either. They think it's an upwardly mobile way of streaking."

Ronald shrugged. "I'm not like other men. Do you mind if I smoke?"

"Go ahead. There's an ashtray over on the bookcase."

Ronald crossed to the other side of the room and picked up the ashtray. As he did so, he inspected Nancy's collection of books. *Advertising Art. The 100 Greatest Advertisements. The Techniques of Persuasion.* Then he came back, tucking a Russian *papirosi* cigarette between his lips and lighting it one-handed with a folded-over matchbook. The tricky technique of a man who thinks appearances are all-important, a man who can toss peanuts in the air and catch them in his mouth.

"So you're in advertising?" he asked as Nancy completed her call to the tow-truck company and put down the phone. "The second-oldest profession."

"I'm a designer," Nancy said. "I paste eentsy little bits of lettering onto slippery sheets of overlay and draw a lot of lines and get paid for it."

She was obviously waiting for him to tell her what *he* did but he stood there silent, his hands in his pockets, puffing at his cigarette and looking at her unblinkingly.

"Shall we have some dinner?" she suggested.

"Sure. What do you like to eat?"

"Could you bear Mexican?" Nancy asked. "Alfonso's is good."

"I could bear Mexican," he said.

They drove down to Alfonso's even though it wasn't more than a five-minute walk to the tourist stretch of Prospect, with its fashionable boutiques, high-priced restaurants, art galleries and realty offices. The sidewalks were crowded with evening promenaders and there were no free parking spaces so in the end Ronald parked the Lincoln in a reserved area outside La Galeria art gallery.

As he locked the car, he nodded toward the art-gallery window. "How about that?" he asked.

They crossed the sidewalk to look at the window display. On a blue burlap-covered stand, under a single spotlight, stood a bronze statuette of the Great God Pan, cloven-hoofed, goat's-horned, dancing and playing his pipes. His face was sly and sharp, and infinitely wicked.

"It's terrific," said Nancy. "A classic." She was being sarcastic. She thought it was awful. She wouldn't have bought it even as a doorstop.

Ronald said nothing but nodded and stood staring at the statuette, his hands at his sides as if he were somehow mesmerized. Nancy waited patiently. She didn't like to urge him on too much since he was buying.

Eventually, without explaining what it was about the statuette that had interested him, Ronald turned away from the window and offered Nancy his arm. As they walked along the noisy, brightly lit sidewalk, Nancy found herself feeling unexpectedly cheerful. Perhaps fate had been taking care of her after all when she had argued with John and when her car had broken down on the freeway. Perhaps at last (*please*, fate!) she had found someone special because there was no doubt about it—Ronald DeVries was special.

They shared *fettucine* and *linguine* smothered in Alfonso's thick, secret sauce. They ate *carne asada* and washed it down with strong red Chianti. They talked about advertising and office affairs and cars that broke down and childhood embarrassments. They laughed and they held each other's hands across the table, their eyes sparkling in the lights from the candles that flickered between them. Ronald ordered more Chianti and Nancy went to the restroom. She looked at her face in the mirror and said out loud, "I hope you're not becoming infatuated, my dear."

When she came back to the table, Ronald poured her another glass of wine and chuckled. "You know something?" he said. "You know what our Christian names are? Ronald and Nancy! Can you believe that? Isn't that too presidential for words?"

"You were telling me all about those old W. C. Fields radio sketches," Nancy reminded him.

"Oh, sure. They were terrific. There was one where Fields says he always collapsed at the sound of the word 'work.' In his family they wouldn't say it out loud, they always referred to it as 'W.' Otherwise he would pass clean out and the only remedy was a deep dipper of dogberry brandy diluted with straight gin."

Ronald did a passable W. C. Fields impression. "I remember the first drink of it . . . I turned a little pale."

Nancy laughed. She hadn't felt so happy in months. She took Ronald's hand again and asked, "How do you know all this stuff?"

He shrugged. "I guess I always enjoyed the radio."

"But they don't have that kind of program on the radio these days, do they?"

Ronald made a disinterested face and took out a cigarette.

"Do you have tapes?" asked Nancy. "I mean, could I listen to some of them?"

Ronald shook his head. "I just heard it, that's all."

It was clear that he didn't feel like talking about it any longer so Nancy tried to change the subject. "You haven't told me anything about Mexico, what you were doing down there."

He looked at her as if surprised that she had asked. "I wasn't doing anything down there," he replied after a short pause.

"I'm sorry," she said. "I didn't mean to be nosy. I was interested, that's all."

"Well, don't be. It wasn't at all interesting."

"Okay, I'm sorry," Nancy said, rather put out. She couldn't understand why the mention of Mexico should have made him so unsettled all of a sudden, and so sour. He had enjoyed his Mexican meal but it seemed as if the country of Mexico itself was a platinum-plated downer. He puffed quickly at his cigarette and then crushed it out, half-smoked.

"Well, let's talk about something else," Nancy suggested. "We don't have to talk about Mexico."

Ronald stared at her sharply. "Look, what is it with you? I said I didn't want to talk about Mexico. I thought I made it perfectly clear that I didn't want to talk about Mexico. And all I'm getting is Mexico, Mexico, Mexico."

"For goodness' sake—" Nancy put in, trying to calm him down. "I asked you in all innocence. I didn't know it was going to upset you. Listen, I don't care what you did or didn't do down in Mexico. I was only making polite conversation and if you don't want to talk about it—"

Ronald's face was expressionless, unreadable, as blank as a headstone.

"Ronald?" she queried, reaching for his hand.

At that moment the waiter came bustling over. "Is there anything else, signor? Did you enjoy your meal, signorina?"

"Just bring me the check," Ronald said shortly.

The waiter glanced worriedly at Nancy. "Is everything to your satisfaction, signor? Signorina?"

"Everything's fine. Just bring me the damned check."

Nancy said nothing until they were walking back to the car. "Did you have to talk to the waiter like that? I was embarrassed."

Ronald was tossing his car keys in the air and catching them again, over and over, with an irritating slap-jingle, slap-jingle. He didn't answer and it was plain that his mood had drastically changed to one of unrelenting coldness.

"What happened in Mexico that upset you so much?" Nancy persisted. "I mean, whatever happened, you don't have to take it out on the rest of us. It wasn't *my* fault. And it certainly wasn't that waiter's fault."

"You don't think so?" asked Ronald. "It's been your fault all along, people like you and him."

"I don't understand you," Nancy remonstrated. "A half-hour ago I thought you were fantastic, the nicest, funniest guy I'd ever met. A half-hour ago, if you can believe it, I even thought I was going slightly crazy over you. But the way you're acting now, what can I say? What are you blaming me for? Something that happened in Mexico that I don't even know anything about? I never saw you before tonight, how *could* I be responsible? And the way you're going on now, I don't think I ever *want* to see you again."

Ronald stopped beside the car and regarded Nancy over the top of the white-vinyl roof with an expression that had altered yet again. The coldness had gone. In its place was self-satisfaction and patronizing smugness.

"You *will* see me again, whether you want to or not."

"I don't think so," said Nancy. "Now, I think I'll walk home, thank you. Do you want me to pay for my share of the dinner?"

Ronald unlocked the car. "Forget it. The condemned lady ate a hearty meal."

"Now what in hell is *that* supposed to mean? Are you trying to frighten me or what?"

"Nobody—ever—has accused me of *trying* to frighten anybody," Ronald said.

Nancy stood where she was. Ronald climbed into the car and slammed the door. His last reply hung in the air like a complex carillon of bells. He had placed unusual and provocative emphasis on the words "ever" and "trying." He had sounded to Nancy as if he had really meant "ever." Not just a human lifetime but hundreds of years, even thousands of years, maybe even eternity. And he had emphasized "trying" as if he had meant that it was unnecessary for him to try, that he frightened people without any effort whatever.

As he leaned forward to insert the ignition key, she caught a glimpse of his face, and the bright streetlight seemed to catch him at an unusual angle so that he appeared suddenly drawn, old and inexplicably unpleasant. He looked up again and the oldness vanished but in that brief moment—what had it been? insight? revelation?—she had felt she had seen him as he really was, and she was unhappily glad of it. All right, so fate hadn't been good to her after all. Ronald had turned out to be just as much of a macho bastard as John Bream and all the rest of them. But at least he had revealed himself quickly, before she became entangled. Fate might have been playing with her but at least it had spared her the long-drawn-out waiting and hoping she usually had to suffer.

She swung her bag over her shoulder and started to walk north along Prospect. It was only a five-minute walk back to her house. She didn't wave, she didn't turn around. She had encountered Ronald by chance, she was going to part with him the same way. Casually, like two people who have talked together on a plane and then go their separate ways. She heard the car start up behind her and the squealing of the tires as he pulled away from the curb but she kept on walking steadily. Ronald turned the Lincoln around in the middle of the road, suspension bucking, and then drove past at high speed without looking at her.

Good-bye, she said to herself, knight in shining armor thou never wert. Still, she was grateful to be back in La Jolla instead of marooned on Interstate-5. She owed him that much, whatever his complexes were, and for the dinner. She wondered why he was so incredibly sensitive about Mexico. What could have happened to him there that was so appalling?

She thought about something else, too, as she followed the curve of Prospect Street, her hair blown by the cool sea wind. She thought about Ronald standing in front of the La Galeria window for minutes on end, staring at that statuette of Pan. On reflection, his behavior seemed really strange, although it hadn't struck her as particularly peculiar at the time. He had stared at it and stared at it, and she could still picture his expression: contempt, but fascination too, as if he couldn't tear himself away from it no matter how incompetent a piece of work it was.

She reached her house and walked up the driveway to the front door. There were no lights in the front windows. Most of the tenants were out for the evening. The woman who lived directly below Nancy had found herself a wealthy

Indian petro-geologist (married, of course), who had taken her with him to an oil seminar in Phoenix.

She took out her keys but as she stepped up to the front door, she was surprised to find it slightly open. She hesitated. Nobody ever left the front door open. It was not that they didn't trust their neighbors or the local inhabitants. Out of the tourist season, La Jolla was as peaceable a community as you could find anywhere in Southern California. Boondocks-on-Sea, one of her friends called it. But the summer brought casual theft, purse snatching, spasmodic outbursts of aggravated assault, and rape.

At length Nancy pushed the door open a little wider. The hallway was dark and silent. She could just make out the lower part of the staircase, faintly illuminated by the stained-glass window at the turn in the stairs. She called, "Hello? Is anybody there?"

Silence. She waited a moment longer and then pushed the door as wide as it would go. Now she could hear the grandfather clock ticking, wearily, wearily, and see the intermittent reflection of its pendulum. She remembered Ronald's curious warning—*You will see me again, whether you want to or not*—and she had an irrational fear that he was waiting for her under the stairs, ready to pounce on her.

"Ronald?" she called, feeling foolish.

There was no answer. Holding her breath, she slid sideways into the hallway and reached for the light switch.

The lights flicked on. The hallway was deserted. Drab and shabby, and smelling, as it always did, of cooking.

There was a note on the hall stand. She walked across quickly and picked it up. It was addressed to her from the Tecolote Road Wrecking Company, Inc. It was written in a careless, scrawled hand and advised her that her vehicle had been towed as she had instructed to their downtown auto-repair shop, where it would be fixed and ready for pickup in approximately four days. She tucked the note back in its envelope and looked around. The tow-truck crew must have called here and somebody had answered the door for them and then failed to close it properly. She could hear, faintly, the sounds of *Matt Houston* from old Mrs. Oestreicher's television, first floor back. It had probably been her.

Nancy closed the door behind her and climbed the stairs to her apartment. She opened it up and went inside, throwing her bag onto the sofa. Kicking off her shoes, she went through to the kitchen and took a bottle of white wine from the Frigidaire. There were three neatly washed wine glasses on the drainer, the only three wine glasses she owned. She filled one with Paul Masson's best and went back through to the living room.

She kept thinking about Ronald DeVries and how his mood had swung so violently. One minute he had been infinitely charming, the next he had seemed capable of strangling her. Oh, well, her mother had always warned her about accepting rides from strange men. "The white slave trade's still thriving, Nancy, and don't let anyone tell you different." Nancy finished half her glass of wine in three thirsty swallows, then refilled it.

She tried to watch television for twenty minutes or so but she was tired and restless, and woozy with wine, so she went through to the bedroom, lowered the raffia blinds and undressed. She hung her blue suit carefully in the closet and parked her blue shoes neatly side by side beneath it. She had a fragment of music on her brain, the introduction to Bob Dylan's song, "What's a Nice Girl Like You Doing in a Dump Like This?" She hummed it again and again as she ran a bath and went back and forth from the bathroom to the bedroom, cleaning off her nail polish, curling up her hair, wiping off her lipstick.

She spent ten luxurious minutes in the bath, watching the drips from the leaky faucet and the steam rising up to the ceiling like a succession of embryonic ghosts. She found herself thinking again of the statuette of Pan, with its hoofs and its beard and its wicked, slanting eyes. She seemed to have an image of it caught in her mind, like the shuddering frame of a video film on pause, an image that wouldn't go away no matter how hard she tried to dismiss it.

She dried herself and sat naked at her dressing table, dusting herself with iris-scented talc and smoothing her face with Clinique cream. Look at me, she said to herself. Twenty-six years old, fashionable, good-looking, intelligent. Big green eyes, sensual lips, a model's figure. What is it about me that proves irresistible to all the wrong men? Why am I sleeping alone tonight for the one hundred and fifty-seventh time this year? I don't know why I even bother to take the pill.

She cupped one hand over her left breast. If you touch me, am I not aroused? If you kiss me, do I not respond? I'm a woman, a fully equipped, highly emotional woman with all the passions of a woman. Yet I expect to be treated like a human being too, not the way John Bream tried to treat me. Not the way Ronald DeVries treated me either. Why do men blame me for everything? John, for being sexually ungrateful for a Carte Blanche bill of seventy-eight dollars and twenty-five cents, including gratuity. Ronald, for some inexplicable hardship he suffered down in San Hipolito, Mexico.

She tied a scarf around her hair and went to the closet to take out a clean shirt. She always slept in men's shirts, partly because they made comfortable nightwear and partly because she liked to go into Sears' menswear department and buy them, as if she had a husband or a steady boyfriend. She climbed into bed with the book she had been reading for the past seven months, never progressing more than two or three pages a night: *An Analysis of Contemporary Advertising*.

"Ogilvy's 1958 advertisement for imported Rolls-Royces contained nothing but facts, without adjectives . . ." she began to read. But then she thought about the statuette of Pan and Ronald's voice saying, "Nobody—ever—has accused me of *trying* to frighten anybody." Of *trying* to frighten anybody.

She tried harder to concentrate on her book. "The agency was faced with an antiquated image of Rolls-Royce as a boxlike car that sold for $20,000 and over, and required a chauffeur to drive it . . ."

"Nobody—ever—"

She read about a page and a half and then yawned and put the book aside on the night table. She switched off the bedside lamp and wriggled under the comforter. She lay on her side for a while, watching the patterns of light dancing on the wall. They danced there every night: the streetlights shining through the yuccas in the backyard. On stormy nights they flickered wildly, but tonight was temperate, only slightly breezy, and their dance was sedate. Nancy's eyes closed. She jerked once and frowned, and then she slept.

Her sleep was dreamless at first but soon she found herself somewhere on a windy hill miles from anywhere. In the distance she could see the red-and-white lights of traffic flowing along the freeway, but something told her it was the wrong freeway and that she was walking in the wrong direction. She tried not to panic but she knew she was lost and that it would take hours to find her way back.

She reached an old-fashioned house standing isolated, silent and derelict. She glided up the steps and found that the door was open. Glancing to the side, she saw a wicker-seated rocking chair lying on its side on the derelict veranda and gray rats tugging at the seat with their sharp teeth. "Someone has died," she thought, and as a thick feeling of darkness and claustrophobia came over her, she knew she would have to enter the house and try to find a telephone.

She opened the door. The interior was gloomy and suffocating. There was a tall display cabinet standing by the side of the stairs. Its glass windows were obscured with grease, dust and the patina of hundreds of years of neglect. She glided toward it and tried to peer inside. She could make out dark and twisted shapes but even when she wiped her hand across the greasy glass, it was impossible to see what the shapes were. For some reason, she found them frightening.

"Nobody—ever—" whispered a voice, a voice as cold as the drip of a faucet in a long-abandoned bathroom. "Nobody—ever—has accused me of *trying*—"

She ascended the staircase without moving her legs and passed a lighted window halfway up in which a bronze statuette of the Great God Pan was dancing. The statue remained motionless but she was sure it would pursue her once she turned her back on it. It seemed, for some reason, to be poisonously evil, the very essence of corruption and terror.

"To frighten anybody—to *frighten* anybody—"

She rose to the second-floor landing. She tried to turn around to make sure the Great God Pan wasn't following her but she found it impossible to turn her neck. She felt as if all her muscles had seized up and that she was powerless to prevent herself from gliding across the landing, not quickly but steadily, silently and irresistibly, toward the door of her own apartment.

The apartment door dissolved like brown fog and she passed through it into the living room. She suddenly thought of the naked portrait of herself by the telephone. Suppose somebody saw it and was scandalized? Suppose somebody saw it and thought she was immoral and that she would have sex with any man who asked her? She tried to turn around to see if the portrait was still there but her neck remained locked in a painful muscular cramp. She forgot that she was supposed to be looking for a telephone.

She went gliding into the bedroom. It was dark in there, impenetrably dark, and the door closed behind her, firm and airtight. She strained her eyes to see where her bed was but the darkness was complete and she had to make her way cautiously across the room with her hands outstretched, feeling her way. She found the bed at last and climbed into it but she had the strangest sensation now that this was no longer a dream, that what she felt was real. She stroked the bed and felt the wrinkled sheets. She could hear the alarm clock ticking. All that was missing was the streetlight dancing on the wall.

Then she heard a sound. It was a scraping, rustling sound—faint but sufficient to convince her there was somebody, or something, in the room. She lay still, listening, her eyes wide, her breath tight. Was that somebody breathing down at the foot of the bed? Or was it simply the echo of her own breath?

She waited. The hands of the clock crept toward half past eleven.

Silence, except for the rushing of her own blood.

Then there was another scraping noise, louder this time. She held her breath again and lifted her head off the pillow, holding it up so her neck ached, peering into the darkness.

I'm dreaming, she thought. This is a dream. All I have to do is wake up.

But then suppose I wake up and find out that it's real, that it's still happening, that there's something in the room with me?

A wind began to blow softly, lifting one of the raffia blinds away from the window so the faintest of lights penetrated the room. It was so dim that Nancy couldn't see anything she recognized. Either that or the room was completely changed. Cautiously she propped herself on her elbows. Was that a mirror where the door should have been? Was that a chair standing in the corner? And next to the chair, that curving shape looked like the side of a large terra-cotta vase.

Scrape, rustle.

Nancy jerked her head around to the other side of the bed, the side where the shadows were. And suddenly he was standing there, right next to her, as white and naked as a corpse, his eyes glowing dull red in the darkness, his teeth catching the light—Ronald DeVries, or a kind of creature that looked like Ronald DeVries.

The wind died down, the blind fell back and the room

was buried in darkness again. Nancy clutched herself close, pulled her legs up under her, shut her eyes and screamed, *"No!"*

Something clawed for her in the blackness. She felt fingernails lacerate her thigh. She tried to twist out of the way but powerful hands gripped her wrists and forced her onto her back. She felt a sharp knee force itself between her thighs, and then one of the hands that gripped her wrists adjusted itself so her upper arm was pinned against the bed by an elbow, and the hand snatched an agonizing, eye-watering clutch of hair. She screamed, or thought she screamed, but how could anybody hear her scream if this was only a dream?

Her shirt was pulled open at the front, the buttons twisted off. Then she felt a heavy, cold, bristly body lying on top of her, a body like a dead pig's. She tried to scream again but she didn't seem to have the breath for it and when she looked up into the darkness, she could see those dimly glowing eyes, like torches shining through a thick blanket, and she could smell winey breath and some other unutterable odor that tightened her throat, knotted her stomach and made it almost impossible for her to speak.

"Don't," she begged in a strangled whisper. *"Don't."*

The creature on top of her dragged at her hair even harder and said something deep in its throat—strange, guttural words that she was unable to understand but that sounded obscene. She thought of John Bream shouting at her down the stairwell. She thought of all the men who had turned and looked at her, a thousand pairs of eyes, all of them calculating, all of them remorseless, all of them wanting nothing but to relieve the urgency of their lust inside her.

"Oh no," she whimpered as the creature's calloused hands began to twist her breasts. "Oh no, oh no, oh *no!"*

She tried one last furious struggle, throwing herself from side to side, tossing her body back and forth, clutching and tugging at everything she could reach. But the creature was too heavy, too strong. It loomed above her, chilly and rank, its eyes hovering only inches from her face, and it pronounced those incomprehensible words again and she could feel them reverberate against its hairy rib cage.

"Please let me wake up," she cried. "Please, dear God, please let me wake up."

But now the creature was leaning forward, pinning her shoulders, and she could feel its tangled beard scratch against her neck and cheek. She could feel it push itself between her legs. It felt as if somebody were forcing a clenched fist into her very being.

"Please, it's too big," she wept. "Please, you're going to kill me. Please!"

She felt pain so intense she thought her pelvis had broken. Her head jerked upward involuntarily and her spine arched. She was hurt too badly to do anything but shudder and gasp, and she had to cling to the creature's shoulders to prevent it from thrusting itself too far inside her.

There was nothing she could do to save herself; she was powerless. She couldn't even wake herself up. All she could do was to hold on tight to the very creature that was torturing her and pray, and pray, and pray.

The creature suddenly cried out *"Sabazius!"* and roared, and she felt its muscles bunch and wriggle like snakes smothered in cold lard. It cried out again, and again, and then it drew itself out of her with a noise she never forgot, liquid and viscous.

She lay where she was as the creature climbed up off the bed, the springs crunching under its weight. *Oh God, oh God, please don't let it kill me. Please let it go away now. Please, God, let me wake up.* She babbled silently like a mad and penitent nun.

It seemed as if she remained hunched up on her bed for hours. She opened and closed her eyes, never knowing for sure whether she was asleep or awake. Gradually the raffia blinds began to lighten and after a while the sun filled the room. She sat up and ran her hands through her hair. Had it been a dream? She looked down at herself. Her shirt was unbuttoned but not torn, and when she turned her hands this way and that, there were no scratches on them, no bruises, nothing to bear witness to a furious struggle with a sharp-nailed beast. She stood up, walked through to the bathroom and looked at herself in the mirror. Her eyes were a little puffy as if she hadn't slept well, but apart from that, she looked quite normal.

Just to make certain, she reached one tentative hand down between her legs. She was moist, as she usually was when she had been dreaming about sex. But there was no trace of the spurting liquid flood with which the creature had filled her. Nor was she sore.

She stared at herself in the mirror. "A dream," she said. "It was nothing but a dream. Can you *believe* it?"

She stepped into the tub, drew the pink-vinyl shower curtain around herself and turned on the faucet, hot and hard. Although there was no evidence that what had happened to her was anything but a vivid nightmare, she made sure that she washed herself thoroughly. She felt polluted by what she had imagined about Ronald DeVries.

She also felt frightened.

She toweled herself and dressed, choosing light-beige slacks and a white short-sleeved blouse. She brushed her hair but didn't blow it dry. It was only seven o'clock and by the time she had made coffee and called a taxi to take her to work, it would be practically dry anyway. She switched on the radio and went through to the kitchen. She hummed along with "We Are the World."

The telephone rang. She went back through to the living room to answer it. "Hello?" she said. Because she was a single girl living alone, she never gave her name until she knew who was calling.

"Nancy? Is this Nancy?" The voice sounded far away.

"Who is this?"

"Don't you recognize my voice? This is Ronald, Ronald DeVries."

Nancy felt a cold prickling across her back. "Ronald? What do you want?"

"I just wanted to know whether you enjoyed yourself, Nancy."

She pressed her hand against her forehead. "Well, yes, as a matter of fact, I did enjoy myself. That is, until you decided to lose your temper and accuse me of all kinds of ridiculous things."

"No, Nancy, not then. I wasn't talking about then. I was talking about afterward."

"Afterward? What do you mean, afterward? There wasn't any afterward. I came home and went to bed."

"And you dreamed, Nancy, didn't you? You dreamed!"

A sensation of pure, slow dread began to crawl through Nancy's veins, branching gradually toward her heart.

"How do you know that?" she demanded shakily. "How do you know I dreamed?"

"Most people *dream*, Nancy."

"But how did you know *I* dreamed?"

Ronald was silent. She could hear the long-distance wires crooning and warbling.

"Ronald," she repeated, frightened and impatient, "how did you know *I* dreamed?"

Ronald laughed. For an instant she could have sworn that his laugh turned into a snarl. Then he said, "I know you dreamed, Nancy, because you dreamed about me. That's how I know you dreamed."

7

Two days later Henry was sitting in his living room listening to Beethoven and drinking chilled vodkatinis when there was a buzz at the door. He closed his eyes in long-suffering martyrdom and let the buzzer go five or six times before he finally heaved himself out of his chair and walked with dragging footsteps into the hall.

"Who is it?" he bellowed, swaying on slippered feet.

"It's me, Gil Miller."

"Ah, the redoubtable Gil Miller. Hold on for just a moment and I shall furnish access."

Henry unchained the door and opened it. Gil hesitated for a moment when he saw him unshaven, wearing a frayed blue bathrobe and holding a large glass of vodka, but Henry said, "Don't mind me. It's Friday morning and I'm having fun." He led the way into the living room, leaving Gil to close the door, and he waved his arms expansively, sending a neat splash of vodka down one of the sofa cushions. "Beethoven! Ludwig van Beethoven!" he proclaimed.

Gil nodded toward the frosted jug of vodkatinis. "How many of those have you had?" he asked casually.

"I don't count my drinks," Henry said. He sat down abruptly, spilling more vodka on his bathrobe. "Drink cannot be measured like days of the week, or like linoleum, or socks. Drink is an endless river flowing majestically toward the sea. From mountaintop to ocean, via the kidneys of a million million devotees. And when I fall, exhausted by my pleasurable duties, there will always be another to take my place."

Gil said, "I've been thinking about Springer."

"Ah," Henry replied with alcoholic sagacity. "*You've* been thinking about Springer. Well, I too have been thinking about Springer. In fact, I have hardly been able to think about anything or anyone else other than bloody Springer."

He touched Gil's chest lightly with the flat of his hand and said, "Sit down, please. I implore you."

"You're drunk," Gil said.

"I know."

"Maybe I should come back tomorrow morning when you're sober."

"Don't! You won't get any sense out of me then."

Gil blew out his cheeks, thought about it and then reluctantly agreed to sit down. Henry lifted the jug and waved it in the air so wildly Gil was sure he was going to spill it all. "Would you care for a . . . libation, m'dear boy?"

"I'm fine. I have to drive."

"Ah, well," said Henry. "Driving is a chore I have long since abandoned. I have a car though, you know. A Mercury, nineteen-seventy-one vintage. Nine thousand miles on the odometer, that's all. It's in the garage, draped in a tarpaulin, waiting for the day I finally make up my mind I have drunk sufficient for one lifetime."

Gil asked, "Has Springer called on you?"

Henry looked truculent. "Springer never stops calling on me. And each damn time he looks different. Three visits in two days. First he looked like a nun, all dressed up in white. Then he looked like the Dalai Lama on his day off. All saffron-yellow robes. He called again this morning—about an hour ago—wearing some kind of black apparatus. Well, I say 'he,' but he isn't really a 'he,' is he? He's more of an 'it.' He could even be a 'she.' ''

Gil sat down, crossing his bare, tanned legs. "And each time he called on you, he asked you the same question?"

"That's right. Just that one question: 'Have you made your mind up yet?' And when I told him no, to wait a little longer, he left. No argument, no bother. No oratory. But he left each time with me feeling guiltier than I had the time before. So now I'm feeling very guilty. And I expect to feel even more guilty as the day wears on."

Gil asked, "Do you think we ought to do it?"

Henry shrugged. "How should I know? Chase some mythical beast? It doesn't even sound sane, let alone logical. It doesn't even sound *real*."

"Then why do you feel guilty when Springer asks you if you've made up your mind?"

"Because—" Henry began harshly and then stopped, pouting. "Because . . . I don't know. I don't know what he is, what he represents, what he's doing here, or why. He simply has that way of making me feel guilty. You have to understand that it doesn't take very much to make me feel guilty. My ex-wife makes me feel guilty. You make me feel guilty."

He drained his glass, burped, and said, "Drink, the endless river . . . flowing with awful majesty . . . toward the sea. Taking a detour, of course, through the human kidney. That's what they call . . . a pleasant diversion."

Gil watched him for a while as the music came to a mighty crescendo and then died away. Casually he said, "Springer's been around to see me too. He asked me the same question. I guess he's talked to Susan as well."

"I see," said Henry. "And what did you tell him? Or her? Or it? Do you know what *I* told him? Or her? Or it? I told him that everyone has his own path to follow. Everyone has his own duty to perform. And that my path did not wend its way anywhere near mythical beasts or killer eels, and that my duty was certainly not to search for invisible rapists."

"I told him I'd do it," said Gil.

Henry stared at him blearily. "You did *what?*"

"I told him I'd do it," Gil repeated.

Henry opened and closed his mouth as if he were stupefied. But then he said, "My dear young man . . . you don't even know what hunting this beast *entails!* Remember that policeman on the beach, the one who lost half his face. Remember the girl. Believe you me, this beast, whatever it is, is no mean opponent. Come on, we're not hunting rabbits here. We're hunting something that as far as I can determine is supernatural. Like a poltergeist. Or a vampire. Or—or, or the Devil himself!"

Gil uncrossed his legs and sat up straight. "You've agreed to do it too, haven't you? That's why you're drunk and listening to all this music."

Henry slitted his eyes.

Gil said, "I bet you agreed to do it before I did. You went away and you thought about it, the same way I did, and in the end you couldn't think of a single decent reason for saying no." Gil looked around. "I mean, Henry, what do you have to lose?"

Henry came over and laid a trembling hand on Gil's T-shirted shoulder. He looked down at Gil with watering eyes. Somewhere beneath those heaped-up blankets of alcoholism that were smothering his emotions, he felt genuinely touched by Gil, the son he should have had and never did. He had always been too selfish to have children, too preoccupied with Marx and Engels and Russell and Kant.

He quoted Kant now as one of his justifications for having agreed to do as Springer demanded. "Two things fill my mind with ever-increasing wonderment and awe—the starry heavens above me, and the moral law within me."

"What's that?" asked Gil. Henry had been speaking very indistinctly.

Henry said, "My reason, I suppose, for saying yes. That and the fact that I believe what Springer says, although don't ask me why."

"And this . . . Ashapola?" asked Gil. "What do you think about that?"

Henry shook his head. "You can call God whatever you like. You can think of him in any way you want. He's still God." He paused for a moment and then said, "We're talking about the never-ending struggle between good and evil, Gil. That's why I told him yes. Whatever Ashapola happens to be, he obviously stands for enlightenment, kindness and protecting the innocent. That girl on the beach was an innocent and look at what happened. If nothing else, other young girls should be protected, and she . . . well, she should be revenged."

He sighed and then added, "You're right, of course, my dear boy. I have nothing at all to lose. A few books, most of which don't really belong to me. A few heaps of paper. A good pen and about forty bottles of vodka. No life anymore, nothing worth worrying about anyway. I couldn't ever kill myself, don't think that, but I'm no longer afraid of dying."

Gil said, "I agreed to do it because I'll never have the chance again. And because of that girl. And . . . well, because, that's all."

Henry sat down next to him and they fell silent. Then at last Henry suggested, "We ought to call him. Or her. Or it. We ought to meet him now that we're both decided."

"What about Susan?" asked Gil.

Henry said, "No. She's too vulnerable. She wouldn't make a very good beast hunter, believe me. I was taken caribou hunting once, you know, in Canada, and there were two women with us, appalling liabilities. They did nothing but chatter and complain about how far they had to walk."

"I don't think hunting this beast is going to be much like a caribou hunt," Gil said, trying not to sound facetious. He didn't quite know why, but he was beginning to like Henry, to even feel protective toward him. He had never come across anybody like Henry before, somebody who could spout philosophy, reel off lines of poetry and make smart remarks without even hesitating, and at the same time act with such lack of reverence for everything, including himself. He didn't necessarily admire Henry, but he would like to count him as a friend.

"It could be very dangerous, you know," Henry said.

"Maybe so. But Springer wants Susan to help us, doesn't he? And he must have a reason. He wouldn't have suggested she get involved if he didn't think she could hack it."

Henry stood where he was, thinking, tilting now and then from side to side as if standing on the deck of an ocean liner in a mild swell. "Has it occurred to you what Springer actually is?" he asked Gil, changing the subject.

"Well, no, I don't know. Just some sexless kind of guy, that's all. Like a Buddhist monk or something."

Henry raised his eyebrows. "I think he's more than a Buddhist monk. And I don't think he's sexless. I think he's a mixture of all sexes, known and unknown. I think he's a microcosm of everything we ever wanted, an encyclopedia rather than a book."

Henry came close to Gil now and clasped his shoulder. Gil could smell the drink on his breath and see the tracery of bloodshot capillaries in his eyes. "I think Springer is what, in medieval times, they called an angel."

"You're kidding," Gil said, pulling away. He turned around on his heel and then stared at Henry again. "You're kidding, right?"

Henry slowly and emphatically shook his head. "Springer is an angel. You look up 'angel' in your dictionary and see how angel is defined. A messenger from God. And that is exactly what Springer is. A messenger from Ashapola, who to all intents and purposes *is* God. So, my friend, when you are talking to Springer, you are talking only one step removed with the Supreme Being, the Creator of the universe. You should tremble! This is like Moses and the burning bush!"

"You're kidding me," Gil repeated.

"Well, you can think what you like," Henry said. "The only way to find out is to confront Springer himself." He put down his drink and looked around the room, patting his shirt pockets in an imitation of jungle drums. "Now, where are my glasses?"

"I'll call Susan," Gil suggested.

"You really think that's wise?"

"We have to, Henry."

Henry sighed. "Very well," he agreed. "But I will tell

Springer this—and I will tell him loud and clear—Susan is not to come along with us if there is the slightest risk. I am not having the life of a young girl on my conscience. Especially one so personable."

"You like her, don't you?" smiled Gil.

Henry frowned at him. "Yes," he said pugnaciously. "What's it to you?"

While Henry rummaged around for his glasses, his shoes and his crumpled linen coat, Gil telephoned Susan. Her grandmother answered and wanted to know who it was.

"A friend, that's all."

"A boy?"

"The last time I looked, ma'am."

"Don't you be fresh with me. Susan's out right now. She's having lunch with the Morgensterns. You can call back later if you want to, but I'm not giving you any guarantees she'll be here."

"Yes, ma'am. Thank you."

Henry said, "Not in? Oh well, it's probably all for the best, you know. I wouldn't like to see her get hurt."

He thought about what he had said and then added, "I wouldn't like to see *me* get hurt either, come to that."

They drove down to Camino del Mar in Gil's yellow Mustang, parking outside the house where Springer had showed them the re-created memory of the girl they had discovered on the beach. They climbed out of the car and stared at the dark-windowed, rundown facade. For the first time, they asked themselves if Springer was going to be here. In fact, Henry was asking himself if Springer had existed at all.

They walked up the weedy pathway and rang the corroded doorbell. They could hear no sound from within the house, no bell jangling, no chimes. The day was hot and humid, with a layer of high cirrocumulus warning of unsettled weather to come. Henry was sweating and took out a balled-up handkerchief to dab at his forehead. He loosened his necktie.

"Don't know what you're wearing a tie for," Gil remarked.

"I am a professor," said Henry with mock pomposity. "A necktie is my symbol of respectability. Besides, if I follow it upward, it enables me to find my head."

They waited and there was still no reply. "Ring again," Henry suggested but just as Gil was about to do so, the front door swung open and Springer stood there in the hallway, white-faced, dressed in solid black.

"You are early," he smiled.

Henry lifted his left wrist and frowned at it. He had forgotten to put on his watch. "How can we be early if we didn't have an appointment?"

"What I mean is, I didn't expect you so soon."

They stepped inside. There was a dusty, lingering smell of patchouli. The banisters were draped with sheets as if the house were being closed for the summer.

"You knew we would come, then?" asked Henry.

Springer nodded. "Your friend is here as well. She came even earlier than you. She is waiting for you upstairs."

Gil and Henry exchanged glances of surprise. Springer smiled at them and led the way upstairs to the large back room where he had shown them the death agonies of the girl they had found on the beach. Susan was standing by the window looking out at the overgrown yard. She wore a simple white T-shirt and a white skirt, and her hair was tied up with ribbons. As they came in, she turned around.

"Hello. Springer said you would come."

Henry briskly rubbed his hands. He had found his own predictability rather upsetting, especially since he had planned to do no more today than sit in a chair, listen to Beethoven and get astonishingly drunk. Susan came over and kissed Gil on the cheek, almost ceremoniously, and then she kissed Henry in the same way.

"Excuse my . . ." Henry said, rubbing his unshaven chin, "prickles."

Springer closed the door. "You have come because it is

your chosen destiny to come. You have come because there is something within each of you that demands it. Susan, you have lost your parents. Your mind is still asking for explanations and you have a strong feeling that if you embark on this adventure, many of your questions will be answered. In some ways, this may be so."

Springer approached Henry and stood looking at him benignly. "You, Henry, are afraid that your life may have been wasted, that all your learning and intellect may have gone for nothing. To track down this beast would be an achievement. And apart from that, you are glad of the company of these two young people. You would have had children if your marriage had been happier. These two are quite acceptable substitutes."

Henry said nothing. He was too good a philosopher; he knew it was no use arguing against the absolute truth. Springer moved on to Gil and laid a hand on his shoulder.

"You seem to have a far more contented life than Henry and Susan. You have parents who love you, a stable home, and you are working hard at your schooling. But still, you are discontented. Unlike your father, you will never be satisfied with anything as mundane and restricting as a store. You expect more. You expect excitement, and danger. What did your father say before you came to meet me? What did he advise you to do?"

Gil flushed in embarrassment. "Guess he didn't realize how you were going to turn out. Guess *I* didn't either."

Springer smiled. "Your father has always told you to take precautions. Not just sexually, of course, but in everything you do. But you are tired of playing it safe. You want to test yourself. Hunting this beast, you think, will be a worthy test."

Springer raised his hands. His face was as smooth as a sea-washed pebble, expressionless but peaceful. "Now you see why you were chosen, why your footsteps were directed that morning toward the beach. Now you see why you have agreed to help me."

Henry thrust his hands in his pockets and rocked back and forth on his heels. "I was surmising earlier this morning that you were a messenger of sorts. A *divine* messenger."

Springer looked back at him with interest. "Go on," he said.

"Well, this may be preposterous. In fact, it sounds completely lunatic now that I'm saying it directly to your face. But I surmise that you are an angel."

Springer seemed to take this remark quite seriously and in good part. He considered it for a moment and then nodded as if he liked it. "Not an angel in the sense that you perhaps understand it. No wings, no robes, no trumpets. More like a collection of projected information, a living hologram. But if you wish to use the word angel . . . I would be flattered."

Susan said, "What I want to know is, if Ashapola is so powerful, why can't he find this beast himself? Why do we have to do it for him?"

"He is all-powerful, but also powerless," Springer explained. "He created the world and everything in it, but for the most part, he allowed his creation to have freedom of choice. If humans choose to believe in him, he is pleased. But he has allowed them *not* to believe in him and to believe instead in other gods if that is what they find most comforting. Ashapola is a god who does not intervene, as a rule, in the destiny of his creatures, and *cannot* intervene any more than a parent can intervene in the life of his children."

"He seems to have intervened quite considerably in this particular situation," said Henry.

"Yes," Springer acknowledged, "because this situation is different. It is no exaggeration to say that this situation is a direct threat to Ashapola himself, to the future of this world and to everybody who lives in it. Without Ashapola's guidance, there was a considerable risk that you would not have discovered the nature of this threat until it was far too late. Ashapola cannot grapple directly with the beast itself, but through me he can give you the power that will enable you to do so, and, with luck, overcome it."

"The beast," said Susan quietly. "Is the beast the same as the Devil?"

"There has never been one single Devil," Springer explained. "As it says in the Bible, the Devil is legion. But today most of the demonic manifestations that once plagued this earth have been destroyed, or somehow contained, and until this poor girl's body was discovered, the only active Devil we knew of was Asmodeus, who has been causing havoc in Israel and the Middle East for years now, in spite of the efforts of the exorcists to track him down."

Springer's face seemed to alter subtly from masculine to feminine. He walked gracefully over to the window and when she spoke, her voice was much higher-pitched and precise, although neither Henry, Gil nor Susan found the sudden change disconcerting. They had accepted her for what she was, a living image rather than a real person.

Springer said, "It appears that a Devil whom we usually call Yaomauitl has reappeared in Southern California. Every Devil has his own way of spreading his evil. Yaomauitl is the veritable emperor of nightmares. By day he is as ordinary as you or I. By night, when people are sleeping, he can enter their dreams and do to them whatever he desires. He can kill them in their sleep; he can infect them with terrible sicknesses; he can blind them. He can also impregnate them with his own seed and that is what happened to the young girl you found on the beach. The seeds devour the womb that nourishes them and make their escape. If they can find a hiding place, they grow, and after six months or so, they emerge as fully grown as their parent."

"And then what happens?" asked Gil.

"The same process is repeated through nightmare after nightmare until there are sufficient Devils to dominate the dreams of an entire nation. That is what happened in Iran. That is what happened in Hitler's Germany. Whoever holds a nation's dreams holds that nation's power. That is why

Yaomauitl is so called: His name means 'Dreaded Enemy.' "

Susan asked, "How do we find Yaomauitl? Especially since he's so ordinary during the day."

"I have no idea," Springer confessed.

"Well, that's up front for you," Gil admitted.

Susan asked, "What do we do with him once we find him? *If* we find him?"

"There I can help you," Springer told them. "Through me you will be invested with the traditional powers of the Night Warriors."

"The Night Warriors," Henry repeated. He liked the sound of that. There was a magnificent warring darkness to it, like black-plumed horses, black-painted shields and thunderous rides across midnight fields.

Springer came away from the window. "Once there were many Night Warriors. There were enough of them to have a secret society of their own; they had their own rules, their own legends, their own particular chivalry. Of course when Yaomauitl was finally defeated, there was no longer any need for them, and although much of their secret lore was passed down from one family to another, the Night Warriors themselves died out."

She paused for a while and then said, "Another reason you three were chosen was because you have ancestors who were Night Warriors. Henry, your paternal great-grand-father was Kasyx, the charge-keeper, one of the greatest of the Night Warriors. Gil, your great-great-great-grandfather on your mother's side was Tebulot, the machine-carrier. And Susan, your great-great-grandmother was one of the last of the Night Warriors, Samena, the finger-archer."

Henry, in spite of himself, laughed out loud at Springer's seriousness. "I'm sorry," he said, "I'm sorry. You're really stretching my credulity here. I feel like any moment now the whole philosophy faculty is going to come bursting into the room shouting 'April fool.' I'm sorry."

"Well," smiled Springer, "your skepticism is understandable. Your mind has been educated to challenge everything. But if I can ask you to suspend your disbelief for a little while longer, you can judge what I am saying from a practical demonstration."

"A practical demonstration?" asked Gil. He had kept quiet and listened so far but Springer was rapidly losing him. Tebulot, the machine-carrier? He was beginning to think, like Henry, that somebody was taking them all for a long and ultimately hilarious ride.

But Springer glanced at Gil, sharp and amused, almost as if she could read what Gil was thinking, and then she said unabashedly, "Kasyx, the charge-keeper, is the power center of the trio. It is Kasyx who draws power from Ashapola at any one of the nine hundred power sources, of which this house is one, and keeps it ready for his comrades to use in their battle against Yaomauitl. If you like, Kasyx is the battery that Tebulot and Samena use to charge up their night weaponry."

"So, Kasyx . . . has no weapon of his own?" asked Henry.

"His power can be used as a weapon," said Springer, "but only in the last resort. This is because it can only be discharged in one total blast, leaving all three of you powerless. So if the discharge fails to have the desired effect, you are left without any means of defending yourselves. Also, the release of energy is tremendous and it is usually far too powerful for normal combat. It can demolish a building. Several famous explosions in the past were explained as natural phenomena but actually they were charge-keepers fighting a last battle with the Devil."

"What about Tebulot?" asked Gil.

"Yes, the machine-carrier. The machine is a weapon, but also a tool. It uses power from Kasyx to cut through walls and doors if that becomes necessary, to make welds and repairs, and also to fire controlled bursts of pure energy. The machine, if you like, is a power controller but it cannot be carried by Kasyx himself because any attempt by him to use it would result in the instant discharge of all his power."

Gil folded his arms. He was finding everything Springer was telling them impossible to believe. His excitement of only a few minutes earlier had flattened out completely and he could have happily gone home. He should have gone bowling with Bradley.

Susan didn't believe any of it either, but unlike Gil, she wanted to stay and listen. Springer's stories of Kasyx, Tebulot and Samena were almost like fairy tales and she found them fascinating. She smiled at Springer as she approached her and kept on smiling as Springer laid her hands on her shoulders.

"Samena is the quickest of eye, the fastest runner, the athlete. Where Tebulot is a heavyweight destroyer, Samena is a lightweight sniper. She too draws her energy from Kasyx. But her weapon is her finger."

Springer held her arms straight out in front of her and crossed her right wrist over her left wrist, keeping her left hand loosely held in a fist. She pointed her right index finger rigidly and took a sight along her right arm.

"That is how Samena uses her weapon but it is better to demonstrate it for real."

She took Henry's arm and led him to the center of the room. He stood beside her, his hands on his hips, embarrassed. "I'll bet you dinner at Anthony's that nothing happens," he said.

Springer stepped around lithely and drew Gil and Susan closer to Henry, placing one on each side of him.

"Now you are ready," she said. "You will normally be dreaming when this happens. Your physical body will be lying asleep in your bed while your Night Warrior manifestation goes out into the darkness looking for the Devil. Your power will be greater when you have left your physical body because the energy will not have to pass through the resistance of solid flesh and bone. But this will give you some idea of what you will be able to do."

She came forward and touched Henry's forehead. "When I have trained you, you will know how to build up your power by yourself. Right now I am having to do it for you. It might help you if you closed your eyes."

Henry hesitated at first but then he closed his eyes. Well, he thought, I might as well get this over and done with. When I open my eyes again, the whole of my freshman philosophy class is going to be standing around laughing at me. But I think I'm still drunk enough not to mind.

Charge-keeper, he thought to himself with mounting skepticism. The only things he got a charge out of were vodka, beautiful women and Beethoven, and not always in that order. Still, he had come here, he had listened to what Springer had said, and so there must be some part of his mind that was still open to argument, no matter how eccentric that argument might be.

Springer's fingers against his forehead began to vibrate. Henry could almost imagine that a high-voltage electric current was running through them and coursing into his brain. He had to admit it, Springer was a genius at stirring up illusion and self-suggestion. He could almost have believed that he was growing, that he was straightening up, that his body was glittering with thousands of volts of stored-up energy.

He slowly opened his eyes. Springer took her hand away. There was a burned, metallic odor of lightning, gunpowder and cauterized copper. Gil and Susan were staring at him in astonishment; he had never before seen faces so dumb-struck.

"Come," said Springer and beckoned Henry over to the far wall of the room. She opened a white built-in closet, empty of clothes, and showed him the full-length mirror on the back of the door.

"This is you—Kasyx, the greatest of the Night Warriors," she told him.

Henry stared at himself. Slowly, slowly, he lifted his hand toward his head, and the figure in the mirror lifted its hand too. It was actually him: Henry Watkins—threadbare professor of even more threadbare philosophy, alcoholic and far-too-frequently frustrated genius—as Kasyx, the Night Warrior. Not taller, although he was standing straighter than usual, with his shoulders thrown back. No more muscular, although his expression was somehow more determined than before and there was a look of power about him, the look of a man who could handle himself in a fight. What was really extraordinary about him, however, was the semitranslucent armor that covered him from head to foot, including a wedge-shaped helmet. The armor appeared heavy and elaborate, with a slab-sided breastplate, jointed hips like lobster tails, and scores of power points, cables, racks and hooks.

He could scarcely see the armor and he certainly couldn't feel any weight. Yet when he moved, the armor moved with him as if he were really wearing it. He turned to Springer and said, "This suit . . . it's like it doesn't exist."

"It exists only in dreams," Springer said. "What you can see of it now is nothing but my memory of it, just as the girl I showed you was only a memory too."

Henry stared at himself. "It's true, then," he said with great simplicity. "The Night Warriors actually existed."

"Yes, Henry, they did, and they will again. Kasyx, Tebulot and Samena."

Springer beckoned Gil to come forward. Gil hesitated at first but then stood beside Henry, glancing at his armor from time to time with fascination. This was absolutely amazing. This beat burning up Interstate-5 at 120 mph, riding his dirt bike all around the Del Mar fairgrounds, Montezuma's Revenge at Knott's Berry Farm and any other thrill he could think of. This beat *everything*.

"Kneel down beside him, on one knee," Springer instructed Gil. Gil did as he was told, looking up at Henry through eyes wide with excitement.

"Now, Henry," said Springer, "lay your left hand on Gil's right shoulder."

Henry complied and Gil immediately felt a tide of energy surge through his nervous system. He opened his mouth and blue sparks crawled around his teeth like crackling caterpillars. His hair stood on end.

"This is you—Tebulot, the machine-carrier," Springer announced, and Gil stared at himself in the mirror. He seemed lither and stronger, and there was a deadly look of conviction in his eyes that almost made him smile. He wore a helmet similar to Henry's but white, with two triangular wing plates on each side of it. His breastplate was white and decorated with tactically placed triangles, but he wore no leg armor, just clinging white tights for quickness of movement and a pair of wedge-soled shoes that looked like the most fantastic Nikes ever designed.

In his hands he carried a massive piece of shining machinery shaped like a machine gun but larger and longer, with one T-shaped lever like a gearshift on top of it and all kinds of slots, bolted-on clips, and slides and switches.

He tried to heft the machinery in his hands but like Henry's armor, it weighed nothing.

"Raise it up and aim it," Springer said. "It will fire a weak charge if you pull the trigger."

Cautiously Gil lifted the machine and squinted along the sights. Springer stood directly behind him and said, "Pull back the T-bar; that charges it. You can see a linear charge scale along the side there, glowing gold. That tells you how much charge you've got. All right, aim it at the wall there and fire it."

With trembling hands Gil tugged back the T-bar until he felt it lock. The charge scale glowed dimly and registered only about a tenth, but that was enough for a demonstration. He touched the trigger. There was a sharp, soft *zzafff!* and a bullet of bright-yellow light zipped across the room and exploded against the wall, punching a two-inch hole through to the brick.

"In a dream the charge will be much more powerful," Springer said. "You will also discover that the machine has many functions. It was created in a dream and therefore its capabilities are limited only as a dream is limited, which is hardly at all."

Gil turned the machine from one side to the other, admiring it.

"Quite a weapon, huh?" Henry remarked.

"Unbelievable," said Gil.

Springer now brought Susan forward. She had been watching the other two cautiously and sensed the newly born comradeship between them, but she had not yet understood the fatherly concern Henry felt for her, nor the fact that Gil thought she was pretty and cute and that if Springer hadn't appeared and turned the routine of Gil's daily life totally upside down, he probably would have wanted to date her. She caught his smile, however, as she came to stand on Henry's other side, and she realized that he was trying hard to show her he cared about her.

Without the need for Springer to tell him, Henry laid his right hand on Susan's left shoulder. Susan watched herself closely in the mirror as the power with which Springer had charged Henry began to flow through to her. Her eyes sparkled as she blinked; a shower of tiny white sparks cascaded from her hair.

Gradually, faintly, her own costume of Samena, the finger-archer, began to appear. She wore a triangular cocked hat laden with ostrich feathers, eagle feathers and peacock plumes. She was fitted with a tight leather bodice decorated with sequins, studs and oddly shaped pieces of metal and laced across her cleavage with tight leather thongs. She also wore a high-cut pair of tight leather briefs around the waistband of which were clipped twenty or thirty different types of arrowheads: hooked, barbed, triangular, flared and smooth. A broad scabbard also hung at her waist, containing a double-bladed knife with a velvet cord attached to its handle. Her legs were bare except for a pair of soft leather boots with turndown tops.

"Samena," Springer said with undisguised pride.

Susan asked breathlessly, "Could I try shooting? Is there enough power left?"

Springer touched Henry's forehead and nodded. "One shot. Use an arrowhead; see if you can hit the wall where Gil hit it."

Susan unclipped a sharp triangular arrowhead. Its body was hollow so she could fit her index finger into it, making it appear that she had a long metallic fingernail. As Springer had instructed her, she crossed her wrists, using her left arm to steady her right. She pointed her arrowhead finger directly at the spot on the wall where Gil had blasted a scar in the plaster, and concentrated.

Nothing happened at first. "What do I do now?" she asked Springer in disappointment. "How do I fire it?"

Springer smiled. "You have to *think* it, that's all. It isn't difficult, and after a while it will come so easily to you that you will be amazed to remember you ever had any trouble."

Susan aimed her finger again. Again nothing happened.

But Henry suddenly pressed his hand against her shoulder as forcefully as he could and shouted *"Fire!"*

Instantly, with an ear-piercing whistle, the arrowhead flashed across the room, followed by a three-foot shaft of golden light. It buried itself in the wall only two inches from the hole Gil had made, at which point the light immediately vanished, leaving the arrowhead deep inside the plaster.

"Yay-y!" shouted Gil and applauded. Susan danced and jumped about. "I did it! I did it!"

Springer said, "You needn't necessarily use an arrowhead. The shaft of light alone—depending on how much charge you put into it—will kill, stun, or frighten people away. But you must train very hard. To take the part of Samena, you must be highly skilled, highly sensitive, and so quick that nobody can catch you. Samena is the most emotional of all the Night Warriors, the one whose nerves have to be stretched to the tautest pitch. But she is also the most deadly."

Henry closed his hands together as if in prayer, and what

was left of the charge Springer had given him began to flow toward the ceiling from his fingers, crackling and spitting.

"Springer," he said, "if I ever doubted you, which I did, please forgive me. This is all quite astonishing. This is like a child's imagination come true."

"I regret that the ultimate purpose is far from childish," Springer said. Her voice had become deeper again, and there were barely discernible changes in her face that made her appear more masculine. "Yaomauitl is by far the most malevolent of all the Devils. He is the Devil of madness, greed and genocide. He came over to the New World with Cortes in fifteen nineteen. Some stories say that Cortes himself was the Devil, walking the earth in the guise of a man. Certainly Cortes was responsible for the murder of countless thousands of Aztecs; and even if he was not the Devil himself, he took the Devil with him when he discovered Baja California in fifteen thirty."

Henry asked, "Why has he reappeared now?"

"There is no telling," Springer replied. "The ways of the Devil are masked from the eyes of Ashapola. That is why only you, the Night Warriors, can discover how he has returned and what his evil intentions are: that is why only you can destroy him."

Henry laid his hands on Gil's and Susan's shoulders. "You have given the three of us a terrible responsibility. You know that, don't you?"

"I do not think you will fail me," said Springer.

Susan asked, "How do we start? I mean, what do we actually *do*? You've said that we're Night Warriors now and that we can leave our bodies when we're asleep. But how do we do that? And how can we meet each other when we're asleep?"

Springer said, "You will use this house as your rendezvous. When you retire to bed each night, you will repeat to yourself the time-honored battle hymn of the Night Warriors, and the influence of that hymn will make sure your dreaming presences meet at the nearest point of sacred power, which is here. After that, you will journey through the dreams of others to seek out Yaomauitl and any of his minions who may have already been spawned."

Gil said, "I think I'm dreaming already."

Springer smiled. "You will soon grow used to the landscapes of the night. You will come here every night for the next two months and I will train you in the mental and physical skills of the Night Warriors. I will teach you their history, their traditions and their lore. I will tell you of their greatest victories and their most terrible defeats. By the time you have completed your training with me, you will feel that your real self is the self who exists in dreams and your waking personality is nothing but a flesh-bound parody of who you really are. Your concept of awake and asleep will be completely reversed. At the end of the night, when you return to your earthly body, you will be doing so to rest, and many times you will feel that this resting is a chore. There is so much more to your mind than the intelligence necessary to carry your body through the waking day. Your mind is a powerhouse, a limitless store of talent, skill and inspiration. Asleep, as a Night Warrior, you will begin to realize that power. No matter how much you have failed during the day, no matter how meanly other people regard you, you will be heroes and heroines in your dreams. Understand this, my friends—you are the people of legends, just as every human being can be once he has understood the strength and the majesty inside his own head."

Gil asked, "This strength, this skill, once we've achieved it, will it affect our everyday lives?"

"Of course," Springer answered. "Once you have gained confidence and power in the dream world, your abilities will not be forgotten during the day. Your life will be changed immeasurably, whether you want it to be or not. But you will find that the success you achieve during the day will count for little compared to the success you achieve during the night. The greatest of adventures awaits you, my friend, as soon as the sun begins to set."

"That first time you came to see me," Gil said to Springer, "that time you looked like a girl . . . you mentioned that book De-what's-its-name?"

"*De Sortilegio*," Springer nodded. "Yes, I did. That was to trigger the memories you inherited from your great-great-great-grandfather. I did not mean to trigger them violently but you went to your Mexican friend Santos, didn't you, and smoked a drug, and that of course heightened your inherited memory to the point of immediacy and violence."

Springer paused for a moment and then said, "*De Sortilegio* was written by Paul Grilland in fifteen thirty-three, after the return of some of Cortes' men from Baja California to Europe, and Grilland's tract takes into account the frightening stories some of the Spaniards told him about Devilish Sabbats that took place on the West Coast of America in those early times. Although some refused to say exactly what had happened, it appears that Cortes initiated Black Sabbatical rites and summoned a manifestation of the Devil, or himself became such a manifestation, and that during the course of those Sabbats, native women were forced to have sex with him.

"Sixteenth-century theologians were always arguing amongst themselves over how it was possible for a Devil to have sex with human women. But Paul Grilland said there was irrefutable evidence of it from stories he had been told, and William of Paris, the confessor of Philip le Bel, supported him. So did the Salmanticenses, the lecturers of the theological college of the Discalced Carmelites at Salamanca, in their *Theologia Moralis*. And Dom Dominic Schram said he had personally known several persons who had been compelled against their will to endure the foul assaults of Satan."

Springer smiled sadly. "St. Augustine himself said that anybody who did not believe the Devil could appear in the night and have carnal relations with a woman was deluding himself. The evidence of history is overwhelming. When the Devil is free and able to travel abroad, no woman is safe from his desires."

Susan asked, "When do we start? Do we start tonight?"

"Do you want to start tonight?"

Susan said, "Yes." She had never felt so motivated, so inspired. She had suddenly been shown that there was something above and beyond her grandparents' upbringing, something far more rewarding and exciting than school, hanging out with Daffy and sitting on the beach hoping to be noticed by Tad Summers and Gene Overmeyer. She felt that Springer had lifted her up and shown her a vista beyond the rooftops of Del Mar, a dazzling vista of mountaintops and great achievements. It was intoxicating, dizzying—and to think that Daffy had talked about "really getting my life together" with aerobic dance!

Gil nodded. "I'd start now if I could get to sleep."

"Henry?" Springer asked, his eyes watchful, guarded.

Henry said, "It seems that I'm in a minority whatever I think."

"Don't you want to begin tonight?" asked Susan.

Henry cleared his throat. "If you want to know the God's honest truth, I'm frightened."

Gil said, "So am I, Henry, but it's something we've got to do. It's a chance in a million grillion. Henry, supposing they said you could go to the moon?"

"The moon?" Henry echoed. He shook his head. "I wouldn't go to the moon. Believe me, Gil, the best view of the moon is through the bottom of an upturned glass of vodka."

Springer said, "You'll start tonight though, won't you?"

Henry thrust his hands into his pockets. "Of course I will. It's wonderful. It's amazing. But don't forget that I'm frightened as well as impressed."

Springer touched his hand in a strange, furtive way that put Henry in mind of an early Christian secretly passing him a communion wafer. "You will have no fear tonight, my friend. Kasyx, the charge-keeper, is fearless."

Henry said, "That's what I'm afraid of."

8

Henry managed to unlock the front door of his cottage just in time to catch the phone, which had been ringing ever since he turned the corner by the promenade. He left his keys hanging in the door and scrambled across the back of the sofa to grab the receiver.

"Henry? Is that you, Henry? I almost hung up."

"Andrea! I was out. I just this second dived in through the door."

"You dived? I wish I could have seen it."

"Let me close the door," Henry said. "There's somebody outside using a power saw. I can't hear you too well."

He laid down the receiver, went to the front door and closed it, then crossed over to the liquor cabinet, lifting out a bottle of vodka and a moderately clean glass. Picking up the receiver again, he opened the bottle and half-filled the glass one-handed in midair without spilling a drop.

"Got your drink?" Andrea asked sharply.

Henry ignored her. "Did you find out anything about the eel?"

"That's why I'm calling. You don't think I would have called you to make small talk, do you?"

Henry swallowed vodka and shivered. Don't let her intimidate you, he thought. Tonight while she slept, he would take on the form of Kasyx, the charge-keeper, the central core of the newly resurrected Night Warriors, and everything Andrea had ever done to hurt him would be meaningless.

"I promised to tell you about the eel," she said.

"Yes," agreed Henry, "you did." He drank more vodka, then put his glass down.

He could hear her shuffling papers. "First of all," she said, "it isn't an eel. That is, it isn't a member of the teleost

138

order *Anguilliformes*, like conger eels or moray eels or freshwater eels. Neither is it a gulpen eel of the order *Saccopharyngiformes*, nor a spiny eel of the order *Mastacembaliformes*, nor a cuchia of the order *Symbranchiformes*."

"Is it a hagfish?" Henry suggested.

"No, it isn't a hagfish either."

"Well, now that you know what it *isn't*, do you have any idea of what it *is?*"

"Nothing positive, no. It isn't a species any of us have come across before."

Henry waited for her to say more. When she remained silent, he said, "Is that it? You don't know what it is, and that's it?"

"Let me put it this way, Henry. It has well-known characteristics. It has a skull with jaws, and it possesses an internal skeleton and a digestive system. It is an amphibian rather than a pure fish in the sense that it possesses lungs, and rudimentary limbs that would enable it to balance itself on land, like a eusthenopteron."

"A what?"

"Oh, Henry, you're still as ignorant as ever. A eusthenopteron, an advanced fish of the late Devonian period, about three hundred sixty million years ago. They were capable of crossing stretches of land from one lake to another during droughts."

"And that's what this so-called eel has turned out to be?"

"No. It simply happens to have rudimentary limbs like a eusthenopteron does. The rest of it is quite different."

Henry was silent for a moment. He of course knew what the eel actually was, or at least he knew what Springer had said it was: one of the seeds of the Devil, already part-grown. And what had Springer told them? *If they can find a hiding place, they grow, and after six months or so, they emerge as fully grown as their parent.*

"You had some people digging on the beach," Henry said.

"That's right," Andrea replied. "So far, though, they haven't found any more of the eels. They're going to dig a little further but they don't hold out much hope. It seems as if the eels have managed to escape deep into the sand."

"I thought you said they weren't eels."

"They're not but that's what everybody calls them. Here in the laboratory we've christened them plourdeostus because they have skull similarities to some of the first fish that evolved with jaws, in the Silurian period."

"Well, that all sounds very much like your usual scientific mumbo-jumbo to me," said Henry amiably. "But then you always were way ahead of me, weren't you, in the department of applied tomfoolery?"

"Now you're being rude again," said Andrea. "You're drunk, aren't you?"

"Not at all," Henry replied. "Not enough, anyway. It just struck me that you people at Scripps can never bear to admit you don't know what something is. So to make up for that shortcoming, you always call it by some mystifying name. Plourdeostus! Why don't you just call them biters? Or vicious bastards, which is what anybody with any sense would call them."

"You're being rude again," Andrea repeated.

"Well, you drive me to it," Henry said. "I'm a paragon of courtesy until I start talking to you. Then, I don't know. I don't know what it is you do to me. Perhaps I should christen you 'dentireversioptus' because you always set my teeth on edge."

"Good-bye, Henry," Andrea warned.

He took a deep breath. "I'm sorry," he told her. "Thanks for keeping your promise. Just forget you ever knew me."

"I did that a long time ago," Andrea retorted and hung up.

Henry sighed. He put down the phone, sat on the sofa and stared at the framed poster for Lucky Strike cigarettes on the opposite wall. He wished he hadn't drunk so much today. On the other hand, there wasn't much point in stopping now; he had reached that state of inebriation when to stop suddenly would guarantee a pounding headache by evening. Better to go on drinking and to ward off the hangover until tomorrow morning. It would be far worse tomorrow but at least it wouldn't interfere with tonight's bit of business.

Gil and Susan leisurely strolled along The Boardwalk at Solana Beach. He had taken her along to the Taco Auctioneer for lunch and now he wanted her to meet his family.

"I just can't wait for tonight," she kept telling him. "Did you see my costume?"

Gil lifted an eyebrow. "Pretty sexy, I thought."

Grinning, she pushed him off the sidewalk. "Well, what if it is?"

"Terrific," Gil joked. "I'm not complaining. The sexier, the better."

"What do you think you look like in those tights of yours?" Susan retaliated. "The Rudolf Nureyev of Solana Beach?"

"Hey, listen, lady, that's the last time you get a taco out of me!"

They kidded along until Susan suddenly turned serious. "Do you think Henry's going to be all right?"

"In what way?" Gil asked. There was chili sauce on his T-shirt and he was trying to rub it off with spit.

"Well, it seems like he's drunk all the time."

"He had a bad divorce or something, that's all."

Susan brushed at her hair. "I'm not saying I don't like him, because I do. I'm not saying I don't trust him either. But you heard what Springer said about this being so dangerous. Do you think Henry's going to be able to handle it if he's drunk?"

"I don't know. I get the feeling that Springer's going to get him off the sauce during training. I mean, the reason he drinks is because he's bored, right? and because he doesn't feel he's worth anything to anybody, and because he doesn't have any companionship. What else is there for him to do except sit at home and get drunk? But now Springer's offered him a challenge . . . I mean like he's offered the challenge to all of us, hasn't he? We've agreed to go hunt for this Devil or whatever because we want something more out of our life. We want some answers. We want some questions too, questions we never even thought about. Have you ever sat down and thought to yourself, is this it? Is this what my life adds up to? Isn't there any more? That's the question Springer's given us, right? And that's the question we want to answer."

Susan reached out and unselfconsciously took Gil's hand. "You know something?" she said. "Ever since my parents died in that car crash, I've never really thought about anything seriously but how to be normal. When you don't have any parents, people are either too sympathetic or they treat you like you're slightly weird, mentally backward or something. Either way, you constantly get treated like you're some kind of abnormal person. I've been to senior citizens' meetings with my grandmother where one of these strawberry-rinsed old ladies used to introduce me to another strawberry-rinsed old lady and say, right in front of my face, 'This is Susan. Her parents were killed in a car crash, poor lamb, but she's taken it so well you wouldn't believe it.' Right in front of my face! As if I needed constant reminding that they died, as if I needed to feel anything but *normal*. I've been reading normal books, wearing normal clothes, watching normal TV programs and hanging out with normal friends. I'm so normal I'm practically a federal statistic on normality. But now that all this has happened—Springer and everything—now that I know about the Night Warriors, I don't want to be normal anymore. I want to find out what I can do if I really stretch myself."

Gil said, "You may have been trying to be normal but you sure didn't succeed. I don't think you're normal at all."

She squeezed his hand. "Is that a compliment?"

He grinned. "Maybe. But not your *normal* kind of compliment."

They reached the Mini-Market. Phil Miller was behind the cash register checking a week's groceries for Mrs. Lim, who ran the Tian Dan Chinese Restaurant along the strip. Mrs. Lim was watching him narrowly, counting up the groceries in her head. She didn't believe in electric adding machines.

"Hi, Gil," his father greeted him, looking at once at Susan.

"Hi, Dad. This is Susan Sczaniecka."

"How're you doing, Susan?"

"Fine, thank you, sir. Gil just treated me to a taco."

Phil said, "A taco? Is he getting serious already?"

"Don't take any notice," Gil said. "That's just my old man being my old man. He thinks he's the natural successor to Don Rickles."

"Little Middles is one dollar sixty-nine cents," Mrs. Lim corrected Phil.

"Oh, I'm sorry," Phil apologized. "That'll teach me to concentrate. Help yourself to a fruit bar, Gil."

"Thanks, Dad."

Susan looked around. "It must be really fantastic, owning a store."

Gil shook his head. "You'd better believe it. You should come down here some Sunday afternoon when we're checking the stock."

They took an orange fruit bar each and then went out through the backyard, which was crowded with wooden crates and empty cardboard boxes, and through the gate that led out to the back alley. This alley took them down to the beach.

It was bright and hot on the shore. Scores of people were out surfing in wet suits and scores more lay on beach towels under the sandy-colored rocks, listening to ghetto blasters, throwing peanuts to the squirrels or simply lying on their backs and baking their bodies. Every few minutes Gil saw somebody he knew. Having been brought up by the ocean, the son of a storekeeper, he knew a lot of people, and Susan was amused by his constant waving and nodding.

"Seems like you're the local celebrity," she said. The sea breeze whipped fine blonde hair across her face.

"We're all local celebrities around here," Gil told her. "We had a gang when we were younger. The Solana Sharks, if you can believe it. I think the worst thing we ever did was to have a pitched battle with a lot of kids from San Elijo, using seaweed instead of car antennas. I don't know if you've ever been hit in the face with a seaweed bullwhip. It hurts."

They walked for over a mile along the shore, finally reaching the police trestles that barred off the beach at Del Mar. Two officers in sunglasses were making time with two high-school girls in small bikinis, but they kept their eyes on Gil and Susan as they approached.

"Sorry, folks, the beach is still off limits."

"Jellyfish, huh?" Gil asked, leaning on the trestle. He knew one of the girls and said, "Hi, Candice." Susan, without really wanting to, stood a little closer to him. She didn't know why, but she felt possessive.

Not far off, three white-coated researchers from the Scripps Institute were probing the sand, accompanied by John Belli, the medical examiner, and Salvador Ortega, and two bored-looking detectives with their jackets slung over their shoulders.

Salvador Ortega, noticing Gil and Susan standing by the barrier, excused himself from the rest of his party and came over. "Mr. Miller," he said, nodding to Gil, "and Miss Sczanieka."

"You pronounced my name right," said Susan. "You're about the first person who ever has."

"My sister married a Pole," Salvador said. "Now her name is Carmen Krzysztofowicz. If I don't pronounce Polish names right, she gives me a hard time."

"How are the jellyfish?" asked Gil, nodding toward the party of researchers.

"We've turned this beach into Swiss cheese. We still haven't located a single one."

"Do you think you will?"

Salvador shook his head. "Those sons of bitches are born survivors if you ask my opinion. They've probably dug their way to Mexico by now."

Gil looked up. "I don't know," he said uneasily. "I've got a funny feeling. Like, we didn't walk down this way by accident. Do you feel that, Susan?"

"I'm not sure," she said. She touched her fingertips to her temples and concentrated. "There's something . . . I don't know what it is. I can't describe it."

Salvador watched them with interest. "You sense something?" he asked, looking from one to the other. "What do you think it is?"

"I'm not certain," Susan said. "It's like the beach is moving under my feet. You know that feeling you get during an earth tremor?"

"Well, we've had enough of those over the past six months," said Salvador. "Maybe you just felt one that I didn't."

It was then that Gil and Susan felt another sensation, an extraordinary sensation, as if an invisible door had suddenly been opened in midair and someone had stepped through. They turned and looked up the beach toward the promenade, and there in the distance was Henry, wearing a turquoise shirt and flapping white Bermuda shorts. He looked like a senior citizen on his annual vacation.

"Did you arrange to meet Professor Watkins here?" Salvador asked.

Gil said, "No, sir."

"You're sure about that?"

"Yes, sir."

Salvador beckoned to the two policemen. "Would you let these people through the line for me? Yes, and this gentleman walking down the beach. Professor Watkins! Henry! Would you come this way, please?"

The cops shifted the trestle aside and Gil and Susan walked through, closely followed by Henry. "Well, well,"

Henry said, "what a surprise. What are you two doing here?"

"I'm not sure," Gil told him. "It just occurred to us to take a walk."

"Me too," said Henry. As the officers dragged the trestle back into place, he stepped forward and shook Salvador's hand. "Well, Salvador, it seems as if something has summoned us. Something imperceptible, like a dog whistle."

"Come and take a look over here," Salvador prompted and they followed him over to the small group of police and researchers who were digging a large hole in the damp sand, looking tired and bored.

"You know John Belli, don't you?" asked Salvador. The medical examiner gave them a tight, unwelcoming smile. "And these three gentlemen are all from the marine biology department at the Scripps Institute."

Three faces—one Caucasian, two black, each bespectacled—greeted Henry, Gil and Susan disinterestedly. Henry came forward and peered down the hole, his hair rising on end in the afternoon wind.

"We'd appreciate it if you didn't stand too close to the edge," one of the researchers said nasally. "The sides, you know, have a tendency to slide."

Henry nodded. "Of course. Don't want to make your work any more tedious than it is already. No sign of plourdeostus, then?"

They stared at him with immediate hostility. "What do you know about plourdeostus?"

Henry beamed. "What I know about plourdeostus is that it's a pretty silly name. Oh, come on, stop looking so amazed. My name is Henry Watkins, department of philosophy at UC San Diego. My wife—or ex-wife, rather—is Andrea Caulfield. Yes, *that* Andrea Caulfield. I was talking to her on the telephone only an hour and a half ago."

"Professor Watkins was here on the beach when the cadaver was discovered," put in Salvador by way of additional explanation.

The researchers appeared to be reassured but not happy. "We'd appreciate it if non-expert observers could be kept out of the way," one of them said haughtily.

"Oh, come on, we're *all* non-expert observers, yourselves included," Henry said with tremendous cheerfulness. "Andrea told me she had never seen anything like this eel before, anywhere, and she knows more about the ocean's more disgusting denizens than anybody alive. We're all in the dark together."

Salvador waited for a moment while digging resumed and then came over and took Henry's arm, leading him aside. "Perhaps you're right, Henry. Perhaps we are all in the dark together. But it seems to me that you three who found the cadaver are slightly less in the dark than the rest of us. Tell me, what made you come down here just at this particular moment?"

Henry glanced at Gil and Susan. They both nodded, so slightly that nobody else would have noticed. "Well . . ." Henry said slowly, "it was just a feeling, that's all . . . it's difficult to know how to describe it."

"Try," Salvador urged.

"I'm not sure I can. It was simply a feeling that I had to be here."

Salvador said quietly, "Mr. Belli is convinced from his examination of the girl's body that she was already dead when she entered the water. He thinks the eels had nothing to do with her death. The only problem he has is that he cannot establish any other cause of death. There is no indication of strangulation, or of battering of the head with a blunt instrument, or of shooting or stabbing. Of course much of the abdomen was missing and it is possible that she was killed by a severe trauma to the abdominal region, but most of her blood remained in her veins and arteries, which suggests that her heart stopped beating before any wounds were inflicted."

Salvador waited for a moment to see the impression this information would have on Henry and then added quietly, "Mr. Belli is extremely angry and frustrated."

At that moment one of the Scripps researchers threw down his shovel and said, "That's it. There's nothing here. Let's call it a day."

Susan stepped forward with one hand raised. "Wait!" she said in a clear, high voice, a voice they could easily hear over the constant grumbling of the surf. "Wait. Don't stop yet. Dig a little deeper."

The Scripps researcher looked at Salvador with an expression that could only be interpreted as "Get this girl out of here, will you please?"

But Salvador turned on his heel, his hands clasped behind his back, and said, "Gil? Henry? What do you think? Should they carry on digging?"

Gil said, "Susan's right. They should carry on."

"Who are these people?" the Scripps researcher wanted to know.

"They found the body of the girl," Salvador told him.

"And that gives them some kind of expertise?" the researcher demanded, climbing out of the hole.

Salvador took out his handkerchief and wiped his nose. "Sir," he said, "if you don't continue to excavate this hole, I shall ask my officers to do so. Of course, if there is anything here, my officers will not perhaps be as delicate in their handling of it as you might be, but that is a risk I shall have to take. I am interested in the biology of this matter of course, but I am investigating a person's death, and that to me is the first priority."

The researcher stared pugnaciously at him and then said, "Very well, have it your way. We'll dig for another half-hour, then we're calling it quits."

They waited on the beach as the sun gradually burned its way toward the western horizon, turning the ocean into dazzling gold. The Scripps researchers dug slowly and systematically, stopping every time they struck a stone or a fragment of buried wood. Salvador came close to Henry and asked, "How about you? Do you think there's something down there?"

"I don't know," Henry said thickly. He was beginning to feel the tight band of a headache around his forehead, and the sun's glaring reflection on the ocean wasn't helping him. He should have brought a hip flask to keep his hangover away, but it was too late now. The membranes around his brain were beginning to tighten and throb and his optic nerves felt as if they were made of chewed string.

John Belli checked his watch. "There's nothing down there, Sal, let's face it. Those eels were totally incidental to the primary cause of death. I vote we forget this digging operation altogether."

"Five more minutes," Salvador insisted.

Three minutes passed, four. Then without understanding why, Susan found herself stepping nearer to the excavation and when she looked around, she saw that Henry and Gil had followed her and were standing close behind. Salvador noticed their move forward and watched them closely.

In the black, wet sand at the bottom of the excavation, something shifted. The researcher touched it with his shovel and it shifted again.

"I've found something," he said, his voice cracking. "It's moving."

Salvador immediately came forward, reaching into his waistband for his .38 revolver and cocking it. "Take a lot of care," he instructed the researcher. "The last one of those things we tried to capture, it took off half of one of my officers' face."

"Thanks for the warning," the researcher said sarcastically. One of his colleagues slid down into the excavation beside him and together they began to clear the sand from the shape at the bottom.

"It's alive," said the second researcher. "There's no doubt about it. I can feel it moving."

"Does it feel like an eel?" Salvador asked.

"No way," said the first researcher. "This is big, much bigger than that eel you brought in to the Institute. I can feel a . . . spine of sorts. Kind of a knobby spine. And ribs."

"Just be careful," Salvador repeated.

Henry thought again: *If they can find a hiding place, they grow, and after six months or so, they emerge as fully grown as their parent.* He didn't have to look at Gil or Susan to know they were thinking the same thing; between the three of them, they had already developed an unspoken rapport.

Cautiously the researchers exposed the shape they had found in the sand. A spinal column, gristly and black. A curved rib cage, each rib separated from the one next to it by dark, semitransparent cartilage. Then a pelvic girdle, attenuated and narrow, and a long, jointed coccyx that almost formed a tail, and bony legs, drawn up under the body in the position of a developing fetus.

Henry could see the creature's heart beating through the thin gristle of its rib cage. He had a feeling of terrible dread and found himself silently praying. He prayed that the creature might die when they brought it out of the sand. He prayed that he wouldn't have to look at it. He prayed that it was the only one and that the others had suffocated in the sand.

"Our Father, which art in Heaven; hallowed be thy name . . ."

The two researchers, working side by side, cleared away the sand from the back of the creature's head. In all, the creature looked as if it would measure about three feet from head to toe.

One of the researchers ran his hand along the knobby spine and then suddenly said, "Look at this." An envelope of papery, scaly skin had fallen away from the coccyx. He handed it carefully to his colleague, who was kneeling by the brink of the pit. His colleague held it up so that the last of the sunlight shone through it. It rustled in the sea breeze as faintly as tissue paper.

"What is that?" Salvador asked.

"It looks like the discarded skin of an eel to me," the researcher said.

"So this is it? This is what we're looking for? And in only two days it's developed as much as this?"

The researcher picked up his rucksack, unbuckled it and took out a long specimen envelope into which he carefully folded the eelskin. "It sure looks like it, doesn't it?"

"But what kind of creature can do that? And what kind of creature can gestate under the sand?"

The researcher gave him a grim smile. "That's what we're here to find out, Lieutenant."

Salvador looked across at John Belli, but the medical examiner stood there with his hands folded across his chest, his lower lip jutting out, and said nothing.

"All right," Salvador said. "You want to get that thing out of there? Duncan, go get the stretcher from the trunk of my car, blankets too. Keith, there's some canvas webbing in the squad car, go get it. We should be able to run it under the creature's body and lift it out real gentle."

Susan whispered, "You *can't* lift it out."

Salvador said, "We sure as hell can't leave it where it is."

"Now that you've found it, you must kill it," Susan insisted. "You must bring wires with high voltage and electrocute it. It's the only way. Electrocute it and then bury it again."

The Scripps researchers shook their heads. One of them said with mock weariness, "First she insists we go on digging so we can locate it. Now she wants us to kill it and cover it up again. Are you sure she's . . . ?" He pointed to his head and twirled his finger.

"You've got to do as she says," Gil insisted in a harsh, loud voice.

"Oh, we do?" retorted the researcher. "Well, this is our show and we run it the way we want to, and we certainly don't take orders from every wandering beach bum who happens to be passing. Do we have that clear?"

Henry touched Salvador on the shoulder. "They're quite right, you know. It's imperative that you destroy this creature at once."

"Now why is that?" asked Salvador. "I'm not saying you are wrong, my friend, but before I decide on any course of action, I want to know why."

"I can't tell you why. I don't even know why myself. But the urgency is great. This creature must not be allowed to live for one second longer than you can possibly help."

"My dear Henry," Salvador said quietly, "I cannot order it to be killed without a sensible reason. It is an integral part of a full-scale homicide investigation; it is a living creature of considerable scientific interest, despite the fact that it has devoured the body of a young girl and mutilated one of my men. It may be the only one there is, or at least the only one we ever find. What will I say to my superiors if I electrocute it and bury it again? That I was instructed to do so by a seventeen-year-old girl and a nineteen-year-old boy and a professor of philosophy at the university? That you three insisted on it as a matter of urgency and that I then decided it was wise to obey?"

Salvador cocked his head questioningly, asking Henry to understand why he could not destroy the creature where it lay. "You understand me?" he asked at last. "You see what I mean?"

Henry felt terrible; he was sweating and chilled at the same time. He wiped his greasy forehead with the back of his arm. "I don't know what to say to you, Salvador. The danger is extreme. If you don't kill this creature now, then believe me, you will regret it for the rest of your life."

Salvador's eyes began to darken. "That is not a threat, I hope."

"A threat?" Henry expostulated. "My dear Salvador, I don't have the power or the means to make any threats, not even to my ex-wife, and certainly not to you. I'm talking about that, that thing down there in that excavation. What do you think it is, Salvador? What do you honestly think it is? You saw what it did to your officer when it was scarcely grown. What do you think it can do now? Look at it! It's the spawn of a Devil, that's what it is! And you must kill it!"

John Belli came over and said brusquely to Henry, "You . . . you and your two playmates. I want you out of here. That creature down there is evidence and it has to be pathologically examined. I don't want any of you anywhere near it, do you understand? You're a potential threat to that creature, in my opinion, and I want you back beyond that barrier, out of my way."

Gil said, "Mister, we're no threat to that creature, but that creature is a threat to humankind."

"He's right," Susan added. "That creature is the spawn of a Devil."

John Belli sighed and rubbed his chin. "*Salvador,*" he appealed with poorly concealed impatience.

Salvador said, "He's right, I'm afraid. You're going to have to back off. It's plain regulations as much as anything else. Just go back behind the barrier; you can see quite a lot from there. But, you know, keep it quiet or I'm going to have to move you farther, or even take you downtown for obstruction."

Henry looked at Salvador steadily. "One last appeal," he said with a dry mouth.

Salvador said, "I'm sorry, but no."

Henry, Gil and Susan reluctantly backed away from the excavation and Salvador escorted them to the police line. "These people are allowed to stay here," Salvador told the officers, "but no closer, you understand?"

They waited behind the line while the Scripps researchers continued their careful clearing of the damp, black sand. John Belli walked off after a while and then drove back onto the beach in his station wagon, backing up toward the excavation until he was only fifteen feet from it. He climbed out of the wagon and let down the tailgate.

"Let's just pray that the creature can't survive once they've taken it out of the sand," Henry said.

"It'll survive," Gil said tersely.

Susan said, "We can still pray."

"Who to?" Gil asked. "God? Or Ashapola? Or the San Diego Police Department?"

John Belli took blankets from the wagon, shook them out and handed them down to the researchers, and even though Henry couldn't see what they were doing, he guessed they were wrapping the creature up so they could lift it out of the hole. After a lengthy pause and a long, inaudible discussion, one of the officers went off to Salvador's car to fetch a coil of canvas webbing, and this was lowered to the researchers too.

Eventually, just as the sun touched the edge of the sea and began to flatten across the horizon, the blanket-covered creature was lifted out of the hole by the combined efforts of the three Scripps researchers, the two policemen, John Belli and Salvador Ortega. From the way they immediately lowered the creature onto the stretcher, Henry knew it was enormously heavy in proportion to its size.

"That looks like it really weighs something," Gil remarked.

Henry nodded, biting his lip.

There was another conference between the police and the researchers and then they gathered around the creature and carried it over to the station wagon, sliding it carefully into the back. John Belli closed the door. Henry saw Salvador say something to him and then he locked it. Henry also noted how far the rear suspension of the wagon dipped.

It took another ten minutes for John Belli to drive off the beach. His rear wheels sank so far into the sand that the policemen had to wedge pieces of driftwood under them for traction. At last, with a spray of sand, the vehicle whinnied off up the beach and jounced onto the road.

Salvador walked over to the police line, his hands in his pockets. "Well, my friends," he said, "that is all there is to see for today."

"Where is Belli taking it?" Henry asked.

"He'll take it downtown first. But the Scripps people have a claim on it too. Once Belli has examined it in relation to the death of our Jane Doe, he will transfer it to La Jolla. There they will be able to analyze it biologically and tell us something about its life cycle." He smiled. "I am sorry you were asked to come over here, but John Belli is very sensitive when it comes to interference of any kind."

Gil said, "We weren't interfering, sir, believe me. If anybody's been interfering, it's those Scripps people and your friend Belli. This creature isn't a joke, sir. It's a living epidemic."

Salvador looked at him sternly. "Nobody suggested that it was a joke, my boy. There are no jokes when it comes to the death of a human being, believe me."

"I'm sorry," Gil said, "but you should have listened. We know what we're talking about."

"You don't know anything," said Salvador. "And just remember that you are permitted to stay as close as this only through my good offices."

Henry put in quietly, "Was the creature still alive when you lifted it out of the hole?"

"As far I could tell," Salvador told him. "Its heart was still beating."

Susan said, "Its face—did you get a look at its face?"

Salvador shook his head. "It was wrapped up in blankets. They soaked the blankets with water and then bundled them tight around its head. I guess they supposed this would simulate the effect of having wet sand all around it."

"Well," Henry said in resignation, "I suppose you have done what you consider you legal duty. But, please, may I ask you to make sure the creature is kept firmly locked up and that there is always somebody present to guard it."

Salvador stared at him narrowly. "What *do* you know, Henry?"

"I know nothing except that this creature is destructive and malevolent and that it will very quickly grow into something neither you nor I nor anybody else is capable of handling."

"And who told you this that you're so certain about it?"

"I can't tell you that. I promised not to. But believe me, it came direct from the highest authority."

Salvador said, "I recognize only two authorities, Henry. The San Diego Police Department and God. If it wasn't either of those, I'm really not interested."

Henry said, "It wasn't the San Diego Police Department."

Salvador laughed. His driver had started his car and the Scripps men were tidying up their equipment. "I have to go now," he said and waved. "But I am sure I will bump into you again. Thank you for all your frightening warnings! I am sure you annoyed John Belli no end."

When he had gone, Henry, Gil and Susan walked back up the beach to the promenade.

"Would you like a drink?" Henry asked.

Susan said, "No, thanks. And you should stay off it too. We're going to be Warriors tonight."

"That's all very well for you to say," Henry protested, "but I have the ancient ancestor of all the hangovers that ever were."

"You won't get rid of it by drinking."

"I won't get rid of it by *not* drinking either. So I might just as well drink."

Susan took his arm and walked along the promenade with him toward his cottage. It was growing dark now. The glow of sunset was gradually fading and the gulls were turning against the breeze in their last search for insects. Susan said, "Just for me, as a personal favor, will you not have any more to drink tonight?"

Henry made a face. "I'm not sure I could cope with being a Night Warrior without a drink."

"Don't tell me you're that much of an alcoholic."

"Did I ever say I was an alcoholic? Of course I'm not an alcoholic. I didn't drink at all last Tuesday, not one drink all day. I'm a heavy drinker, sure, but I drink because I like it. It makes me feel good. I'm not furtive about it. I don't hide bottles of vodka down the back of the sofa. And I don't drink anything I don't like. I had a bottle of Malmsey in the house for months and never even touched it. Now your genuine alcoholic, he'll drink anything."

Susan squeezed his arm closer. "The trouble is, Henry, we're really going to have to depend on you tonight. You're the center of the whole thing, the charge-keeper. Supposing something goes wrong because you've had one too many drinks?"

Henry said, "I promise you, I can handle it. There are some people who can and there are some people who can't. I happen to be one of those who can."

Susan said, "You know that I lost my parents?"

They had reached the corner by Henry's cottage now. Gil had been walking a little way behind them and he kept his distance, pretending to be looking out to sea where a dark, curling cloud hung in the shape of a question mark.

Henry said nothing but looked at Susan with a serious face.

"They were in a car crash," she said. "They were coming back from a dinner party at Escondido and they went off the road by Lake Hodges."

"Well, I'm truly sorry," Henry told her.

Susan lifted her head and looked him straight in the eye. "The medical examiner said that my father had twice as much alcohol in his blood as the legal limit."

Henry laid a hand on her shoulder and attempted a smile. "Well," he said, "I guess there isn't any answer to that."

Gil came forward and held up his left arm, showing his wristwatch. "We have to arrange a time," he said. "How about ten o'clock?"

"That's a little early for me," Henry said. "Let's make it eleven, shall we? Otherwise there won't be a hope of my being asleep and you two will be left on your own."

"Eleven's okay with me," said Susan. "My grandparents go to bed at ten-thirty and that's when the televisions get switched off. There isn't much hope of getting to sleep before then anyway."

Henry said, "Eleven it is then," and quoted from

Macbeth: "When shall we three meet again—in thunder, lightning, or in rain?"

Susan quoted back at him, "When the hurly-burly's done—when the battle's lost and won."

Henry took his hand from her shoulder. "I'm afraid you might be right."

He watched the two young people walk back along the promenade toward Solana Beach. It was still light enough for them to make their way along the shoreline, and the tide was well out. Romantic, he thought, on a warm night like this, a night full of expectations and promises.

But also a night of fear, he thought, as he unlocked his front door and stepped into the silent living room. There gleaming in the dusk were the curve of the television screen and the half-empty vodka bottle on the table. They shine, he thought as he closed the door behind him, the two placebos for every sickness know to man, physical or mental. A fifth of vodka and half an hour of *The $100,000 Pyramid,* and insensibility will supervene, guaranteed.

He switched on the lamps beside the sofa. His wristwatch was where he had left it last night, next to a dog-eared copy of Spinoza's *Ethics.* He picked up the book. For some reason he couldn't remember, he had underlined the words, "We feel and know that we are eternal." Then he picked up his watch. Seven-eighteen. Nearly four hours to go. How was he going to occupy himself for four hours?

He could work on his thesis. He could read more of Spinoza. He could take a shower and wash his hair. He sat down and slowly unlaced his sneakers. He looked up, and there was the vodka bottle, shining at him.

9

She was pushing her shopping cart through Ralph's when the young man came around the corner pushing his cart and collided with her.

"Oh, I'm sorry," he apologized. He was tall and curly headed, and he put her in mind almost instantly of Elliott Gould. "I guess I'm not much of a driver. Did I hurt you?"

"I'll live," she smiled.

She went on, pushing her cart past the herb and spice shelves. She was giving a small dinner party tomorrow, not that she particularly felt like it. Paul had been away for a week in Las Vegas, negotiating a new lighting contract with the Desert Hotel Group, and he would bring back three of his clients so they could inspect the full range of his latest fixtures out at his engineering works in Burbank.

She hated business dinners. Mostly the clients were short and fat and coarse, and they drank too much and smoked too much and tried to grab her behind. Afterward she always felt that she and her house had been gang-banged. She had begged Paul to take his clients to restaurants— "They'll be so much more impressed with a restaurant"— but Paul believed implicitly in the personal, family touch. When men were away from home on business, he argued, they saw far too many restaurants. They wanted to feel comfortable and relaxed. They wanted to feel they were friends rather than mere business clients.

So it was that several times a month Jennifer was expected to prepare a four- or five-course dinner of *boeuf carbonnade,* or glazed duck with baby vegetables, or roast rack of lamb Provençale. She had Inez to help her of course, but even if she had run a kitchen staff of twenty, her feelings about business dinners wouldn't have changed. It was the loud laughter, the crass remarks, the blue jokes and the sub-

Rabelaisian table manners. Whenever she thought of business dinners, she thought of the president of Northern Frate and how he had crushed out his cigar in the Madeira sauce left on his plate.

Jennifer thought she deserved better: a better home, a better husband, a better life. When Paul wasn't making business-dinner demands on her though, he was still amusing and gentlemanly, and she believed he still loved her, as much as he could love anybody. It was just the unrelenting sameness of every day that depressed her: the sameness of housework and then the sameness, once the housework was finished, of wondering what on earth to do to occupy her spare time. She often tried to spin out a small embroidery project for days on end, unpicking the stitches unless they were absolutely perfect. She had plenty of friends, but they were caught in the same predicament. Their children were away at school, their husbands were away at work, and let's face it, not every woman could write *Scruples* or head up Twentieth Century Fox or play championship tennis.

She used to look out the window of the plane when she flew back from visiting her sister Nesta in San Francisco and try to count the bright-turquoise swimming pools that studded the Valley, thinking to herself that by each of those pools there stands a house and in each house there sits a woman waiting out the rest of her life in emptiness.

Jennifer stopped beside one of the store's mirrored pillars and studied herself. "Brunette, dark-eyed, with excellent bone structure, seeks amusement. Dresses tastefully, talks intelligently, makes love with enthusiasm when required. Will not consider embroidery or business catering. Prefers hunting rhinoceros, sailing uncharted oceans, dancing until well past dawn and running naked through breeze-blown fields of golden poppies."

She focused her eyes in the mirror. The young man who had collided with her only a few minutes earlier was standing behind her, watching her. She blushed suddenly and turned around, hoping she hadn't been making her usual faces.

"I'm sorry," he said. "I was thinking how attractive you are."

"What?" she asked as if he were mad. God, he probably was.

"I have to cook this meal tonight," he told her, and he said it in such a way that she wasn't sure of what he had said. "It's lamb," he added distractedly.

She stared at him. "What is?"

"This meal I have to cook tonight. My fiancée's folks are coming over. I can't afford to take them out to a restaurant so I thought I'd cook."

"And you were going to cook lamb?"

"I have this recipe, look. I cut it out of last Friday's food section."

He held out a well-folded cutting from the *Times*. She took it but couldn't read it because she wasn't wearing her glasses. She fumbled in her pocketbook and finally managed to find them. "Now then," she said, peering at the cutting. "What is this?"

She read it quickly. It was Lamb en Croûte, a boned leg of lamb smothered in pâté and herbs, wrapped in pastry and then baked. She gave the recipe back to him. "Do you cook much?" she asked.

"Only burgers."

"Don't you think Lamb en Croûte is rather ambitious for somebody who cooks only burgers?"

"I guess. But I thought that if I followed the instructions carefully and used frozen pastry instead of trying to make my own . . . well, that it would probably turn out okay."

"Maybe, with lots of luck," smiled Jennifer. The young man amused her. He was gentle and earnest and good-looking, and he spoke to her as if he respected her advice as a person, not the way Paul spoke, as if she were lucky that he deigned to share his priceless conversation with her.

The young man scratched the back of his neck, thinking

hard. "It's just that this meal is real important and if I cook something dumb, what are her parents going to think of me?"

"You don't have to cook anything so complicated," said Jennifer. "Most people prefer plain food anyway. I give dozens of dinner parties and the most successful ones are always the simplest ones. Ham or tenderloin of pork or—"

"They're Jewish."

"Well, in that case you can always do something simple with beef or fish."

The young man looked down wistfully at the recipe he held in his hand. "You're right," he said. "Maybe I should cook something simple, broiled ribs of beef or something."

Jennifer watched him for a moment. In the bottom of his shopping cart he had already collected liver pâté, Herbes de Provence and frozen pastry as well as snow peas, baby carrots and russet potatoes.

"Let me make a suggestion," she heard herself saying. "Why don't you come back to my house this afternoon and I'll prepare the Lamb en Croûte for you? You have to partly cook the lamb before you wrap it in the pâté and the herbs and the pastry. I'll do all that and decorate it for you, and then all you have to do tonight is put it straight into the oven."

The young man stared at her. "You'd do that?"

"Why not? I don't have anything else to do this afternoon. It should be fun."

"Well, that's terrific. But you don't even know me. I could be the Hollywood Hatchetman or somebody like that."

"Oh, sure," Jennifer said briskly, pushing her shopping cart ahead of her. "The Hollywood Hatchetman wanders around Ralph's wondering how to cook Lamb en Croûte for his parents-in-law-to-be."

The young man followed Jennifer along the aisle. "Even Charles Manson used to shop," he said breathlessly.

Jennifer stopped and their carts collided again. "You're

not a friend of Charles Manson's, are you?" she asked half seriously.

He clapped his hand against his chest in horror. "Me? No, of course not."

"Listen," said Jennifer, "we'd be better off with just one shopping cart. Otherwise there could be a serious traffic accident before we've finished."

It took them ten minutes to finish their marketing. Then the young man pushed the shopping cart out to Jennifer's car, a metallic-green Eldorado, six months old.

"Where's your car?" she asked.

He flapped one hand diffidently toward a scabrous Le Sabre, twelve years old, with a collapsed suspension. Jennifer smiled. "You want to leave it here and come back in mine?" she asked.

"No, that's okay. I'll follow you. Not too close. I wouldn't want to embarrass you."

Jennifer said, "I really ought to know your name. And I guess you ought to know mine. I'm Jennifer Shepheard."

They shook hands. "Bernard Muldoon," the young man told her. "I'm a business-studies student at UCLA. Training to be a captain of industry."

"Good to know you, Bernard."

They drove out of the parking lot onto Hollywood Boulevard, heading west. Jennifer kept her eye on Bernard's limping Buick, making sure she didn't leave him behind as she turned up La Brea. She didn't live far away, just up the canyon on Paseo del Serra. But by the blue smoke coming out of the back of Bernard's car, she thought she ought to keep the pace sedate. In five minutes, however, they were parking on the sharply sloping driveway outside Jennifer's split-level, ranch-style house and Bernard was helping her carry the groceries around the back to the kitchen.

He glanced around as Jennifer opened the door for him. "The neighbors won't gossip, will they?" he queried.

"You're not bent on giving them anything to gossip about, are you?" she smiled.

Bernard flushed. "Well, no, of course not. But I know what some of these suburban neighborhoods are like. They live entirely on gossip and Stouffer's candies."

"You think I'm like that?" asked Jennifer, thinking of the afternoon last week when she had put her feet up, read *Lace 2* and eaten a whole box of violet creams. She didn't binge like that very often; she wanted to keep her figure as well as her mind. But she swore now that she would never let herself do it again.

The kitchen was tiled in Thanksgiving Brown, with glazed pictures of golden poppies beside the sink (the poppies through which she sometimes imagined herself dancing naked). There was a cookie jar with a silly rabbit's face on it, an egg rack with ten brown eggs in it and a Currier & Ives calendar that Sammi, her middle daughter, had given her in a teenage attempt to teach her mother some taste. Jennifer unpacked the groceries on the tiled central island and told Bernard where to put things away.

"Would you like a glass of wine?" she asked. "There's some Chablis in the refrigerator. Or there's beer if you'd prefer. The glasses are in that cupboard next to the scales. That's it. And could you pour one for me, please?"

They spent the afternoon in the kitchen preparing the Lamb en Crôute and chatting about politics, art, television, how good Raquel Welch looked for her age, contraception for underage girls, nuclear energy, Greenpeace, the meaning of other people's lives and the meaning of their own. Jennifer could hardly believe it when she looked up at the wall clock and saw that it was past five. Bernard had kept her continuously interested, continuously amused. If only . . . but then "if only" was as far as a married woman was allowed to think, as far as Jennifer was concerned anyway. Beyond "if only" there was excitement and pleasure, but there was insecurity and danger as well.

"What time is your dinner?" Jennifer asked him as she

glazed the pastry with egg. "You should put this in the oven at least an hour beforehand, at two hundred twenty degrees."

Bernard stood with his hands tucked into his back pants pockets and looked down at the lamb for a long while, saying nothing. Jennifer stopped glazing it and asked, "Is anything wrong?"

"Well . . ." he began.

"Well what? Is there something wrong with the lamb? You don't like the way it looks? Maybe those pastry flowers are too fussy. It was supposed to have been cooked by a man, after all. We don't want your fiancée's parents thinking there's anything limp-wristed about you, do we? You know what people are like when it comes to carrying on the good old family tree."

"Nothing like that," said Bernard. "The truth is, I have a confession to make."

"A confession?" asked Jennifer. She went over to the sink and washed her hands. Then she untied her apron strings and said, "You don't owe me anything, you know. Not even the truth."

"The truth is," Bernard told her with great simplicity, "that I have no fiancée."

Jennifer said "Oh" and looked at the lamb. "But if you have no fiancée, that means your fiancée's parents aren't coming to dinner."

"That's right."

"But if your nonexistent fiancée's nonexistent parents aren't coming to dinner, who is?"

"I was hoping that I was, with you."

Jennifer stared at him openmouthed. "You were hoping that . . . you mean you . . . I don't believe it! You picked me up in that supermarket and got me to invite you home to dinner! You even got me to cook it! I just don't believe it!"

"I told you that you're beautiful. At least I was honest about that."

Jennifer shook her head. "I really can't believe it. I thought I was hearing things when you said that. I couldn't believe that a total stranger—I *still* can't believe it! I need a drink! Pour me another glass of wine before I pass out!"

Bernard hurriedly splashed Chablis into a glass and handed it to her. "I'm real sorry," he said. "I didn't know how else I was going to approach you. You can throw me out if you like. You can even keep the lamb. I'm sorry. You just attracted me. I thought you were so fantastic-looking and I didn't know what else to do."

Jennifer perched on the edge of one of the kitchen stools, still shaking her head. "I have to admit that you succeeded. What a line! But how did you know I was going to invite you home? I guess you must realize that I'm married."

"Oh, sure," said Bernard. "I was in the drugstore yesterday, you know the drugstore on Sunset, and I saw you talking to a friend. I came up close and I heard you saying that your husband was away until Saturday. That decided me, I guess. I had only one day and I had to think of something pretty fast. So that's what I thought of."

"Well, now," Jennifer told him, "what are we going to do? Morally, I guess, I should take you up on your offer and throw you out. Immorally, of course, I should say to hell with everything and since I've spent all afternoon preparing this damn lamb, I may as well cook it and invite you to share it with me, which is not as generous as it sounds because you bought it in the first place. On the other hand, what will the neighbors think? Those feeders on gossip and Stouffer's candies? On the other hand, who gives a damn what they think?"

"It's your choice," Bernard said a little sadly.

Jennifer said, "You've thrown me. You've really thrown me. Nothing like this has ever happened to me in my whole life. Listen, stay. Let's cook the lamb, let's have some more wine, let's talk a lot more. I haven't talked so much in three years, not since my last daughter left home. There's only one thing I'll ask you to do, if you don't mind doing it, and that is to drive your car away from here and maybe park it on Orchid Avenue, you know where that is? At least then the gossip will be kept to a reasonable minimum."

Bernard said, "You're some lady. I mean that. I knew when I first saw you that I wouldn't be disappointed."

They ate dinner in the dining room. Jennifer set the table with a fresh white-linen tablecloth embroidered at the edges with columbine. The lamb was too much for the two of them but she assured him that her husband would be quite happy with curried lamb next week.

"Three nights running?" asked Bernard.

Afterward they sat on the sofa in the living room, which overlooked the pool patio, and Jennifer played Frank Sinatra records and offered Bernard a glass of Paul's Courvoisier brandy. She sat on the floor close to him, humming along with "My Way." Bernard sipped his brandy and told her about his business studies.

"You have to grow when you're in business. You know what Roger Falk said."

"No," smiled Jennifer. "What did Roger Falk say?"

"Roger Falk said that many executives think they have ten years' experience whereas in fact they simply have one year's experience ten times over."

"Well, I think that's true," Jennifer said. "I mean, take Paul, for instance—"

"Do we have to talk about Paul?"

Jennifer turned and looked up at him. "What does that mean?" she asked. The lamplight was shining in her eyes and she knew she was looking attractive.

Bernard shrugged. "It means I don't particularly want to talk about Paul, that's all."

Jennifer laid her hand on his knee. "Paul is a long way away," she said.

Bernard laid his hand on top of hers. But quite unexpectedly he said, "It's late anyway. I'd better be going."

Jennifer said in undisguised bewilderment, "It's only eleven o'clock."

"Sure, but I have to get all the way to Venice."

"Bernard," Jennifer protested, "eleven o'clock is early."

"Well, I know, but I have a morning class tomorrow and you know how it is."

"No, I don't know how it is. You've gone to all the trouble of tricking your way into having dinner with me, we're alone together, there's music and wine, my husband isn't due home until tomorrow, and you're *leaving?*"

Bernard finished his brandy and set the glass down. "I'm sorry. I enjoyed every minute of it, but I really have to go."

Jennifer turned around so she was kneeling, clutching his hand. "What are you trying to do?" she demanded. "Are you trying to get me to beg you to stay?"

Bernard slowly shook his head. "I have to go, and that's it. I didn't mean to upset you."

Jennifer took a long, deep breath. Then she said, "You haven't upset me. As a matter of fact, you haven't upset me at all. Go on, you'd better go. And don't forget to put on your sneakers. I'd hate for any of the neighbors to see you leaving the house with your shoes in your hand. They would definitely get the wrong idea."

She stood up, flustered. She had to face up to the fact that Bernard had aroused her to the point where she was ready to go to bed with him, that she had been mentally and physically prepared for adultery. She felt guilty, cheated and unutterably relieved, all at the same time.

Bernard hopped around on one foot, trying to lace up a sneaker. "I'm sorry," he said. "I've made you angry and I didn't mean to."

"You haven't made me angry at all," Jennifer told him tightly.

"You're married," he said. "I didn't expect—"

"I don't care what you expected or didn't expect. Just go. You can take that lamb with you. I'll get you a doggie bag from the kitchen."

At the back door, the doggie bag clutched in his hand,

Bernard turned around and said, "I guess I'm not very good when it comes to seduction."

"No," said Jennifer, "you're not."

"I'll go, then. Thanks for everything. Thanks for the dinner."

Jennifer began to feel less frustrated, less punitive. She had at least spent a cheerful and talkative afternoon with Bernard. For the first time in years she had been able to think about something other than her isolation and boredom. She should be grateful to him for that at least.

"Good-bye, Bernard," she said softly and kissed his cheek. "And . . . you know, don't be a stranger."

"I won't," he told her and kissed her back. Then, without even a wave, he was gone and she heard the wrought-iron gate at the side of the house clang shut behind him.

She closed the door, locked it and put on the security chain. Frank Sinatra was still singing in the living room. She cleared away the dishes with a lump in her throat, then switched off the lights and went through to the bedroom with a large glass and what was left of the wine. The bedroom was white, with a white fluffy carpet, a white frilly bedspread and white seersucker drapes. She switched on the television and then went across to her dressing table, where a white poodle with a red-felt tongue and a zipper in its belly was jealously guarding her nightgown.

She undressed, watching herself in the mirror. How many businessmen's wives are doing the same, she wondered. All over Hollywood, all through the canyons, all across the Valley, a hundred thousand women stepping tired and lonely out of their clothes, studying themselves in their mirror.

She tied up her hair in a pink-chiffon scarf and walked through to the bathroom. She showered, standing in the steam thinking at first of nothing at all. But when she washed between her legs, she held her hand there for an extra moment, closed her eyes and thought of Bernard. She should have known when she first saw him that he wasn't sufficiently macho to make her a new lover.

She dried herself and went back to the bedroom. She disemboweled the white poodle, taking out the pink transparent baby-doll nightie that Paul liked best. Her nipples showed through the nylonlike cherries on top of two white ice-cream sundaes. There were matching briefs with the nightie but she rarely wore them.

She climbed into bed and reached over to the bedside table for a magazine. She flicked through *Western Living* and *Los Angeles* and *Cosmopolitan,* her glasses perched on the end of her nose; then she tossed the magazines aside and watched television for a while. It was almost midnight. They were showing *See Here, Private Hargrove* on 11 and *Horror Hospital* on 9. She watched both movies for five or ten minutes, flicking with remote control from one to the other; then she changed over to the news.

She wasn't quite sure when she fell asleep, or even if she had. She felt herself dozing, felt her head sliding sideways on the pillow. Then she recovered, blinked, and tried to focus on the television screen. A newsman was saying, ". . . given the rich diversity of Asian immigrants' backgrounds, it is impossible to generalize about their experiences in becoming Americans . . ."

She drank a little more wine but it tasted vinegary. She listened to the news again and then her head began to slide on the pillow once more. She slept but she wasn't sure of how long. She dreamed she was crossing a wide, polished floor and that her footsteps echoed around her. On all sides tiers of balconies rose up, draped with gaily colored blankets and bedding. She heard music, Italian music like her father used to play when she was a child.

She reached the end of the polished floor and opened a door. Inside, her family was sitting down to lunch. She looked around the room and realized that she had never been away, that she had always been a child and that she had never grown up and left the Astoria neighborhood, never moved West and married. Her father was sitting where he always sat, his back to the door, his shirt bunching out of the triangles made by his crisscrossed suspenders, his bald patch shining because it was hot. On the dresser, the same yellow-and-blue plates were propped up, and the porcelain Madonna stood where she always stood, her holy baby in her arms.

Her sister Grace and her brother Michael were there too, waiting at their places. Only Momma was missing. Jennifer moved through the room and heard herself ask, "Where's Momma? Isn't Momma here? It's lunchtime."

She looked down at the table. Their plates were empty, cold, and the vegetable tureens were empty too. "Where's the food?" she asked. Her father raised his head and told her in a reverberating voice, "It's lamb."

She thought, "My God, he's sick. I can hear the sickness in his throat. Doesn't he realize he has to eat or he's going to die?"

She ran to the door. Her black dress rose up and down with every step, making a slow, thundering sound. She snatched at the door handle and swung the door wide. She found herself running along a narrow tunnel, her shoes splashing through ice-cold puddles, her footsteps echoing. She was panicking now; somebody was after her. She could hear him close behind but she didn't dare turn around in case he was really there, closer than she had feared.

She reached the end of the tunnel. Her eyes were blinded by a sudden dazzling whiteness and she had to press her hands over them to protect them. She slid backward, stumbling over something white and furry like the body of a polar bear. She opened her eyes and she was lying in her own bed, in her own bedroom, but she was sure she was still dreaming for outside the window the landscape was blood-red. Blood-red sky, blood-red garden, blood-red palm trees. Even the swimming pool was blood-red.

Someone's been killed, she thought. Someone's been killed and his blood has splashed everywhere, over the sky, over the houses, over the ocean too. Someone has died and his death has colored the world red.

She wondered if there was anything about the killing on the news. Slowly she turned her head toward the television. The screen was flickering blue-gray and she heard the muffled sound of waltz music.

As she stared at the television, however, specks of colored light began to fly off the screen and into the room. Gradually they assembled themselves into a blurred shape standing in the center of the white fluffy carpet. A body, a rib cage, a pelvis, a head, two muscular legs, all slowly created out of flying particles of light. The waltz music went on and on, dim and crackly like a shellac record from the 1930s.

Jennifer sat up in fascination and terror. The shape that was slowly manifesting before her was at least eight feet tall; its head almost touched the ceiling. It was broad-shouldered and as it became more distinct, she could see that it was muscular and lean, with skin as purplish-brown as if it had been stained with dogberries. Its face was pointed and malevolent, with slitted eyes that gleamed the same blood-red as the landscape outside the window, and two horns slanted back from the top of its head. Its thighs were thick with fur, and from between them reared a huge reddened phallus, below which hung two purple testicles as big as oranges.

The creature stank. It stank of sweat, greasy fur, foul breath and sex: an odor so overwhelming that Jennifer retched. She thought with mounting horror, how can I smell this stench when I'm only dreaming? How can I see this creature so clearly? I can see every hair of its beard, I can make out every wrinkle around its eyes! My God, it's just like the Devil in fairy stories but it came out of the television, and it's here in front of me, and it's *real*.

She heard a voice inside her head coax, *"Jennifer. This is what you wanted, isn't it? This is what you were longing for all day. You wanted to take him to bed, didn't you, Jennifer?*

*You wanted him on top of you! You wanted sweat and pain
and the feel of another man's body! This is what you
wanted, you whore! This is what you wanted, you slatternly
bitch!"*

Jennifer clutched at the sheets and screamed but no sound
came out of her mouth. The creature approached the bed
and it was so grotesque that she kept on screaming silently.
It sat down on the edge of the bed. It must be real, I can feel
the comforter pinned under it, I can feel its weight. Then it
slowly pulled back the top part of the covers, revealing
Jennifer in her baby-doll nightie.

"Don't kill me!" she begged. Her screaming had stopped
now; her voice was hurried and low and erratic, like water
tumbling down a dry creek bed for the first time. "I beg you
in the name of the Holy Mother, please don't kill me."

The creature's eyes appeared to flare as Jennifer mentioned the name of the Blessed Virgin. It reached out and
touched her cheek with its left hand. The skin on its fingers
felt as hard and rough as the skin on the paws of a farm dog.

"Silence," said the voice inside her head. *"I am your
Master One and your Master Many. You will do whatever I
say. I have to come to you today in two guises, the guise of
your friend and the guise of the goat, but I have as many
faces as the ocean has waves, and each one changes as the
waves change."*

For a liquid second Jennifer thought she could see
Bernard's features flowing across the creature's face. Then
the face returned to its narrow, pointed, menacing self, with
eyes that were filled with blood.

"You see the Devil you believe in, my love," the voice
continued. *"Did you not wish today that you could lie with
the Devil rather than with your husband? Well, this, my
filthy dear, is what you can do."*

The creature took hold of her just behind the knees,
gripping her with bruising strength and spreading her legs
so wide she heard the muscles crack. Then it reared up over
her—heavy, huge and evil-smelling—and glared down at

her with a face so old and wicked that she found herself unable to speak, unable to cry out, unable to do anything but lie there and shiver.

"Now you will be my little mother," the voice whispered, and Jennifer stared down at herself in freezing disbelief as the creature's massive member slid into her, right up to the shaggy fur that clung to the lower part of its protuberant stomach.

She closed her eyes. It was pain, solid pain, but it was also something else. Deep down beneath the pain there was a dark-running rivulet of pleasure, a rivulet that trickled through the forbidden recesses of Jennifer's mind, down her spinal column and into the nerves that were feeling the size and the power of the creature's penis.

The creature began to thrust in and out of her, slowly at first but then faster and faster, and even more brutally, like a mindless mechanical piston. The dark rivulet flooded the lower chambers of her brain and then began to rise up from beneath, flooding chamber after chamber until all of her body and brain seemed to be darkness. The creature let out a guttural, indistinct shout and held itself rigidly still for a moment, pumping deep inside her. Jennifer was a hair's-breadth from a climax, clinging to the very edge of it, her eyes tight shut, her face clenched, her chest flushed. Her nipples protruded and the muscles in her pelvis were tightly bunched in readiness for her final release.

But the final release never came. She opened her eyes and the creature was gone. Slowly, inch by inch, as she looked around in mystification, her muscles began to relax. But she was still shaking and her mind was still contracted for that ultimate moment of orgasm, and at first she couldn't understand what had happened, or even if anything had happened. The television was tuned to *The Rose Tattoo*. Her drink remained untouched on the night table. Outside in the darkness, a dog was barking, monotonously and hopelessly.

Jennifer touched her body. The covers had been dragged

back and her baby-doll nightie had been pulled up to bare her breasts, but had there really been anything here? A creature? A Devil with horns and hair? It wasn't possible. She sniffed once or twice but the rank smell, if it had ever been there, had vanished. She touched herself tentatively between her legs. She was wet and a little sore, but no wetter or sorer than she would have been had she been urgently masturbating.

She pulled down her nightie and covered herself again. Dreaming, she thought. I must have been dreaming. I *was* dreaming. The house is locked, nobody could have come in. And there is nothing and nobody in the whole wide world that can manifest itself out of a television.

She thought of her dream about her father. Somehow it must have gotten mixed up with a dream about Bernard. She had wanted to take Bernard to bed and so her unconscious mind must have created the Devil for her—the real, live, hairy Devil—to express what she really felt about adultery. Pleasurable, exciting, dangerous, frightening . . . and wrong. In the old days adulterers had been stoned. These days God sent them bad dreams and nervous breakdowns.

Jennifer went to the bathroom, took two Valium pills and washed them down with warm Perrier. Then she switched off the television, turned off the lights and climbed into bed. She lay awake for a long time listening to the dog.

Then, abruptly, she switched on the light again, sat up in bed and wondered whether she ought to call Father O'Hare. She looked at the clock. Two twenty-five. It was too late to call anyone and try to explain that she thought she had been raped by Satan.

And apart from that, she felt more than a little guilty about what had happened, or what she had dreamed had happened. It was one thing to explain to Father O'Hare that the Devil had appeared in her bedroom and forced her to have sex with him. It was quite another to say that although she had been frightened, although she had been shocked, she had taken out of it some wild and perverse pleasure, a pleasure as urgent as the human appetite for self-destruction and as deep as sin itself.

She turned out the light again. She slept, but she didn't dream.

10

Susan told her grandmother she was feeling nauseous and went to bed early. She was too excited about what was going to happen tonight to stay in the living room watching television and listening to her grandfather's interminable drolleries about every program that came on. He was a devotee of the kind of humor once called "ribbing," the sort of pointless, deadpan, tall-story humor favored by old men who sit in rockers outside small-town general stores.

"That Jack Lord, do you know how he keeps his hair so thick? He insists as a condition of their contract that every guest star who appears on *Hawaii Five-O* give him a plug of scalp to add to his hair transplant."

Susan closed her bedroom door and wondered whether she ought to lock it. She didn't know what would happen if her grandmother came in to check on her when she was asleep and her Samena personality was away, somewhere out in the night. She knew it was supposed to be dangerous to wake a sleepwalker but she wasn't sure if waking a Night Warrior amounted to the same thing.

Perhaps she wouldn't wake up at all and then her grandmother would panic and call an ambulance. On the other hand, if she locked her door, her grandmother would likely start banging on it and if Susan failed to reply, she would almost certainly try to force it open.

It was probably better to leave the door unlocked and hope her grandmother didn't disturb her while she slept and that it wouldn't affect her Night Warrior personality if she did.

She tugged off her T-shirt and was about to take off her shorts when her grandmother knocked at the door and came in. "How are you feeling?" she wanted to know. "Would you like some Pepto-Bismol? Is it that kind of nausea? You

177

haven't been eating those chili dogs again, have you, the ones that made you sick the last time?"

"It's not that, Grandma," Susan said. "I think it's just my period coming on."

"You ought to see the doctor if you're feeling nauseous."

"I'm okay, Grandma. It's just my period, that's all."

"So long as it *is* your period."

"I'm not pregnant," Susan smiled.

Her grandmother was flustered. "I do try to look after you the best I can."

"Grandma, I know you do, you're wonderful. Don't worry about it."

Her grandmother blinked behind her glasses. It had been a long time since Susan had said she was wonderful. Pleased, disarmed, she retreated to the door and gave Susan a little wave. "You can have some tea later if you'd care to."

"I don't think so, Grandma. I'll just get some sleep."

"Okay then. I'll see you in the morning."

Susan finished undressing, rummaged around in her drawer for a clean T-shirt, put it on and jumped into bed. It was twenty after ten. In ten minutes or so her grandfather would reach over, lay his hand on her grandmother's knee and say, "Well then, Dolly, I think it's time to strangle the chickens." That was what he always said when he was suggesting they turn off the television and go to bed. Why going to bed should have anything to do with strangling chickens, Susan never knew.

She lay in bed with the light on for a while, her hands clasped behind her head. Then she switched off the light and lay in the dark. She could hear the traffic along Camino del Mar, and the cicadas chirping, and the steady blowing of the air-conditioning through the vent in the ceiling. After a while the television in the living room was switched off and she heard her grandmother and grandfather walk past her door murmuring something about doctors and hepatitis, and how some people never washed their hands after going to the bathroom.

"One hamburger out of every ten will make you ill. An old friend of mine proved that. He ate nine hamburgers and he was perfectly okay, but when he ate the tenth, he became violently sick."

"You and your stories," Susan's grandmother chided.

The old couple took a long time getting to bed. There were teeth to be taken out, corns to be planed, curls to be wound up in heated rollers. By the time the toilet had been flushed for the last time, it was almost quarter of eleven and Susan was growing anxious that she would miss her rendezvous with Henry and Gil.

At last, however, the house was silent and dark. She lay back on the pillow, looking up at the ceiling, and repeated the words Springer had given her to memorize. They were strange and simple words. Springer had said they had been translated from the Latin and carried to the New World in 1601 by the first of the Night Warriors.

"Now when the face of the world is hidden in darkness, let us be conveyed to the place of our meeting, armed and armored; and let us be nourished by the power that is dedicated to the cleaving of darkness, the settling of all black matters, and the dissipation of all evil, so be it."

Susan repeated the words three times as Springer had instructed and then she closed her eyes and lay still. I'll never get to sleep in time, she thought to herself. I'm going to be late and the others will go off without me. The luminous hands of her bedside clock said six minutes of eleven. How can I possibly get to sleep in six minutes?

Curiously, though, her eyes began to close and even when she wanted to open them again to look at the clock, she found that she couldn't. Her body slowly began to relax, all the way through, as if it were a building in which the lights were being extinguished floor by floor. Her heartbeat slowed, her respiration became flat and shallow, and she began to feel as if she were slowly moving backward inside her head, backward into the darkness that every human being carries inside himself. As she went back faster and faster, ever deeper into inner space, she heard a high-pitched, metallic singing sound, an inanimate choir.

She rose now, dark and invisible, through the ceiling of her room, through the attic and up into the night above Del Mar. To the south she could see the dim surf gleaming as far as La Jolla and the lights of San Diego sparkling beyond. To the north she could see the long curve of Cardiff, San Elijo Lagoon and Encinitas. The traffic poured along I-5 like streams of fireflies. Beyond the highway the inland hills were wrapped in shadows and crowned with condominiums.

Susan didn't feel as if she were flying. The sensation was more one of being *absorbed* through the evening air, as if she were no more substantial than ink that was quickly being absorbed by blotting paper. She felt as if the molecules of her personality were mingling with those of the night through which she was passing, as if nobody could tell where the night ended and Susan began. But she could see the landscape below her clearly and as she spun slowly down toward the house on Camino del Mar and passed through its roof and into the upstairs room, she was aware of an extraordinary friction.

The room was lit by a single naked bulb that threw stark shadows in all directions. Springer was there in his male manifestation this time, dressed in a plain black suit. Gil had arrived too, but as yet there was no sign of Henry.

Susan went straight to the mirror and looked at herself. She had not yet taken on the guise of Samena but she was delighted, frightened and fascinated to see that she was transparent, that she could see the opposite side of the room through the outlines of her body. Gil was the same: substantial enough to recognize and talk to, but unreal. A dream figure, a living memory of himself.

Springer said with a small nod of his head, "You are both

to be congratulated. It is not easy to leave one's body for the first time."

"Will we be safe?" asked Susan. "Our actual bodies, I mean. I was worried that my grandmother might try to wake me up."

Springer smiled. "All you need worry about is someone physically destroying your body. That would give you nowhere to return to. But I don't think your grandmother is likely to do that, do you?"

"Of course not," Susan smiled and then added, "I feel like I'm dreaming."

"You *are* dreaming," Springer told her, coming up behind her and laying a hand on her semitransparent shoulder. "Your mind is here, your spirit is here, but your material substance remains at home, sleeping."

Gil said, "There's no sign of Henry yet."

"Henry will be here," Springer assured him.

"I hope he wasn't doing any more—you know," Susan remarked, making a drinking gesture with her hand.

Springer ignored her words and held out his hands to both of them. "Now is the time for you to prepare yourselves, Tebulot and Samena, for your first training as Night Warriors. Come here, each of you, and kneel in front of me."

A little hesitantly, they knelt side by side. Springer raised his hands, palms facing outward, and chanted the ancient words of the Night Warriors. *"Now when the face of the world is covered in darkness, let us prepare ourselves here at this place of our meeting; let us arm and armor ourselves; and let us be nourished by the power that is dedicated to the cleaving of darkness, the settling of all black matters, and the dissipation of evil, so be it."*

"So be it," Gil and Susan repeated.

"You are Night Warriors now," Springer said. "You are members of that great and glorious host who captured and chained all nine hundred and ninety-nine manifestations of the Devil and who earned for all time the gratitude of

Ashapola and the Council of Messengers. You have dedicated your dream selves to the extinction of evil, and in particular to the pursuit and capture of Yaomauitl, the Deadly Enemy."

Springer circled his hands in the air, and over their heads two golden circles of light appeared and then slowly faded.

"Tebulot, stand," Springer instructed Gil, and Gil rose to his feet and found as he did so that he was mantled in the hard, gleaming-white armor of the machine-carrier and that in his arms he was carrying the huge weapon with which he would protect himself from harm and which he would use to track down Yaomauitl. This time the armor felt solid, although it wasn't excessively heavy; it was fashioned out of a thick, lightweight alloy and brightly enameled. The machine, though, was a different matter. It weighed at least thirty pounds and even though its odd horn-shaped handles made it easy to hold, it was not readily maneuverable.

"Whoever dreamed this up, he could have dreamed it up lighter," complained Tebulot.

"Its weight is necessary in order to stabilize it when it fires," Springer explained. "At full strength, it can vaporize the walls of a fortress."

He turned now to Susan and said, "Samena, stand," and Susan rose to her feet to assume the identity of Samena, the finger-archer. Her plumed hat gleamed in the light from the naked bulb, and the arrowheads hooked around her briefs jangled as she turned around.

Now that her costume had materialized fully, she could see that the soft leather from which it was made had been perfectly tailored to fit her snugly and that it was elaborately decorated with semiprecious stones: opal, turquoise and jet.

Springer said, "The design of these costumes and this armor goes back hundreds of years. It is the combination of many men's and women's dreams. Parts of Tebulot's armor can be seen in the drawings of Leonardo da Vinci, and some of Samena's jeweled decorations match those seen at the

Kandariya Mahadeva temple at Khajuraho, in Bundel-khand, dating from one thousand A.D."

Tebulot asked, "What time is it now? Henry's late."

"Give him a chance to leave his body," said Springer. "Remember that he is older than you, and much more set in his attitudes. It is not easy for a man of his age and his customs to leave his body while he sleeps. There are many chains that have to be broken first. Chains of habit, chains of doubt, chains of apprehension. The mind argues, 'Why should I take the risk of facing the Devil when I would much rather stay asleep in the safety of my own bed?'"

But Springer had hardly finished speaking when there was a soft noise like someone dragging the hem of a silk cape along a polished floor and Henry slid into the room through the ceiling, wearing a pair of pale-blue pajamas.

"I couldn't get to sleep," he told them apologetically. "I tried and I tried but my brain was free-wheeling so fast I thought I was going to burn out my cortex. Even after I repeated the incantation, I stayed awake. I'm sorry."

Springer said, "It was not your fault, my friend. Your difficulty was quite understandable. But we should hurry now. The quicker we prepare, the more time we will have to train you. Kneel, please, Henry, and I will recite the words that will transform you into Kasyx."

Samena touched Henry's arm. Under her plumed hat her eyes were bright and serious. "Henry?" she said. "Are you all right?"

Henry shook his head. "If you mean am I drunk, the answer is no. I spent the whole evening staring at a bottle of vodka but I didn't open it once. I remembered what you told me about your parents. Then I looked around my house and remembered what Gil had told me when we first decided to be Night Warriors. He said that I had nothing to lose and he was right. So I thought to myself this evening, I've been alive for nearly half a century, and to have nothing to lose at the age of fifty is not much of an achievement. In fact, it's a pretty miserable thing to have to admit. So even if I have no real duty to you two, or to the girl who died on the beach, at least I have a duty to myself."

Springer was waiting for Henry patiently, so Henry said, "That's all of it," and knelt down as Springer had told him to.

Springer repeated the ancient words of the Night Warriors. He swept his hand around and drew the golden halo over Henry's head. "Stand, Kasyx," he said, and Henry stood up in the armored paraphernalia of the charge-keeper, the source of all righteous energy. Kasyx's armor was a dull metallic crimson, and fingers of electrical energy played repeatedly across his chest and around his shoulders, crackling fire creatures of sheer hairraising voltage.

Instinctively Kasyx laid his left hand on Tebulot's right shoulder and his right hand on Samena's left shoulder, and for a moment they stood in silence as the vast amounts of power Kasyx had been given by the god of gods, Ashapola, coursed through their bodies. At last the charging was complete and they saw now that they were no longer transparent, that their flesh and muscle were as real as any wide-awake human's.

Springer said, "I will take you first into a nightmare so you may see and hear for yourselves what the landscape of dreams can be like. I have scanned the sleeping minds of thousands of people in Del Mar—children and old people, blacks and whites—and I have found for you a nightmare that will challenge your abilities but not be too dangerous."

"We're going to do that now?" Samena asked nervously. "I thought we were just going to train. You know, like learning to use our weapons."

"In the landscape of dreams," smiled Springer, "the only useful training is through practical experience. I can tell you anything you like. I can tell you about nightmares in which terrible monsters appear and absolutely refuse to die, no matter what you do to them. I can tell you about nightmares in which you can be torn apart, or in which you *think* you've been torn apart. I can tell you about tortures and spiders and drowning and fire. But I can never re-create for you in words that which you would ultimately have to face in the real world of dreams."

Springer walked around them and showed them how to grip their hands together so that as they passed from dream to dream, they would be inseparable.

"The night is full of dreams; they are like a huge, invisible palace of a million rooms, one room for every dream. It is not difficult to lose one of your Warriors as you move from one dream to another. Sometimes this can be perilous. Occasionally it can be fatal. It takes a long time to trace your way through to any one particular dream, and by the time you have returned to where you left your stray Warrior . . . well, dreams change, and many dreams are more frightful than you can possibly imagine."

He faced them for one last time and said, "I have asked you to take up the task of being Night Warriors because each of you has inherited something of those mystic qualities that make you a natural hunter of Devils. But you may still choose not to take up your dream identity; you may still return to your sleeping body, even now, and never again wear this armor and never again carry these weapons. It is yours to decide. There is much terror ahead of you, and much struggle. But if you succeed in your adventures, you will know the ecstasy of great achievement and you will become exalted."

Kasyx raised the visor of his helmet and said, "I'm going to continue, thanks. I didn't spend the whole afternoon staring at a full bottle to back out now."

Samena said, "I want to go on."

There was a pause. They turned and looked at Tebulot.

"You have the most to lose, Tebulot," said Springer gently.

"Yes," replied Tebulot, "but also the most to gain. I'm coming."

They stood close together and clasped hands. Only Springer stayed apart. He looked at them one by one, and his eyes were frightening and remarkable, as dark as windows that looked out into infinite space. Beyond his eyes there were galaxies, spinning star systems and light-years of impossible distance.

"Follow me," Springer said simply. "Be wary. Trust nothing, for nothing will be as it seems."

Springer began to rise into the air and fade. For a moment the Night Warriors hesitated, uncertain of how they were going to follow him. But then Kasyx heard the clear words inside his head, words bright and sharp: *Rise up, Kasyx. Use your power and rise up.*

Kasyx closed his eyes and concentrated on rising. His concentration was far more intense than needed because the Night Warriors rocketed up through the roof of the house and soared high into the night, hundreds of feet above Del Mar, spinning off to the right as they did so because Samena was so much lighter than the other two.

Springer came looping up to join them. Kasyx noticed that as Springer passed through the air, he seemed to leave behind him a trail of absolute darkness that took several seconds to dissipate. The thought occurred to him for a jagged half-second that they had not yet been given any proof that Springer was actually what he, or she, claimed to be, that for all they knew, Ashapola could be the Lord of Darkness instead of the Lord of Light. Quite innocently all three of them could be setting out to help the Devil instead of fighting him.

But the words of Springer cut into his mind again, this time speaking in the lighter tones of a woman: *You will always question; you will always doubt. Ashapola expects you to. Faith should never be blind as it is in Christianity and so many other religions. Faith should come through questioning and criticism, through the proof of intellect and experience. Gods should be tested as well as men. The moment of religious ecstasy comes when you know for certain that your God is infallible.*

They hung high in the air like four dark kites. Below

them traffic twinkled, surf gleamed and Southern California edged closer to midnight.

Springer said, "To enter a dream, you must first encounter the dreamer. Follow close behind me. I am going down now to that apartment building on the corner. You see it? The one with the roof garden. On the fourth floor of that building a man is sleeping. He is exhausted. He has been working hard to keep his business from bankruptcy. Two years ago he was divorced by his wife because of his adultery with his secretary. He has a son, whom he sees only twice a month. He is haunted again and again by guilt and by responsibilities that are not even his."

They sank slowly through the warm evening wind. Kasyx found that he was able to control the movements of all three of them quite easily with only a minimal consumption of power. Together they soared and circled, descending all the while, until at last they faded through the walls of the building and into the bedroom of the man whose dreams they were going to penetrate.

The room was in darkness. The windows were closed and the air-conditioning was set to sixty-five degrees; after the warmth of the night outside, it felt chilly. The man lay on his back on a crumpled sheet, wearing nothing but jockey shorts. He was dark, with a bald patch that shone white in the darkness, and a dark, hairy body. By the side of the bed there was a copy of *Reader's Digest*, a bottle of Nytol sleeping tablets and a glass of water.

Springer leaned over the man and touched his eyelids with his fingertips. "He is experiencing the worst of his nightmares even now. You can see by his eye movements that he is dreaming. This is what is called REM sleep—for Rapid Eye Movement."

"How do we get into his nightmare?" asked Tebulot, shifting the weight of his weapon.

"More important, what do we do once we get in?" Kasyx wanted to know.

Samena asked, "Will he know we're there? Will he be able to see us in his dream?"

Springer said, "He will see you in his nightmare as clearly as everything else he can see. As for what you may and may not do, once you have penetrated his sleeping mind, the rules are quite simple. You may explore the dream in the same way you can explore the waking world. If you are threatened in the dream, you may defend yourselves and fight back. There are virtually no limitations except one, which is that you must not hurt the dreamer himself if he happens to appear in his own dream as a separate personality. You must be very wary of this for sometimes the dreamer will appear in his own dream as a child, or as somebody of the opposite sex, or in some kind of disguise."

"What happens if we hurt the dreamer?" asked Tebulot.

Springer looked at him through the darkness of the bedroom. For a moment Springer was neither he nor she but something quite ethereal. "If you hurt or kill the dreamer, the dream will collapse in on itself, with you inside it. In the early days, before the symbolism of dreams was fully understood, many inexperienced Night Warriors were lost in that way. Today, of course, even untrained people like yourselves are aware that much of what appears in dreams and nightmares is metaphoric rather than literal."

They looked down at the sleeping man. He groaned, turned and muttered to himself.

"Shall we go?" asked Kasyx.

Springer nodded.

"You, Kasyx, will use your power now to create a nexus between your dream and his. All you have to do is draw an octagon in the air with both hands, the hands separating at the top of the octagon and joining at the bottom. Then place your hands back to back in front of you and slowly prize them apart."

Kasyx did as Springer instructed. Allowing a steady current of power to flow from his hands, he described a large eight-sided figure in the darkness. His fingers crackled and danced with bright blue sparks, and as he drew the octagon, it remained suspended in the middle of the room, flickering like illuminated barbed wire.

Then he held his arms in front of him, thrusting his hands into the center of the octagon and gradually parting them. He felt extraordinary resistance and he had to double the power to keep his hands from being pushed together again. As he opened them out, however, he suddenly saw what he was doing. He was tugging the substance of the waking world apart as if it were a heavy but invisible curtain, because beyond the octagon, where his hands had drawn the molecules of reality aside, he could glimpse a grim, rainy landscape of rocks, mountains and wind-lashed trees.

"Now," said Springer, "you must enter. I shall not be coming with you, I am forbidden. But I shall follow you with my thoughts and I shall advise you and instruct you whenever it is necessary. Remember, all you are doing now is familiarizing yourselves with the world of nightmares. Take no risks and use no weaponry unless you are forced to for your own protection."

Kasyx, Tebulot and Samena now linked arms again and stood in front of the glimmering octagon.

"By the will of Ashapola, enter the world of dreams," Springer intoned, and the octagon rose slowly and turned sideways until it was over their heads. Then it gradually sank toward the floor, encircling them as if a conjuror had passed a hoop over them to show there were no strings, no mirrors, no tricks.

The instant the octagon touched the floor, the screaming of the wind exploded in their ears and they were hit by a solid wall of pelting rain. Still clinging together, ducking their heads, they looked around trying to orient themselves. The rain drummed against their armor and the wind blew the plumes of Samena's hat into a fury of boiling feathers. In the distance there were broken crags, towering mountains and a whitish building that looked like a fortress or a monastery standing at the head of a valley.

"What do we do?" Samena shouted against the wind.

"Head for that building, if you ask me," Kasyx shouted back. "That seems to be the core of what he's dreaming about."

They released each other's hands but stayed as close together as they could. Slowly, trying to acclimatize themselves to walking through the uncompromising terrain of somebody else's nightmare, they made their way across sharply sloping granite foothills until they reached a wind-blasted promontory from which they could look down at the wide valley that led up to the building. They could hear a bell tolling from the building's tower, a soulful, melancholy bell that reminded Kasyx of Edgar Allan Poe's lines on *"iron bells/ what a world of solemn thought their monody compels/ for every sound that floats/ from within their rusted throats/ is a groan."*

Tebulot touched Kasyx's shoulder and shouted, "Look, down there!"

Kasyx wiped the rain from his visor and strained his eyes to see down into the valley. In the shadows, in the slanting sheets of rain, he could make out a slow procession of figures. They were dressed in long, white robes, and hooded, ten or eleven of them, gradually climbing the valley floor. The two leading figures dragged behind them a large wooden cross and on the cross a naked man was spread-eagled.

Kasyx held his left hand against the side of his helmet and immediately his vision was altered to close-up. He could now see the hooded figures as clearly as if he were standing only a few feet from them. They seemed to be tall, much taller than ordinary men, and no matter how narrowly he adjusted his vision, he was unable to see anything inside their hoods except absolute blackness. He thought that once he caught sight of something like a curling black lock of hair, or a tentacle, but as quickly as he adjusted his focus on it, it disappeared.

Now he turned his attention to the wooden crucifix and the man who was stretched upon it. The two leading figures were dragging the crucifix with its top bumping on the ground so that the man's head was lower than his feet. He had been nailed to the cross through his forearms and feet, and there were diagonal marks on his body as if he had been whipped. His eyes stared wide in agony. Every jolt along the rocky ground must have been punishment. Kasyx recognized the man as the dreamer himself.

Samena said, "They seem like they're heading toward that building too."

"They'll reach it before we do," Tebulot commented.

"Are we supposed to save him or something?" Samena asked. "I mean, it seems as if Springer has put us into this dream for a reason, to see what we do."

Kasyx shook his head. "We're not supposed to intervene unless our safety is threatened."

"Sure," argued Tebulot, "but what are Night Warriors for? Isn't their whole reason for existence to go into dreams and save people?"

"I don't know," said Kasyx. "That man down there on the cross, he's the one who's dreaming this dream. Maybe he needs to have dreams like this to express his sense of guilt. Maybe if he didn't have them, he'd wind up a head case. Look at what's happening to him down there, he's being punished. You heard what Springer said: Things in dreams aren't always what they appear to be. Maybe those hooded figures are nothing more than his feelings of guilt."

"So meanwhile we stay here and let them drag him across those rocks? Is that it?"

"We're not supposed to interfere," Kasyx insisted.

"Well, I still think the whole purpose of our being here is to interfere," Tebulot told him.

"Let's get to the building first," Samena suggested. "Then we can make up our minds about what we're going to do next, whether we're going to help him or not."

"They're going to get to the building way ahead of us," said Kasyx. "Supposing they don't let us in?"

Tebulot lifted his weapon. "You heard what Springer

said. This thing can vaporize the walls of a fortress. We can get in there whether they want us to or not."

Bent against the wind and rain, they scrambled down noisily from the rocky promontory and headed toward the building along a narrow spine of gray granite. Below them and to their left, the procession with the crucifix was now close to the head of the valley and when the wind dropped from time to time, the Night Warriors could hear the hooded figures chanting in Latin. The bell still tolled dolorously from the building's tower, over and over again.

At last, more than two hundred and fifty yards ahead of the Night Warriors, the procession reached the outer walls of the building and crossed an extraordinary suspension bridge to reach the high main gate. In fact, as the three Warriors drew closer, they could see that the entire building was extraordinary. It was constructed of granite, the same granite as the mountains around it, but highly finished so it glistened wetly in the rain. Its walls were smooth and unscalable to about seventy feet from its foundations, but above that height there were hundreds of openings on dozens of different levels, and these openings were connected by external stone staircases without railings or supports. Up and down the staircases in a never-ending stream climbed men and women in sackcloth robes, chained, shackled and crowned with thorns.

At the top of the walls there were battlements on which more of the hooded figures came and went and from which wet, black flags snapped in the wind.

"I told you," said Kasyx as they crouched behind the last protective jumble of rocks, "this man is punishing himself. That's what this nightmare is all about. We don't have to save him at all. Look at this place. Punishment Palace. I've seen the symptoms a hundred times. He probably likes to wear ladies' garter belts and to have his fingers trodden on with stiletto heels."

"I don't know," frowned Samena. "I think there's more to this nightmare than that. I can sense something, I don't quite know what it is."

Kasyx said, "Believe me, Samena, he's probably loving every minute of it."

But Tebulot put in, "Don't dismiss Samena out of hand, Hen—I mean Kasyx. Just remember what Springer said, that Samena is the most sensitive of all of us. She could be picking up something that's out of our range."

Kasyx looked at Samena and she smiled. He had to admit that she looked more than becoming in that plumed hat and that tight, decorated bodice. "All right," he admitted. "Maybe I should stop being so much of a lecturer and start being more of a listener."

Samena said, "I can't describe it to you but I get the feeling there's some other presence inside that building, something apart from the dreamer himself, something stronger than the dreamer, something that's taken over his dream."

Kasyx said uneasily, "Maybe that's why Springer brought us here. Maybe Yaomauitl's hiding in this dream."

"He said we had to train first," Tebulot protested. "He wouldn't send us out against Yaomauitl on our very first night."

"Well, I'm not so sure about that," said Kasyx. "In fact, I'm not so sure about Springer. We don't know who or what he really is, do we? And we've allowed ourselves to be beguiled into this incredible adventure, haven't we, without checking his credentials."

Tebulot held out his armored hands. "He can do *this*, he can practically turn us into superheroes, and we have to check his credentials? Come on, Kasyx, why are you doubting him all of a sudden? Don't you feel fitter, don't you feel better? Don't you feel that you could do absolutely anthing you wanted to?"

Kasyx lifted his visor. He looked at Tebulot with steady eyes while the rain dripped persistently from the rim of his crimson helmet. "I guess you're right. I do feel better. I guess that's why I found myself volunteering to be a Night Warrior all the way down the line without even asking myself why. Have you realized how calmly we've accepted all this and yet how incredible it actually is? We've been calm because we feel this is something we've been waiting for, this is our chance to break free."

He paused and then said, "I don't think I'll ever stop doubting. It's part of my nature and it's most of what my job's all about. But all right, I'll accept what Springer has done for me and I'll go along with this until someone shows me that I'm making a dangerous idiot of myself. Just one thing, though: Don't ever ask me to lay down my life for Springer or Ashapola, not as a one-to-one choice, because the answer will always be, forget it."

"Nobody asked you," said Tebulot.

"No," Kasyx replied, "but there's always a chance that somebody might."

Samena touched her fingers to her forehead. "That feeling . . . it's very powerful. It's very evil too."

"What do you mean, evil?" Kasyx asked.

"I mean it's frightening. It's cold and vicious. It's like the feeling you get when you're walking along a sidewalk and you suddenly realize you have to pass a really mad-looking dog. I mean, you're scared but you can't run away."

"Well," said Kasyx, "the question is, what do we do about it?"

"Didn't Springer say he was going to keep in touch?" asked Tebulot. "Maybe you should try to ask him."

Kasyx closed his eyes and concentrated on communicating with Springer. But even after two or three minutes, he heard nothing but silence, a silence as empty as the infinite look he had last seen in Springer's eyes.

"He's not there," Kasyx said. "At least he's not keeping in touch."

"In that case I vote we go into the building and see what's going on," Tebulot urged. "Come on, we may not have much time. This guy might wake up soon or turn over and start dreaming about hootchie-kootchie girls."

Kasyx lifted his head and narrowed his eyes against the wind. "I'm not sure I'd object to that."

Nevertheless he laid his hands on their shoulders and gave them as much of his charge as he felt was safe. Naked electricity wriggled across his chest and sizzled in the driving rain. Tebulot checked the glowing charge scale and saw that it registered one-hundred-percent full. Samena unhooked an arrowhead from her waistband, a simple triangular point, and fitted it over the end of her right index finger.

"Very well then. Let's go see what we can find in the way of evil influences," said Kasyx.

They rose from behind the shelter of the rocks and headed diagonally across the valley floor toward the strange suspension bridge at the front of the building. They ran quickly and kept their heads down, which was all they could do to minimize detection. Kasyx was thankful that the rain was coming down even harder now, although he slipped once or twice on the rocks.

They reached the bridge without being seen, at least as far as they could tell. They ran across it without hesitation, their feet slapping on wet stone. The bridge spanned a deep, artificially cut ravine in which lay stagnant water black with slime. The surface of the water was circle-patterned with raindrops, and occasionally furrowed as if something were swimming deep below its surface.

The Night Warriors found themselves approaching a narrow, curved gateway. Kasyx was aware of the Freudian symbolism of gateways in dreams and noted to himself that this one was remarkably similar in shape to the female vulva, but he said nothing and led his two companions through to a long, dark corridor. At the far end of the corridor they could see an inner courtyard, cobbled and puddly, and two or three of the hooded figures apparently standing guard.

"What do we do now?" asked Tebulot, nervously lifting his weapon.

Kasyx said, "We approach them, that's all. But we keep ourselves right on edge. Any hostile movements, let them have it."

"That sounds like good basic American thinking," commented Samena with noticeable sharpness.

"Well, what do you suggest we do? Go up and shake hands? As far as we can make out, those jokers crucified the man who's dreaming this dream and for all we know, they might be quite happy to do the same to us."

Cautiously they walked the remaining few yards along the tunnel and emerged into the rainy courtyard. Tebulot glanced up. On the walls that surrounded the courtyard there were twenty or thirty small balconies and on each of those balconies stood a hooded figure with a weapon similar to a crossbow.

"I think this is what they call a trap," he said, nudging Kasyx's armored elbow.

"You're probably right," said Kasyx. But by now they were less than ten feet from two hooded figures standing in the center of the courtyard and the option of turning back seemed more dangerous than the option of going on.

Kasyx stopped and raised his hand.

"They're not Comanches," Tebulot protested.

"For God's sake, this is a universally recognized gesture of greeting," Kasyx snapped back.

The hooded figures regarded the Night Warriors from the black depths of their hoods without revealing their faces, without making a sound. The wind spiraled down inside the courtyard, raising leaves and litter and ruffling the hems of their pilgrims' robes. Kasyx said loudly, "We wish to see the dreamer. We wish to ensure that he is safe."

Still the hooded figures said nothing. But one of them raised its sleeve and made a beckoning gesture, and then both of them turned and began to walk across the courtyard toward another tunnel on the far side.

"Do we follow?" asked Kasyx.

Samena glanced up at the hooded figures surrounding them with their crossbows.

"I think we ought to," she suggested.

Tebulot nodded. "Springer talked about practical experience, didn't he? This is obviously it."

Kasyx said, "Keep a lookout behind us. I don't want to get boxed in."

The hooded figures glided faster and faster and then disappeared into the tunnel. Kasyx touched Tebulot's shoulder and said, "Keep that weapon of yours ready. This could be an ambush."

They hesitated at the mouth of the tunnel but then, without further discussion, they entered it, knowing that whatever their destiny was, it lay somewhere beyond and that they would have to follow it regardless of their fears.

11

The interior walls of the tunnel were soft and slimy, with a distinctive aroma that reminded Kasyx of the female vagina. Whatever the dreamer's obsessions, they were obviously sexual as well as financial. In fact, the farther they penetrated the dream, the more urgent the erotic atmosphere became. Somewhere deep within the building there was a rhythmic pounding sound, more like that of a human heart than a mechanical apparatus, and Kasyx was aware that the building was gradually transmogrifying into a gigantic body.

At the end of the tunnel they emerged into a vast, enclosed gallery that had a dark, domed roof laced with pipework resembling veins and arteries. Dominating the gallery was an elaborate machine of wood-and-metal construction, fifty or sixty feet high, with gears, cogs, pulleys and winches, and massive black, greasy pistons that churned back and forth on eccentric wheels. The machinery set up a low, rumbling noise overlaid with a high-pitched sizzling of lubricated steel sliding against lubricated steel.

"Where did those two jokers in hoods go?" Tebulot asked, keeping his weapon raised.

"There," said Samena, pointing across to the other side of the gallery. On a balcony supported by spindly staircases of iron and brass, the two hooded figures watched them dispassionately.

"Where's the dreamer, that's what I want to know," said Tebulot, looking around.

Kasyx lifted his head and scrutinized the machinery. "I see him," he said at last.

Tebulot and Samena followed his gaze. At the very top of the machinery there was a jointed wooden track that rattled over rows of revolving wheels. Into this track the dreamer's wooden cross fitted, like an automobile axle on a production line, and the dreamer was still nailed to it. Gradually the cross and its human burden were carried along to the end of the wooden track, where they were lifted so they were standing upright, and then they were carried down on an endless toothed belt into the very heart of the machinery.

As he was transported through the huge device by tracks and pulleys, the dreamer suffered continuous punishment. The cross was passed through a tunnel of lashing leather whips attached to endlessly revolving wheels. Then he was repeatedly stabbed by flailing arms that looked like hairbrushes except that they were fitted with spikes instead of bristles.

Kasyx watched the cross descend through the framework of the machinery level by level. Then he turned to Tebulot and Samena and said, "That's enough. This guy doesn't need saving. Not by us anyway. Maybe a shrink would do him some good."

"So what do we do, split?" asked Tebulot. He was almost disappointed that the dream hadn't turned out to require a rescue mission after all.

But Samena said, "There's still something evil here. I can feel it. It's close now. Much closer. Maybe it's not in this dream . . . but it's very near."

Kasyx said, "My vote is that we leave it for now. Come on, we don't have any real experience yet. If Yaomauitl turns up in this dream, what the hell are we going to do?"

Samena touched her fingers to her forehead and closed her eyes. She could sense the evil almost as distinctly as the heartbeat that pounded through the building. It was like an intense black coldness inside the front of her brain. She could almost see grotesque faces somewhere just out of focus, faces that whispered and conferred with each other, speaking of blasphemies, tortures and cruelties beyond human imagination.

Yet there was some curiously *alluring* quality about this darkness, this evil. It promised sensations of intense pleasure, of delirious self-indulgence, of nakedness, passion and danger. The voices whispered of the "little death" and of moments of humiliation so extreme that the pleasure centers of the brain craved for extinction to make the humiliation complete.

Kasyx reached out for Samena and drew her toward him. "What is it?" he asked. "Is it really strong?"

She nodded. "I don't know whether it's good or bad. It seemed like it was evil at first . . . but now I'm not so sure."

"Maybe we should check it out," Tebulot suggested.

Kasyx shook his head. "Enough for one night, okay? Let's get back to Springer. I want to know why he hasn't kept in touch."

They turned back toward the tunnel but as they did, two hooded figures stepped out of it and barred their way. The Night Warriors cautiously approached them and then halted. It was clear that the figures were not going to move out of the way.

"Do you want to stand aside?" Kasyx asked.

One of the figures raised its arm and pointed to the opposite side of the machine gallery. There was another tunnel entrance there, slightly narrower but just as dark.

You will go that way, the hooded figure commanded.

"Sorry, pal," Kasyx replied. "We're going back the way we came."

You will go where you have been told, the figure insisted.

"And if we refuse?" asked Tebulot.

The two hooded figures, already tall, began to stretch taller, and the shadowy mouths of their hoods widened until they were leaning over the Night Warriors like blind, man-eating worms. They swayed as they came nearer and Kasyx again glimpsed those writhing black tentacles where their faces should have been.

Tebulot didn't wait for orders. He wrenched back the T-bar on his weapon, lifted the weapon to his shoulder and fired it at the nearer of the figures. There was a soft, sharp *zzaffff!* and a white bolt of pure energy was swallowed up by the darkness inside the figure's hood.

For a moment Tebulot thought the figure had absorbed his shot without injury, but then suddenly the hooded cloak began to collapse. It fell to the ground as if it had been completely empty, a magical trick, but at the last second there was a nauseating wriggling from under the robes and something emerged, something gristly, black and tangled. Tebulot tugged back the weapon's T-bar and fired again, and another bolt of white energy scored a direct hit. There was a crackle, a sickening odor of burned fat and a shriek.

The second figure had hesitated when its companion was attacked but now it swayed ominously over Samena, and score after score of greasy tentacles began to unroll from the front of its hood as if it were vomiting snakes. Samena screamed, lifted her arms, stiffly crossed her wrists and aimed her right index finger directly at the heart of the tentacles.

She let fly with almost all the energy Kasyx had given her—far more than she needed—but then, she was inexperienced and terrified and the creature was almost on top of her. There was an explosion of power from the tip of her finger, and the arrowhead she had fitted earlier lanced into the creature's body, followed by a six-foot shaft of pure, dazzling light.

The arrowhead tore into the creature's flesh, opening a path for the concentrated energy to follow. The energy zapped out of sight, burying itself beneath the surface of the creature's skin; then it detonated. With an ear-splitting crack, pieces of unraveled tentacle were spattered in all directions. Some of them struck Kasyx's helmet, making a slapping sound like fragments of wet wash.

"Come on now!" shouted Tebulot and they ran into the tunnel, which was very dark and seemed narrower and moister than it had been before. Their feet slipped on the ribbed, muscular floor and several times they had to put their hands out sideways to prevent themselves from falling.

At last they reached the end and were back at the cobbled courtyard. It was still raining, a torrential downpour that filled the courtyard with a rising mist of spray. Kasyx reached out and held Tebulot's shoulder to caution him not to go any farther, and then he clasped his hand over the brow of his helmet. In this way his vision switched to infrared for detecting enemies by heat rather than by light.

He scanned the brightly colored green-and-yellow courtyard that the infrared displayed before him. There was nothing that gave off calorific energy, although Kasyx was aware that because they were nothing more than monsters in a dream, the hooded figures might radiate no body heat. In which case they could be waiting outside in the rain, ready to attack.

"I can't detect any of those tentacle creatures out there," he told Tebulot and Samena, "but we ought to come out of the tunnel ready for anything. Remember those figures up on the balconies; they might try firing down on us, or stretching down and trying to grab us. So we've got to sprint across that courtyard like goddamned ostriches and set up as much attacking fire as we can."

Tebulot cocked his weapon and frowned in concentration as he set it for rapid side-to-side fire. There were no instructions on the switches or levers but he seemed to know intuitively how to operate it. The weapon was partly mechanical and partly imaginary; it was capable of doing whatever its carrier could think of. If Tebulot had wanted his energy bolts to fire out forward and then U-turn and hit a target somewhere behind him, it was capable of carrying out his command.

Samena, who had been alertly protecting their rear, fitted her finger with a multiple arrowhead that would burst apart in midflight and send a dozen wicked barbs hurtling in a deadly hemispherical spray.

"All right," Kasyx said tensely. "Now *go!*"

They threw themselves out into the driving rain and were instantly met by a flying forest of thick black arrows fired from the balconies above. The arrows zipped through the rain with such velocity that they were invisible until they struck their targets, and each one set up a hair-raising screech as it flew toward them.

Tebulot's machine was defensive as well as offensive. Dropping to one knee, he lifted it and fired a spray of energy bolts that intercepted almost all of the next shower of arrows so that they came clattering down harmlessly. For the first time, Samena showed her speed and skill in movement, dodging and ducking between hurtling arrows to reach the middle of the courtyard, lift her stiffened arms and let loose a multiple burst of arrowheads at the overhanging balconies.

There were cries and screams from above and four empty robes came floating down through the rain to settle wetly on the cobbles. Tebulot adjusted his weapon and fired a short but punishing burst of energy at each of them. There were searing sizzles and eternally echoing shrieks. Only one of the tentacled creatures managed to escape him, dragging itself like a deformed octopus across the courtyard and into the shadows.

Kasyx deflected several arrows by raising his arm in front of his face and discharging power. With a violent snapping of static electricity, the arrows lost their atomic integrity and vanished. But the drain on Kasyx's charges was too high for him to defend himself much longer and he took advantage of Samena's next flurry of arrowheads to run for the tunnel that would take them out of the building.

Once in the shelter of the tunnel, he looked back. Tebulot had almost reached shelter, pausing now and again to fire off a tremendous fusillade of dazzling white energy at the hooded figures clustered on the balconies. Samena was farther away but she was so light and agile that Kasyx felt sure she could reach the tunnel without difficulty.

The courtyard flashed and crackled with blinding lights. The pouring raindrops were caught by the flashes in midair as if picked out by strobes, and Tebulot and Samena appeared to be fighting in a cage of silver needles. There was a strong smell of burning linen and some indescribable odor the tentacle creatures gave off when Tebulot hit them, like scorched snail.

More arrows screeched down into the courtyard; more robes tumbled and billowed down from the balconies. But Tebulot checked his charge scale now and saw that it was glowing only faintly, which meant that he had used up most of the energy Kasyx had given him before they entered the dream. He loosed a final flash of energy and then came running toward Kasyx, his head down and his arm held up to protect himself from random arrows. An arrow hurtled close and crunched deep into the cobbles next to his running foot but he managed to make a final football-tackle leap into the tunnel, his weapon clattering down next to him.

"Power!" he said breathlessly. "I'm out of power!"

Kasyx said, "Hold on. I don't have much left. We're going to need quite a dose of it to get out of this dream; I don't want to use that."

They anxiously watched Samena, who was almost halfway across the courtyard now, weaving and dodging among the swarms of arrows the hooded figures were firing at her. She was unable to see the arrows but her sensitivity was such that she could pick up the tiny surges of emotion that came from the hooded figures just as they released their crossbows, and she could also sense the hustling of the air molecules as they were pushed out of the way by the arrows' 300-mile-per-hour flight.

Kasyx and Tebulot were mesmerized for a moment by Samena's stunning ballet, but then Kasyx realized she was no longer firing her arrowheads. Like Tebulot, she must be out of charge.

"Samena!" he shouted. "Samena! You have to run for it!"

Samena glanced at him quickly, her face tight with tension. He could see her judging in that flick of the eye the distance to the tunnel, trying to choose the best way to make her escape.

"Now, Samena!" Kasyx bellowed. "Now!"

Then, however, the courtyard began to change dramatically. The balconies withdrew into the walls like closing eyelids and the hooded figures vanished with them. The tops of the walls high above their heads began to lean toward each other and close in until at last they joined to form a vaulted roof. Beneath their feet the heartbeat drumming grew louder and more insistent, and the courtyard grew darker until Kasyx and Tebulot could make out only the whiteness of Samena's arms and legs as she came struggling slowly toward them.

Kasyx called, "Samena! One last effort!" But now the floor of the courtyard began to drop and curve and she was having to climb her way uphill to reach the entrance to the tunnel. The cobbles rumpled up into soft, fleshy folds, slippery with mucus, and after only two or three steps she lost her grip and slid back down again. Kasyx leaned forward and looked into the deep, curved reaches of the courtyard but Samena had dropped out of sight.

Tebulot shouted to Kasyx, "Give me some charge! Just a little! I have to go get her!"

Kasyx lifted the visor of his helmet. "Supposing we don't have enough charge to get out of this dream? What then?"

"I have to go get Samena!" Tebulot yelled. "For Christ's sake, give me some charge!"

Kasyx hesitated but Tebulot said fiercely, "We're in this together, Kasyx, like the three musketeers. One for all and all for one. If we don't take Samena with us, we don't leave. We're Night Warriors, don't you understand that?"

With a nod of acceptance, Kasyx held out his hand. Tebulot took it and placed it directly against his breastplate. "Now," he said, and Kasyx allowed a subdued flow of power to leave his body and pour into the machine-carrier's energy system.

"More," Tebulot urged.

Kasyx took a sharp breath but gave him more, even though he could feel the power shrinking in his own body with every passing second.

Tebulot checked the charge scale on his weapon. It

glowed up to the halfway mark and he took Kasyx's hand away. "That's enough. Now I'm going after her."

The walls and ceiling of the building were steadily closing in, heavy, suffocating and dark. Kasyx touched the center of his forehead and a bright beam of light shone out from the rim of his visor, narrow but spreading out. It lit up redness, wetness and ridges of soft flesh.

The courtyard had now been completely transformed. Between Kasyx and Tebulot and the place where Samena had disappeared, the tunnel was gradually tightening like a muscular sphincter. As Tebulot struggled toward it, knee-deep in scarlet flesh, it drew together until the aperture was only two feet across.

"It's closing!" Kasyx shouted at him.

Tebulot yanked back the T-bar of his weapon with a slippery hand. He fired a brief burst of energy at the sphincter and momentarily it recoiled and shuddered as if it were alive. But then it tightened even harder, until the tunnel was completely occluded.

"One more burst!" Kasyx called.

Tebulot fired again but even though the sphincter winced, it remained tightly closed.

Now Kasyx came running forward, breathing heavily, panicking at the thought that Samena might be lost. He was charge-keeper, she was his responsibility, and what would happen to her earthly body if her soul were irretrievably lost in some strange man's nightmare?

He had sufficient power left to take Tebulot and himself out of the dream, but that was not what he was going to use it for. He was going to release it all—all of it at once—and hope it would open the tunnel sufficiently wide for them to rescue Samena. After that . . . well, he didn't know what would happen after that. But loyalty was more important than survival; the cause was greater than those who fought for it.

Tebulot shouted, "What are you doing? Kasyx!" But Kasyx was now too scared and exhilarated to answer. He was going to discharge all his energy in one shattering explosion, not only the energy Ashapola had given him but the stored-up energy of his own intellect and personality. If he was going to go, then by God he was going to go spectacularly. Nothing left but the smoking soles of his shoes.

He closed his eyes and said a silent prayer. But just as he summoned the power inside him, he felt the muscular sphincter relax and open.

Tebulot scrambled up beside him and together they stared into the widening cavern. It was dark red, almost black, and so hot that steam was issuing from the complicated intaglios of flesh. In the distance, over the irregular crusted surface, knelt Samena. Kasyx touched his hand to the side of his helmet and focused on her in close-up. She was bound with ropes, her hands behind her back and a slipknot around her neck.

Behind her the air began to waver and gradually take on the shape of a standing figure. Kasyx focused more sharply and saw that it was a young boy not much older than twelve or thirteen, dressed in gray. The boy had a curiously unformed face, as if a sculptor had not yet decided on the expression he should mold into his clay or what meaning his creation should have. One meaning, however, was unmistakable: The boy's left hand held the end of the rope that was fastened around Samena's neck.

Tebulot said, "What the hell is that?"

"A boy of a sort," Kasyx replied.

"Sure, but what sort?" Tebulot asked, peering through the night.

"Let's go find out," Kasyx suggested and they walked toward him.

Calmly the boy watched them approach. When they were less than twenty feet away, however, he lifted one hand and at the same time tugged on the rope around Samena's neck with the other. The implication was unequivocal and Kasyx and Tebulot halted where they were.

"Samena!" called Kasyx, "are you all right?"

Samena stayed where she was, silent, her head bowed.

The boy said in an oddly gruff voice, "She is well for the time being but she cannot speak. She cannot hear either, or see."

"What have you done to her?" Kasyx demanded.

"You looking to have your brains blown out or something?" Tebulot put in with undisguised aggression, lifting his machine.

The boy smiled, almost wistfully. "Those must have been great days when the dreams of whole nations were guarded by Night Warriors, the Devils were free, and mighty battles were fought through all the landscapes of the human imagination. Sad that I should have no more adversaries than three, and those three inexperienced and weak."

"Inexperienced perhaps," said Kasyx, "but not so weak."

The boy shook his head. "I know how little power you have left, old man. You have barely enough to return to the waking world. Even if you were to unleash all of it, I would deflect it as easily as you deflected those arrows from the Monks of Shame."

He tugged at Samena's rope and added, "You would be powerless and I would be able to snuff you out like a candle."

"Who are you?" Kasyx asked. "What do you want with Samena?"

"You know me quite well," the boy replied. "You saw me on the beach at Del Mar. Not as I appear to you now, but like this."

For a photographic instant they saw what the boy really was. They saw the face of a demon with flaring eyes; they saw a skeletal rib cage with a half-developed heart that beat against the translucent skin like an embryo chick throbbing in its albumen; they saw clawed hands and curved thighbones. Then the image of the boy blotted it out, the demon was gone and they were standing on this dream desert, the wind blowing soft as a funeral lament, wondering if they had gone to hell or if hell had instead come to them.

"You are the spawn of Yaomauitl," Kasyx said thickly.

"Well, well, my inexperienced friend, you are more knowledgeable than I thought," the boy replied. "In that case, the contest between us will be keener and much more exciting. There is no pleasure in destroying the dull-witted or the uninformed."

"What are you doing here?" Tebulot challenged.

"You really don't know? You have no idea of who the dreamer is? Why, you are innocents! Ask you friend called Springer."

"*You* tell us," urged Tebulot.

The boy shook his head. "That would spoil the pleasure."

Kasyx asked, "What are you going to do with Samena?"

"I intend to keep her for a while, until I am fully grown. A hostage, you might say, to allow me to finish my gestation and reach the height of my powers."

"Then you are not as powerful as you pretend to be," Kasyx said slowly.

The demon's eyes burned bright. "I could still destroy you, old man!"

"Perhaps you could, but you are not powerful enough to destroy all three of us. If you were, you would do it. That is why you need one of us for a hostage, to keep the other two at bay."

"Well, you are perceptive as well as knowledgeable," said the boy.

Kasyx said, "I want you to let go of that rope now and release Samena. Otherwise I'm going to give you the energy flash to end all energy flashes."

The boy looked up at the night sky. The stars were beginning to whirl away as if they were dandelion plumes being blown off a creosote-painted fence. The desert was beginning to shift and tilt beneath their feet.

"You feel that?" asked the boy. "The dreamer is waking up. His deepest sleep is almost over."

"I'm still going to burn you," said Kasyx and took two or three steps forward.

But it was Tebulot who said, "No, Kasyx. Not now."

Kasyx turned. "Wasn't it you who said that we were the three musketeers? If one goes, we all go?"

"That's exactly why you can't use your energy flash now," Tebulot told him. "If he deflects it, which he says he can, he'll kill you and he'll probably manage to kill me. But what's he going to do with Samena?"

Kasyx slowly lifted the clear visor of his helmet and turned back for a moment to look at Samena and the demonic boy.

Tebulot said, "It's too risky, too unpredictable."

"But he has her as his hostage!" Kasyx exploded.

"I know . . . but as long as he keeps her as his hostage, she's safe. We can try to get her back tomorrow night in another dream. Come on, Kasyx, you can see that it's too dangerous. Back off."

Kasyx slowly retreated. "This is unlike you, Tebulot," he said.

Tebulot didn't look at him. "Maybe it is," he replied quietly, "but before, I thought Samena was dead. Now I can see she's alive, and as long as she's alive, she has a chance."

Kasyx nodded. He understood. The passions of the young were often wildly uneven but they were strong, and he admired strength, even in the pursuit of impossibilities. He had never had very much strength himself, and he had never tried to pursue the impossible. Not before tonight anyway.

Taking a breath, he said clearly, "We are forced to leave you here, Samena. For your safety as well as ours, we have to return to the waking world without you. But I make you this promise: I will come back and Tebulot will be standing by my side, and we shall free you from Yaomauitl's bastard offspring, *in the dark and holy name of the Night Warriors!*"

The boy lightly applauded, patting the fingers of his right hand into the palm of his left, which was the hand in which he held the rope. "Believe me, she didn't hear a word of that, my poor old man. But a fine speech all the same."

Then, still smiling, he folded his hands against his chest and he and Samena immediately began to recede into the middle distance. They shrank, faster and faster, until they reached the desert's far horizon and were gone.

Kasyx watched the horizon for a long time and then turned to Tebulot. "I've lost her," he said, and he was desolate.

Tebulot said, "Not you, Kasyx. Us. *We've* lost her, but we're going to get her back. You can promise yourself that."

The floor of the desert began to ripple and waver. "It's time we left," Kasyx said. "I just hope to God that Devil does nothing to harm her."

"I don't think it will," Tebulot said. "Not until it's fully grown, and not while you and I are still around. If you ask me, it was a lot more worried about us than it pretended."

Kasyx formed the octagon in the air, using his penultimate reserves of power. The octagon hung in the air like an eidetic image and then lifted over their heads and encircled them. As it touched the ground, the desert vanished and they were back in the dreamer's bedroom. The dreamer himself had tossed and turned; he was sleeping on his left side now, his mouth open, his eyelids flickering in the last vivid dreams of night. Outside the window, the sky was beginning to pale.

"Let's go before he wakes up," said Tebulot.

"No," Kasyx replied. "First we're going to find out who he is."

"But he's going to wake up in a minute. Suppose he finds us here?"

"Then we can vanish," Kasyx said impatiently. He walked across to the dreamer's closet, opened it and began to rummage through the clothes.

"Nothing here, no name tags," he said, closing the doors and going over to the bureau. He opened one drawer after another, lifting up socks, shorts and T-shirts. On the bed the dreamer began to snuffle and tug at his pillow.

"Hurry up, Kasyx, for God's sake," Tebulot urged.

"I don't see you helping," Kasyx retorted. He opened the topmost drawer of the bureau and found what he wanted. "Eureka, here we are: wallet, ID card, social-security card, credit cards, everything."

He lifted one of the ID cards out of the wallet. Tebulot could see his lips moving as he read the words on it. Then slowly he tucked it back into its plastic holder, folded the wallet and returned it to the drawer. When he looked across at Tebulot, his face was serious.

"Who is he?" asked Tebulot.

"His name's Lemuel F. Shapiro and that card identifies him as a senior medical examiner for the San Diego County coroner's office."

"What?" Tebulot whispered. "I thought Springer said he was a . . . businessman, a bankrupt—"

"That's what Springer said, sure. But Springer was spinning us a yarn, wasn't he? And it makes me wonder just how many other yarns he's been spinning us. You see what he did, don't you? He guided us into the dream of one of the few people likely to have nightmares about that embryo Devil they dug up from the beach today. He knew we were bound to come up against it sooner or later and he didn't give a damn what happened to us. He didn't warn us, he didn't give us enough power to fight back."

Lemuel F. Shapiro opened one eye and lay on his bed listening, like a man who can't be quite sure if he hears voices. Kasyx beckoned to Tebulot to clasp his hand and together they rose slowly through the wall, their molecular structure disassembling to let them through, and then sailed almost invisibly over the dawn streets of Del Mar. The sky was the color of iced tea, the ocean splashed listlessly against the shore. At last they descended, scarcely stirring the morning air as they vanished through the tiled roof of Springer's house on Camino del Mar, through the ceiling of the upstairs room, and materialized side by side, their arms upraised.

There was no sign of Springer. The house was empty. A thin film of undisturbed dust lay everywhere, as if in proof that nobody human had passed that way.

"We'd better get back to our beds," said Kasyx. "But— as soon as you can—I want you to go up to Susan's place and check out what's happening to her body. If there's any problem, call me. They may think she's gone into some kind of coma if she doesn't wake up. I just don't want them to think she's dead and try to cremate her or do something stupid. You heard what Springer said, that she won't be in any danger unless they destroy her physical body."

"Can we believe anything Springer said?" Tebulot asked, taking off his helmet and running his hand tiredly through his hair.

"I don't know," Kasyx answered. "But I sure want to ask him some questions. Now, you won't forget to call me about Susan, will you? In fact, call me anyway."

Tebulot raised one hand until it was level with his eyes, the back of it facing toward Kasyx. Although Kasyx had never seen such a gesture before, he knew what it was: the farewell salute of the Night Warriors, the salute always given as day breaks and the adventures of the night come to an end. It means, *"May you be taken safely through the hours of the sun, to preserve you and keep you for the hours of the moon."*

Kasyx made the same gesture and then the two Night Warriors rose and faded through the roof of the house, wheeling over it for a moment before each returned to his own bed. Kasyx sank into his physical body with relief and regret just as his alarm clock began to bleep. He reached out with an unexpectedly heavy hand and switched it off.

12

Henry sat up in bed licking his dry lips. The sun fell in zigzag patterns across the rumpled comforter and on the framed print of "Fragrance of Love" by Christine Nasser. He washed his face with his hands and was surprised at how thick and coarse his skin felt, as if it were a latex mask.

He went to the bathroom and stared at himself in the mirror. He was still the same Henry as yesterday evening, the same man who had sat staring at a bottle of vodka and defying himself not to pick it up, turn the screw cap and give himself the courage and confidence that lay distilled within it. But during the night he had found a different courage, a different confidence. During the night he had penetrated the nightmares of Lemuel F. Shapiro and fought against the worst that his imagination could offer. During the night he had faced the Devil.

He showered, sudsing himself slowly and evenly. Then, wrapped in a towel, he walked through to the kitchen to make coffee. Just as he was spooning it into the filter paper, the door buzzer sounded. He went to the door and called out, "Who is it?"

"Lieutenant Ortega. Do you mind if I come in?"

Henry drew back the security chain and opened the door. Lieutenant Ortega looked more summery today in a pale-blue seersucker jacket and a dark-blue pair of permanent-press pants. He wore mirror-lensed sunglasses, and a folded handkerchief in his breast pocket, both of which were telltale signs of his age.

"I was passing by on my way to headquarters and thought I would drop by to see how you are."

"Oh, yes?" asked Henry a little suspiciously. He let Salvador pass by him into the living room and closed the door. "You'll have to excuse the way I'm dressed."

214

Salvador's eyes darted around the room as if checking for clues that would tell him how Henry had spent yesterday evening. Henry said, "I'm making some coffee. Do you want to join me?"

"Sure, that would be nice."

Henry went back to his bedroom and dressed quickly in a short-sleeved shirt and banana-yellow slacks. He came back into the living room combing his hair. "Did the coroner get a chance to look at that creature you dug out of the beach yesterday?" he asked.

"They're starting on tests this morning, so I understand."

"Do they have any idea of what it is?"

Salvador lifted his head slightly. "Why did you ask it like that?"

"Why did I ask it like what?"

"You asked me do they have any idea of what it is as though you yourself *knew*."

Henry pulled a face. "Did I? I didn't mean to."

"There was an intonation in your voice," Salvador persisted.

Henry paused by the kitchen door. He said nothing. But Salvador sat where he could watch him as he made the coffee, his legs crossed, and Henry could tell by the expression on his face that he was still expecting an answer.

Henry brought the coffee in and sat down opposite. "Whatever it was, it looked as if it grew out of one of those eels," he said, trying to sound conversational.

Salvador nodded. "John Belli is quite convinced of that too. The eel had obviously secreted itself in the sand, down where it is damp, and then sloughed its skin. Of course John Belli's only problem is to find out what kind of creature goes through such a life cycle. He is beginning to wonder if the eels found their way into the body of the girl not as predators attacking her flesh from the outside, but from the inside as growing elvers. Children, as it were, who had an insatiable appetite for their mother."

Henry said, "That's impossible. A woman can't be impregnated with eels."

"Nevertheless there are indications on the girl's remains that she was devoured from the inside of her abdomen outward rather than the other way around. The pattern of the teeth marks, for instance, and—if your stomach can bear it at this time of the morning—the amount of waste material the eels excreted *within* the abdominal cavity rather than outside it."

"Why are you telling me this?" asked Henry.

Salvador looked at him steadily. "I am telling you this because your interest in what has happened here has been unusual. I keep asking myself, why does Professor Watkins wish to come down to the beach and inspect the evidence for himself? What does Professor Watkins know about these creatures that he is declining to share with his friendly neighborhood detective?"

"I used to be married to a marine biologist, that's all," Henry said. "I guess I have a taste for the aquatic."

Salvador put down his coffee cup. "I am not a fool, Henry. I want to know why you and those two young friends of yours are showing such a keen interest in following this investigation."

Henry tugged at the wet hair at the back of his neck. "This creature . . . what are you going to do with it once you've finished examining it?"

"As I told you, it will be taken to the Scripps laboratories for full biological tests."

"Are you going to kill it?"

Salvador's eyes flickered. "How do you know it is still alive?"

"I just assumed. You didn't tell me it was dead."

"You would like to see it dead though?"

Henry said nothing. Salvador leaned forward and repeated, "You would like to see it dead. On the beach you begged me to destroy it. Destroy it, destroy it, that's what you said. It's the spawn of the Devil. Now don't you think you owe me some kind of explanation for that? The spawn of the Devil?"

Henry said, "I was . . . rather the worse for wear. You know, more vodka martinis than were good for me. I was just . . . well, letting my imagination run away with me."

Salvador slowly shook his head from side to side. Henry noticed how neatly clipped his fingernails were. "I don't think you were drunk, Henry. And I certainly don't think Ms. Sczaniecka was drunk. Yet she said the same thing. Destroy it. It's the spawn of the Devil. Now what did you both mean by that?"

"Well, spawn of the Devil, that's a figure of speech. Just like calling somebody an s.o.b. I guess we felt that what that creature had done to that poor girl on the beach . . . well, you know. I guess we felt disgusted. We wanted to see it destroyed, the same way anybody would want to see a mad dog destroyed if it had killed a child."

Salvador leaned back and laced his hands behind his head. "Really, Henry, this is very weak. You are the kind of man who always says what he means. If you say spawn of the Devil, you mean spawn of the Devil. What I want from you now is some kind of clear explanation of what that means. You said it loud. You *shouted* it. Why won't you talk about it now?"

"If I told you, Salvador, you wouldn't believe me."

"You can always try me."

Henry stood up and went across to the window. He drew back the drapes and stared out at the glittering ocean. "There's a legend about the Devil," he began. "It goes back hundreds of years. Apparently if the Devil wants to reproduce, it appears to young women in the night and impregnates them. The Devil's sperm grow like eels. They eat the mother and then escape into the outside world, where they find themselves a burrow or a hidey-hole and grow."

"And you believe that what we have discovered on the beach is a Devil . . . a growing Devil?"

Henry didn't answer but kept on staring at the sea.

"Who told you this legend?" asked Salvador.

"I looked it up," Henry told him. "I was interested in finding out something about those eels, that's all."

"And you believe it?" Salvador persisted.

"I didn't say I did and I didn't say I didn't. So far, though, it's the only independent explanation I've come across that fits all the circumstantial facts."

"But . . . Devils?" Salvador smiled incredulously.

"What else?" asked Henry. "Only Mr. Belli and the people at Scripps can tell us any different."

Salvador stood up and brushed off his pants. "Well," he said, "it seems that you have given me something to think about if nothing else. Do you have the reference to the Devil here so I could look at it?"

"I'm sorry, it was in a library book at the university," Henry lied.

"Perhaps you could give me the title."

Henry came over and patted Salvador in a friendly, paternal manner on the shoulder. "It escapes me for the moment. But I'll check it today and have somebody call you."

"Better still, perhaps the university could photocopy the reference for me," Salvador suggested.

"Dollar-fifty a copy," Henry said, opening the front door for him.

"I think the police-department budget can stretch to that." Then Salvador hesitated in the doorway. "We have managed to identify the girl, you know."

"Oh, yes?"

"Her name was Sylvia Stoner. She was twenty-two, a fashion model from Houston, Texas."

"Do you have any idea of what she was doing in Southern California?"

"Oh, yes. She was on vacation, visiting friends in San Diego."

Salvador took out his spring-bound notebook and wetted the tip of his finger so he could flick quickly through the pages. "She stayed with them for six days and then disappeared. They didn't alert the police because they thought she'd simply gone freewheeling around for a day or two. According to them, she was something of a fun girl."

"It was no fun the way she ended up," Henry said. As Salvador lowered his notebook, he caught a glimpse of the name "Esbjerg," underlined twice, and part of an address that started with the name "Market." Salvador flipped his notebook shut and Henry couldn't see any more.

"Are you releasing this to the media?" Henry asked.

"Not so far. Not until we know what that creature actually is. If we go public with what we know so far, we're going to look like the Looney Tunes department. We had enough sardonic laughter over that Ramirez business last month."

"Oh, I remember," smiled Henry. "The bordello bust."

"Don't remind me," Salvador said. Then, with a brief wave of his hand, he walked off down the path. Henry closed the door and went immediately to the bookcase for the San Diego telephone directory. He took it into the kitchen, where he filtered fresh coffee. His finger ran up scores of Espinosas and Esmeraldas until at the top of the page it peaked on Esbjerg, K., 603 Market Street. There were two other Esbjergs but one was out on 44th Street by Holy Cross Cemetery and the other was on Gamma at 39th.

He picked up the phone and dialed Gil Miller at the Solana Mini-Market.

Gil had arrrived back in his body to find his mother worriedly shaking him and saying, "Gil? Gil? Are you all right?"

He opened his eyes, blinked and yawned. "Sure, sure I'm all right. What's the matter?"

"I've been calling you and calling you. Your father wants you to help him unload the van. I thought you were sick or something."

Gil sat up. He had a tight headache, unlike any other

headache he had ever experienced. It felt as if someone were gripping his head and squeezing it. He frowned at his watch and saw that it had stopped.

"What time is it?" he asked his mother as she tugged back the drapes.

"A quarter after six. I'll make your breakfast while you help your father."

Gil tossed back the sheets and stood up. He had a small but brightly lit bedroom, with a large window facing south and a smaller window facing east. The walls were painted pale yellow and there was a large cork bulletin board running the length of the bed, with school pennants, pictures of Lamborghinis and Maseratis, and postcards from friends as well as a poster of Karen Velez, *Playboy*'s Playmate of 1984.

Mrs. Miller went downstairs while Gil dressed in a clean pair of shorts, yesterday's chopped-off denims and a brown-and-orange Padres T-shirt. Walking into the kitchen, he poured himself a large glass of Minute Maid grapefruit juice and drank it in three long gulps.

Phil Miller was in the backyard stacking vegetables. "You sleep good?" he asked. "There's ten boxes of lettuce to come out next."

Gil climbed into the back of the van and began shifting boxes. He kept thinking about the nightmare from which he had just returned, and about Susan, still trapped in that nightmare somehow. In the light of the morning, in the back of his father's van, it seemed so far away and so bizarre that he could have easily convinced himself it had never happened.

"You're quiet," said his father.

"Something on my mind, that's all," he replied, passing down a carton of radishes.

Phil Miller looked at his son closely. "Anything a father ought to know about?"

Gil shook his head. How could he possibly explain to his father that only a couple of hours ago he had been Tebulot, the machine-carrier, and that he had been killing creatures in a torrential rainstorm in a castle that didn't exist? How could he tell him that he was worried about a girl whose dreaming personality had been taken hostage by an embryo Devil? His father's imagination was capable of encompassing price changes, new grocery products and baseball scores, and occasionally a random episode of *V,* but that was about as weird as it went.

"You're not sick?" his father asked.

"No, no. I'm fine. Listen, do you need me in the store today?"

"I was hoping you might help out with the deli counter."

"If I got Lisa to do it?"

"Then, sure. If you get Lisa to do it."

Lisa Dalwick was a school friend of Gil's; her father was one of the most successful of the local realtors. Lisa's father didn't particularly approve of Lisa mixing with Gil, but since Lisa thought the sun rose and set with Gil, there was little Dalwick *père* could do about it. Gil drove around to Lisa's house after breakfast and promised her a whole afternoon's swimming together if she helped out at the market. Lisa was okay. She was cute and petite and her figure turned heads, but right now her mouth was crowded with more braces than the Coronado Bay Bridge.

Once the problem of the deli counter had been settled, Gil drove up to Del Mar Heights and parked outside Susan's house. He jogged up the steeply angled driveway and rang the doorbell, still jiggling from foot to foot.

After a long wait Susan's grandfather came to the door.

"Is Susan here?" Gil asked.

The old man shook his head. He was carrying a copy of *The National Enquirer* in one hand, folded over. "She's in the hospital," he said. "They took her away about an hour ago."

Gil felt a sensation of dread slide through him as if he had swallowed a mouthful of mercury. "Hospital?" he asked. "Is she sick or something?"

"They don't know," the old man told him. "They can't understand it. She just wouldn't wake up this morning, that's all. She's breathing okay. Her blood pressure and all the rest of it, they're okay. But it's like she went into some kind of coma when she was asleep."

"That's terrible," Gil said, thinking to himself, if only this poor old man knew just how terrible.

"They, er, took her to the Soledad Park Clinic," said Susan's grandfather. He took off his glasses and stared at Gil with bleary, widely cast eyes. "They said any friends of hers would be welcome to visit. You know, like a familiar voice might snap her out of her coma."

"Sure," said Gil. He touched the old man's arm. "I'll find out what time visiting hours are. I'm real sorry this has happened. Can I keep in touch? You know, call you now and again to see how she is?"

Susan's grandfather nodded. "You're welcome to. Do I know your name?"

"Gil. Gil Miller." He was almost tempted to say Tebulot.

It was nearly eleven o'clock by the time he reached Henry's cottage and buzzed the doorbell. Henry opened the door with relief when he saw him. "I've been trying to call you. Your mother said you were out."

"I went up to Susan's place."

"And?"

Gil lifted his hands in resignation. "She's in the hospital. When her grandparents couldn't wake her up this morning, they called a doctor. She's okay as far as I can make out. She's still alive and all her vital signs are normal. But she's—what do you call it—comatose? Her personality hasn't come back yet, which means that Devil's still keeping her hostage."

Henry didn't say anything for a while. Then he slowly nodded, sat down and said in the bleakest of voices, "All we can do is hope that it keeps her hostage until nightfall."

"What I want to know is, where is it keeping her?" Gil said. "It took her out of that desert dream but where did it go from there?"

"Into another dream maybe," Henry suggested. "There's

always somebody asleep somewhere, even during the day. Shift workers, nightclub staff, prostitutes."

"Another question is, how do we find out what dream she's in?"

"I don't know, but there must be a way. I mean, surely the original Night Warriors must have had some form of system for detecting where the Devils were. After all, how many millions of dreams do you think there are in just a single night? It would take you a lifetime to search through them all, even if you were sensitive the way Susan is."

"I'm glad you said is and not was," Gil remarked.

"We need to talk to Springer, don't we?" Henry said. "I vote we go to the house to see if he's there. But there's something else I want to follow up too. Lieutenant Ortega was here this morning, poking and prying as usual, but this time I think I got more out of him than he got out of me. He's found out who the girl was, the girl we discovered on the beach. And I've found out where her friends live, down in San Diego. After we've been to talk to Springer, maybe you could drive us down there. I have a feeling we may be able to get a little more out of them than the police did. After all, you and I know what this business is really all about, don't we?"

"Speak for yourself," Gil said unhappily. "I think I'm about as oh-fay with what's going down here as a blind-folded gopher in a six-foot hole."

Henry went across to his desk, took his wallet out of the top drawer and counted the money in it. Then he pushed it into his back pants pocket. "I feel agonized about Susan," he said. "I feel like I mismanaged the whole thing. We should never have gone into that building to begin with."

"You didn't mismanage anything," Gil protested. "For starters, you're not in charge. Just because you're older and you're a professor, you feel you're responsible for everything we do. But this is different. Whatever we decide, we decide together, and that makes us all responsible for what happened, including Susan herself."

"Well, I guess you're right," Henry told him, "but it doesn't make me feel better."

They drove in Gil's Mustang down to Camino del Mar, parked across the street from Springer's house and crossed to knock at the door. They waited and knocked again but there was no reply. When they tried the handle, they found the door was firmly locked.

Gil said, "Looks like Springer's left us out on our own."

"Maybe that was his plan right from the beginning," suggested Henry. "Not to train us at all but to throw us in at the deep end. Sink or swim."

They left the house and headed across to I-5 to drive south to San Diego. As usual, the interstate was teeming with traffic.

As they passed the Mission Bay exits, Gil asked, "Aren't you drinking anymore?"

Henry shrugged. "I haven't made any conscious decisions about it. But, no, I haven't had a drink."

"You should stick it out," Gil told him. "I like you better when you're sober."

"I think I'm dull when I'm sober," Henry replied. "God knows how I'm going to lecture to my philosophy classes without the jolly old verbal lubricant. Do you know what sheer unadulterated torture it is having to explain Strawson's *Individuals* and the shortcomings of linguistic philosophy to two dozen nodding twenty-year-olds? Even when you're smashed?"

"What *are* the shortcomings of linguistic philosophy?" Gil asked, overtaking a tractor trailer from Toys R Us.

"Well, the major criticism is that it fails to address the serious and traditional problems of mainstream philosophy," said Henry. "In fact, some of the questions it attempts to answer are not just trivial but completely factitious."

He stopped and stared at Gil, the slipstream blowing his hair. "You don't want to know all this, do you?"

Gil smiled and shook his head. "I just love to hear people sound off about their favorite subjects even when I don't understand them. You should hear my dad talk about retail price maintenance and bar codes. You wouldn't understand that anymore than I understand philosophy. But he sure gets complicated, and mad."

Henry smiled. "You get on well with your parents?"

"Sure. I'm not going to run a market, though, when I leave school."

"After what we've been through already, I don't think any of our lives will be the same again," Henry said. "You can't blast nightmare monks by night and sell Danishes by day."

They left the freeway at the Tecolote Road exit and drove into San Diego on the Pacific Highway. The streets were hot, dusty and rundown looking. A black man in a grubby Hawaiian shirt was standing by the side of the road hopelessly holding out his thumb for a ride. Henry said, "Given all the sociological factors, the ratio of blacks to whites, the local history of crime, political attitudes, etcetera, I wonder what the mathematical probability of that poor fellow's being offered a ride actually is?"

"Henry," said Gil, "you've got a strange mind."

They drove along the harbor front, passing the tuna docks and the *Star of India*. They took a left just before they reached Seaport Village, into Market Street. The 600 block was right on the corner of Kettner. Number 603 was a narrow, flaking building with a secondhand auto-parts store at street level, a decaying remnant of the old San Diego. Gil U-turned the Mustang and parked outside.

Inside, the auto-parts store smelled of grease, exhaust and sweat. A thin young man with spiky blond hair sat behind the counter dressed in greasy jeans and a greasy T-shirt, listening to Bruce Springsteen and reading *Aquaman*. He was surrounded like an Arabian thief by all his riches: differentials, steering linkages and engine blocks. Steering wheels and mufflers hung from the ceiling, and a smeary glass cabinet was crowded with side mirrors and decorative hubcaps.

"Help you gentlemen?" the young man asked, tossing his comic book onto the counter.

"I hope so," said Henry. "We're looking for somebody by the name of Esbjerg."

"Tommi or Ericka?"

"Either. Both. We're friends of Sylvia's."

"Ah . . ." the young man nodded. "Requiescat in parchay."

"Yes," said Henry. "We were pretty cut up about it too." He looked around the store and the young man followed his gaze with thinly concealed interest.

"That your Mustang out there?" he asked. "I got an almost-new set of four anthracite-steel, low-profile wheels, make your Mustang look like a million dollars. Hold the pavement better too. Grip like glue."

Henry shook his head. "I just wanted to talk to the Esbjergs, that's all."

"Well, they're not here," the young man said. "They took off last night after the cops came around. They took their camping gear, everything. They didn't say where they were going or when they'd be back. My guess is Yosemite, or maybe even Mazama, up at Crater Lake."

"Oh, that's too bad," Henry said. "I was hoping to talk to them about Sylvia."

"What about Sylvia?"

"Well, we hadn't seen her for quite a while. The cops won't tell us anything. We were wondering exactly what happened. She went off on vacation and the next thing we knew, she was dead."

The young man sniffed and arched his backside off the metal chair to chivvy two sticks of Juicy Fruit from his back pants pocket. He unwrapped them, tossing the wrappers over his shoulder, and folded the sticks into his mouth.

Henry said, "Was she here the day before she died?"

The young man shook his head, his mouth full.

"Can you tell us where she was?" Henry persisted.

The young man nodded. But then he said, "I can, for sure. But I ain't about to."

"Why not? We were friends of hers."

"Oh yeah? From where?"

"From Houston."

"From Houston, huh? Then of course you'd know what high school she went to in Houston? And of course you'd know what street she lived on, and what her daddy did for a living?"

Henry was silent. The young man laughed, chewed noisily and said, "I knew you for what you were the moment you walked in here."

"We're not police if that's what you think. We're not private investigators either. But we do have an interest in finding out what happened to her. You see, we have reason to think that a friend of ours is being threatened by the same person who was responsible for killing Sylvia."

The young man chewed thoughtfully, then said, "How much do you think those wheels 'ud be worth? You know, current market value?"

Henry was no fool. "How about a hundred?" he suggested.

The young man shook his head. "They're worth two hundred fifty, absolute minimum."

"Two hundred," Henry countered.

"Two hundred fifty."

Henry reached into his wallet and counted out a single hundred, two fifties, three tens and a dollar. He made up the difference with a handful of quarters and dimes. The young man scooped the money across the counter and arranged it into neat piles, pressing the creases out of the bills with the side of his hand.

"Sylvia came here about three months ago from Houston. She said she'd been having some kind of long-running argument with her parents about going to school, snorting coke and stuff like that. Tommi and Ericka were always easygoing so they asked her to stay, and in any case, Tommi had some kind of a mild thing going for Sylvia, you know? She was a pretty good-looking chick."

"We know what she looked like," put in Gil.

The young man paused for a moment as if interruptions annoyed him. But then he went on, counting up the loose change as he did and arranging it into piles of a dollar. "Anyway, soon after she got here, Sylvia met some guy at one of those rock shows they hold up at the Planetarium, and the two of them—Sylvia and this guy—they both went to Mexico for the weekend. I don't know what happened to her in Mexico because she wouldn't say, but I never saw the guy again and she was kind of strange afterward, like somebody who's had some kind of what do you call it? . . . some kind of religious renovation."

"Revelation," said Henry.

"That's right, revelation."

Henry said, "Is that all? She went to Mexico for the weekend and came back strange?"

"That's not exactly two hundred fifty bucks' worth," said Gil in a tone more threatening than he had ever heard himself use before.

The young man glanced up shiftily and then said, "All I know about Mexico was that she went as far as a place called San Hipolito, you know? And apparently what happened was she met some other guy, apart from the guy she went with, and I don't know, there was some kind of argument. Sylvia was never too clear about it. She was pretty doped up most of the time, you could never say when she was telling the truth and when she was fantasizing. She used to tell all kinds of stories, how her father secretly bought himself a ride on one of the space-shuttle missions, that kind of stuff."

Henry said, "Is that all you know? Listen, I need everything—absolutely everything—even if it sounded like a fantasy."

The young man shrugged. "She stayed here for—what? a couple of months?—but she kept talking about going back to Mexico. She said she had terrible nightmares all the time and that she was pregnant. She kept having stomach cramps but when Ericka told her to go to the doctor, she wouldn't on account of being so high all the time. She was afraid the doctor would take her off the stuff."

"Did she ever go back to Mexico?" asked Gil.

The young man said, "Not as far as I know. But she lit out of here maybe two or three days before they found her dead, and she could have been anywhere during those two or three days. Mexico, L.A., who knows? She was always going places just on impulse."

"What about the police?" asked Henry. "Did you tell the police about any of this? About Sylvia going to Mexico and about those nightmares?"

"Uh-uh," the young man told him. "I just said that she stayed here, that's all. I don't tell people nothing, not for free anyway. I've got a living to make."

"Sure you do," said Henry. "It's a pity you don't take Visa. I'd have bought those wheels just for the hell of it."

They left the auto-parts store and climbed back into Gil's Mustang.

"What do you think?" Gil asked. "It sounds to me like Sylvia could have gotten pregnant with those eels when she was down in Mexico."

"My feelings exactly," Henry agreed. He checked his watch. "It's just after twelve now. Provided there isn't too much of a hold-up at the border, we could make it to San Hipolito and back in maybe five hours. I know where it is. It's only seventy miles southeast of Tijuana, just past Ojos Negros."

Gil said, "I want to make sure we get back in time to go looking for Susan tonight."

"I don't think it matters where we are, Gil; our dream personalities can travel a lot faster than our waking bodies. Even if we get stuck in Tijuana tonight, we can still make it to Springer's house. And when we're flying, we don't need to go through border control."

"Okay," Gil said. "Let's get back home. I have to tell my parents I'm going to be late. Then we'll pick up everything we need, I.D., and stuff, and go straight through to Mexico."

He started up the engine and headed the Mustang back toward the Pacific Highway and I-5. It occurred to Henry as he watched the dry summer hills flash by that he had never worked as well with anybody in his life as he did with Gil, and as he had with Susan. The thirty-year disparity in their ages made no difference. They worked as one person, their minds and their actions interlocking so there were scarcely any wasted words.

All those years of teaching philosophy had given him a narrow and distorted view of how young people thought and behaved, and he had never seen such a practical demonstration of how alert and wide-ranging their thinking processes could be. Until now the only time he had been in any real contact with anyone under forty was when that person was struggling to understand Heidegger and Kierkegaard. Faced with less speculative problems, however, that same person was apt to be quick, creative and instantly decisive.

"I should have had children, you know," he told Gil as they sped over the bridge that took them across the Inland Freeway.

"Oh, really?" Gil asked, glancing behind him. "What makes you say that?"

"Encroaching old age, I guess."

"You're not old at night, are you?"

"Old? If I have to go through any more nights like last night, I'll wind up dead, not old."

Gil gripped Henry's shoulder for a moment. "You're Kasyx, the charge-keeper, and don't you forget it."

"Could I ever?" asked Henry.

13

"We have suffered many earthquakes here this year," the priest told them without expression. His English vocabulary was perfect but he had not had enough conversational practice to be able to emphasize the right words. "The earth has opened here, and here. A wall of the church fell here. And there, you see, we lost one complete row of houses. Four people were hurt. One was killed. Do you wish to look at his grave?"

Henry flapped his Panama hat in front of his face to cool himself. Beside him, Gil was dressed in nothing but his chopped-off denim shorts but still his face was squinting against the mid-afternoon glare and his forehead was studded with sweat.

They had reached San Hipolito after a dusty, winding drive up into the Sierra de Juarez. The sky was as dark blue as concentrated copper-sulphate solution, and utterly cloudless. They could have driven through San Hipolito without even realizing it was there: two rows of adobe houses, a small dust-colored church, a farm gate and a collection of rusted milk churns. A monotonous bell rang far away across the hills, reminding Henry uncomfortably of the bell that had tolled in last night's dream.

Their first surprise was to see that the soil around San Hipolito was deeply riven with cracks. On the northwest side of the village, half a hillside had broken open and dropped away, and there were deep crevices running across the main highway. As the priest had explained, one of the far walls of the church had collapsed. A deserted wheelbarrow stood beside the rubble waiting for the siesta to finish so it might once again be put into the service of the Lord.

The priest was short, only five feet five, but thickly built, with a large head and penetrating eyes. His principal flock, he explained, was at Ojos Negros but he had been born in San Hipolito and the people here had known him all his life.

"We've been looking for a friend of ours, an American girl named Sylvia Stoner," said Henry. "We heard she might have come this way. Maybe a month ago, maybe longer."

The priest said, "Come inside," and led them through the churchyard, where stone crosses and blind-eyed angels baked in the hundred-degree sun, through the heavy, dried-oak door and into the church itself. Although a large rhomboid of sunlight fell across the nave from the half-collapsed wall, the church was cool and they sat down with relief in one of the polished pews.

"I wondered when somebody would come to find out what happened," the priest said.

"Oh, yes?" asked Gil, looking around at the single stained-glass window, the simple altar and the silent confessionals.

"Do not understand this wrongly," the priest went on. He coughed and cleared his throat. "Everything was properly reported to the church authorities and to the police at Ensenada."

"What was properly reported?" Henry inquired.

"You came because of the girl, yes?" the priest asked, his thick eyebrows crowding together in perplexity.

"That's right, Sylvia Stoner. Pretty girl, blonde hair. Always wore a silver chain around her ankle."

"And you do not know what happened here?" the priest asked.

Henry shook his head. "I think you'd better tell us."

"Well . . ." said the priest, licking his lips anxiously, "if you do not already know . . ."

"Father," Henry put in, "this information is vital. A friend of ours is in serious danger and it could be that this danger has something to do with what happened here in San Hipolito."

"I suppose it can do no harm if I tell you," the priest said, frowning.

"It certainly won't do anybody any good if you don't," Gil pointed out.

"Very well then, come with me," said the priest. He stood up and beckoned, and they followed him along the nave to the end of the church where the wall had collapsed. They could see that the ground gaped open to a width of nearly fifteen feet and that there was a sixty-foot crevice zigzagging from the middle of the graveyard to the foot of the front pew. It looked as if part of the crevice had once been a vault of sorts because six or seven feet of the wall were lined with terra-cotta tiles, salt-glazed to a shiny black.

"Of course you know how bad the earth tremors have been," said the priest, standing at the edge of the crevice. "You have probably felt them in San Diego."

"I had no idea they were as strong as this," Henry said.

"Well, they have been less frequent lately, and not as powerful. But the night this wall collapsed, there was quite a severe tremor, three point four, and many houses and outbuildings were destroyed throughout this district and beyond. When I felt the tremor in my house at Ojos Negros, I had a strange feeling that something terrible had happened, and sure enough, I was telephoned to come at once."

"There's no damage here that can't be repaired," Henry commented, shading his eyes to look out of the church and into the sun. "A couple of truckloads of concrete should put you right."

The priest rubbed his hands, slowly and nervously. "I am afraid that something happened here that all the concrete in the world could not put right. In this vault there rested a box, a long wooden box, carved and sealed. I still have it; it has been taken to my house at Ojos Negros for safekeeping. Until the night of the earth tremor, the box was hidden below the ground and covered with an iron trap three inches thick and tiled over so that it was indistinguishable from the church floor. But *crack!* When the earth shifted, the iron trap was broken in half and the wooden box was exposed to view. The church curator, Miguel Estovar, ran here to the church as quickly as he could but he was too late. The trap had been broken, the seals had been damaged and the wooden box was empty."

Henry asked in a quiet voice, "Tell me, Father, what was inside the wooden box?"

The priest stopped wringing his hands and chivvied his fingertips anxiously against his sleeves.

Even more quietly, Henry asked, "Was it Yaomauitl?"

The priest stared. "You know about Yaomauitl?"

Henry nodded. "We are Night Warriors. When the sun sets, I am Kasyx and this is Tebulot."

Immediately, without further questions and without ceremony, the priest went down on one knee and clasped Henry's hands. Then he clasped Gil's hands and kissed them. As softly and quickly as if he were reciting his rosary, he said, "The legends always said the Night Warriors would come if ever Yaomauitl was freed but I never believed them." He looked up at them, the sunlight shining around their heads like halos, and said with the deepest of emotion, "You have restored my faith. It is like a miracle."

"We're not *that* miraculous," Gil said. "We only started training last night."

The priest stood up and gripped each by a shoulder. "I know you will defend us. God be praised."

"Tell us something about Yaomauitl," Henry said. "Was he buried here for long?"

The priest said, "He was buried here in sixteen eighty-seven. It happened after a dream battle in which it is said that sixty of the finest Night Warriors lost their lives. He was placed inside a box of elmwood, through which evil manifestations may not pass, and the box was sealed with the nine holy seals of God. The iron trap was then lowered over his tomb and the iron trap was blessed by nine priests and crossed ninety-nine times with holy water. The church of San Hipolito was built on top of the tomb to further sanctify this place. Yaomauitl has lain here ever since, until he was freed by that earth tremor."

"Do you know what he looks like?" Henry asked.

"Come with me," said the priest. "I have a contemporary woodcut of the entombing of Yaomauitl in my study. It shows the Devil quite clearly. It also shows the nine seals and the Night Warriors who entrapped Yaomauitl at last."

They left the church and walked across the glaring courtyard at the back until they reached a small adobe house shaded by scrub trees. A Mexican woman was outside on the veranda cleaning moths off the oil lamps. She watched Henry and Gil with suspicious silence as the priest took them into the house.

"Maria is like most of the people of San Hipolito," the priest explained. "She doesn't readily take to strangers."

"You still haven't explained what any of this has to do with Sylvia Stoner," Gil said.

"Well," said the priest, ushering them into his house and leading them through to the living room, "this is because you have to understand the background of what occurred before you can come to the same conclusion I did. There are no easily explained facts. There are no reliable witnesses either. But everything indicates that my assumption is correct, and I have to say that Monsignor Del Parral in Ensenada concurs with my opinion."

The inside of the small adobe house was cool and musty. The furniture was simple: rushwork chairs and plain wooden sofas. The walls were painted white and hung with brightly colored native paintings of Biblical scenes: Joseph and his coat of many colors, Moses in the bulrushes, the Pièta. The floors were tiled dark brown and there was a basket of eucalyptus logs beside the hearth.

Henry and Gil waited while the priest went through to his study. He returned with a red cardboard folder that he laid on the low table in the middle of the room and opened.

Inside it there was a sheet of thick art paper, yellowed at the edges and badly foxed but printed with the most richly detailed woodcut Henry had ever seen. It was in the style of Dürer's "Apocalypse" and although it was not nearly as accomplished as a work by Dürer, it clearly showed the Devil Yaomauitl being imprisoned in his elmwood box.

"How old is this?" asked Gil quietly.

"The print is relatively new, eighteen eighty or thereabouts. But the original woodcut from which it was taken—which is now in the Museum of Religious Art in Mexico City—that was dated sixteen eighty-seven. The artist was Paolo Placido, SJ."

Henry and Gil examined the woodcut with gradually increasing dread. It depicted a long, coffin-shaped box, with rich and fantastic carvings of ivy, mistletoe and other holy plants as well as the figures of angels and saints. The box was being lowered by derricks into a tile-lined crevice in the ground. There were twenty or thirty people standing around the box, some of whom were dressed in elaborate armor and winged helmets. Henry and Gil both recognized a much earlier form of Tebulot's armor and a weapon that was primitive by the standards of the weapon Tebulot carried now but that must have been the most powerful machine ever dreamed of at the time.

The illustration of Yaomauitl himself was unmistakably disturbing. He was tall, with dark, slanted eyes that even after three hundred years seemed to stare out at them with glistening malevolence. His body was gristly and had protruding ribs and a grotesque pelvic girdle from which depended a long, sinewy penis. His hands and feet were like claws with curved, razor-sharp nails, the kind of nails that could disembowel with one flick.

Henry and Gil recognized the Devil at once. He was older and more battle-scarred but he was indisputably the parent of the creature that had taken Susan hostage, the "boy" who, for one split second, had revealed to them the real shape of his body and the real wickedness of his soul.

Henry said, "Yes," gently and handed the woodcut back.

"You recognize him?" the priest asked.

Gil nodded. "We saw one of his kids, if that's what you can call them."

The priest stared at the woodcut with an expression of solemn apprehension. "Then it has already started, the spreading of his seed."

"Yes, Father," said Henry. "That was how Sylvia Stoner died."

The priest looked up at him. "Night Warriors," he whispered with reverence. "Perhaps you won't believe this but I have been dreaming that you would come. It says in *De Daemonialitate* that the Night Warriors will always rise in response to a reappearance of the Devil in any of his manifestations. And here you are. You will forgive me if you are no surprise to me."

"It's more helpful that we're not," Henry smiled and grasped the priest's shoulder. Perhaps there was still some residue of Ashapola's power in Henry's hand for the priest glanced at it quickly and smiled the smile of the reassured.

"Now then," the priest said, "you wish to know what connecton was formed between Yaomauitl and your friend, Sylvia Stoner. Let me tell you what happened as far as I know it. Then I will take you to see Ludovico, who is the only person in the village who knowingly encountered Yaomauitl after the box was broken open. But before that, would you care for some wine? We grow our own vines here, you know. I cannot guarantee that it is as smooth as anything from Napa Valley but it is quite refreshing."

He poured each of them a glass of dark-red pinot wine, fruity and aromatic, and then sat back and said, "Your friend Sylvia and her man companion arrived here in the last week of April. I remember that, of course, because of Easter. They came in a wagon—you know, four-wheel drive—and they said they were touring Baja California on vacation. They asked me if I knew where they could stay for a day or two and I directed them to Señora Rosario's house.

Her two boys left home to work in America, her husband died and so she has many spare rooms."

"What did Sylvia's companion look like?" Henry asked.

"Well, you could say that he looked like a tennis player who has let his training go by the way," said the priest. "Curly hair, not too tall, handsome but very untidy. Unshaven, crumpled clothes."

"Did you catch his name?"

The priest shook his head. "She called him 'baby.' They came to take pictures of the church and the village but they took no care with their pictures, and they spoke too loudly of what they were going to do on their vacation."

"What are you trying to imply?" Henry asked.

"Simply that they were not genuinely here on vacation. They came, like a few other Americans before them, because they heard that some of the villagers have another crop, apart from grapevines."

"You mean—?"

"Yes, my friends. Marijuana. The fragrant strain known among connoisseurs as San Juarez Paradise Number One. Very difficult to find, very expensive. And not many Americans know that it is grown in the hills around San Hipolito."

Neither Henry nor Gil said a word about the priest's apparent approval of the marijuana crop but the priest himself sipped his wine and smiled at them over the rim of his glass.

"I can see you are surprised that I condone the sale. Well, I do not condone it but I do turn a blind eye to it. There is no money in San Hipolito, my friends. Because most of the soil is stony and barren, conventional farming produces little reward. Without the sale of San Juarez Paradise Number One, this village would die, the people who live here would be dispossessed and the church would fall into ruin. I have to make a practical choice between a trade that transgresses the laws of men and a state of poverty and suffering that would transgress the laws of God."

"So Sylvia and her companion were here for grass?" asked Henry.

"Of course. There is nothing else here that would entice an American tourist, no matter how eccentric, to stay in San Hipolito for even a few minutes."

"Then what happened?" asked Gil.

The priest spread his hands. "They stayed for two days, maybe three, and I heard from one of the little birds who tell me such things that they were negotiating with the Perez family to buy two thousand dollars' worth of marijuana, first quality. Perez of course was holding out for more money, and Sylvia and her companion were constantly telephoning to America to see if they could drum up more promises of sales."

He paused for a moment and then said gravely, "There came then the day of the earth tremor. The ground split and everybody in the village rushed into the surrounding fields lest their houses fall on them. When they returned, they found that the church wall had fallen and that Yaomauitl had escaped from his elmwood box. They sent out dogs, and men with shotguns, but there was no trace of the Devil, or even of his passing."

"Sylvia and her companion were still in the village?" Henry asked.

The priest nodded. "They stayed for one more night and one more day. But certain things about them were strange. The night after Yaomauitl escaped, Señora Rosario heard them upstairs in their bedroom. They seemed to be arguing, or at least the girl Sylvia seemed to be arguing. Señora Rosario did not recognize the other voice. It was a man's voice, very harsh and loud, and it sounded as if it were coming from everywhere at once. She said it frightened her to hear it. However, it did not last for very long because the argument finished with great abruptness and then Señora Rosario—well, she usually does not listen to such things— but she heard Sylvia and her companion on the bed. She said it sounded very violent, like rape. She could hear

Sylvia crying out in a muffled voice as if there were a hand or a pillow over her mouth. She could hear the man cursing her in the same harsh voice. And she could hear the frame of the bed shaking as if they were trying to break it to pieces. The next morning she went upstairs and told them they must go."

"Sylvia's boyfriend was still with her?" asked Henry. "In spite of the way he had sounded the night before?"

"Ah, you are quick, Mr. Watkins," said the priest. "Yes, her companion was still with her, but when they left Señora Rosario's to drive back to America, they made one mistake. One serious mistake."

"What was that, Father?"

"Come," said the priest. "Now is the time for us to talk to Ludovico."

They finished their wine and the priest led them out of the house and across the highway. He pointed out Señora Rosario's house, a large, secluded adobe at the end of one of the two rows of houses that made up the village, trailing with creeper and surrounded by a high wall. Although it was well past siesta time now, there didn't seem to be anyone around, only a small, bare-bottomed boy playing in the dust and a thin, mangy-looking dog that kept prowling and barking around one of the houses. The priest waved a fly from his face and then pointed down the street, close to where Gil had parked the Mustang.

An old man was sitting in a shadowy doorway. His face was withered and his eyeballs were as white and vacant as hard-cooked eggs. He wore a freshly pressed suit of pale-beige linen and his shoes had been highly polished even though they now bore a thin film of dust. His hands rested on the gleaming brass knob of a walking cane.

"This is Ludovico," said the priest. "Ludovico, these two gentlemen are special friends of mine from El Norte. I would like to introduce them to you."

Ludovico blindly shook hands with Henry and Gil and then asked, "What are they looking for, these special friends of yours, Father?"

"They have been asking about the girl who came here, the American. The girl who was here when the earthquake came and damaged the church."

Ludovico licked his deeply lined lips and said, "You said that somebody would come one day to ask about her, didn't you, Father?"

"Yes, Ludovico, I did."

"Can you trust this pair, Father? I sense something unusual about them. I sense something to do with electricity."

Henry smiled. "You're right, sir. Is there anything else you can sense?"

The old man touched his own face as if to reassure himself it was still there. "I sense many strange things. Strange duties, strange ambitions. I sense danger too."

"Did you sense something the day the earthquake damaged the church?" asked Henry.

"Not then, not then," Ludovico answered. "But the day afterward when they left. That was when I sensed something. You see, they had passed by me several times during their stay in the village and I had come to know them quite well. Their voices, their footsteps, the sound of their clothes."

"And?" asked Gil when the old man seemed to hesitate.

"And they made the mistake of passing close by me when they left the village for the last time. Because I heard them, both of them, quite distinctly, and I sensed something I never wish to sense again. It was the same girl, of that there was no question. Perhaps not in soul, but certainly in body. The man, however, was completely different. People say he looked just the same but when he passed me by, I heard hard skin rubbing on hard skin; I heard the sharp clicking of claws on the road; I heard hissing breathing and a terrible rustling sound that filled me with fear. Worst of all, I felt a dead coldness as if somebody had opened an icebox door in front of my face and closed it again. There was no doubt about it. That afternoon, regardless of what anybody else perceived with their eyes, I knew that a Devil had passed by me."

Henry turned to Gil. There was no need for either of them to speak. The pieces of the fateful puzzle were coming together now, and they had learned something new about their Deadly Enemy, something Springer had either failed to tell them or didn't know. He had admitted, after all, that even Ashapola was not always able to anticipate the ways of Devils.

That something was that Yaomauitl could take on the form of a human being—so effectively, it seemed, that everybody who saw him was deceived. Only those who were unable to see him were not taken in. Only the blind could detect the distinctive sound of a demon from hell.

"So Yaomauitl escaped from San Hipolito in the guise of Sylvia's boyfriend," said Henry. "And Sylvia's only crime was that she came here looking for high-quality grass."

"At the wrong time, I regret," said the priest. "But if it had not been her, it would have been somebody else. Yaomauitl is indiscriminate in his choice of familiars."

"Did you find out what happened to the boyfriend?" asked Gil.

The priest said, "That was the only time we did not involve the police. We ask you, too, not to pass this information on to any law-enforcement agency because it will only cause suspicion and distress, and may even lead to a wrongful arrest. Victor Perez, you see, had many arguments with Sylvia's companion about the price of his marijuana, and that could easily be misconstrued as a motive for her friend's murder."

"You found him dead, then?"

The priest said, "Yes, we found him dead."

"And you're certain Yaomauitl did it?"

"No human being could have killed a man in this fashion, my friends."

Henry said nothing but it was obvious that he wanted to know how the Devil had destroyed Sylvia's traveling companion. The priest thanked Ludovico for his evidence and they all shook hands with him. Then the priest led Henry and Gil farther down the village street until they reached a stony side turning that led down beside a vineyard. They walked alongside the vines under a baking sun, their feet crunching on the bone-dry soil.

"We haven't moved him yet," said the priest over his shoulder. "Nobody will touch his remains because they believe they contain evil; and in any case, I didn't think it wise. If anybody did come asking questions about him, I wanted to be able to show that it would have been impossible for Victor Perez, or indeed for anyone, to have murdered him."

They reached the end of the vineyard. Along the lower edge of it for about half a mile, the boundary had been marked out with staves six or seven feet high and fifteen feet apart. Halfway up the end stave there was a large, dry lump—a papery-looking excrescence resembling a wasps' nest. They approached it with a mixture of mystification and alarm. But even on close inspection, Henry and Gil couldn't make out what it was. It was some sort of desiccated tissue, twisted and snarled with tendons, and there were some dark-maroon lumps on the side of it, but it bore no resemblance to anything they had ever seen.

Henry stared at the priest in perplexity. But the priest beckoned him around to the other side of the pole and pointed.

Although it was squashed and distorted, Henry could discern the face of a man in the middle of the dried-up flesh. The man's eyes were shut tight, his nose was pressed into an indeterminate lump and his mouth was dragged down sideways by the intrusion of five curled nodules that must have been his fingers.

The priest crossed himself and said, "He was found here three days after Sylvia and her companion had left San Hipolito. Yaomauitl could have hidden the remains of course, but I believe he left them here as a warning." He looked away, out across the mountains. "Now you know what a man looks like when every single ounce of moisture is taken out of him. We don't amount to much, do we, for all of our pride?"

They trudged back up the hill. Only Gil turned to look back. Tonight they were going to have to face the offspring of the creature capable of doing that to a man and he wanted to keep the image sharp in his mind. It would ensure that he didn't hesitate when it came to pulling the trigger of his machine.

The priest invited them back for more wine but it was growing late and they wanted to return to San Diego as soon as possible.

"I will pray for you," the priest told them.

Gil started up the Mustang. Henry said, "Thank you, Father. We appreciate your prayers."

"There is one thing more," the priest added. "Wait here for just a moment and I will bring it for you."

He hurried off toward his house. Gil and Henry sat silent while they waited for him to return, each pondering the dried-up remains of Sylvia's friend, each thinking of the Deadly Enemy, Yaomauitl, and how he had stared at them so malevolently from that woodcut made so many years ago. That woodcut alone was proof of the longevity of utter evil. Evil could be contained, evil could be banished, but evil could never be destroyed.

The priest returned, perspiring and out of breath. He handed Henry a brown-felt satchel fastened at the front with a fraying cord.

"Take these," he said. "These are the nine seals the Night Warriors placed on the elmwood box to keep Yaomauitl from breaking out of it. They were brought over to Mexico by Jesuits who had heard of how the Devil was causing havoc in the New World. They are beyond price, my friends, so please guard them well."

When Henry untied the cord and looked into the satchel, he saw a collection of small tissue-paper packages. He took one out and carefully opened it. The priest watched him anxiously as he laid the seal across the palm of his hand.

It looked like nothing more than a blob of black, cracked sealing wax stuck onto an old piece of twisted fabric. The priest said, "They were found in Jerusalem in the year nine hundred. They are said to be fragments of the robes of nine of the twelve disciples, one from each, taken from their hems on the night of the Last Supper. Three are missing, those of Judas, Peter and John."

Henry touched the seal with his fingertip and turned it over. "What happened to those three?"

The priest said, "Nobody knows. But the saying is that if anybody could get all twelve together, he would be able to exile the Devil forever."

"Perhaps God has the other three," said Henry. "Perhaps he doesn't want us to exile the Devil forever. Perhaps from time to time we need to be reminded of the ultimate evil so we can appreciate the ultimate good."

"You should have taken the cloth," smiled the priest.

Henry wrapped up the seal and dropped it back into the satchel. "In a peculiar sort of way, I think that I just did."

They drove back down through the San Juarez mountains, their sun visors lowered against the burning sun. They reached Mexican Highway 1 at Ensenada and drove north to Tijuana. It was dark when they reached the border and they had to wait an hour before they could get through, but at last they were back on I-5 and heading for Del Mar and Solana Beach.

"Those seals," said Gil, "what do you think of them?"

"Phoney probably," Henry replied. "Have you ever come across a religious relic that isn't? If they joined all the pieces of the so-called True Cross, they'd have a crucifix as tall as the Sears building. And as for fragments of cloth from Jesus' robe, you'd have thought Jesus owned a seamless-robe warehouse."

"You believe in Yaomauitl though, don't you?"

"Do I? I don't know what to think. I know that something

terrible's been prowling around and that something killed Sylvia Stoner and her boyfriend. But don't let's be too naive about it. Don't let's jump to hasty conclusions. Springer set us up once and he could be doing it again.''

"You really don't trust anybody, do you?" Gil asked.

"Yes, I do. I trust you and I trust Susan, and I also happen to trust myself. But that's about as far as it goes. Don't think I'm getting cynical on you. I'm not. The more I see, the stronger my belief becomes. I believe in the Night Warriors and the task the Night Warriors have to perform. I believe in them implicitly. But if so much supernatural stuff is proved to me so unequivocally, why should I accept any other supernatural stuff that isn't proved so well? It would certainly make life easier for us if everything that priest said was one hundred percent, but supposing it isn't? Supposing he's left out one or two absolutely crucial facts? Supposing he's lying to protect a real murderer? Supposing none of it ever happened and you and I were being suckered from beginning to end?"

Gil said, "Henry, somewhere along the line we have to take one or two things for granted. Otherwise we're not going to get anywhere."

"Well, you're right," Henry agreed. "But let's not automatically take everything at its face value, huh? Especially not priests and men who seem to be messengers from God."

When they reached Henry's cottage, Gil parked outside and Henry said, "I have an idea. Why don't you call your folks and tell them you're staying over tonight with friends? I'm rarely disturbed here so there isn't much chance of somebody bursting in on us and thinking we've gone into a coma."

"That sounds like good thinking," Gil said.

Henry unlocked the front door and reached around to switch on the lights. "The phone's at the back of the sofa. When you've finished, maybe we could go out and get ourselves an egg foo young to go."

The lights blinked on and there he was, or rather she, because this evening she was wearing a plain white costume more like a dress than a suit and her face was more finely featured than usual. She was sitting in Henry's favorite chair, her legs crossed, watching and waiting as if she had been there for hours.

"Well, well," she said. "The return of the Night Warriors."

Henry was taken off guard. "Springer," he said. "I thought we'd seen the last of you."

"The last? What on earth made you think that?"

"What on earth do you *think* made me think that?" Henry retorted. "You abandoned us last night . . . left us tangled up in some goddamned nightmare with no power and no way out. And thanks to you, Samena's been captured— and held hostage—by that Devil they dug up on the beach. You *knew*, didn't you? You knew right from the very beginning that we were going to come face-to-face with that Devil. I mean, you lied about it. You went out and tracked down one of the pathologists who was working on that Devil, and of course he was bound to have a dream about it . . . and now look at what the hell's happened."

Springer listened patiently, her hands pressed together in simulation of prayer.

"Is that all you have to say?" she asked at last.

"There could be more," Henry snapped. "It depends on the quality of your explanation."

"My explanation is very simple," said Springer. She rose from her chair and walked toward Henry and Gil with an effortless glide. "Please, Gil," she said, "do call your parents. They would like to know that you are safe, and it would be a good idea if you were to spend the night here."

"Well?" Henry demanded.

Springer smiled. In her asexual way, she was really very attractive, Henry had to admit. She had a beauty no human being can ever achieve. Faultless, pale and perfect.

"I confess that I deceived you and that I took you into

248

Mr. Shapiro's dream in the full knowledge that you would encounter the creature from the beach. I didn't tell you because I didn't want you to overreact. I believed, you see, that you would be able to cope quite easily with a Devil who is still only an embryo or—what do they call the offspring of kangaroos?—a joey.''

"Maybe we could have coped with it with some forewarning and a little more power," Henry protested.

Gil said fiercely, "We were completely fucked. There was nothing we could do. We had to make up our minds whether we wanted to kill ourselves for no reason or come back here to safety and leave Susan behind. That was some kind of choice, huh?''

"Well, that part of it I regret," Springer said. "But even *I* cannot be in two places at one time, no matter how many different faces I wear. I had to leave you because I had located the descendant of yet another Night Warrior and it was essential that I recruit him as quickly as possible. He will join you tonight. His name is Xaxxa, the slide-boxer.''

"What is the point of recruiting another Warrior when it costs you one you've already got?" Henry asked bitterly.

Springer said with a touch of sharpness, "I am your trainer, Kasyx, not your nursemaid. I fully expected the three of you to be able to deal with that nightmare and to overcome the creature too.''

"Whatever you expected, Springer, the simple fact of the matter is that I don't trust you anymore," Henry told him.

"Me neither," said Gil.

Springer thought about that for a moment and then said, "Do you consider it essential for your task that you trust me?''

Henry said, "Not essential, no. I've been a Night Warrior for only one night but I get the feeling that it's a much bigger thing than both of us.''

Springer nodded. "In that case, you will give me the opportunity to prove to you that I *am* trustworthy. You will go out tonight with Xaxxa and you will rescue Samena from the spawn of the Devil. I will guide you to the right dream and this time I will advise you in advance of the true identity of the dreamer."

"It's not our leather-and-lashes friend, Lemuel Shapiro, again, is it?" asked Henry.

Springer said, "No. The creature was moved today from the coroner's laboratories to the Scripps laboratories. Your dreamer will be one of the people who is studying it there. Most probably Doctor Caulfield."

Henry stared at him in disbelief. "Doctor Andrea Caulfield?"

"You know her?" asked Springer, mildly surprised at Henry's reaction.

"I should think so. She was my wife for four years. And now you want me to go into one of her nightmares?"

Gil slapped Henry on the back. "Jeez, who knows, Henry, you might even come face-to-face with the monster she thinks you are!"

14

They went to bed at ten-thirty after a quick Chinese supper Gil brought back from Chung King Loh. Henry took the bed and Gil bunked down on the sofa. Gil was happy to stay over at Henry's cottage; it made him feel more relaxed even though he suspected part of the reason Henry had invited him was so he could act as watchdog in case Henry felt tempted to take a drink. Henry was fighting his alcoholism hard; he even regretted having accepted the priest's offer of red wine. As he told Gil, "Once you've taken that first drink, it's ten times more difficult to say no to the next."

Springer had left them with a promise to meet them at the house on Camino del Mar at eleven. She would say nothing further about tonight's assignment nor their new Night Warrior, Xaxxa. She wouldn't even explain what a "slideboxer" was. "When you come tonight, you will see for yourselves."

In the darkness of their separate rooms, Henry and Gil said the words that would transport their dreaming personalities out of their earthbound bodies:

"Now when the face of the world is hidden in darkness, let us be conveyed to the place of our meeting, armed and armored; and let us be nourished by the power that is dedicated to the cleaving of darkness, the settling of all black matters, and the dissipation of all evil, so be it."

They closed their eyes and felt the tides of sleep steadily overwhelm them, just as the Pacific steadily overwhelmed the shore. They rose, as silent and transparent as ghosts, leaving their bodies in the cottage, and sailed high above Del Mar, darker tonight because of cloud cover, following the bright network of traffic toward the house where Springer would be waiting for them.

They were absorbed through the roof of the house and sank into the second-floor room.

Springer, as promised, was already there, looking even more feminine than she had in the afternoon. She had combed her hair into luxurious waves and she wore an extraordinary white knee-length jacket with wide shoulders and a loosely tied belt, with nothing underneath but a white garter belt and white stockings.

"You're early," she said with pleasure. "That will give you time to meet your new Warrior, Xaxxa."

She turned and ushered forward a tall, well-muscled black boy, dressed at the moment in nothing but pale-blue shorts. His hair was cropped short, emphasizing the thickness of his neck. His face was flat, short-nosed, one of those highly photogenic faces like Muhammad Ali's. But although he was obviously athletic and intensely fit, there was a cautious expression of humor around his mouth, an expression that contradicted the idea that anyone with this kind of physique had to be serious and dull.

"Xaxxa," said Springer, nodding her head. "Xaxxa, this is Kasyx, the charge-keeper, and Tebulot, the machine-carrier."

"You didn't tell me they was white," said Xaxxa suspiciously.

"I didn't tell you they were black either."

"Well, Night Warriors, I guess I kind of assumed they was all black."

Gil said, "Does it matter—our being white?"

"That depend," said Xaxxa. "I mean like that depend entirely on your attitude. I mean for instance if you think that because you *white*, you can start giving me orders, then you can forget it. You can forget this whole Night Warrior thing completely. My father was in Viet Nam and believe me man he took nothing but three years of shit from white men, and he always said to me never go joining nothing where there's a white man in charge because you going to be sweeping the floor even if you some kind of genius."

"*Are* you a genius?" asked Henry.

Xaxxa said, "No, but that's if I was."

"Do you have a name, apart from your Night Warrior name?"

"Sure. My name's Lloyd Curran."

"I'm Henry," said Henry, "and this is Gil. I'm a teacher and Gil's a student, and neither of us are geniuses either. The only other thing I can say is that the Night Warriors aren't like the army. We don't have officers and we don't have rank. We work together no matter our age and experience and—now that you've joined us—no matter our color. What do you do, Lloyd?"

"Trainee photographer," Lloyd said, still suspicious. It was obvious that he had been expecting something rather different. Certainly not a skinny storekeeper's son from Solana Beach and a blotchy-faced philosophy professor in creased pajamas.

"Springer said you were a slide-boxer," put in Gil. "Did you try it out yet? The suit? The slide-boxing?"

"Kind of," said Lloyd.

"Can we have a demonstration?" Henry asked. "We don't even know what slide-boxing is."

Springer walked around and touched Henry's arm. "If you charge up, Henry, you'll be able to show each other what you can do."

Henry knelt down and Gil and Lloyd knelt beside him. Springer stood over them and recited the words that would transform them into Night Warriors. Three golden halos shone over their heads and then faded. At last they stood up.

Kasyx's crimson armor crackled alarmingly with static power. Springer said, "I have given you the maximum charge this time. You have two powerful combatants to supply and you will need it. The only reason I gave you less last time was because I did not expect you to have to fight so violently, and also because there is always a risk with an inexperienced charge-keeper of accidental discharge, which can not only kill you and your Warriors, but the dreamer too."

Kasyx laid his hand on Tebulot's shoulder and Tebulot's weapon immediately hummed with full power, its golden charge scale glowing bright. Now they turned to Xaxxa, the slide-boxer.

Xaxxa seemed even more muscular and well-developed than he had earlier. His chest bulged and gleamed, his stomach was flat and hard. He wore a white, domed helmet that sparkled with bursts of silver light as if it had been lacquered with flakes of chrome. There was a curved white bar around the brown of the helmet, and around this bar dozens of tiny colored lights endlessly teemed.

On his shoulders Xaxxa wore white protective pads, overleaved like the scales of a dragon. His torso was bare and all he wore around his loins was a tight white protective codpiece of the same sparkling substance as his helmet. It was fastened in place by a thin leather waistband and a thin leather strap that cleaved deep between his muscular buttocks. His calves were clad in white boots, the sides of which were clustered with complicated insets of silver and copper in patterns that reminded Kasyx of microcircuits.

"The boots are the key to Xaxxa's talent," said Springer. "If you will charge him up, Kasyx, he will show you something of what he can do."

Kasyx laid his hand on Xaxxa's shoulder. Xaxxa watched him closely as the power of Ashapola thrummed into his body. "I always got to depend on you for power?" he asked Kasyx.

Kasyx nodded. "Just as I, in my turn, have to depend on Springer's god of gods, Ashapola. As Night Warriors, old buddy, we are all dependent on each other."

As Xaxxa's body was infused with power, the metallic patterns on his boots began to sparkle and glow. At last Springer said, "Enough," and Kasyx drew away. Springer stepped foward and lowered the white bar from the brow of Xaxxa's helmet to the level of his chin. Over his face there appeared a curved visor of absolute energy, which from the outside was an optically perfect mirror. When an opponent faced Xaxxa, he would see only his own face.

"Now watch," said Springer. "I will pretend to be Xaxxa's adversary. Xaxxa will defend himself and then attack me in his turn."

Springer poised herself in an attacking position, her knees bent, her hands raised. Xaxxa crouched down too, gradually moving away from her in a diagonal, his open hands tensely circling in the air.

There was a split second of tension. Then Springer flashed in toward Xaxxa, her hands flying in a style that looked like hyper-complicated kung fu. But there was a sharp *veeeowwfff!* and Xaxxa slid instantly to one side on a shining two-foot-wide strip of pure golden power. Then with a long whistle, curving and high-pitched, a strip of power zipped across the room, twisting itself into a corkscrew loop, and Xaxxa slid along it at high speed like a two-hundred-mile-an-hour surfer. He actually turned upside down at the top of the loop, then came hurtling back toward Springer on a streaking strip of power that brought him right up behind her, poised to dropkick her in the back even before she had recovered enough to turn around.

He allowed the power strip to fade and came to a standstill. He lifted his visor and grinned widely. "Slide-boxing," he announced. Then, *"Wow!"*

"That's something," said Kasyx. He was impressed.

Tebulot was almost envious. "Here you've got me lugging this damned great machine around, and look at him *go!*"

Springer touched each one of them on the forehead. "Each Night Warrior has his part to play. You are several, but you are one."

"Well, then," said Kasyx, "isn't it time we went looking for Samena?"

"Yes," said Springer.

"Whose dream?" asked Kasyx, looking at Springer meaningfully.

"Your ex-wife's, I'm afraid. Out of all of those who have been studying the creature at Scripps, hers is the most vivid response. She was tired tonight; she went to bed at nine-thirty and is already asleep."

"We going into his ex-wife's nightmare?" asked Xaxxa. Springer nodded.

"You said we were going into black dreams as well as white. How come the very first dream I get has to be white?"

"You'll have a really good time," said Tebulot. "White people dream about other white people, so you'll have plenty of crackers to knock around."

"You trying to be funny?" asked Xaxxa.

"What are you going to do?" Tebulot challenged him. "Loop-de-loop and smack me in the back of the head? This weapon fires backward, in case you're interested."

"Jive ass," Xaxxa retorted.

Kasyx said, "For Christ's sake, Xaxxa, stop trying to act like Mr. T."

"Mr. T?" Xaxxa yelped. "Where this man been?"

"He's a philosophy professor," said Tebulot. "That is, during the day. But tonight he's Kasyx, your charge-keeper, and you need him, just like you need me and I need you. So let's go find Samena."

Xaxxa made no more complaints. Tebulot recognized that he was only playing the part of the aggressive ghetto kid because he was nervous, excited and a little afraid, the same way he himself had been just yesterday and, to a great extent, still was. He saw strength in Xaxxa, and resilience, and humor, and all those qualities would make him a good man to rely on in case of a crisis.

The three Night Warriors gathered close and clasped hands. There was no animosity on Xaxxa's face as he interlaced his fingers with Kasyx's and Tebulot's, only anticipation, excitement. They rose up through the ceiling, through the rafters and the roof, and then they were out in the night, more than a hundred feet high and turning south.

This time there was no need for Springer to direct them to the house of their dreamer. Kasyx had Andrea's address engraved on his bank balance.

"I keep thinking this can't be real," Xaxxa whispered.

"Me too," said Tebulot.

"I mean this is Peter Pan, right? This is real flying. I only wish I could bring my Pentax. The pictures you could get, you know? The shots!"

They followed the curve of the coastline south to La Jolla, perched on the headland overlooking La Jolla Bay. They turned inland when they reached the cove, flying over the glittering balconies of the fashionable restaurants, over Prospect Street to Pearl Street, where they spiraled down at last toward a small, whitewashed house with Spanish-style arches and a red-tiled roof. Andrea's Volkswagen Rabbit was parked in the exact center of the well-swept driveway.

They faded in through the red-tiled roof and into the master bedroom. Andrea was lying on her back on the carved double bed, her hair in curlers, her pale-green nightgown rumpled up around her thighs. A paperback copy of Hardy's *World of Plankton* lay on the bedside table next to a jar of cold cream and a small Cartier alarm clock that had once belonged to Henry. The room smelled of Estée Lauder perfume, which gave Kasyx something of a familiar shock. So did the sight of Andrea in her nightgown. Ever since their divorce, she had always been fully dressed when he met her, smart, neat and businesslike. To see her like this reminded him uncomfortably of the four years they had been married.

"Your ex?" Xaxxa whispered. "Not bad-looking, if you don't object to a second opinion."

Kasyx looked at her curiously. He supposed, after all, that she wasn't all that bad-looking. His impression of her face had been distorted by acrimony and alimony; if he had been asked to draw her, she probably would have turned out uglier than Yaomauitl.

"Let's get into the dream," he suggested. "How about you, Xaxxa? Are you ready for this?"

"Do your worst," said Xaxxa.

Kasyx lifted his hands and across the darkness of the bedroom drew the crackling blue octagon of light. Then he pushed his hands forward and divided the darkness inside the octagon like a curtain, stretching it apart. Slowly a sunlit street scene appeared, although none of the sunlight fell into the bedroom. Kasyx beckoned Tebulot and Xaxxa to stand close beside him and then he raised the octagon over their heads. They held hands tightly as the light descended and gradually enveloped them in Andrea's dream.

Xaxxa breathed, "Holy shit."

The instant the octagon touched the floor, the Night Warriors found themselves in a dusty, hot, brightly sunlit square in what appeared to be a North African city, like Tangiers or Marrakesh. A mosaic fountain splashed in the roasting wind and palm trees rattled above the white-domed rooftops. They could hear the hoarse, throaty tremolo of a bamboo *chebaba* and the clamor of a street market not far away. Figures in green-and-white *djellabas* hurried through the square wearing dark, masklike sunglasses. There was a smell of heat, sewage and roasted meat.

Xaxxa looked around in awe. "This is a dream? This is actually a dream?"

Kasyx said, "It is, and we're right inside it."

"And we going to find this Devil character inside this dream?"

"That's what Springer says."

"Fee-*eew*," said Xaxxa.

Tebulot suddenly pointed across the square to a wide archway. "There," he said. "Isn't that your wife?"

Kasyx pressed his hand to the left side of his helmet and his vision jumped to close-up. He glimpsed a woman's back as she disappeared into the crowds of the *souk,* a woman in a *solar topi* and a white bush shirt. He didn't see her face but he saw the green feather in her hatband. Andrea's trademark color had always been green.

"You're probably right," he told Tebulot. "I guess we'd

258

better follow her, see where she goes. But will you please remember she's my *ex*-wife."

Tebulot smiled and beckoned to Xaxxa. Together, keeping shoulder-to-shoulder, they crossed the square and went through the archway, elbowing their way past crowds of Arabs. The sorrowful music of the *chebaba* grew louder and was joined by the tremulous playing of pipes. Panpipes from the Atlas mountains, magical pipes, whose music could convey the listener into dreams beyond dreams. The crowds jostled even closer and the Night Warriors found themselves forcing their way along a narrow market street, sheltered from the midday sun by layers of striped awnings and lined on each side by stalls selling bronze dishes and copper jugs, strange bead embroidery, leather shoes and intricate camel harnesses, caged birds that whistled and piped, and sweetmeats studded with flaked almonds and blowflies.

At the end of this street they saw the white woman disappearing into the doorway of a shop. They followed her to the front of the shop, pushing aside dark-skinned children who danced around them for money. There was Arabic writing across the doorway, and from inside there was the sound of a radio playing Arab music, and the fragrance of *kif* resin burning in a pipe.

"What do we do, go in?" asked Xaxxa.

Tebulot slung his weapon across his back. "I don't see that we have any choice, Kasyx, do you?"

Kasyx shrugged. "I just want to be careful. There's no telling what my ex-wife might do to me if she finds she's got me cold, right inside her own dream."

"Just so long as she don't wake herself up," said Xaxxa.

Kasyx cautiously entered the shop doorway. "Anybody there?" he called loudly.

Inside the shop it was gloomy and hot and smelled even more strongly of *kif*. The walls were lined with scores of mahogany drawers, rather like an old-fashioned apothecary's, and each drawer was labeled in Arabic. A long flypaper hung from the center of the ceiling and dozens of flies struggled on it fitfully. Some of the flies had white heads and Kasyx realized they were humans who had been genetically tangled up with insects in the same way as that scientist had been in *The Fly*. He remembered that Andrea and he had started to watch *The Fly* on late-night television once after coming home from a dinner party and Andrea had switched it off, saying it was disgusting and puerile. Disgusting and puerile it may have been, but she had obviously remembered it.

They poked around the shop but there was no sign of the white woman. Tebulot picked up a brass camel's bell from one of the shelves and shook it. Almost at once a door opened at the back of the shop and two Arabs appeared, both wearing dark glasses. They were dressed in green-striped *djellabas* and one of them wore a *fez*.

"We're looking for a white woman who passed through here," Kasyx said.

The Arab in the *fez* shook his head. "No white woman has passed through here, Lord."

"There was a white woman. I saw her myself."

"No white woman, Lord. But there are many white women at the Hotel Delirium."

"One special white woman, the dreamer of this dream," Kasyx insisted.

"No, Lord."

"Tebulot, Xaxxa, look in the back," Kasyx said.

"No, Lord! You may not look there!" the Arab cried out, lifting his hands.

"Why not?" Kasyx demanded.

"*Mektoub*, it is written."

Tebulot heaved his weapon off his back and tugged back the T-bar. "Sorry, buddy, but it's just been unwritten. Come on, Xaxxa, let's go take a look."

The Arab stared at them in hostility. "*Eshkoon?* Who are you?"

"The dreamer of this dream knows who we are," said Kasyx.

Tebulot and Xaxxa opened the door at the back of the shop and went through to the corridor behind it. Kasyx said to the Arabs, "Stay where you are," and followed them. Tebulot had already reached a large back room, windowless, lit only by *kinki* lamps suspended from the ceiling at different levels. At the side of the room, almost in darkness, there was a bed draped with a homespun woolen blanket. On this, still fully dressed but with her baggy *sarouel* pants drawn over to one side, the white woman lay, her eyes closed. An Arab girl crouched between her legs, a tinker's wife, a prostitute, her tongue lapping furtively like a cat's. The white woman's *solar topi* rested on a wooden table in the middle of the room on which there were plates of food: roasted spiced lamb, dates and *couscous*.

A thin boy sat on the opposite side of the room on a bright-turquoise cushion, playing the full-bellied Arab lute called a *gimbri*. The music was hypnotic and repetitive, the same glissando over and over again, to accompany the barely audible licking.

Now Kasyx knew why the Arabs had tried to prevent him from coming in here. They were the guardians of Andrea's innermost secret. No wonder his marriage had been so barren; no wonder he had suffered four years of coldness and isolation. Andrea had lived in Morocco for two years before she had taken up her appointment at Scripps. In Morocco she had obviously found the forbidden pleasures and secret satisfactions she was looking for, and she had never forgotten them.

Tebulot asked uneasily, "What are you going to do?"

But Kasyx had no time to reply. The white woman on the bed had opened her eyes and was staring at them, and in an instant the room, the bed, the boy and the tinker's wife had folded up like figures in a child's pop-up book and shrunk out of sight, a rectangle of patterned darkness flying in the wind. Instead of standing in the corridor at the back of a shop, they were out in the desert under a glaring sun and there was nothing but sand wherever they looked.

"What happened?" asked Xaxxa.

"My wife suddenly realized we were there," said Kasyx.

"Your *ex*-wife," Tebulot corrected.

Kasyx said, "Yes, my ex-wife. And judging by that, my wife that never really was."

"You don't want to feel bad about it, man," Xaxxa told him.

"I don't. I just feel embarrassed."

They shielded their eyes against the throbbing brightness of the desert, wondering which way to go. There were dunes upon dunes, ribbed by the wind and stretching for miles. And there was that extraordinary *sound* the desert made, as if it were a huge, distant dynamo thrumming on and on. It was the sound of heat and distance and wind blowing through the *foggara*, the mysterious underground waterways built by the people of the Sahara in the centuries before the white imperialists began to crisscross the sand.

Then, one by one, twenty or thirty horsemen appeared on the brow of a distant ridge, their outlines melted by the rising heat so they looked like a frieze cut out of thin, black tissue paper. They paused for a minute or two and while they did, Kasyx pressed his hand against his helmet and examined them close-up.

"Can't see their faces," he said. "They're draped all around with muslin."

"Are they armed?" Tebulot asked.

"Muskets of a kind," Kasyx replied. "Hard to tell what sort of firepower they've got though. Andrea never did like guns. Maybe they're just decorative."

In an extraordinary way, the sand dunes between the horsemen and the Night Warriors began to move up and down in a kind of carousel motion and the ridge on which the horsemen were standing was carried nearer and nearer, without the horsemen actually having to ride. Within a short time, the horsemen were standing only fifteen feet away, silent, unmoving, their hands on their saddle pommels, their heads completely hidden in *tegelmousts*.

"Allah akbar!" the tallest of the horsemen proclaimed. "There is no other god but Allah, and Mohammed is his prophet!"

Kasyx stepped forward across the sand, closely followed by Tebulot and Xaxxa.

"We're looking for a white girl," he said. In the dry desert air, the air that could turn the inside of a man's nose and throat into sandpaper, his crimson armor crackled louder than ever with static electricity.

"You are unbelievers," the horseman retorted. "We have come to escort you away from the desert, away from this land."

"No way, José," said Tebulot. "We came to look for our friend Samena and we're not leaving until we've got her."

Without warning, the horseman reached into the folds of his *djellaba* and whipped out a long, curved sword. *"Bismillah!"* he cried, his voice as harsh as a hawk's, and spurred his horse forward. Behind him there was a teeth-grating ring of steel against steel as twenty swords were drawn from their scabbards. They flashed in the desert sun like pieces of exploding glass.

Tebulot lifted his machine and fired a heavy bolt of energy. There was a crack that echoed and reechoed across the desert, and the horseman flared up into an incendiary ball of fire, leaving only a smudge of black smoke. His horse reared, whinnied and then broke into a thousand tiny bricks that scattered across the sand.

"Allah akbar! Allah akbar!" shrieked the horsemen, whipping their mounts toward the Night Warriors. But now Tebulot set his machine to fire a multiple spray and under a deafening fusillade of pure power, a dozen horsemen burst into flame and their horses shattered beneath them. As Tebulot reset his weapon, Xaxxa slid up and away to the left of the horsemen on a shining strip of energy, pulling down his protective face mask as he went. He curved thirty feet into the air and then came streaking down toward the Arabs, his knees bent like a champion surfer's, his body precisely

balanced, and as he flashed past them, he punched and kicked in a flurry so fast that seven horsemen were hurtled off their steeds before they could even take a swing at him with their swords.

"Night Warriors!" he crowed as he rode his energy strip up again and turned a loop high in the desert air. Only three horsemen were left and they were already yanking at their reins and turning their horses around to make their escape. Xaxxa whistled down on them as fast as a jet fighter and dropkicked the nearest of the three so he was hurled headlong into his two companions. All three of them collapsed to the sand in a tangle of *djellabas* and flying limbs.

Tebulot methodically fired a single shot at each of the fallen horsemen. Their robes flared up one by one and they vanished. Puffs of smoke blew across the desert. Kasyx walked across the sand, occasionally kicking one of the bricks that had so recently been horses. From a hundred yards away, Xaxxa came slowly sailing back toward them, six inches off the ground, holding his hands over his head like a boxing champion.

"Who *were* those dudes?" he asked as he came to rest beside Tebulot. "Don't tell me your wife sent them."

"Ex-wife," said Kasyx. Then, "No, I don't think she did. Her response to finding us inside her private dream was to hide, to run away. These horsemen were aggressive and ready to cut our heads off. They were sent by the Devil, if you ask me."

"So he's here somewhere," said Tebulot. "The question is, where?"

"He's back in that Arab city, in my opinion," Kasyx replied. "That's where my ex-wife's greatest guilt is located; that's the kind of place the Devil would find attractive."

"Question is, where is it?" asked Xaxxa. "I mean, she could even have stopped dreaming about it, in which case it won't even be there anymore."

But, strangely, they turned around and the city was only a half-mile behind them. Their thoughts about it must have drawn it closer, which made Kasyx realize that no matter how substantial anything appeared to be in a dream, it was really no more than a creation of the dreamer's imagination and that, as such, it could be moved, shifted and switched on and off as easily as the image from a movie camera. Tebulot glanced at him in surprise but Kasyx said, "Come on, while we still have the chance."

They entered the city by a wide gate at which crowds of leprous beggars sat and shook their wooden bowls for *dirhams*. Again they plunged into the twisting alleyways, pushing their way past children, merchants and hunched-up creatures in long woolen *djellabas*. They were about to give up the search as hopeless when a high, clear voice called out, "Lords! Are you seeking someone?"

They turned to their left to see a narrow alley between two buildings, cluttered with broken pottery and discarded bedding. At the end of the alley a stone staircase rose to a green-painted door outside of which stood a pale, handsome boy in a simple white robe and a white headdress, beckoning them.

Kasyx stepped forward. "We seek a white girl called Samena."

"She is here," the boy acknowledged. He turned and glanced inside the half-open door and then beckoned again.

"Could be a trap," Tebulot suggested.

"I don't see that we have any alternative," said Kasyx.

"Come on, man, they give us any jive, we can always beat the shit out of them," added Xaxxa enthusiastically.

"This guy definitely thinks we're the A Team," Tebulot complained.

In single file they went down the alley and climbed the stairs. The boy held the door open for them and they could smell the strong, cheap perfume that drenched his hair and his clothes, a favorite in the Sahara, *Bint es Sudan*. Inside the house it was stuffy and gloomy. Decorative shutters had been closed over the windows so that only a few thin flower patterns of sunlight shone on the blue-and-yellow mosaic floor and the figures who sat in heaps of dusty cushions around the walls.

One of the figures they recognized immediately and Kasyx felt a surge of sheer relief. It was Samena, blindfolded and gagged, her hands bound behind her back, but apparently safe and well. The other three figures were unknown to him: a fat European, unshaven, in a grimy white suit; a young man, his face covered in a muslin *tegelmoust*; and an older man, thin and elegant, either Moroccan or European, wearing a combination of tailored gray Savile Row jacket and baggy *sarouel* trousers. He was smoking a thin, clay-headed *sebsi*, a *kif* pipe, and the stony blankness of his eyes showed that his mind had already retreated into the dream within a dream.

Kasyx stepped down into the room and faced the three men. "I am Kasyx," he said. "I have come to demand the release of my fellow Warrior, Samena. Which one of you is the spawn of Yaomauitl?"

The European cleared phlegm out of his throat and gave Kasyx a buttery smile. "You have extraordinary bravado, my friend Kasyx. Are you not aware that any child of Yaomauitl is always closely watched by his father and that anything you do to the child, the father will repay seven hundredfold?"

"We are Night Warriors," said Kasyx. "We have no fear of Yaomauitl or of anything Yaomauitl can do."

"Then that tells me you are very inexperienced Night Warriors, my friend Kasyx. A Night Warrior who knew Yaomauitl well would take far more care than you. Turn around and see for yourself."

"Kasyx," Tebulot muttered, and Kasyx turned around.

The door through which they had entered had been locked. The handsome youth stood beside it, jangling the keys in his hand. Worse than that, between the Night Warriors and the door stood four tall creatures dressed in close-fitting black hoods and suits, with eyes that gleamed yellow and malevolent like the eyes of panthers.

"The Black Ones, the Afreets from the desert," the fat European explained nonchalantly. "They are the stuff of Arabian nightmares, the beings who wake up even the most Westernized of Moroccans in the middle of the night, sweating and trembling."

The thin man with the *kif* pipe began to repeat a *zikr*, a magic phrase that, endlessly chanted, would eventually take the *kif* smoker into a state of magical trance. Behind them the Afreets began to move forward, their feet silent on the mosaic floor. The fat European smiled and began to waggle his foot in time to the *zikr*.

"The Afreets destroy their victims by twisting their heads around until they are facing behind them. You can always tell the victim of an Afreet because his head is around the wrong way."

"Tebulot," Kasyx advised, "get ready to hit them and make sure you're quick."

"Give me a little more power," said Tebulot, and Kasyx reached over and grasped the machine-carrier's shoulder for a moment. The deep energy of Ashapola poured through his fingers and into Tebulot's body. The charge scale on Tebulot's machine glowed golden and he slowly pulled back the T-bar until it clicked into the fully armed position.

"It is a pity that the new generation of Night Warriors should die thus," smiled the fat European. He shook a cigarette out of an untidy paper package and scratched a match on the sole of his shoe so that it burst noisily into flame. "However, it is always the least-principled who survive."

"*Kaluakaluakalua!*" the thin man suddenly cried out in a high, penetrating voice.

The Afreets pounced forward, bounding noiselessly through the air as if they were shadows of invisible creatures. Tebulot swung around and let fly a dazzling burst of energy, a squiblike shower of detonating sparks and lancing fire. One of the Afreets screeched and tumbled over, his body ripped into cinders and tatters of fabric. Xaxxa swung up off the floor, sliding his feet upward until they were on the same level as his head, then hurtled himself around like a propeller. His feet caught a second Afreet in the back of the head, audibly snapping his neck. The yellow-eyed creature twisted and collapsed to the floor as if he were a marionette whose strings had been abruptly cut.

A third Afreet leaped on Kasyx, seizing his upper arms with hands that gripped like metal pincers. Kasyx heard his crimson armor buckle and felt the supernatural pressure of the Afreet's fingers against his muscles. But then he discharged a controlled burst of energy and his armor suddenly jumped alive with blue snakes of electricity. The Afreet shuddered and dropped to his knees, his hands burned and smoking. Tebulot turned and fired from the hip with his heavy machine, blasting the Afreet's head from its shoulders in a spray of ashes.

"Get that last one!" Kasyx shouted, but as Xaxxa twisted around on a corkscrew of glowing energy and Tebulot swung his weapon into place, the last surviving Afreet lithely rolled over behind Samena and seized her head.

"*Stop!*" roared Kasyx as the Afreet started to twist her head to one side.

The thin man said something quickly in Arabic and the Afreet stopped, its eyes smoldering like *kinki* lamps.

The fat European drew in a leisurely fashion at his cigarette and then slowly blew out smoke so it issued from his mouth and disappeared up his nostrils. "I see that you are not prepared to sacrifice the life of even one of your fellow Warriors," he said. "This makes you very vulnerable, does it not?"

"Tebulot," Kasyx instructed, "point your weapon at the one in the middle, the one with the scarves wrapped around his head."

Tebulot did as he was told.

"Full charge?" asked Kasyx.

"Ninety percent," said Tebulot. "Enough to wipe out everything standing in my line of fire for two miles. Including, of course, our pal here."

"Xaxxa," said Kasyx and indicated the fat European and the thin man with the *kif* pipe.

Xaxxa poised himself ready and said, "I can take 'em out before you can blink, man."

Kasyx now approached the young Arab in the *tegelmoust*. "Can I speak to you directly, spawn of Yaomauitl?" he asked. "Or are you going to persist in using these two interpreters?"

The young man raised his head slightly. Behind the veils of muslin, Kasyx could make out the chilling, slanted eyes of the Devil himself.

"We have been to San Hipolito and seen your father's tomb," said Kasyx unsteadily. "We know who and what you are, and we also know how to defeat you. Before another week is out, we shall have cornered your father Yaomauitl too, and believe me, he's going back to that box and that vault and this time he's going to stay there forever."

"You are accursed," the young Arab said in the coldest of voices. His breath fumed through the muslin as if the room were refrigerated. "You are a dog of Ashapola, and my father and my many brothers shall have revenge on you."

"Well, you can threaten what you like," said Kasyx, trying to sound confident. It wasn't easy because he was deeply afraid and he knew that Tebulot and Xaxxa were too, for all their nonchalance. "But if you don't let Samena go this minute, we're going to evaporate you, and that's a promise."

The young Arab said, "Very well, my friend. The finger-archer will be released. But let me warn you, you have made a serious mistake. It is not for nothing that my father Yaomauitl is known as the Deadly Enemy. We shall have our revenge on you, believe me; and the pain you shall suffer shall outweigh ten thousand times the pleasure you are feeling now that you have succeeded in freeing her. I promise you this, Kasyx, by all the torments of hell."

"Let her loose," Kasyx insisted. Tebulot drew back the T-bar of his weapon and lifted it to his shoulder so he could aim it more accurately.

The young Arab raised one hand to the Afreet. At once the Afreet released Samena's head and stood back, an evil shadow. Then the young Arab spoke quickly in Arabic to the fat European, who in turn spoke to the thin man with *kif* pipe. "The girl is to be released and the Afreet is to return to the world beyond dreams."

Positioning his cigarette between his lips, the fat European climbed to his feet and went over to Samena. He took a heavy clasp knife from his pocket and unfolded it, one eye squinched tight against the smoke that rose from his cigarette. All the while, Tebulot's aim never wavered from the young Arab in his enveloping robes and Xaxxa remained poised to strike if necessary at the thin man with the *kif* pipe. The fat European cut methodically through the cords that tied Samena's wrists and then untied the blindfold and the gag. She opened her eyes and stared at Kasyx and Tebulot in agonized relief.

"Oh, thank God!" she said.

Kasyx said to the young Arab, "Let's get rid of that Afreet, shall we?"

The young Arab nodded to the thin man, who recited his *zikr* again and the Afreet twisted and faded like smoke, as if it had never existed.

Kasyx went over to Samena and helped her up. Then he edged his way back behind Tebulot and Xaxxa, keeping his arm protectively around Samena's shoulders.

It was then that he felt the floor shift and stir beneath his feet. He knew what was happening. Morning was approaching and Andrea was gradually beginning to wake up. The North African dream would soon fold and collapse like imaginary *origami* and be forgotten forever in a blatant flood of Southern California daylight.

"Time for us to go, I'm afraid," he told the young Arab.

The young Arab raised his hands. "Revenge shall be mine. *Mektoub*, it is written."

Tebulot asked from the corner of his mouth, "Do you want me to blast him?"

Kasyx nodded and quietly said, "I'm going to draw the octagon now. Wait until it's right up above our heads, then let him have it. That way, if he tries to retaliate—if he *can* retaliate—we'll be well out of the dream."

Kasyx raised his arms and began to describe the electrical blue octagon; it reflected in the silvery face mask of Xaxxa's fighting-helmet and lit Tebulot and Samena in an eerie, supernatural light.

"Are you ready?" Kasyx asked Tebulot.

"One thing!" the young Arab called as Kasyx prepared to lift the octagon over their heads. There was little time left now. The integrity of the dream city was beginning to come apart. Dozing memories of other days in Andrea's life were beginning to intrude on the equilibrium of the building: sudden flashes of walks along the San Francisco Embarcadero; flickers of Paris; lectures at UCLA. Faces, voices, snatches of music. The floor began to ripple like water; somewhere the wailing of panpipes rose again to warn them that morning had arrived and that all through the Western time zones, in the minds of millions of sleeping people, whole imaginary landscapes were crumbling and vanishing, whole metropolises were collapsing. The Atlantis of the night was again sinking down into the seabed of the collective unconscious.

Tebulot lifted his weapon and aimed it at the young Arab's head.

"Fire when I give the word," Kasyx murmured.

But the young Arab said in a strange, strong voice, "You would not break the code of the Night Warriors, would you, *effendi?* The code of the Night Warriors honors a deal struck, and the deal you struck was to give me my life in exchange for your finger-archer."

He turned toward the door of the room and beckoned, and the pale, handsome boy who had first admitted them appeared. He was nudging in front of him the woman in the white *solar topi*, the dream personality of Andrea herself. In one hand the boy held a large, curved knife, and he was smiling.

"If you attempt to kill me, this lady will die too," said the young Arab.

Kasyx turned to Tebulot and then back to the Arab. "If you so much as touch her," he warned, "this dream will collapse, with you in it."

"Ah, yes, but at least I will take you with me."

Xaxxa said, "He's got us, man."

"Your black friend speaks the truth," the young Arab told Kasyx. "You have got what you came for, the finger-archer, Samena. Be satisfied with that."

Kasyx said, "If you so much as *touch* that woman—"

But now the dream was falling apart on all sides. Kasyx quickly grasped the hands of his companions and initiated the slow descent of the octagon to take them out of the dream and back to the real world. Behind the young Arab the wall of the room had disappeared. There was a beach there now, a windswept shoreline somewhere down East, where Andrea lived as a child.

A split second before the octagon descended in front of his eyes and blotted out his view, Kasyx saw the young Arab unwind the veils that covered his face, and for one heart-swallowing fraction of a moment he glimpsed the hideous face of Yaomauitl's embryonic son as it really was: bulbous, malevolent eyes; cheekbones and gristle and semitransparent skin; and a mouth that was stretched with two layers of developing teeth.

Tebulot dropped to one knee, ready to snap off a last shot if Kasyx ordered him to, but then they heard a thin, high, distinctive scream and Kasyx shouted, "No, Tebulot, leave it!"

"Henry!" Andrea shrieked. "Henry, for God's sake, don't leave me!"

Then the octagon touched the floor and they were back in Andrea's bedroom, looking at each other in shock and helplessness.

"Kasyx, there was nothing you could have done," said Tebulot. "Believe me, you did everything you could."

But Kasyx turned at once to the bed. Andrea was still asleep but she was mumbling, tossing, and thrashing her legs.

"That bastard," breathed Kasyx. "That *bastard!*"

"Wait," said Samena. "She's waking up."

Tebulot said, "You're right, look. She's opening her eyes. She's okay. Yaomauitl hasn't kept her hostage after all."

Kasyx stood over Andrea's bed, watching her gradually awaken. To Andrea, the Night Warriors appeared only as the faintest of ghosts, the subtlest of shifting outlines in the air. She frowned at Kasyx and tried to focus her eyes, but then Kasyx turned around and grasped the hands of his fellow Warriors and they rose up together through the ceiling of the house like vanishing memories.

It was past dawn as they descended through the roof of the house on Camino del Mar. Springer was waiting for them, cross-legged, meditating. His head was closely shaven now, revealing the bumps of his angular skull, and he was wearing a plain white-cotton robe, like a monk.

"Ah, you have brought back Samena," he said, rising to his feet. "Are you safe, Samena?"

Samena said shakily, "They scared me but they didn't hurt me. I'm not sure of where they kept me. They took me out of that desert in the first dream and locked me up in some kind of room that looked as if it was made out of fog. I sat there for hours and hours and then they came to get me again and I was taken to that room in Arabia somewhere."

"It sounds as if you were imprisoned during the day in the dream of someone who was brain damaged or in a coma," said Springer. "But at least you are free now and the Night Warriors are four again."

Kasyx said, "They tried to take my ex-wife Andrea too, but I don't think they succeeded. We saw her wake up normally."

Springer frowned at him. "You actually saw the Devil take her captive?"

Kasyx nodded. "Yes, but if he'd held her, she wouldn't have wakened, would she? She would have stayed asleep the way Samena did."

"No," said Springer emphatically. "There is a great difference between capturing someone's dream personality when he is inside his own dream and capturing someone when he is inside somebody else's dream. When he is inside somebody else's dream—as Samena was—his dream personality remains in the dream state because he is unable to return to his waking body. But when he is inside his *own* dream, he appears to wake up as normal and to behave as normal. The only difference is that when he goes back to sleep at the end of the day, his dream personality is still in bondage to whoever captured him the previous night. Your ex-wife is as much at the mercy of the Devil as Samena was."

"And he said he was going to get his revenge on you too, Kasyx," Xaxxa reminded him.

Kasyx looked at Springer anxiously. "Is there any way I can tell for sure that Andrea's dream personality is being held hostage? Can I tell while she's still awake?"

"There are ways. Can you get to talk to your ex-wife this morning?"

"I can try."

"If the Devil threatened revenge on you, you must," Springer said. "Yaomauitl is known throughout history for his callousness and his brutality. His offspring are just as cruel. When she sleeps tonight, believe me, he will torture or kill your wife's dream personality, which will have the effect of destroying her mind completely. Her body will live but her imagination will be extinct."

Kasyx asked, "How do I tell if she's been captured or not?"

"Go talk to her. It doesn't matter what excuse you make. Talk about anything you like. But in the middle of the conversation, make sure you ask the question, 'What are the seven tests of Abrahel?'"

"What good will that do?" asked Kasyx.

Springer laid a hand on his shoulder. "It is the first question of the Demonic Interrogation, which was devised by the Catholic Inquisitors to determine who was possessed by Satan and who wasn't. If her dreaming personality has been held hostage by the spawn of Yaomauitl, she will answer, 'The seven tests of Abrahel are his and his alone.' And she will refuse to say any more about it."

"But supposing she says something else altogether?"

"Then you will know that the spawn of Yaomauitl has failed to capture her. There are twelve questions in the Demonic Interrogation and every person whose soul is possessed *must* answer them."

"But what if she answers in the way that proves she's being held hostage? What then?"

"Then you have several choices. Either to leave her to the Devil's devices, in which case she will more than likely be killed; or to wait until nightfall and go to rescue her in the same way you did Samena; or to kill the spawn of the Devil himself during the day so he may no longer dream he has captured her."

"The Devil's under police guard at the Scripps laboratories," put in Tebulot. "How can we possibly kill him?"

Kasyx said, "I don't know. But we can try, can't we? Listen, Tebulot is staying at my place; he can come along to the laboratory with me and see if we can get access to the Devil. Samena, try to get some rest. You're going to have a difficult time today, going back into your body and trying to prove to your grandparents and your doctors that you're perfectly okay. Xaxxa, maybe I can call on you if I need you."

"Anytime, man," Xaxxa acknowledged.

The four Night Warriors talked for a while longer and

then first Xaxxa and then Tebulot broke free from the room and floated out into the daylight. Kasyx and Samena were the last to leave except of course for Springer, who prowled up and down at the far end of the room, thinking deeply.

Samena said, "I haven't really had a chance to thank you."

"What for?" asked Kasyx.

"For saving my life. That Devil was threatening to eat me alive. *Literally*, inch by inch."

"I guess you shouldn't always believe what Devils tell you, should you?"

Samena reached out and held his hand. "I was frightened, Kasyx. I was sure they were going to do something terrible to me."

"Did they talk to you?"

"They talked to each other all the time but not very often to me. There were always at least three of them—the fat man with the dirty suit, the thin man with the pipe and the Arab. But sometimes there were more, although I couldn't see who they were; their faces were masked behind those veils. The young Arab spoke to them in strange languages. I mean they weren't French and they weren't German and they weren't Italian."

Kasyx said, "None of them touched you?" It was the question any father would have asked his daughter after an assault and they were both aware of it.

Samena shook her head. "They swore at me, some of them. One of them tried to touch me but the young Arab warned him off."

Kasyx was thoughtful. "He needed you, that's why. He isn't yet ready to fight us. He isn't strong enough." He rubbed his hand against the side of his neck and then asked, "How many others do you think you counted?"

"At least ten," said Samena. "They were just the same, all wrapped up in those veils."

Springer put in, "That means at least ten of those original eels managed to dig themselves into the beach and survive. They must still be there now, gestating."

276

"In that case we'd better start digging them out," said Kasyx.

"You won't find them easy to kill," said Springer. "They are arch survivors, with a ten-thousand-year history of staying alive against all odds."

"I'll find a way," said Kasyx. "Believe me, Springer, I'll find a way."

15

Samena blew Kasyx a ghostly farewell kiss as they parted company over the rooftops of Del Mar. She would now return to her earthly body to recuperate after her ordeal as the Devil's hostage, and Kasyx would return to his earthly body and attempt to find out if Andrea had been captured by the Devil in Samena's place.

Samena turned toward La Jolla and flew like a wraith toward the university. The Sisters of Mercy Hospital was a large white building on the slope overlooking the freeway, with cedars of Lebanon standing around it and windows that reflected the hills and the traffic and the morning sky. Samena could feel the tug of her body somewhere within the hospital, and she allowed that tug to guide her down through the building's roof, its concrete floors, its electrical conduits and its air-conditioning pipes. At last she located the private room on the fourth floor in which her body lay comatose, connected to a saline drip and scores of electrical contacts that measured her heartbeat, respiration, blood pressure and the electrical impulses that flickered within her brain.

Although it was only six-thirty in the morning, her grandmother was there, sitting beside the bed watching her. There was a half-empty cup of coffee on the bedside table, which showed Samena that her grandmother must have kept a vigil all night. This fussy, irritating woman who had built her whole life around television soap operas had been watching over her, praying for her, ever since she had failed to regain consciousness yesterday morning.

Samena hesitated for a moment, the scene was so poignant. Her grandmother said nothing but sat with her hands clasped, her eyes red with tiredness and tears.

Slowly, silently, invisibly, Samena sank into Susan's

body. Susan's skull encased her mind; Susan's flesh enrobed her limbs. She waited with her eyes closed, feeling her muscles, her nerves, the blood that circulated around her arteries and veins, feeling the suppressed thumping of her heart.

And then she opened her eyes. Her grandmother's head was bowed and she was whispering something that sounded like the Lord's Prayer. Susan watched her for a while, then reached out her hand and said, "Grandma?"

Her grandmother slowly lifted her head. At first she couldn't believe Susan had spoken. Then she said, "Susan?" and clutched Susan's hand tightly, bursting into tears. "Susan, than God, you're awake! Nurse, she's awake! Oh, Susan, thank God! Thank God!"

Susan and her grandmother clung together and in spite of herself, Susan started sobbing too, releasing at last all the terror she had felt during her long day in the hands of Yaomauitl's bastard. She wept uncontrollably, and it was only when the doctor came in to see her and administered a sedative that she gradually settled down.

The doctor stood beside her bed and kept watch on her until she had stopped crying.

"You gave us quite a scare, young lady," he remarked. "We thought we might have lost you for good."

"I was just as scared as you were," Susan said.

The doctor gave her an uncertain smile. "I'm not quite sure what you mean by that."

"I just mean that I was scared too."

"You were unconscious, my dear. You can't actually be scared when you're unconscious."

Susan realized she was making things dangerously complicated. "I was dreaming, that's all," she told the doctor. "I was dreaming, and I was scared in my dream."

"I see. Like Dorothy in Oz."

"Yes," said Susan and thought to herself: If only you knew how right you are, Doctor. "Just like Dorothy in Oz."

* * *

Kasyx returned to his sleeping body barely in time to be awakened by his alarm clock. He sat up. There was a good smell of fresh coffee in the air and he suddenly remembered that Gil had spent the night at his cottage instead of going home. Henry stretched, pushed back his comforter and stood up. When he went through to the living room, he found Gil sitting at the table eating a large bowl of *muesli* and reading the paper.

"Ah, you're back," said Gil. "There's coffee in the kitchen. I just made it."

Henry poured himself a cup of coffee and then came back in. He sat down on the opposite side of the table and said nothing for a while, watching Gil read.

"Anything interesting in the paper?" he asked eventually.

"Padres licked hell out of the Braves."

"Well, that's one bit of good news."

Gil folded the paper and tossed it aside. "They've had more earth tremors down in Baja. Two winos were found dead in Balboa Park. Shamu, the killer whale, has been suffering from flatulence."

"Thanks for the précis."

Gil said, "I'm real pleased we got Samena back. I'm sorry about you ex-wife though."

Henry shrugged. "It had to be her, of all people. Still, I'm going up to the laboratory as soon as I'm dressed. Maybe she hasn't been taken over by that Devil after all. It happened pretty much in the very last second of that dream, didn't it?"

"That stuff about asking her that question," said Gil. "Do you think that's really going to work?"

"Don't ask me. But what else can I do?"

Gil was silent for a time and then he said, "You know something, Henry? This is all crazy. Here are you and I and Susan—and now Lloyd Curran too—risking life, limb and sanity to fight off some insane creature that appears only in people's dreams. I mean, why the hell should we?"

"You want to quit?" asked Henry.

"I didn't say that."

"Well, *I* don't want to quit," Henry said. "That creature we were fighting last night is only one out of ten, maybe a dozen. He's only a fledgling too. Imagine what kind of power he'll have when he's fully grown. He's going to get inside people's heads while they sleep and he's going to make them think and feel anything he damn well wants them to. Come on, Gil, we spend one third of our lives alseep. That creature and his brothers are going to be able to dominate one third of our existence, and probably the other two thirds too."

Henry stared at Gil steadily. "Somewhere, Gil—somewhere not too far away—Yaomauitl himself is prowling around, and he's impregnating more women with Devils every day. God knows how many he's managed to fertilize already. So think about it. Each woman has a dozen eels, each eel becomes a fully grown Devil within only a couple of months; how long, mathematically, before we have Devils in the *thousands* and those Devils are dominating the minds of nearly everybody in the country? Let me tell you something, Gil, this is nothing short of an invasion."

Gil said, "But why *us*, that's what I want to know! Why does it have to be *us* who have to try to stop it?"

Henry finished his coffee, looked at Gil for a moment and then turned and stared out the window toward the sea. It was a bright, sharp, glittery morning.

"I guess it has to be us because it was always written that it would be us. What did those Arabs say last night? *Mektoub,* it is written."

"You really believe that? I didn't think philosophers believed that."

"I don't think you want a long lecture on determinism and historical inevitability, do you?" smiled Henry.

Gil shook his head. "The point is, whether it's written or not, what are we going to do about it? I mean, what *can* we do about it?"

Henry said, "Do you want to drive me up to La Jolla? We can start by trying to find out if this creature's gotten any kind of hold on Andrea."

Gil checked his watch. "Let me call my mom and dad first. Then . . . okay, I'll drive you. If it's written, I guess it's written and there's nothing we can do about it."

They reached Scripps Institute of Oceanography shortly after eight. There were three police cars in the parking lot, which Henry took as a bad omen. Gil parked the Mustang and heaved himself out without opening the door. Henry sat in the passenger seat for a while and then awkwardly clambered out in the same way.

"Hey-y-y . . ." Gil complimented him. "*The Dukes of Hazzard* strike again."

They went into the marine biology department. It was cool, air-conditioned and almost silent. At the far side of a wide reception area a Mexican security guard was talking to a newly arrived receptionist. She kept saying, "Well, they won't even *think* of changing the lunch break, I know that. They won't even *think* of it. I've tried, I've tried asking them, but they won't even *think* of it."

Henry and Gil waited for a minute and then Henry noisily cleared his throat.

"Yes?" asked the receptionist, plainly irritated at the interruption.

"We'd like to see Dr. Andrea Caulfield, please," said Henry.

"Who shall I say wants her?"

"Her husband, if you don't mind."

"Ex-husband," put in Gil, and Henry dug him sharply in the ribs.

It was nearly ten minutes before Andrea appeared. She was wearing a white lab coat with a row of pencils in the breast pocket and her hair was severely tied back with a green ribbon.

"Henry," she said in an odd tone of voice.

"Hello, Andrea."

"What are you doing here? This is most peculiar."

"What's peculiar about it?" asked Henry.

"I—" Andrea began and then stopped. But Henry could see in her eyes the unspoken mystification she was feeling. Last night she had dreamed, and in her dream she had seen Henry, clad in extraordinary armor, and this unfamiliar youth who was now standing here next to him—here, in real life, among the potted plants of the Scripps Institute's reception area.

Henry said, "I wanted to know how the work was coming along."

"Work?" asked Andrea, still a little dazed.

"Your investigations . . . the creature they dug up on the beach."

"Oh, that. Well, we're waiting for two or three digestive experiments as well as a full electroencephalograph and some skin and blood analyses."

Henry thrust his hands into his pockets and tried to look affable. "I was wondering if you'd had any preliminary ideas, made any guesses about it."

"Henry, you know very well that I simply don't work that way . . . and listen, why on earth are you here at eight o'clock in the morning asking such peculiar questions? And who on earth is this?"

Henry turned around and looked at Gil as if he had never seen him before in his life. *"This?"*

"Yes, Henry, I—" she leaned forward and peered at Gil. "I'm sorry to sound rude," she said, "but have I met you somewhere before?"

Gil said, "I'm Gil Miller. Your husband, your ex-husband and me, we were the ones who found the girl's body on the beach." He put out his hand and Andrea rather distractedly shook it.

Henry asked nonchalantly, "Is there any chance that we could take a look at the creature?"

"A look?" said Andrea. "No, I'm sorry, that's out of the question. The police are here, guarding it. They've been here ever since it was brought over from the coroner's office."

"Surely a look won't do any harm," Henry persisted.

"I'm sorry, Henry, no. They won't allow it."

"Oh, well," Henry sighed, "I guess this is a wasted journey."

"Yes," Andrea agreed, still baffled. "I guess it is."

"You, er . . . don't happen to know when the police might release some information?"

"Henry, I don't understand why you're asking me these peculiar questions."

"You're right, they *are* peculiar," Henry told her, suddenly smiling. "Like—what are the seven tests of Abrahel?"

Andrea stared at him for what seemed like minutes. He could almost feel the world turning under his feet. She didn't even blink; her eyes remained fixed on him as if she were trying to set him on fire with X-ray vision. He stared back at her but it wasn't easy. There was such force in her eyes—or in whatever was concealed behind her eyes—that he could scarcely prevent himself from looking away, turning around and hurrying out of the building.

Gil sensed the tension between them and stepped back, a response he suddenly realized was one that Tebulot would have made, not Gil. And he could sense the evil too, the increasing coldness; and whether Andrea answered Henry's question from the Demonic Interrogation or not, he knew the Devil was here and that the Devil had possessed her.

"I—" Andrea began. Her voice was deep, thick and turgid as if her throat were filled with frozen slush. "The—"

Henry tried to smile, but his face was rigid. "The seven tests of Abrahel, Andrea? What are they? That's all I want to know."

"You . . . want to know . . ." Andrea said hoarsely, "if—"

"If what, Andrea? Come on, you can say it. Don't be

afraid. We used to be man and wife, remember? We shouldn't have any secrets, even now."

Terrified as he was, Henry stepped closer to her, until he was no more than a foot away. Andrea still didn't take her eyes from him, and now they were dark and glistening like the eyes of a predatory beast. He could feel the coldness pouring off her like liquid oxygen, that coldness those who have come close to Devils always remember: *"uerie cold, like unto yce."*

Andrea said, quickly and quietly, "The seven tests of Abrahel are his and his alone. Now go, both of you, and don't let me see you here again, do you understand?"

Henry rested his hand on her shoulder. She slowly turned her head sideways to stare at it but made no move to push it off.

"Andrea," Henry said, "I know all about your dream last night. I know what happened to you. I've come to help."

She looked back at him. "You *know* . . . how can you know?"

Henry smiled. There was enough residual energy in his body for him to warm her, to dissipate the coldness of Yaomauitl's bastard offspring. The Devil may have captured her dreaming personality but he had not yet captured her earthbound body, or her soul.

"It's hard to explain," Henry said, still smiling, "but all you have to know is that I understand what's happened to you and that I can help you."

"You're lying," she said. "You're *mad.*"

"Remember Morocco?" Henry asked. "Remember the back room of the shop?"

Andrea stiffened. She took Henry's hand and lifted it off her shoulder as if it were something inanimate: a hat, or a dead bird. Henry could tell there were two distinct forces inside her, tumbling, turning and raging against each other. Her indecision was catastrophic. She turned around and began to walk away, and then she turned again and began to walk back.

"You *can't* . . ." she said, "you can't *possibly*—"

It was then, however, that Lieutenant Salvador Ortega appeared from the direction of Andrea's laboratory. Today he was wearing a green-and-yellow-plaid sportcoat, green slacks and a green bow tie. He came up to Andrea in a matter-of-fact way, not noticing her intense agitation, and linked his arm through hers.

"Now then, Doctor, I'm going to start getting jealous. We were supposed to be running through these pathology tests, weren't we? And what do I find? You're out here making time with your husband-as-was."

Andrea tugged her arm away. For the first time Salvador realized that something was wrong. "Dr. Caulfield?" he asked. But Andrea stalked away, back to her laboratory, leaving Salvador with Henry and Gil and his own perplexity.

"What did I say?" he asked Henry.

"It was not what *you* said," Henry told him.

"Well then, what did *you* say? She was fine when she came in this morning; now look at her."

"Salvador," Henry said, "I want you for once in your career to stand logic and procedure on their heads. I want you to believe that what you've got in there—that creature—has already had a serious effect on my ex-wife's mind and that unless you destroy it—and I mean right away, now—it could very well kill her."

Salvador turned and looked back toward the laboratory. Then he asked, "Do you have any evidence of this, Henry?"

"What kind of evidence do you want?"

"Concrete evidence, Henry. Something in black and white that I can show to the chief of police."

"You know that's impossible."

Salvador folded his arms across his chest and gave Henry and Gil a brief, resigned smile. "John Belli's in there too. We're doing a complete forensic examination and trying to come up with some kind of explanation for this creature's appearance that will satisfy the media and the public and—most of all—us."

"Salvador, I beg you to kill that creature before nightfall. Do you hear me? I'm begging you. Otherwise Andrea will certainly die."

"He's telling the truth, Lieutenant," Gil added.

Salvador said, "I believe you. Can you understand that? I *believe* you. I don't know why, but I do. However, there's nothing I can do without substantive evidence. My hands are tied."

Henry ran his hand through his hair. "Is that your last word?"

"I'm sorry, yes, that's my last word. I don't have any alternative."

"All right," Henry said and reached out for Gil's arm. "Let's go, Gil. We have other fish to fry."

Salvador stood watching them as they left, his arms still folded. "I'm sorry, you know?" he called after them as they reached the revolving doors.

Henry nodded without answering, and they went back out into the sunlight.

"What are we going to do now?" asked Gil.

"For the moment, nothing. At least not as far as *this* Devil is concerned." Henry checked his watch. "But I want to come back here before they close at six o'clock. We're going to destroy this creature tonight, you and I, and that's all there is to it."

"You're going to break into the laboratory?"

"If I have to."

"Okay then," Gil said. "I'm with you. I may be nuts, but I'm with you."

"Let's drive down to Prospect Street," Henry said. "You know that little shell store down by the cove? I want to talk to somebody down there."

They climbed back into the Mustang without opening the doors and Gil swerved out of the parking lot and back toward Torrey Pines Road. The morning was clear and two students were flying Japanese fighting kites. The kites' tails swirled and corkscrewed in the warm, breezy air: indecipherable messages of oriental peace and contentment.

Henry found the man he was looking for outside the La Jolla Shellerie hanging a row of shiny pink conch shells from the store's front awning. A carousel of postcards whirled in the wind, making a clattering noise. The man was thin and rangy, with a bulbous nose and close-set eyes. He wore a striped T-shirt and a shapeless yachting cap.

"Good morning, Laurence," Henry said, climbing out of the Mustang.

"Good morning, Henry," Laurence said as casually as if Henry visited him every morning. He went on twisting wires around conch shells.

"How's business?" Henry asked.

"So-so," replied Laurence. "Had a busload of Episcopalian ministers here Thursday and sold out of sand dollars." Sand dollars were white, chalky shells supposedly marked with symbols representing the apostles and the life of Christ.

"Laurence," said Henry, "I was thinking this morning and I remembered something you told me about digging up clams."

Laurence narrowed his eyes and stared at Henry with caution. "Clams?" he asked, tying the last of the conches and propping his hands on his bony hips.

"You said you could detect clams under the sand by tapping the beach in a certain way."

"That's right. Clam-drumming, I call it. But it don't apply just to clams. Any creature under the sand you can detect the same way. Clams, crabs, mussels, lugworms, you name it."

Henry said, "How much would you charge for a day's detecting?"

Laurence shrugged. "Hundred maybe, hundred'n'fifty."

"All right then," Henry said. "How about today?"

"*Today?* What in hell are you looking for today?"

"Will you help me?"

Laurence looked at Henry closely, then at Gil, and then back at Henry. "What are you trying to dig up, Henry? Tell me that."

"I'll show you when we dig it up, Laurence. Otherwise you won't believe me."

"You're not looking for buried treasure? I only do living creatures. You need a metal detector for buried treasure."

Henry said, "We're looking for living creatures, Laurence. Hundred and fifty. And I'll throw in two bottles of Chivas Regal."

Laurence took a long, deep, thoughtful breath and at last he nodded. "Okay," he said. "Let me go get my stuff. Nancy can take care of the store for today. She always makes more money than I do anyway. She's hard-bit. She won't never give no tenderhearted discounts to small kids with not enough pennies for a sea horse."

Laurence collected a heavy, shapeless bag from the back of the store as well as a six-pack of Michelob with one can already missing, and a dry salami sausage. "Rations," he remarked laconically. He sprawled out on the Mustang's rear seats as Gil turned out of Prospect Street and back toward Del Mar.

"You and me haven't been fishing in a while," Laurence remarked to Henry as they roared down the long hill toward the beach.

"Been busy," said Henry.

Laurence made a face. He knew what Henry meant by "busy." "Drunk," that's what he meant by "busy." With one hand steadying his nautical hat, Laurence leaned forward and said, "Fishing in a small boat in a good strong surf is the world's A-number-one cure for a hangover."

They reached the beach where they had found Sylvia Stoner's body and parked. It had been almost a week now, and because no more eels had been discovered, the police barriers had been taken away. There were one or two joggers around, and a small gang of dedicated surfers, but as yet it was too early for the mother-and-baby crowd, and much too early for the school lunch-break brigade.

They walked across the beach, leaving imprints on its immaculately smooth surface. The tide was well out and still retreating. Clouds were reflected in the wet sand like fragments of a jigsaw puzzle.

"It would help to know what kind of creature you're looking for," Laurence said. "Is it big or small? Shellfish or worm?"

Henry shielded his eyes against the sun and looked around the beach, trying to remember where it was that the writhing eels had buried themselves.

"It's big," he said. "More like a lizard, I guess you could say."

Laurence wrinkled up his nose. "You're wasting your time in that case. Ain't no lizards on these beaches."

"You'd be surprised," Gil said.

"Lizards?" Laurence demanded. "You're putting me on."

Henry pointed to the sand in front of him and said, "Try rousting them out here."

Laurence lifted his bag off his shoulder. "If you say so. You're paying the money. But I can promise you one thing. If it's lizards you're after, you're going to be real disappointed. I never did see no lizards on these beaches, not once in forty years."

He hunkered down on the sand and began drumming on the beach with the palms of his hands. Gil looked across at Henry and raised a questioning eyebrow but Henry gave him a look that meant, "This may seem ridiculous, but bide your time and watch."

"Rousted some clams there already," remarked Laurence, nodding toward a slight disturbance in the surface of the sand. "See, what this drumming does is simulate the sound of the sea coming in and the clams get all excited and prepare to come up. Least that's the theory. Some people say it don't do nothing but irritate them, like a snake charmer tapping his foot irritates the snake and makes it come out of the basket. Snakes is stone deaf, same as clams. Never saw a clam with ears anyhow."

He kept up this bantering commentary as he moved crabwise in a wide semicircle, his left leg leading the way, his hands pattering on the sand in a light, insistent rhythm.

"Not everybody can do this. It's what you call an acquired skill. You remember Gene Krupa, the famous drummer? Well, he came down to San Diego once and he wanted to know how to do it but he couldn't work up that rhythm for anything."

Gil suddenly touched Henry's arm. "Look," he said. "Over there."

Only twenty feet away, in the center of the sloping beach, the sand was beginning to shiver and crack. Whatever was causing the vibration, it was at least three feet long, maybe longer, and it was moving deep beneath the sand with a restless, spasmodic, jerking motion.

Laurence peered at the movement and said, "Now that's something. I never saw nothing like that before."

He walked over to the patch of disturbed sand and prodded at it with the toe of his sneaker. "Now that's really something."

Out of his bag he took a small metal shovel that he used for digging clams. He began to quickly and methodically dig a narrow, deep trench.

"What did you say this was? Some kind of lizard? It's sure buried itself way down deep."

Henry and Gil waited by the side of Laurence's excavation, shivering slightly in the sea breeze. Their bodies may have been sleeping peacefully during their exploits in North Africa last night but their minds were tired; Gil would have done anything to go back to his own bed and sack out for the rest of the afternoon. But he was determined to stay by Henry. Between them, they were the core of the Night Warriors and if they didn't hold together, they might as well give up their fight against Yaomauitl and his buried offspring.

After twenty minutes Laurence suddenly said, "I got something. There's something down here all right."

"Laurence, be careful," Henry warned.

"Feels like something knobby," Laurence said. "That's right. Jesus, you're right. It's like the back of some kind of lizard or something."

He swung himself out of the hole in the sand and then stared down inside it. "Jesus, you see that? Well, you can't see too much of it but that mother's *big*. What is that, Henry? Jesus, that gave me a scare when I realized the size of it."

Henry said diffidently, "It's a kind of a lizard, that's all. Now do you want to fill in that hole in again? I just wanted to make sure it was down there."

Gil stared at Henry in surprise but Henry lifted his hand to indicate he knew what he was doing. Laurence sniffed, wiped his nose with the back of his arm and said, "You want to fill it in again? What in hell for? That must be some kind of rarity, that lizard. Must be worth something. They pay good money for specimens at Scripps, and at the San Diego Zoo too."

"Laurence," Henry insisted, "I want you to bury it."

"Could be a thousand dollars in a rare specimen like that," Laurence protested.

"Bury . . . it," Henry repeated. Laurence huffed, picked up his shovel and reluctantly obeyed.

Gil took Henry aside. "Why are we covering it up again? I thought you wanted to dig them up and kill them."

Henry nodded. "I *do* want to kill them but I've had a better idea than digging up all of them. You stay here; I'm going to see a friend of mine in the chemistry department at the university. You don't mind if I borrow your car, do you?"

Gil looked doubtful but Henry asked, "Have you seen me take one single drink this morning?"

"No, I guess not," Gil said and handed him the keys.

"Keep an eye on our friend Laurence here," Henry told

him. "As soon as he's finished covering up this Devil, get him to drum up some more. Cover the whole beach as far as the cliffs. When you find one of the Devils, mark the place with stones or something. I'll be back well before the tide starts coming in. You should be able to locate at least ten. That's about as many as I can remember and it tallies with what Susan said about the creatures in her dream."

Henry jogged off up the beach. Gil thrust his hands into his pockets and turned back to Laurence.

"You have any idea what the hell these critters are?" Laurence asked.

"Search me," said Gil. "I'm only the chauffeur."

"Strange guy, that Henry Watkins," Laurence observed. "Good fishing partner because he fishes and drinks and keeps his mouth shut. Last thing I like is a gabby fishing partner. But very brainy. I mean, at least as brainy as somebody like Einstein, if you ask me. I reckon if he didn't drink, he could've been famous. Could've won a Nobel prize or something like that."

He finished filling up the excavation, dropped his shovel onto the sand and went across to his bag to twist out a can of beer. He made no attempt to offer one to Gil. He popped the top and drank half the can without breathing.

"Want to roust out some more?" Gil asked after Laurence had finished the can, pressed the flat of his hand against his belly and loudly eructated.

"You're paying the money," said Laurence.

Gil stood by and watched with his hands in his pockets as Laurence slapped away at the sand in gradually progressing semicircles. Maybe Gil was just tired but it occurred to him that the dream world of the night and the waking world of the day were beginning to overlap. It was almost as weird pursuing the Devils out here on the beach in the sunshine and the wind as it was pursuing them through the labyrinths of people's nightmares. It was more frightening, too, in a way, because to go after them in daytime meant that they were real flesh and blood, not just the fractured pieces of somebody else's imagination.

What's more, he was unarmed and unarmored and if any of those Devils decided it objected to being disturbed by Laurence's drumming, there was nothing he could do to protect himself except run like hell.

Laurence suddenly said, "Here's another, and another."

Gil stepped forward. There were two shivering disturbances in the sand, close to each other. They were unmistakably similar to the first one they had located. Gil made a pattern of stones over each one. A crucifix, as if he were hunting vampires.

"I wish you'd tell me what these darn things are," Laurence grumbled. "It's unnatural to go clamming and not know what kind of critter you're after."

Gil said nothing but forced a smile. He was still smiling when Bradley Donahue appeared, weaving along the beach on his bicycle. He was wearing a T-shirt with "Let My Fingers Do the Walking" printed on it. He whistled when he saw Gil, and whooped.

"Hey, Gil, haven't seen you for *days,* compadre. Where you been?"

"Hi, Bradley. How are things?"

"Well, they're okay, I guess. You didn't come to Donna's party last night. Everybody was asking where you were. And guess who was there? Shirleen! You remember Shirleen, she used to go to school with the Kaiser brothers. Really enormous cakes. She went off with Jay McDonald, of all people, what a smooth-ass. I swear to God he puts rolled-up socks in the front of his pants to give himself profile."

Bradley stopped talking for a moment, looked around at Laurence and frowned. "Is that guy with you?"

"Kind of," Gil said.

Bradley leaned closer. His breath smelled of orange-flavored Bubble-Yum. "What's he doing or is it impolite to ask?"

"He's drumming up clams. He slaps the sand, see, and the clams come up to the surface."

294

"This isn't the season for clams, is it?"

"Not really, but we're practicing."

"I see," Bradley said, although clearly he didn't. He watched Laurence for a while longer and then said, "Where were you anyway? Your dad said you were staying the night someplace. Not with some lady of ill repute, I trust, I trust?"

"I was just doing some studying," Gil said uncomfortably. He realized how far he had grown away from Bradley after his experiences as a Night Warrior. He suddenly thought of firing his weapon up at those Monks of Shame and the way they had come fluttering down through the rain. He thought of those Arab horsemen flaring like magnesium.

"Hey, you coming to Ken and Lillian's barbecue tonight?" Bradley wanted to know.

But Gil didn't answer. His yellow Mustang had reappeared and Henry was making his way down the beach toward them, carrying a large glass carboy and a length of shiny glass tubing.

Bradley saw that Gil wasn't looking at him but at Henry, and suddenly he frowned. "Gil? What the hell is going *down* here, Gil?"

Gil slapped him on the back and tried to look cheerful. "Just a little experiment, that's all."

Bradley looked back at Laurence, who was still slapping the sand. "Experiment? What kind of experiment?"

"I'm sorry, I can't tell you. It's kind of secret."

"Can I watch?"

Henry came struggling up to them and set down the carboy on the sand. "Whew," he said, "that's darn heavy. There are two more of them in the trunk."

"Henry," said Gil, "this is my friend Bradley."

"Pleased to know you, sir," said Bradley, holding out his hand.

"Well, absolutely likewise," Henry replied tautly. "But do you think you could make yourself scarce? What we're doing here is rather . . . well, you know, unorthodox."

"You want me to leave?" asked Bradly, hurt.

Gil said, "I'll tell you what, Bradley. Go back to the store, help yourself to any magazine you like. Tell Dad I said it was okay and that I'll pay for it out of my allowance."

"You mean any magazine? *Hustler* or something?"

"You got it."

Bradley mounted his bicycle, waved, whooped and went wavering off. Henry said urgently to Gil, "I want to be quick, before any lifeguard patrols come past and ask what we're up to. How many embryos have you located?"

"Six so far. Laurence is still drumming away."

"Okay then, I want you to help me," said Henry. "This carboy contains concentrated sulphuric acid. I borrowed it on permanent unofficial loan from the chemistry department at the university as payment for a favor I once did for one of the lecturers. A horrible man called Kinsky."

"What are you going to do with it?" Gil asked.

"Very simple. Wherever Laurence has located an embryo, I'm going to push this glass tube down until it touches the Devil underneath. Then—with the aid of this funnel— I'm going to pour down a hefty beakerful of acid. Look . . . we might as well start here, where we dug up the first one."

"Do you think it's actually going to work?" Gil asked dubiously.

"My dear fellow, this stuff will burn its way through the trunk of a giant sequoia, from one side to the other. There isn't a creature alive that can withstand it."

Henry handed the glass tube to Gil, who hesitantly positioned it over the spot where they had found the first of the Devil's offspring. Slowly he pushed it into the soft sand, inch by inch, until he felt resistance against it. The sand shifted and cracked, and he knew he had located the Devil.

"Is that it?" Henry asked, and Gil nodded.

"Very well," Henry said, and he carefully filled a half-liter chemical beaker with the fuming, straw-colored acid.

Gil watched him as he fitted a glass funnel into the top of the glass tube and prepared to pour the acid down it.

"You're really sure this is a good idea?" he asked.

"It's the quickest and most effective way I could think of," Henry replied, his face grim.

"Okay then," said Gil. "You'd better do it."

Keeping tight control over his trembling fingers, Henry slowly emptied the beaker into the funnel. The funnel filled up for a moment and then gradually emptied as the acid drained down the tube and into the cavity where the Devil's embryo was concealed.

The last of the acid disappeared and Henry said, "All right now. Take the tube out." He was white with stress and he accidentally dropped the beaker onto the sand.

"Found another one!" Laurence called to them from across the beach.

"Thank you, Laurence," Henry replied. "We'll be right there."

Gil watched the patch of freshly dug sand. "Is it working?" he asked Henry. "What are we going to do if it doesn't work?"

But his answer came from the sand itself. Suddenly and frighteningly, it started to heave and boil, and to kick up in sprays. Henry and Gil stepped back and watched the commotion with increasing dread, but the creature did not emerge from its hiding place. Instead, it twisted and thrashed deep below the surface, invisibly, and there was no sign of its death agony but the sand furrowing, humping and rippling.

At the very last though, as the disturbance began to die away, Henry and Gil heard a scream unlike anything either of them had ever heard. It was a purely mental scream inside their heads, but it set Gil's teeth on edge as if he had been biting limes, and it cut through Henry's thinking processes like a sharp cleaver. Both of them shut their eyes tight as the scream went on and on, and in those moments of blindness both of them saw hell itself, the real hell of degradation and disappointment, pain and despair, the hell of cancer and fire and love gone cold. In the instant before the creature died, there was something else though, something that chilled them even more, something that wrapped their foreheads in wind-chilled sweat. It was a chilling sensation of mockery, of bloodthirsty taunting, promising that by killing the Devil's child they had achieved nothing whatsoever, only the bringing down on their own heads the revenge of Satan and his nine hundred and ninety-eight evil associates. The Devil's children were also the children of death, and so they returned gladly to the charnel house of hell. They could be tortured, they could be imprisoned, they could be burned into raw fat by concentrated sulphuric acid, but they could never truly be destroyed.

When the scream at last died away, shrinking into the back of their occipital lobes, Gil wiped his face with his hands and looked at Henry with undisguised fear and deep respect.

"Oh, boy. Yaomauitl is really going to go for us now, isn't he?" he asked.

Henry said, "It would seem so, if you experienced the kind of feeling I did. But I had a pretty good idea this would happen. These embryos are not real embryos, not in the sense that each one of them is a separate individual. At least I don't think they are. They're more like replicas, endless copies of Yaomauitl, which are closely connected through their unconscious minds with the master himself, their father. If one of them dies, if one of them gets hurt, Yaomauitl knows about it just as surely as if it had happened to him."

Gil looked around at Laurence, who was patiently standing beside another disturbance in the sand.

"That makes eight," he called.

"Are we going to kill them all?" asked Gil.

"Yes," said Henry. "Help me."

16

They left the beach when the tide came in. They had emptied two and a half carboys of concentrated sulphuric acid and burned eleven embryos beneath the sand. It was four-forty in the afternoon when they climbed into Gil's Mustang and turned around for La Jolla to take Laurence back to his shell store. The sky had clouded over and a cool wind was blowing off the sea.

They had twice been obliged to halt their acid-pouring when lifeguard patrols came past, and once during the lunch break, when a gang of school kids decided to make camp close by and to horse around on top of the very places the Devil's embryos lay concealed. But Henry had been patient and by four o'clock they had succeeded in destroying every one of the embryos they had located, and Laurence had drummed the beach for a second time to make sure they hadn't missed any.

Henry turned around in his seat and counted out Laurence's money. "I'll bring you the Chivas Regal tomorrow," he promised.

"That's okay by me," Laurence said, licking his thumb and counting through the bills, tidying them up and turning them around whenever they were upside down. "Just glad to be of service."

"One thing more," Henry added as they turned down Prospect Street. "I don't want you talking about what we did today. It wasn't exactly illegal but it wouldn't quite please the police department if they happened to find out about it. What the police don't know, the police aren't going to grieve over, if you get me."

"I get you," nodded Laurence. "Besides—to tell you the truth—I still don't have the first goddamned idea what you guys were actually doing."

"Good, let it stay that way," said Henry as Gil brought the Mustang to a halt outside the store. He climbed out of the car so Laurence could struggle out of the back, heaving his bag over his shoulder.

"Hasta la vista," Laurence said and disappeared inside the store, leaving the conch shells swinging on the awning.

"What do you think?" Gil asked as they drove back to Del Mar. "Do you think you can trust him?"

"Laurence?" asked Henry. "No, I don't think so. But find me somebody else who could have done what he did today."

Gil said, "There's just one thing . . . you kind of thought all of that acid thing up on your own."

Henry glanced at him. "I know what you're going to say," he answered. "You're going to say that I should have involved you from the moment I first thought about it. You're going to say two heads are better than one and four heads are better than two. You're also going to say that because I'm older, I seem to have taken charge of the Night Warriors and that I expect all of you to do whatever I tell you."

Gil thought about it and then nodded. "Yeah, that's pretty much it."

"Well," Henry said, "I've been thinking about it as much as you have and all I can say is I'm sorry. I should have discussed the idea with you earlier. I should have discussed the idea with *all* of you. Being a teacher, I'm used to being in control and I guess I expect to have things my own way automatically, without thinking. But from now on I'll try to give the Night Warriors the benefit of my experience without the authoritarianism that seems to come along with it."

"Henry," Gil told him, "I like you a lot. Don't misunderstand me."

"Well, I'm pleased about that because I like you too."

They returned to Henry's cottage, where Henry went through to the kitchen to make bologna-and-pickle sandwiches while Gil called Susan's house to see if she was home from the hospital.

"She's back," said her grandmother, "but the doctors say she has to rest for at least a week, and in three days she has to go to the clinic for more tests."

"I'm really pleased she recovered," said Gil.

"Thank you," said Susan's grandmother and Gil could hear that her tone had softened. "We praise the Lord that she's well again."

"Is it possible I could talk to her, just for a minute?"

"I'm sorry. Maybe tomorrow."

"Okay then. Could you just tell her eleven."

"Eleven?"

"It's a little joke between us, that's all."

"All right then. I'll tell her eleven, whatever that means."

Henry came in with the sandwiches as Gil put the phone down. "Any luck?" he asked. "How is she?"

"She's fine. She has to rest but she should be able to join us tonight."

"Excellent," Henry said. He took a mouthful of sandwich and passed the plate to Gil, saying, "Mmhh-hmmuhh, help yourself," with his cheeks crammed.

When he had eaten two sandwiches and drunk a large glass of milk, Henry checked the time. "I want to get back to the Scripps Institute before it closes. I'm afraid we'll have to play this one by ear since we don't know where they're keeping the creature or how well it's guarded."

"Do you have a gun?" Gil asked.

Henry shook his head. "I used to have a Japanese sword that my brother brought back from Tinian."

"My father has a gun behind the counter in the Mini-Market. A three-fifty-seven Python."

Henry thought about this and then slowly shook his head. "It's too risky, carrying a gun. Far too risky."

"Well, how else are we going to kill this creature? Chop

its head off? An ax is going to be a lot more conspicuous than a gun."

"Maybe you're right," Henry agreed. "But the question is, how are you going to get hold of the gun?"

"What's today? Thursday, right? Tonight's the night my father goes off early, to his sports-club meeting. I can get in there, lift the gun and nobody will even notice."

Henry picked up a slice of pickle that had escaped from one of his sandwiches and popped it in his mouth. "Well . . . very much against my better judgment—"

"There's something else," said Gil. "Why don't we get Lloyd in on this? He looks like he's pretty athletic and pretty bright. I think we ought to involve him too."

"Do we know where he lives?" Henry asked.

"Not far, somewhere on Lomas Santa Fe Drive, I think he said. I'll look it up in the telephone directory."

So it was that a little after five they left Henry's cottage and drove to the Mini-Market at Solana Beach, where Gil handed over his Mustang to Henry and went into the store. Henry then drove over to Lomas Santa Fe Drive and pulled up just past the fire station at a small, white-painted house with a green roof and green shutters. He made sure nobody was looking and then he hopped out of the Mustang without opening the door.

He walked up the short, sloping driveway and rang the chimes. After a minute or two, a black woman in a purple-and-white dress answered the door and stared at him suspiciously. "Yes?" she asked.

"You're Mrs. Curran?" he smiled, straightening his necktie.

"That's right. What do you want?"

"I'm looking for Lloyd Curran. My name is Henry Watkins and I'm a professor at the University of California at San Diego."

"What do you want with Lloyd?"

"I was talking to him yesterday. We were discussing educational prospects, university degrees, things of that sort. I have some information he asked for on university curriculae."

Mrs. Curran stared at him without saying a word. Then she turned back into the house and called, "Lloyd! Some professor wants you!"

Lloyd came to the door wearing a bright-red T-shirt and smacking his fist into a catcher's mitt. He didn't recognize Henry at first but then Henry lifted his hand in the unique salute of the Night Warriors, palm facing behind him, and Lloyd suddenly understood that he was receiving a house call from Kasyx, the charge-keeper.

"Hey, come on in," he said but Henry could hear the sounds of television, rock music and arguing children inside and he shook his head. "Just come out and sit in the car for a minute. We can talk there."

"Well . . . okay," Lloyd agreed reluctantly. They walked down the path together and climbed into the Mustang. Lloyd ran his fingers over the custom dash cut out of machine-turned aluminum and the special sport steering wheel and said, "Are these *your* wheels, man?"

Henry shook his head. "I haven't driven my own car in years. Up until the time I was initiated into the Night Warriors . . . well, I had a little drinking problem."

Lloyd was obviously impressed by Henry's candor. He said, "I smoke a little *ganja* now and again, but . . . you know, nothing heavy."

"When you're a Night Warrior, you don't need anything like that," said Henry. "The high comes with the power. Your slide-boxing is something special."

Lloyd asked, "Can I tell you something?"

"Go ahead."

"Last night in that dream I was scared. I mean I was really-truly scared."

"You had every right to be."

"Well, I know that, man, but the strange thing is, when I woke up this morning, I felt disappointed. I felt that I wanted to be back there where the action was. I couldn't believe it but that was the way I felt. I was scared but I loved it. I felt like I was really somebody, doing something."

Henry smiled and nodded. "You were," he said.

"How about your ex-wife?" asked Lloyd. "Are you going to try to rescue her tonight?"

"I'm going to try to rescue her now," Henry told him. "In a minute Gil and I are driving up to the Scripps Institute to kill the creature we met in that dream last night. We were wondering if you would care to join us."

"You mean—without being a Night Warrior? Just as me? No armor, no slide-boxing?"

"Just as you," said Henry. "The only weapon we're taking with us is a gun, and the sole purpose of carrying that is for executing the creature, nothing else."

Lloyd blew out his cheeks and drummed his fingers rapidly on his knee. "You're talking about breaking the law, man."

Henry said, "Yes. But then again, no. We—you, me, Gil and Susan—we are the only people who truly understand the danger of what is going on here. For that reason we have to think of *ourselves* as being the law. Vigilantes, do you see, whose duty it is to protect the world from the Devil."

Lloyd said, "We're taking a gun?"

"That's right."

"And we won't have none of that armor, none of those special skills?"

Henry shook his head.

"Okay then," Lloyd agreed. "You can count me in. Just let me go tell my mom I'm going to be late."

Henry waited in the car. There was some argument between Lloyd and his mother but eventually he came skipping out and climbed into the car again.

"Everything all right?" asked Henry, starting up the engine.

"Mom thinks I'm a kid still. She don't like spooks neither."

Henry U-turned the car and headed back toward Solana Beach. "I don't think anyone ever called me a spook before," he said with an odd sense of satisfaction.

They picked up Gil by the Santa Fe railroad crossing. He was carrying a brown paper sack full of groceries. He waved and ran across the road to meet them.

"Did you get the gun?" Henry asked, heaving himself into the passenger's seat.

Gil lifted a box of Cheerios out of the sack. "Right inside here," he smiled triumphantly. "I told Mom I was staying at your place for another night to revise an English assignment and that we needed some groceries."

"She doesn't object to your staying?"

"Not at all," Gil said, driving the Mustang across the highway. "Once I convinced her you aren't a faggot."

"Thanks for nothing," Henry said.

It took them another fifteen minutes to reach the Scripps Institute. One of the police cars was still parked in the lot but apart from that, the building and its grounds were almost deserted. Henry told Gil to park at the far end of the parking lot, under the shadow of a cypress tree where it would be out of sight from the main entrance to the marine biology department.

"I'll walk in and ask to speak to my wife," said Henry.

"Your ex-wife," Gil corrected him.

"That's right," Henry smiled. "Then I'll walk through to the biology laboratory and as I pass by, I'll open that emergency exit right there—that brown door, you see it?— from the inside. As soon as you hear the door click open, get yourselves inside as fast as you can but don't close the door after you. I'll go back to the reception desk, say that I've finished talking to my, uh, ex-wife and sign out. Then I'll come around to the emergency exit and let myself back in."

"What do we do once we're in there?" Lloyd asked apprehensively.

"To your right, about thirty feet along the corridor, there's a broom closet. Hide in there until I join you."

"That emergency exit, it doesn't have an alarm on it, does it?" asked Gil.

"Not the last time I used it. Soon after we were divorced, I snuck into the laboratory to steal back my gold fountain pen. Andrea never realized it was me who took it. She was always complaining about how dishonest the laboratory staff is."

"What about the gun?" asked Gil.

"You're the gunner, you take it. Tuck it into your belt, at the back, and just make sure you don't sit down too quick. The last thing we want is an assless Warrior."

It was seven minutes of six, almost time for the marine biology department to close. Henry marched inside and Gil and Lloyd watched him through the window as he spoke to the receptionist. At first the receptionist seemed reluctant to let him through, but then they saw Henry sign the visitor's book and make his way back toward the laboratory. They loped over to the emergency exit and waited beside it for him to open it.

"Supposing he gets caught?" Lloyd wanted to know.

Gil turned and looked at him. "Then, my friend, we are well and truly fucked."

But it was only a minute before the brown door abruptly clicked open. They looked around quickly and dodged inside, pulling the door to behind them but not quite closing it. Inside, the corridor was white and fluorescent and smelled of institutional floor polish. On the walls there were framed photographs of dolphins, narwhals and squid.

Their sneakers squeaking on the polished floor, Gil and Lloyd hurried to the broom closet and let themselves in. Gil tripped over a bucket, and when a mop slid sideways down the wall and clattered onto the tiles, they held their breath but nobody came to investigate.

"Next time why don't you just yell out, 'We're here!' " Lloyd whispered.

"It was an accident, for Christ's sake."

They waited for a few minutes and then the closet door

suddenly opened and Henry came in, gasping and out of breath. He nearly knocked over the mop but Gil managed to catch it.

"Security guard was taking a look around," Henry panted. "I had to jog around the building and come up behind him."

"Man, you're not fit at all," said Lloyd.

"You don't need to be an Olympic gold-medalist to teach Kant," Henry retorted with a small show of bad temper. Exertion always made him irritable.

They stayed in the broom closet for almost a half-hour. They heard doors slam, footsteps squeak on the corridor floors and people call good night. Eventually the corridor lights were dimmed and Henry eased open the door and looked out.

"It's all right now. It looks like everybody's gone home."

They walked softly along the corridor until they reached a short staircase on their left with a notice that read "Marine Biology Laboratory—Spectator Seating."

"We'll go up there," Henry said. He remembered Gil's words about always taking charge and added, "If you agree that it's a good idea, that is. There's a balcony there, overlooking the main laboratory. We'll be able to see exactly where the creature is being kept and where the police guard is situated. Then we can discuss how we're going to take the creature out."

"Sounds okay to me," said Gil.

"Me too," Lloyd agreed, and they crept up the stairs until they reached the swinging doors that led out onto the balcony. Through the small, wired-glass windows in the top of the doors, they could see that the laboratory was still brightly lit. Henry held them back for a moment and then eased open one of the swinging doors so he could see the laboratory's main floor. Gil and Lloyd crowded close behind him.

There, below the railing of the balcony, lay the laboratory, about fifty feet square, white-tiled and gleaming.

There were three long, varnished benches stocked with test tubes, chemicals, pipettes and flickering Bunsen burners. At the far end of the room an IBM computer terminal flickered and glowed next to a microfiche retrieval display. To the right, up against the wall, rows of steel shelving held scores of aquarium tanks. Most of the tanks were empty but some of them contained shoals of tropical fish swimming back and forth like showers of brightly colored needles, and turtles dipping and diving in search of food.

In the center of the laboratory stood a large dissection table, flooded in light by bright overhead spots. On this table, facedown, a sinewy black creature lay, its face turned toward Henry and Gil and Lloyd, its eyes closed, its scaly body shining in the light. Andrea was standing over the creature, peering up at an X-ray transparency. She was wearing her reading glasses and she looked tired and drawn. A little farther away, sitting on the edge of a tilted laboratory stool, talking quietly to a uniformed policeman from the San Diego police department, sat Salvador Ortega.

Henry carefully let the swinging door close again. He turned to face Gil and Lloyd and asked, "Well? What do you think?"

Lloyd shook his head. "We don't have a chance the way things stand. If we came down that balcony waving a gun, those cops would waste us before we could make it anywhere near enough to make sure of that beast."

"I agree," Gil said. "We can't risk using the gun until the police are out of the way."

"That means a diversion," Henry said. "Something to get them out of the laboratory just long enough for one of us to nip in there and blow that creature's brains out."

Lloyd said, "I hate to ask at a time like this, man, but what happens after we've blown that creature away? Those cops are going to run us in, right? I mean if we kill that thing, isn't that murder?"

"Not murder, no," Henry assured him. "The creature isn't human, after all. The worst they can get us for is illegal possession of a firearm and tampering with police evidence."

"Those are still offenses, right? They can still lock us up?"

"Well, yes," said Henry uncomfortably. "I suppose they can."

"In that case, I pass," Lloyd said. "I don't know about you guys but I'm not going to be locked up in no cell for nobody, and especially not for the ex-wife of somebody I don't hardly know."

Gil said, "Henry, he may be talking sense. This may not be the right way to do it."

Henry looked from one to the other, thoughtfully. "We have to destroy that creature in some way," he said.

"Well, listen, I've got an idea," Lloyd said. "If you can get everybody out of that laboratory for just about a minute—your wife, the cops, everybody—maybe I can jump down off the balcony and hit it with something, crack it on the head."

"How about setting fire to it?" Gil suggested. "There are Bunsen burners down there, and bottles of methylated spirits. Maybe we could make it look like an accident."

Henry went back to the window in the swinging door and peered down into the laboratory. "You may have a good idea there, Gil," he remarked. "There are two bottles of pure alcohol on the examination table itself. All you would have to do is knock one of them over, make sure the creature is drenched with it and then set if afire. It may not look like a very *likely* accident but there's a good chance nobody could prove anything different."

He turned around. "But it won't be as quick and as effective as a gun."

Gil lowered his head. "Well, I know, but I guess I wasn't too keen on using the gun anyway. I know it was my idea but if my dad found out I'd borrowed it . . . well, he wouldn't trust me again, ever. Especially if I used it to shoot somebody, or something."

Henry nodded. "I understand. Let's see if we can't burn it."

Five minutes later Henry knocked on the doors of the laboratory. "*Andrea!*" he shouted. "Andrea, are you in there? *Andrea!*"

The doors were opened immediately by Salvador Ortega. "Professor Watkins, what are you doing here? This building is closed for the night."

Henry tugged at his sleeve. "I have to see Andrea . . . to warn her."

"Come on, Henry," Salvador cajoled him. "This isn't the way to behave."

Henry seized Salvador's lapels and stared wildly into his face. "Salvador, listen to me. You have to listen to me! Andrea's going to die! You mustn't let her touch that creature anymore! It's going to kill her!"

"Who's that?" called Andrea. "Henry, is that you?"

"Oh, Andrea," Henry babbled. "Andrea! Andrea! I always loved you, didn't you know that? You mustn't touch that creature anymore! You must run, flee! I loved you when I was married to you, Andrea, and I love you now!"

"You're drunk," Andrea said coldly.

"I'm not! I'm sober! I'm stone-cold sober! Smell my breath! Go on, smell my breath! *Haahhhh!* Did you smell that? *Haaahhh!* There you are, nothing but garlic, and that came from two bologna sandwiches."

Andrea came out into the corridor with Salvador. "Henry, listen," she said, "I don't care whether you're drunk or not. I'm a busy person and I have four skin tests to complete tonight before I go home. So would you please be good and go back to your cottage and submerge your senses in whatever brand of distilled grain you happen to be favoring this month."

Henry gripped her lab coat and wound his hands around it. "Andrea, I love you! Haven't I always said so? You mustn't touch that creature anymore! Promise me! Promise!"

Salvador opened the door of the laboratory and called out, "Officer, would you escort this gentleman out of the building. I think he's suffering from nervous strain, not to mention too many vodkatinis."

The uniformed officer came out of the laboratory with a grin, his thumbs tucked into his leather belt. "Yes, sir," he said to Salvador, and then turning to Henry, "Come along, pal. I think you've overstayed your welcome."

Henry glared at him. "Pal? I'm no pal of yours, you uniformed chump! Did you hear that, Salvador? This police officer claimed that he was a pal of mine, or at least that I was a pal of his. Do you know what a serious offense that is? Referring to a member of the public in an overly amicable manner in an attempt to secure his cooperation to waive his rights under the Constitution."

Salvador put his arm around Henry's shoulder. "Come on, Henry. I don't know what this act is all about but it's time to go. I don't want to have to take you down to the cooler, do I? It wouldn't look good in the papers. 'Famous Philosophy Prof in Pokey.'"

Henry melodramatically slapped one hand against his heart. He arched his head back and rolled his eyes. "Aaagh!" he shouted. "Aaagh!"

"Henry, what is it?" Andrea asked anxiously. "Henry!"

Henry allowed his knees to buckle and he took five or six steps around the corridor with his legs bent. As he came around for the second time, he glimpsed orange flames leaping up inside the laboratory and knew his diversion had worked. Lloyd had managed to jump down from the spectators' balcony and splash the creature with alcohol.

"Henry—" said Andrea but before she could say anything else, she was interrupted by an ear-splitting screech. She and Salvador whipped around and the police-man flung open the laboratory door.

"Oh, my God!" Andrea cried. "Oh, my God, the poor thing's on fire!"

They burst into the laboratory. To Henry's horror, the

Devil creature was sitting up on the dissection table, flames pouring out of it like a sacrificial Buddhist, its slanted eyes blazing crimson, its double layer of teeth stretched back in agony, and it windmilled its arms so the flames made a flaring, roaring noise. Henry glanced up toward the balcony but Lloyd and Gil had disappeared.

"Fire extinguisher, for Christ's sake!" Salvador yelled. He tore off his sportcoat and approached the blazing creature like a matador, trying to avoid its circling arms.

The creature screamed and screamed, and in every scream Henry could hear the clashing of hell, the fury of fire, the agony of torture. The screaming was so piercing he wasn't even sure it was audible.

Salvador tried to dance in closer but the heat was already unbearable. It was astonishing that the creature was still alive and able to scream. Its black flesh crinkled and crackled like paint being stripped by a blowtorch; flames gushed out of its chin like a beard of fire; grayish brains began to bubble out of its ears.

"Where's that fire extinguisher?" Salvador roared. He made a pass at the creature, holding out his sportcoat, and over the smell of charring flesh they could smell the distinctive odor of scorched wool.

But before the policeman could reach the dissection table with the extinguisher, every fluorescent light in the laboratory exploded, showering them with broken glass. Ghostly flickers of blue light danced momentarily on the ceiling and then the laboratory was drowned in darkness except for the fiery Devil itself. It rose up, blackened, on the dissection table until it was standing on its hind legs like a goat. Its eyes were burned out, its bare bones gleamed through its incinerated flesh, but it stood there before them still blazing, still mocking them, still defying them to come nearer.

With a succession of ear-splitting crashes, the aquaria along the wall of the laboratory burst open. Henry heard water splash onto the floor and the desperate flapping of suffocating fish. Then, one by one, the Bunsen burners flared with gas and exploded; and immediately afterward every test tube, pipette and bottle smashed into thousands of pieces of hurtling glass.

"Out!" yelled Salvador. "Out!"

Henry awkwardly pushed Andrea toward the door but as she reached it, she turned and screamed at him, "It's locked! I can't get out! Henry, it's locked!"

Henry looked desperately around for something to beat the door open with. He picked up a lab stool by its legs and bashed it at the wooden paneling once, twice, three times. At the third blow the stool's seat flew off and he was left with nothing but a handful of sticks.

Salvador, his coat still held up in front of him, made a last effort to smother the creature's flames. The policeman had managed to bring the fire extinguisher forward but the mechanism seemed to be jammed and he was hitting it again and again with the butt of his revolver.

The scene in the darkened laboratory was like a grotesque marionette show. A small, screaming figure standing on a stage gushing with flames while nobody could do anything but stand around and watch helplessly. The room was filling with thick, black smoke now, choking their noses and filling their throats with the sickening odor of burning bone.

Salvador turned in horror to Henry and shouted, "Can't you get that door open?"

"It's locked!" Henry shouted back. "I've tried breaking it down but it's too solid!"

"We'll have to climb onto the balcony!" Salvador said. But as he lowered his sportcoat and took a step back toward them, there was a sudden rush of flame and the burning Devil leaped off the dissection table and clung to him like a child clinging to its father.

"*Madre mia!*" Salvador shouted and frantically clawed at the creature. But it had wrapped its arms tightly around his chest and was digging its claws into him. His cotton shirt scorched and suddenly flared and he staggered back three or four paces, the Devil still hugging him tightly.

"Help me!" Salvador screamed. "Help me, for God's sake, help me!"

The policeman circled warily around Salvador. Henry glimpsed his terrified face in the light of Salvador's burning shirt. But then the creature lashed out with one of its claws so quickly that Henry saw nothing but a semicircular rush of fire. Its claws caught the flesh of the officer's face and ripped off everything below his eyeballs with a sound like a tearing sack. The officer's hands jerked up to his face in a reflex of agony and horror, and then he collapsed into the darkness.

Salvador wrestled with the Devil and fell suddenly silent now in the depths of his unbearable pain. But the more he struggled, the tighter the burning Devil clung to him. Salvador's hair burst into flame and Henry watched in morbid fascination as it curled and shriveled and his scalp turned patchy and red. Salvador didn't scream even though the Devil's thigh bones burned through to his pelvic girdle and the Devil's claws penetrated his back.

It was then that the laboratory doors swung open and Gil and Lloyd appeared, Gil holding his father's gun. Gil said, "Christ almighty!"

Henry turned to him and shouted, "Give me that!" His voice was almost hysterical. Gil handed him the gun without argument. Henry cocked it and walked up as close to Salvador and the Devil as he dared.

Over the Devil's blackened shoulder blade, Salvador caught sight of Henry lifting the revolver. He nodded his mutilated head up and down in silent supplication. Kill me, *por favor*. Henry held the heavy pistol in both hands, his aim wavering for a moment, and then fired. The recoil was voluminous; the laboratory bellowed with echoes. The top of Salvador's head burst open like a pot of red chili that had suddenly boiled over and he dropped back against one of the benches and then onto the floor, the Devil still clinging to his chest.

The blazing Devil turned, thwarted of Salvador's living

soul, looked up at Henry and screamed again, a vast carrion-crow scream that chilled Henry from his head to his toes. Its claws released their hold on Salvador's body and Henry heard them scratching on the tiles.

He fired once more. His ears sang. The Devil's chest flew open like an exploding bird cage and blazing fragments spewed in all directions. Henry fired again and the Devil's skull was smashed. He fired twice more and at last the creature was nothing but pieces of burning bone.

A wind began to blow. Softly at first, stirring the ashes of what had once been Yaomauitl's bastard child. Then stronger and louder, in a low, doleful shriek like the mistral that blows down the Rhone-Sâone valley in France, eventually driving men mad with depression, or like the sirocco that blows across the Sahara, its flying grit turning glass windows into blind, opaque stones.

Henry lifted his head, his gray hair blown wild by the wind, his eyes watering with heat and emotion.

"Yaomauitl!" he shouted. "Yaomauitl!"

But then the wind died away, whispering into the corners of the laboratory, and Henry knew that Yaomauitl had departed. He turned around and looked at Gil and Lloyd and Andrea, and outside he could hear footsteps approaching along the corridor, and the sound of police sirens.

He laid his hand on Gil's shoulder. Gil stared at him in shock.

"It wasn't your fault," Henry said hoarsely. "Nobody could have known what that creature was going to do."

Gil pressed the back of his hand against his forehead. "It was burning," he said. "It was burning and it wouldn't die."

The officer whose face had been ripped off by the creature's claws started to moan somewhere in the shadows.

Lloyd said, "Oh, my God. It's a real Devil, isn't it? I mean a real, actual Devil."

"Yes," Henry replied. He was conscious that Andrea

was looking at him fixedly, her glasses clenched in her hands.

"Henry," she said in a trembling voice. "Henry, what happened here?"

"You were examining that creature," Henry said. "You must have known what it was."

"I had no idea, Henry. The tests we managed to complete showed that it was nothing more than a kind of amphibian . . . a kind of urodela, like a salamander or a siren. Very highly developed, of course, but—"

"A Devil," Henry interrupted her.

"What?" asked Andrea, perplexed.

"What are the seven tests of Abrahel?" Henry asked her, his voice choking.

"The what? Henry, you asked me that before. I don't know. What on earth are you talking about?"

Henry said, "You're saved, Andrea. You don't know it, but you're saved."

At that moment an arc light suddenly flooded the laboratory and Henry realized that the place was crowded with police, medics and firemen. A policeman came up to him, prized the gun from his hand and said, "Okay, sir. I'll take that."

17

Springer was a woman that night. She wore a complicated gown of white taffeta and silk with a high, ruffled collar and a triangular bodice of pleated lace embroidered with white seed pearls. It looked as if it had been created by the court dressmaker of Queen Elizabeth I in conjunction with the Emanuels.

When they were assembled and transformed into the accoutrements of Night Warriors, she said, "You have been rash."

"We have killed all of Yaomauitl's offspring," Kasyx retorted defiantly.

"You have killed the offspring that came from the body of Sylvia Stoner, but there will be others as long as Yaomauitl is free."

"We know that," Gil said. "That's part of the reason we did it."

Xaxxa put in, "We could have spent years hunting for Yaomauitl without finding him. You know that. Dream after dream with no luck at all. The only reason you found that Devil son of his last night was because you knew where to look."

"Same as the night before," said Samena, "the night you sent us into Mr. Lemuel Shapiro's nightmare with no hint of a warning."

"So what we've done now is, we've made Yaomauitl mad," Xaxxa said. "We've made him *so* mad that he's going to come looking for us instead of the other way around."

Kasyx added, "We plan to bushwhack Yaomauitl, if that's the right word."

Springer paced slowly around the assembled company of Night Warriors, her dark, impenetrable eyes taking in the

316

crimson electric armor of Kasyx, the white breastplate of Tebulot, the plumed tricorn hat of Samena and the tight harness of Xaxxa. When she had walked around them in a complete circle, she said in the sharpest of tones, "Well . . . we speak differently tonight. We speak with independence. We speak with accord."

"Perhaps we're learning who we are and what we can do," Xaxxa replied.

"You killed one man and seriously disfigured another in your new flourish of independence and accord," said Springer.

"No," Kasyx protested. "That's where you're absolutely wrong. We didn't hurt those men, Yaomauitl did. This is a war, Springer, not just a frolic for four people who want to do something exciting at night. This is an invasion. Believe me, I regret the death of that detective more than anybody. He was the first detective with whom I was ever on first-name terms. But in wars, in invasions, people get hurt. You can never win unless you take that risk."

Springer remained expressionless for a moment and then smiled. "You have spoken well, Kasyx," she said. "You have understood the gravity of what Yaomauitl is attempting to do. You have begun to act on your own initiative too, and even though your attack on those buried Devils was hasty and ill-prepared, you were lucky; it worked and you destroyed them. Whether it is owed to luck or not, there can be no serious criticism of success."

Samena said, "Were you planning on putting us into any particular dream tonight?"

Springer shook her head. "You must go out on your own now and choose whichever dream you will. You are not yet fully experienced Night Warriors but you are ready to select a dream of your own. My task is almost finished."

"You're leaving us?" asked Samena. Suddenly she found the prospect of being without Springer unsettling, like driving for the first time without an instructor. Samena had spent a whole day in limbo as a hostage to Yaomauitl's offspring and she was still nervous about going into dreams again. She had not yet been able to explain to any of the others the total fear she had felt, the deathly despair of sitting alone hour after hour in a room whose walls were as intangible as fog and yet as impenetrable as tempered steel.

Springer produced a white peacock fan from her sleeve and began to flutter it before her face. "I am not exactly what you think I am, any more than Ashapola is exactly what you think he is. We are greater and at the same time lesser, yet greater because of our lessness."

Kasyx, trained as he was in philosophy, was equal to that riddle. "I see," he said. "Ashapola is the God of Human Possibilities and you are his messenger."

Springer said, "You make a wise charge-keeper, Kasyx. One day in years to come, your name may be remembered with great admiration."

Kasyx turned to Tebulot, Samena and Xaxxa. "I've learned something else," he told Springer. "I've learned that no charge-keeper can be greater than the Warriors he is appointed to serve. We are one. We are Night Warriors."

Springer took Kasyx's hand and bowed her head. "I wish you good fortune in your fight against Yaomauitl. I shall be watching you."

Now, clasping hands, the four Night Warriors rose through the roof of the house and into the night. There was no moon. They rose high, scanning the sparkling landscape for any intimation that Yaomauitl was coming after them, listening and looking, using their heightened psychic senses. They drifted north, following the luminous line of the coast, dark shadows in a dark sky. They could feel beneath them the dreams and nightmares of the thousands of people already asleep—dreams and nightmares in which the strangest events were acted out in darkness and in daylight, in fear and in happiness, in passion and in agony. Clocks spun, clouds rushed across unimaginable skies, fields of corn waved like fire. There were voices and sobs, and music that sounded as if a great unseen orchestra were tuning up, cellos and piccolos and anguished violins. Shouts. Laughter. Muttering and weeping.

In dreams and nightmares, everything was possible. The dead could walk and talk as if they had never been away. The unborn could open their eyes and stare at their mothers who never were. Loves could be consummated between passing strangers. Fortunes could be won by the poorest, and to the rich could come ruin and humility.

Over these dreams and nightmares the Night Warriors passed, trailing their shadows behind them. Every dreamer who sensed them go by would frown in his sleep and feel in the morning that something unusual had happened to him during the night.

It was Samena who first sensed the presence of Yaomauitl. They had almost reached Beverly Hills and were about to turn east and head out toward Glendale and Pasadena. But Samena suddenly lifted her head, raised her hands and said, "He's here. I can feel it. He's very close."

The Night Warriors slowed their shadowy journey. Samena closed her eyes and slowly sank to the west, following her emotions rather than her eyes. The others stayed close, keeping up with her, looking around for sign of an ambush. They had seen how ferocious Yaomauitl's offspring could be. Yaomauitl himself, the Deadly Enemy, was fully grown and centuries old. They had every reason to be even more frightened of him.

"Left, left," murmured Samena and they spiraled down toward a large, pale-green stucco house on Lago Vista Drive in Coldwater Canyon. There was a free-form swimming pool at the back of the house, an orchid garden, and a Bentley Eight parked in the driveway. There were bright lights on in the house and the Night Warriors could hear the sounds of music and laughter.

"Are you sure this is the place?" Kasyx asked Samena. "I can't imagine that anyone could be sleeping with this noise going on."

"Follow me," said Samena gently and led the way down

through the green-tiled roof, the large attic studio, the ceiling, and into a child's bedroom.

It was a pretty room, decorated with floral-print drapes and an ice-blue wall-to-wall carpet. In the middle of a large brass bed, on top of covers that matched the drapes, a boy of about eight was sleeping. He was blond-headed, sun-tanned and delicate-featured, with skinny wrists and skinny ankles. He wore pale-blue pajamas with wrinkled-up trouser legs. On the pillow next to him a small blue teddy bear stared up at the ceiling. Over the head of the bed there hung a sentimental picture of the four apostles standing around the cot of a sleeping child, with the words, "Matthew, Mark, Luke, and John/The bed be blest that I lie on."

The Night Warriors stood at the foot of the boy's bed and looked down at him.

"The Devil's here?" asked Xaxxa. "In this kid's dream?"

Samena said, "Can't you sense it?"

They were silent for a moment. They could hear people laughing and talking downstairs. It seemed from fragments of conversation that the house belonged to a motion-picture executive who was celebrating the success of a recent production. A woman with a penetrating, high-pitched voice kept saying, "Charlton was *wonderful* . . . I was never a fan of his but he was absolutely *wonderful!*"

Kasyx said, "Very well. The longer we delay, the more chance the Devil will have to prepare himself." He lifted his arms and drew the fluorescent blue octagon in the air while the other three drew close to him.

Kasyx parted the night inside the octagon and the Warriors glimpsed darkness and sinister shadows. Tebulot eased his weapon off his back and held it ready in case they were attacked as soon as they penetrated the dream. Kasyx raised the octagon over their heads and then commanded it to descend around them.

As soon as the octagon touched the floor, the Night

Warriors found themselves in a whirling, cavernous nightmare. They were standing in what appeared to be a cathedral, or a church, with a high, domed roof and a wide floor of black-and-white tiles. The cathedral was filled with a howling noise, echoing and breathy like the sound of a subway train rushing through a tunnel, and shadows and objects hurtled through the air in a mad defiance of the laws of gravity.

As they looked around, a massive rocking horse appeared, the size of a small building, with snarling lips, bared teeth and wild, blind eyes. It rocked thunderously over their heads and when they looked up into its belly, they could see huge, oily springs, groaning gears and scores of small children clinging desperately to its stirrups.

"Some nightmare," said Tebulot. "I bet the poor kid's parents have been forcing him to take riding lessons."

Kasyx asked Samena, "Any idea which way?"

Samena touched her forehead with her fingertips and closed her eyes. "He's outside somewhere. I don't quite know where. He's keeping very still and quiet. He probably knows we're here and he's hiding."

"Okay then," said Kasyx. "Let's head for the door, shall we? But keep a lookout for absolutely anything."

A screaming jack-in-the-box flew past them, its mouth stretched wide in mechanical agony, followed by the running shadows of fierce dogs. A voice was shouting: "Now look what you've done! Now look what you've done! Now look what you've done!"

They reached the doorway and looked back inside the cathedral. Everywhere there were objects flying about: keys, candlesticks, chairs, scissors, toys, shoes; and the walls echoed and reechoed with the sounds of hundreds of conflicting voices, voices shouting, screeching, bullying and nagging.

"Now look what you've done!" "Can't you be more—!" "How many times do I have to—!" "Look at the mess you've—!" "If you don't tidy up your—!" "Don't you be so—!" "If you talk back to me once more, I'll—!"

They glanced at each other, each recognizing the pit-of-the-stomach smallness of being a child. None of them said a word. This was the first time they had been reminded of the real feelings of childhood since they had passed adolescence. For Kasyx, that was nearly forty years ago; for Tebulot, Samena and Xaxxa, it was only five or six. But until now they had completely suppressed the fear, the anxiety and the sense of utter dependence on adults, whose tempers could unpredictably change from friendly to sarcastic to nightmarishly violent for no reason a child could begin to comprehend. It was all here, however, inside this nightmare: the chaos and turmoil of childhood uncertainties.

The Night Warriors left the cathedral, closing its doors behind them, and stepped out into an unkempt cemetery. The sky was slate-gray, carrying impending thunder, and a wind furrowed the dry grass between the headstones like a bony hand. The tombs were enormous: huge stone engines of exalted death, with angels, masks and scythes carved on them, and open stone books in which words were written in strange, indecipherable languages. Somewhere a branch or a gate intermittently tapped in the wind, *tak-tak, tak-tak,* and the Night Warriors felt that Yaomauitl, the Deadly Enemy, was somewhere close.

As they passed through the cemetery toward the crumbling lych-gate, they heard the raspy grating of stone on stone. Xaxxa, taking up the rear, suddenly looked around and quietly said, "Oh, Jesus Christ, man."

Kasyx halted and turned. Tebulot lifted his weapon. But Xaxxa remained where he was, staring at the tombstone beside him. The lid had slid off to one side, leaving a narrow, triangular gap, and inside the gap they could see a yellowish corpse in a winding-sheet, an old woman who glared at them with bloodshot and bulbous eyes.

Kasyx said, "It's just part of the nightmare. Forget it."

Xaxxa slowly stepped away without taking his eyes from the open tomb. As he passed the next tomb, however, there was another grating noise and that tomb opened too, revealing a half-decayed man in a morning suit. Then another tomb opened, and another, until the sliding of stone lids on top of stone catafalques sounded like the relentless grinding of teeth. Over two hundred bodies lay open to the thunderous sky, unmoving but unquestionably alive in the tattered finery in which they had been entombed: wedding gowns and dinner suits, evening dresses and frock coats.

The branch went *tak-tak, tak-tak* as the Night Warriors proceeded cautiously through the cemetery, glancing apprehensively from one side to the other. Suddenly lightning cracked from the clouds, a thick-trunked tree of solid electricity, and earthed itself in a distant hillside. The wind whipped up and leaves rattled. There was a smell of ozone . . . and death. The freshness of allotrope of oxygen mingled with the sweetness of human disintegration.

The dead sat up in their tombs. Whether they had been galvanized into life by the devastating discharge of lightning, like Frankenstein's monster, or by nothing more than a random fantasy that had entered the mind of the sleeping boy, the Night Warriors couldn't tell. Anything was possible in a nightmare. But the dead sat up stiffly, their dry skin audibly cracking, their flesh flaking from their faces like pieces of desiccated fish, and they turned toward the Night Warriors and screamed at them.

It was no ordinary scream. It was a hellish, discordant clamor that lifted the hair at the back of their necks and chilled their bladders with a sudden primitive urge to urinate and then to run. Kasyx had never heard anything like it, not even this afternoon from the blazing Devil. This was a cry of utter despair from those whose lives had been lived out and finished. This was the most elemental human terror of all: the fear of dying, the horror of being dead.

"Come on, let's get out of here," shouted Kasyx, and the Night Warriors retreated from the cemetery, the dead screaming after them. Beyond the cemetery there was a field in which the grass was deep crimson and the surrounding trees pungent yellow, like a photograph printed with the wrong dyes. They jogged through the grass, looking back from time to time to make sure the dead weren't following them.

After a few minutes the screaming died away into the distance. The crimson field began to rise until at last they found themselves standing on a ridge overlooking a strange city. All the buildings were towering, black and sparkling with lights, and walkways connected the upper levels. There were black flags flying in the wind and small aircraft swarming about like hornets. The city ticked with a regular tensile tick and Tebulot turned to his companions and said, "Clockwork. Can you hear that? The whole place is clockwork."

It was then, however, that Samena turned around and touched Xaxxa's arm. Xaxxa turned around in turn and alerted Kasyx.

"They've followed us," he said.

Kasyx looked back at the windblown field of crimson grass. Advancing across it in a single line stretching from one horizon to the other came the dead. They were silent now, and they walked with their heads lifted in defiance, their tattered robes and dresses dragging through the knee-deep grass.

"Tebulot," said Kasyx, "this is no figment of the boy's imagination; this is Yaomauitl's doing. Are you fully charged up?"

Tebulot checked his charge scale and nodded. Samena unclipped a multiple arrowhead from her belt and slipped it over her index finger. Xaxxa stepped to one side and crouched, ready to attack.

Now the distant thunder began to grumble and lightning walked across the far horizon. As the dead came nearer, it began to rain, widely spaced drops that rustled in the grass. Kasyx heard a high-pitched clicking from behind and above him and almost immediately four small planes came curving overhead, their propellers shining in the rain, their stubby black wings buffeted by the wind.

There was another sound too: the tearing of grass. They looked down and saw that handfuls of crimson turf were being ripped away from underneath by skeletal fingers that were demanding access to the world above. Only fifteen feet away a hand broke loose from under the grass, and then another, and then the rotting head of a corpse emerged from under the ground, grinning the grin of the long dead, its teeth, ears and eye sockets clogged with soil. At last it tore aside the turf as if it were opening the zipper of a sleeping bag and rose to its feet, blindly and unsteadily, its head lifted to seek out the scent of living flesh. Another hand tore through the earth by Samena's foot, and then another. Soon the whole grassy ridge was wriggling with decayed hands as the dead struggled out of their burial barrow.

Kasyx said, "This is it. This is Yaomauitl's army. The dead! Look at them!"

Xaxxa wrinkled up his nose. "Man, they got to smell like the *worst*."

Tebulot raised his weapon and aimed it.

"Are you ready?" asked Kasyx. "They'll tear us to pieces if they get their hands on us."

Samena was lifting her arms into the firing position when suddenly she stiffened as if she had heard something and turned around.

"What is it?" asked Kasyx. But then he looked for himself and saw it.

The clockwork city was somehow reassembling itself, changing, interlocking like a child's Erector set. With a mechanical clicking and clanking, it was rising up into the threatening sky, building upon building, chimney upon chimney, whole railroad yards turning on their side and interlocking into bridges; pyramid-shaped office buildings grinding around on their axes and rumbling into diagonal slots next to parking lots. It rose, the city: a huge construction of buildings, highways and bridges, still glittering with light, still teeming with traffic, but a humanoid now, a city in the shape of a man.

The Night Warriors stared up at its staggering bulk and for the first time since Springer had invested them with the power of Ashapola and the ancient armor that had protected their ancestors, they felt helpless.

Slowly two gleaming, yellow eyes opened in the head of the clockwork city and a voice thundered down at them like a succession of trucks crashing off a cliff.

"You have dared to defy Yaomauitl, the Deadly Enemy, the Scourge of the Church! You have dared to destroy my beloved children! For this there is no forgiveness, no mercy! For this there is nothing but eternal punishment and the tortures of hell!"

With another piercing scream, the tattered dead came running up the crimson hill toward the Night Warriors. They were armed with baling hooks, scythes and curves of broken glass, which they waved above their heads as they ran.

"Hit them!" Kasyx shouted. Tebulot dropped to one knee, firing a blinding salvo of power, one charge after the other in a tight quarter-circle. Immediately corpses began to screech, explode and burst into flames. One of them was detonated in all directions, its hands and feet flying one way, its skull tumbling into the air behind it. Another, blazing, cartwheeled away across the grass, a fiery crucifix.

Samena dodged and skipped between the grasping hands still rising from the grass beneath their feet, trying wildly to clutch at their ankles. She crossed her arms and fired a multiple arrowhead at a dozen corpses who had broken into a run up the slope toward Kasyx. The arrowhead whizzed on a shaft of golden power until it was ten feet from her; then it split up like a star-burst so each part of the arrowhead could seek out its target. The running corpses stumbled, collapsed and fell.

Now Xaxxa flashed away from the ground, soaring high above the field on his shining pathway of pure power. He turned to the right, lifting himself higher than Kasyx had ever seen him go, moving like a jet at the top of its turn in an air show. Then he was sizzling back across the thunderous sky, his knees bent in perfect balance, the surfer of the power slide, his face concealed behind his mirrored mask. Kasyx turned his head to watch Xaxxa as he flashed along the line of corpses, just above their heads, and then turned again to come back and hit them with everything he had.

The dead dropped to the ground like harvested corn-stalks, one after the other, and Xaxxa arced up and around again to find more quarry. His last pass along the line of corpses was abruptly followed by a sonic boom that swelled, clapped and then faded.

At this Tebulot began to fire quick blasts, blowing up one corpse at a time with devastating accuracy. Samena took to using flail-headed arrows, which opened out in flight and released spinning wires with weights at each end, like bolos, which whistled through the corpses' necks and sent their heads flying.

Kasyx glanced behind him. The clockwork city was slowly and noisily dismantling itself, returning street by street and building by building to its original form, but it had been an unnerving demonstration of Yaomauitl's power. They were on Yaomauitl's territory now, fighting in the nightmare he had selected, and Kasyx was beginning to feel that they were already outnumbered, outsmarted, snared like flies on a spider's web. Struggling, yes; fighting, yes; but with no chance of escaping unscathed.

More and more corpses rose from the ground, white-faced and maggoty, with earth in their hair. Kasyx shouted, "Back! Let's get back! There are too many of them!"

They fired off three more bursts of power. Corpses flared, shrieked and fell to the grass, guttering and crackling like burned-down candles. But more corpses rose behind them, pale and screaming, a huge, jostling multitude that at last were overwhelming. The Warriors topped the ridge and ran down toward the clockwork city, while behind them the dead swarmed to the top of the hill, shrieking their rage and agony up to the sky.

Now the Night Warriors were running seriously. The slope gradually flattened out into a wide, dismal plain, a place of ashes and wild timothy separating the hill from the city. In the distance, about half a mile away, a clockwork train sped along a tinplate track, the windows of its passenger cars alight, and high behind it a clockwork crane rose up, tick-tocking as it turned.

Their feet crunched in the ashes as they neared the bulky skyline. But as Kasyx glanced behind, he saw that they had little chance of reaching the city. The armies of the dead had come running down the hillside, outflanking them on the left and about to overtake them on the right.

Abruptly Kasyx stopped running. The others went on for a few paces and then stopped and turned back.

"What's the matter?" Samena asked. "Kasyx? Are you all right?"

Kasyx said, "We're making fools of ourselves! Look at us, running! We're doing exactly what Yaomauitl wants us to do!"

"What else are we going to do, man?" Xaxxa demanded. "That's an *army!*"

"Yes, Xaxxa, but so are *we!* As long as we fight together instead of separately."

"What are you trying to say?" asked Tebulot.

"You said it yourself earlier today. We have to fight together, and as equals. So let's do it."

The front-runners of the army of corpses were only fifty or sixty feet away now. Tebulot raised his weapon and zapped off a burst of glittering explosive power that brought down seven of them.

Kasyx said quickly, "What we'll do is this. I'll send out a field of power to bring them all closer together. Xaxxa, you fly behind them and station yourself there. Then Tebulot can fire charges at you, which you deflect with your power slide into the back of their ranks. Samena meanwhile can pick them off from the front."

Tebulot looked uncertain but Kasyx said, "I'm sorry. Maybe I'm being authoritarian again, but it should work if we do it quickly."

"I'm game," said Xaxxa.

Samena said, "I'd rather fight it out than run away. And I don't fancy *that* place one little bit." She nodded toward the clockwork city.

"Okay then. Let's do it to them before they do it to us," Kasyx said.

"Oh, God," complained Samena. "You've been watching *Hill Street Blues*."

Kasyx frowned at her. "What on earth is *Hill Street Blues*?"

Xaxxa took up his slide-boxer pose and flashed off over the heads of the rapidly advancing corpses. Tebulot took an extra charge of power from Kasyx and then knelt, ready with his weapon fitted to his shoulder. Samena armed her finger with more flail-headed arrow tips.

Kasyx stood just behind them and stretched out his arms. As he closed his eyes and concentrated deeply, his armor began to come alive with spitting electrical charges. Samena, who was standing closest to him, could hear a deep generator-hum that meant he was about to build himself up to maximum power.

Kasyx strained harder and harder and when at last he opened his fingers, a vibrating sheet of pure electricity streamed out on either side of him like a cloak. It streamed ever wider until it reached the corpses who had been trying to outflank them. The first corpses who reached it ran right into it, shrieked, pirouetted and exploded into blazing pieces. Behind them the others hesitated and then retreated, shuffling, pushing, panicking and screaming.

Some of them tried to go back toward the hill but Tebulot fired a quick burst of energy at Xaxxa, who dived, swooped in the air and caught the energy against the bottom of his power slide so that it ricocheted off in a shower of sparks and zipped into the corpses like red-hot daggers. Bodies burned and toppled and crackled into fragments.

Kasyx now brought his arms slowly toward each other and the electric fence he was radiating from his fingers began to close in on the corpses from either side. He was using full power, which he knew he would be unable to sustain for long. But this was the only way he could think of to annihilate Yaomauitl's army of the dead.

Soon the screeching corpses had been herded by Kasyx's fences into a narrow corridor a dozen feet wide. They began to wail and mill around in desperation. Although they were already dead, they knew that if they failed Yaomauitl, he would summarily deprive them of their immortal souls. They were doubly afraid now, not just of being dead but of being sent by Yaomauitl to eternal nothingness, the greatest disaster of all.

One corpse—taller and less rotted than the rest, although half his naked jaw was leering from the side of his face— came staggering out from the burning crowds of Yao-mauitl's army and lurched toward Samena, his hands clawing at the air. Samena fitted a simple arrowhead to her finger, straightened her arms and hit him in the middle of his forehead.

The corpse swayed but kept staggering forward. Samena tried to reload but she dropped her next arrowhead into the ashes.

"Samena!" Kasyx yelled at her.

Screaming harshly, the corpse fell against her, wrapping its rotted arms around her. Then it lifted her into the air, shaking her in an attempt to break her back. Samena cried out in agony and pummeled the corpse's arms, and although she broke off chunks of decayed flesh, the corpse still clung to her, shaking her even more ferociously.

"Tebulot!" Kasyx shouted. Tebulot turned and saw what had happened. He couldn't shoot though; the danger of hitting Samena with an energy bolt was too great. But

Xaxxa, flying high above the remnants of the army of corpses, looked to see why Tebulot had stopped feeding him fire power and he understood what was happening in an instant. He circled, paused and then came surfing in across the battlefield at high speed, feet first, leaning back at an angle of nearly forty-five degrees.

There was a moment when Kasyx thought that Xaxxa was attempting the impossible and he was tempted to shout to him to pull clear, to pull away, to not take the risk. But then Xaxxa streaked unerringly up to Samena and the corpse and dropkicked the corpse's head off its shoulders, sending it at least a hundred feet away, rolling and jumping across the ashes and the timothy grass. The severed neck fountained with a yellow-and-gray liquid and then the headless corpse spun around, buckled at the knees and collapsed to the ground, releasing its hold on Samena.

Samena climbed to her feet. She was shuddering and pale but she managed to give Xaxxa a fleeting smile of thanks. She had been captured by the Devil and she understood the power of total evil. Nothing—not even a rampaging corpse—could ever equal the terror of that.

After Kasyx allowed his power fences to die down, the Warriors patrolled the huddled army of corpses, occasionally firing at those still moving. Tebulot's weapon was hot in his hands and almost empty of power but as he looked around the plain of ashes and saw the strewn corpses, he knew the Night Warriors had won a great victory over the forces of darkness.

The wind blew ashes over the bodies and flapped at their funeral clothes. In a day or two they would be buried for a second time, this time forever. Kasyx said, "I suppose we ought to pray for them. They were only ordinary people like us."

No one answered him and Tebulot, stepping over the corpses toward him, said, "Now we look for the big cheese himself, huh? Yaomauitl."

Kasyx looked toward the clockwork city. Although it had

taken on the shape of a huge, recumbent body, it was constantly changing, constantly reassembling itself, which showed that the boy who was dreaming about it was restless and frightened. Highway overpasses disconnected themselves from one intersection and connected to others. Steeples and clock towers rose and sank like the bobbin heads of old-fashioned sewing machines. Lighted trains whirred in and out of tunnels; clockwork ticked; whistles blew.

Samena came forward, the plumes of her hat blowing in the wind. "Yaomauitl is there," she said, nodding toward the city. "The city is made of the scariest things the boy can think of. Yaomauitl has drawn them all together and taken them over. You saw how the city rose up like a Transformer. The city is Yaomauitl and Yaomauitl is the city."

Tebulot came and stood at Kasyx's right and Kasyx laid his hand on the machine-carrier's shoulder to recharge him.

"What do we do?" Tebulot asked. "Do we try to blow up the whole place or what?"

"Wouldn't that inflict damage on the boy—I mean psychologically—if we blew up his most intimate fears?" Samena asked.

"I don't know," Kasyx replied. "Besides, I think the question's academic. We don't have sufficient power to destroy the whole place."

Xaxxa said, "Yaomauitl's got a *heart*, right, like everybody else?"

Kasyx nodded. "I think we can assume he has since his offspring had an anatomy similar to a urodela."

"A what?"

"A species of amphibian creature like a salamander lizard, or a siren, which is a kind of lizard that doesn't have legs."

"Okay then," said Xaxxa. "If the Devil has a heart, we can go into the city and find it, right? And hit him right where he lives."

Tebulot checked the charge scale on his weapon. "That

makes some kind of sense, I guess. If we don't have enough power to destroy the whole city, I don't see that we have any option."

Samena shrugged. "It makes sense to me. We don't have much time left, do we?"

"Question is, can we *find* the heart?" Kasyx said.

Samena armed her index finger with an arrowhead designed to bury itself deep within a building or a body and then explode like a whaling harpoon. "I'll find it," she said. "When the Devil's offspring held me hostage, I think I developed a nose for Yaomauitl and his kind."

They walked away from the plain of ashes where they had defeated the army of the dead and into the outskirts of the clockwork city. Over their heads, they sky was still thunderous and lightning leaped from cloud to cloud. By the time they reached the first buildings, it was beginning to rain, a slow, soft drizzle that glistened on the printed tinplate sidewalks and beaded the printed tinplate walls. They walked cautiously down a dark, narrow street, their weapons raised. They passed under a railroad bridge and a train hurtled above them, its lights shining on the rooftops.

Samena touched her fingertips to her forehead and closed her eyes. "This way," she said, turning to the left. They followed her along a narrow alleyway between buildings crowded with cogs, springs and ticking ratchets. There was a strong odor of oil in the air as well as a curious aroma of tin. Kasyx asked, "Can you smell that? I used to have a windup racing car that smelled exactly like that. Jesus, I feel like I'm six years old again."

So far they had come across none of the inhabitants of the city but suddenly the alleyway ended and they stepped out onto a broad tinplate mall, dimly lit but busy with clockwork trolley cars, buses and automobiles, all life-size. The noise of springs and cogs was tremendous and there was an endless rattling of painted metal tires on painted metal pavement. The buses and trolleys were crowded with vacantly smiling people painted on the tinplate windows.

The bus drivers had been painted in profile on the side windows of the buses and in full face on the front windows.

"This is *weird*," Xaxxa said as they walked past butchers' stores in which the meat was simply printed on the back wall behind the counter, and grocery stores with printed advertisements for Wheaties, Come Brown Rice and Rinso. The drizzle sparkled in the streetlights, forming a soft halo around each globe. Kasyx, as he walked along the wet sidewalk, began to understand that they were making their way through some archetypal childhood, lost and gone forever in the real world but still alive on the fringes of every child's dreams.

This city was the boy-dreamer's creation only insofar as each part of it represented one of his nightmares. It was Yaomauitl, the Deadly Enemy, who had brought his nightmares together and made a city of them. Yaomauitl could take on any form he desired, and that was what Samena had meant when she said that Yaomauitl actually *was* the city.

The Night Warriors followed Samena through the maze of streets, over narrow bridges and mysterious walkways, through silent town squares and clamorous trolley depots. They had been walking through the rain for almost twenty minutes before she raised her hand and said, "Listen! Now you can hear it!"

They strained their ears and knew she was right. Underneath the ringing and clashing of the city's traffic they could detect another kind of mechanical sound: the deep-throated *kachug,* pause, *kachug,* pause, *kachug,* pause, of a massive grandfather clock with a swinging pendulum. This clock was the city's heart: a clock of nightmares, the kind of clock that chimed in echoing hallways, with a pendulum that swung back and forth in a dark, rushing arc from side to side.

They crossed a narrow bridge that took them high above the city's main street. Hundreds of feet below glittered the headlights of clockwork cars and buses. The pale face of a clock on a steeple told them it was already four twenty and that this deep-level nightmare couldn't continue much longer. As dawn broke and the boy-dreamer began to stir, his mind would gradually rise up through the lighter debris of dozing dreams and this malevolent clockwork city would be buried in darkness for all time.

"There!" said Samena, pointing ahead. The bridge led to a curved tunnel running through the sixty-sixth floor of a tall, iron-gray skyscraper on the far side of which there was a balcony with tinplate railings. They jogged through the tunnel, came out on the other side and stepped over to the balcony's edge.

In front of them—out of the black chasm of the city's structure—a massive iron framework rose up; inside this framework a clockwork mechanism steadily and inexorably beat away the minutes of the night. From the center of the mechanism a pendulum swung, a pendulum more than a hundred feet long and bearing on its disc-shaped weight the death mask of a goat-bearded man in corroded bronze.

"Yaomauitl's heart," Samena declared.

Tebulot wiped the rain from the visor of his helmet. "Do you think we have enough power to destroy it?" he asked Kasyx.

Kasyx gave him a thumbs-up sign. "One burst at maximum strength should do it."

Tebulot shouldered his machine while Kasyx stood behind him and placed a hand on each of his shoulders to infuse him with as much of Ashapola's power as possible. The charge scale on the side of Tebulot's weapon shone white, indicating full energy and more. It hummed loudly, eager to be released. Samena and Xaxxa kept watch from opposite sides of the balcony.

"Ready?" Kasyx asked Tebulot. "Then kill him . . . *in the dark and holy name of the Night Warriors!*"

Tebulot fired. There was an ear-shattering *zzhhhwaaappp* and a fifteen-foot bolt of supercharged energy streaked from the muzzle of his machine. But they had reckoned without the strength and the devilish alertness of Yaomauitl, the Deadly Enemy, for as the energy bolt sped toward the massive clock mechanism, there was a metallic flickering sound and a flock of curved metal plates was catapulted through the air like clay pigeons, or frisbees, and across the front of the clock structure. Tebulot's energy bolt hit the first plate in a spectacular shower of sparks and the plate was canted off sideways. But it was enough to deflect the energy bolt by two or three degrees and when the energy bolt hit the next flying plate in another explosion of sparks, it was deflected another two degrees, and then another, in a glittering succession of firework ricochets that set up a loud whistling and crackling.

As it sparkled against the last plate, the energy bolt flashed harmlessly skyward, disappearing into the wind-blown cloud base. The plates themselves, smoking and scorched, tumbled down into the depths of the clockwork city, bouncing off beams, scaffolding and railroad tracks with a deafening clanging.

The Night Warriors were stunned. They stood on the balcony watching the gargantuan clock mechanism continue as before, *kachug*, pause, *kachug*, pause, and they knew that this time they had failed.

"That's it!" Kasyx said. "We're almost out of power! Let's get out of this dream as fast as we can!"

But then the skyscraper on which they were standing began to descend and other towers began to rise. They looked down from the balcony and saw the building sliding smoothly and quickly into the ground, its lighted windows swallowed up story by story, while a tall, thin steeple next to them began to climb into the sky at the same relentless speed. Bridges and traffic intersections swung around and reconnected without even a pause in the flow of clockwork trains and cars. Lightning forked down between the buildings, lighting up the chaos of assembly and reassembly in stark, startling relief.

As the sixty-sixth floor of the skyscraper neared the

ground, the Night Warriors stepped back into the protective shelter of the tunnel behind them, but the balcony retracted of its own accord before the building slid without any hesitation into a sleeve of close-fitting steel plate. They saw a wall of greasy metal speed upward before their eyes as if they were standing in an elevator. Then the building slowed, hissed, and shuddered to a stop and the balcony opened out again, this time into a series of steps.

There was silence. They were deep inside a metallic cavern a little higher than their heads. Cautiously they climbed down the steps and looked around, Kasyx using his helmet to illuminate the farthest depths of the cavern. They glimpsed shadowy archways, massive pillared supports, and shiny black electrical cables that hung from the roof like boa constrictors.

Kasyx looked from one side to the other and said, "There's nothing here. This is way down beneath the surface. The power and maintenance department, if you ask me."

"Shall we call it a night?" Samena suggested anxiously.

"I think so," Kasyx said. "Tebulot? Xaxxa?"

Xaxxa nodded. "Let's face it, man, he outsmarted us this time, but next time we're going to be ready. Next time we're going to blast that mother right where it hurts the most."

Tebulot raised his hand in agreement. He had been fighting hard, his machine was heavy and he was looking weary. Kasyx therefore took a single step back and opened out his arms to draw the octagon in the air.

"We shall return to fight Yaomauitl again," he said. Samena, Tebulot and Xaxxa gave him, bravely, the salute of the Night Warrriors.

At that moment, however, they heard a grinding, clashing sound from the darker recesses of the metallic cavern. Kasyx looked this way and that, his horizontal beam flickering from one shadow to another. Tebulot, tired as he was, lifted his machine again, and Samena unhooked an arrowhead from the jingling collection on her belt.

"What the hell is that?" Tebulot asked, alert and nervous.

His question was answered immediately for out of the darkness, on all sides, ten or eleven gigantic clockwork machines appeared, advancing on them in a whirring rush. Each machine was different but each was nothing more than a huge collection of churning cogs, ticking springs, swinging foliots and spinning crown wheels. The Devil's machinery; it had no purpose other than to mangle or maim anyone caught in its way.

Xaxxa instantly sped away from the Night Warriors on a power slide that illuminated the whole cavern. He banked and turned, keeping his head low, and streaked in to dropkick one of the machines on its side plate. His first kick merely unbalanced the machine for a moment but then he circled again, ducking low, and delivered another two-footed kick, this one against the top of the machine.

The machine teetered on its wheels and for a second Kasyx thought it would regain its equilibrium and keep coming. But the momentum of its cogs swung it to one side and it crashed to the floor of the cavern in a thunderous explosion of flying gear wheels and tumbling spindles.

Samena ran forward, somersaulted between two machines and fired a double-headed arrow. Each arrowhead trailed out behind it a long, thin cable of braided steel that flew into the clockwork mechanisms and hopelessly tangled them. The machines ground and strained at their springs and finally jammed up completely.

Tebulot blipped off several small energy bolts, wrecking one machine and sending another around and around in clattering circles, shedding nuts, bolts and pieces of framework.

Kasyx shouted, "Back! Back! Let's get out of here!" and lifted his arms again to draw the octagon. But Samena screamed at him, "Behind you! Kasyx! Behind you!"

Kasyx heard the machine before he saw it; his ears were suddenly filled with the whirring of flywheels. He turned and saw that one of the machines was almost on him. He tried to stumble clear but the cogs snatched at an ankle, capturing half of one leg between the wheels and the springs. He roared out in pain, hopping on his other leg, desperately trying to push against the mechanism's framework to wrench himself away.

If he hadn't been wearing armor, his leg would have been mangled. As it was, the cogs had crushed the greaves below the knee and twisted the alloy of his sabatons. The machine squealed loudly as its crown wheels tried to pull him deeper inside and the teeth of its cogs rattled against his poleyns, or knee plates. He gritted his teeth and pushed harder against the framework. He felt his muscles crack and sweat streak down the side of his face. His trapped leg felt as if it were on fire and he knew that if he relaxed for even one instant, he would be pulled inside the clockwork and killed.

He considered using his remaining power to disable the machine but he knew that if he did, there would be no energy left to return the Night Warriors to the real world. They would be imprisoned in the clockwork city for as long as the clockwork city lasted and then swallowed up for all eternity when the boy-dreamer awoke.

"Kasyx!" Samena shouted and came running over to help him.

"Get back!" he gasped. "Don't come too close!"

Now Xaxxa and Tebulot came up and in spite of Kasyx's protests, they caught hold of him under his arms and helped him maintain his steady pull against the devouring machine.

"Let me go!" Kasyx demanded. "I can . . . draw the octagon. Then you can— For Christ's sake, let me go!"

Tebulot said, "No martyrs in this cause, old-timer. Hang on tight. Samena, let's have one of those wires of yours to jam up this machinery with."

Samena came up and fired off a wire-trailing arrowhead at close range. The wire lashed itself around the crown wheels as tight as a fusee spring and the clockwork shuddered, snarled and came to a stop.

"Right," said Tebulot. "Xaxxa, see if you can kick those cogs free."

Supporting himself against the machine's framework, Xaxxa kicked out at the gear wheel again and again. At last one of the spindles burst out of its socket and three cogs clattered to the ground. When Xaxxa kicked again, Kasyx's leg came free.

They lifted the charge-keeper out of the machinery. His leg was twisted at an odd angle and he was white with pain.

"Put him down for a moment," Tebulot said but Kasyx shook his head violently and said, "No, no! Let's get back! Just gather around me and let's get back!"

They did as they were told. They came close to him, supporting him this time instead of simply holding his hand, and he drew the sparkling blue octagon in the air in front of them. As he lifted it above their heads, they heard more clockwork machines grind toward them but Yaomauitl had missed his chance. The octagon sank around them and when it touched the floor, they were back in the sleeping boy's bedroom.

The house was quiet now; the lights were out. The sun was just beginning to lighten the sky over the Santa Monica mountains. The boy had buried himself in his covers during the course of the night and now lay hot and tousled, one arm hanging limp over the edge of the bed.

Kasyx winced and half-collapsed. "Jesus, this hurts . . ." he gritted between tightly clenched teeth.

Tebulot said, "Come on, I'll get you home. You should be okay once you're back in your own body."

Samena clasped his hand and said, "Take care, Kasyx. I'll call you as soon as I can."

And Xaxxa put his arm around him, looked straight into his eyes and gave him a short, strong nod that meant more than words could have expressed: "We're brothers; we're friends; we've fought together; we've been scared together. It doesn't matter that I'm young and black and that you're old and white. We're Night Warriors, and when we fight the Devil, we're together."

Samena and Xaxxa rose and faded through the ceiling of the house and were gone. Tebulot supported Kasyx and helped him lift himself slowly into the air and fly out over the early morning canyons of Beverly Hills.

It was a long way back to Del Mar but the wind was warm, the morning was sunny and Tebulot had sufficient strength for both of them. He carried Kasyx back past San Juan Capistrano and San Clemente and Cardiff-on-Sea, slowly and gently, as solicitous as a son.

Nobody could have seen them flying past; the sun was too bright and their images were too insubstantial. But they were as graceful as the transparent wings of dragonflies, as silent as a kind thought, and they carried with them the last hope of returning Yaomauitl, the Deadly Enemy, to his elmwood prison in Mexico.

═══ 18 ═══

Jennifer woke up in the middle of the night drenched in sweat. She had been dreaming that dream again, the one in which the Devil had been lying on top of her, forcing her legs apart and whispering in her ear, "*Now you will be my little mother.*" She had dreamed it two or three times a week since that encounter with Bernard Muldoon at the supermarket and it was always the same: the weight of its body, the feel of its fur, the stench of its breath.

But tonight it was different. Tonight when she woke clutching the tangled sheets, sweating, shuddering . . . tonight she could still feel something. There was a stirring in her stomach, a strange, slithering sensation and a persistent nausea that refused to be swallowed away. As she lay in the darkness with Paul sleeping heavily beside her and only the green eyes of the digital clock for company, she tried to think of what it was she had eaten today that could have upset her. The passion-fruit juice at breakfast? The herb-and-tomato omelet she had eaten at Sandra's for lunch? The filets of veal she had cooked for Paul's dinner?

Usually when she felt nauseous, she had only to think about what she had eaten to identify what it was that made her feel sick. But this sickness was different; it kept turning and rolling inside her stomach as if she were still trying to digest something only half-chewed. This sickness had a movement of its own.

She lay and sweated for another half-hour. The sky outside the tightly drawn drapes began to lighten. She longed to get up, draw back the drapes and make herself a cup of hot, strong lemon tea. But Paul was a hair-trigger sleeper, easily disturbed, and he needed his rest after five straight days in Denver trying to wrap up the Trianon deal. So she lay where she was, rigid, clutching and releasing the sheets, sweating, trying to suppress the rolling and the slithering.

Slowly she moved one hand down until it rested on her naked abdomen. Her muscles were churning all right, she could feel them. Yet they couldn't be her stomach muscles, they were down too low, and this slow, turning-over sensation wasn't at all like gas.

It suddenly occurred to her just what this sensation felt like. She hadn't felt it for a long time, not since the days she and Paul had been poorer but happier. They had lived in a third-floor walkup over on Santa Monica Boulevard, next to the Mexican restaurant. They had wanted a family in those days but that was before Paul had become serious about his promotion prospects, office politics and his status in the air-conditioning industry.

She remembered the happiness. She remembered the sunshine. She remembered the day she had come back from the doctor and told Paul he was going to be a father.

She also remembered the day when it had all ended. The [pa]in, the spasms of labor, the blurred faces in the hospital. [She h]ad heard it cry just once. Too young, too under- [develo]ped to survive. Paul had held her hand. Her mother [had b]rought her walnut candies.

[B]ut now, tonight . . . this feeling, this intermittent pushing and rolling. This was the same, or almost the same. She didn't know how it could have happened. She had taken her pill religiously, and Paul had been away so frequently and for so long that they scarcely ever had sex anymore. *But it was the same!* She couldn't deny it, no matter how she tried to pretend that it was an omelet, filet of veal or plain old flatulence.

She felt as if she were having a baby!

She stared at the ceiling. This was ridiculous. Of course she wasn't having a baby; she had experienced no morning sickness, no weight gain, no swelling of her breasts. She hadn't had a period of course, but then, she took her pills continuously, and even when she did allow herself to menstruate—"to flush myself out," as she liked to think of it—her flow was always light.

She couldn't be having a baby. And yet, what else could it possibly be? It was inside her, and it was moving on its own. She was sure it was shifting around of its own accord, around and around as if it couldn't settle itself for even a moment.

She looked across at Paul. It was light enough now for her to make out his face. His eyes were closed, his mouth slightly open. He wasn't snoring, he never did. Sleeping, he always looked as if he were dead. It took only one wind-rattled door, however, or one dripping faucet, or one foot creaking on a wooden floorboard, and he was instantly and irrevocably awake.

Jennifer whispered, "Paul."

There was a moment's pause. She knew he had woken up instantly and that he was deciding behind those closed eyelids whether to sit up and be angry or keep his eyes closed and pretend he was still asleep.

"Paul," she repeated.

He opened his eyes. Hazel-colored irises, too pal[e] really attractive. He stared at her without speaking. [It was as if] he hadn't yet made up his mind what kind of mood [he was] going to be in.

"Paul, I'm sorry to wake you, honey, but I think I[']m sick."

"Sick? What do you mean? You mean nauseous?"

"Well, kind of but not exactly."

He propped himself on one elbow. "Not exactly? What exactly does that mean, not exactly?"

"It's like my stomach's turning over and over. It won't stop. I feel like I want to throw up but I can't."

Paul dropped his head back onto the pillow. "Jennie," he said tiredly, "I don't expect to be awakened at the crack of dawn just because you have a stomachache. I have a long, hard day ahead of me. I need to get some rest. Now why don't you go to the bathroom and fix yourself some Pepto-

"Honey?" Paul persisted. "Listen, honey, I've called for an ambulance."

"Paul," she whispered. She scarcely moved her lips, as if she were trying to ventriloquize, as if she wanted to speak to him without her body finding out what she was doing. "Paul . . . it hurts so bad . . . I can't stand it."

He started to lift her. "Come on, Jennie. Come and lie down on the bed."

"Don't move me," she whispered.

"Jennie, you can't stay here on the kitchen floor—"

"Don't move me! For God's sake, Paul, don't move me!"

Paul stared at her. "Jennie, honey, you can't just stay here on the floor."

Jennifer began to shake and a long string of saliva dangled from her lower lip. "Oh, God, Paul, it hurts so bad. It's like something's biting me. It's like there's something inside me that's biting me."

"Honey, it's probably food poisoning. That's a symptom of food poisoning, that sharp pain like that. It must've been the veal. You have to be so careful with veal. Was that fresh veal you bought or frozen veal? I'll sue that market for everything they've got."

Jennifer could scarcely hear what he was saying. The pain inside her uterus was growing steadily more severe as nerve after nerve was stripped away. The wriggling grew more excited too, and when Paul gently opened her wrap to look at her stomach, he could see the convulsive movements for himself. It was as if her muscles were turning and contracting in grotesquely exaggerated peristalsis.

She threw back her head—the veins in her neck standing out like dark-blue worms—and screamed. It was the most terrible scream Paul had ever heard, even worse than the screams of the woman on the Ventura Freeway after her arm had been severed in a car crash. This scream was so agonized, so desperate, that Paul found himself screaming too, shouting at the top of his voice, begging her to stop. "Stop it! For Christ's sake, stop it!"

Suddenly, unexpectedly, she did stop. She stared at Paul as if she didn't know who he was and then she slowly lowered her eyes until she was staring at her stomach. An extraordinary hissing noise came from the back of her throat, a low, hoarse hissing as if she were having difficulty breathing.

Paul said fearfully, "Jennie? Jennie, what is it? For God's sake, Jennie, you've got to tell me!"

His eyes followed hers down to her stomach. The wriggling continued but now a darkish lump had appeared under the skin, like a severe bruise or a constricted hernia. Jennifer stared at the lump in horrified fascination, and even though she was suffering pain more terrible than anything she had ever experienced, she remained quiet, expressing her agony by hissing, by clenching her fists, by praying that this was all a nightmare, that it wasn't real and that she would have only to say, "Paul, wake me up," and it would all be over.

She didn't ask him to wake her up, however, because she knew it wasn't a nightmare and that if she did ask him, it wouldn't make any difference. She was awake and the gnawing pain inside her body was real. Oh, Lord, please save me. Oh, Lord, please don't let me die. Oh, Lord, whatever you ask me, I'll do it. *Please, Lord; please, Lord; please!*

Paul heard the distant shrill of the ambulance siren and squeezed Jennifer's hand. "You hear that, honey?" he reassured her. "Only a few minutes longer and the medics are going to be here."

Jennifer lifted her head and said hoarsely, "Too late."

"Now, come on, Jennie, that's no way to talk. Why, they'll have you in the hospital in ten minutes and then you'll feel fine. Come on now, honey, I promise you."

Jennifer repeated, "Too . . . late. Too . . ."

Then she buried her hands in her hair and clenched it so tight that Paul could hear her scalp skin tear away from her skull. She opened her mouth wide and this time she screamed and wouldn't stop. She screamed so loudly that Paul didn't hear the ambulance turn into Paseo del Serra, nor did he hear the paramedics ring at the door.

"Jennie! Stop it! Jennie!" he roared at her, over and over until their faces were only inches apart, she screaming white-faced and agonized, he screaming red-faced and furious.

Suddenly Jennifer's scream turned to a descending moan of sheer terror. She looked down at her stomach again, her hands still tugging at her hair, and the black bulge was bigger than ever, and moving. Paul stared at it too, unable to imagine what it was; all kinds of strange and horrible ideas tumbled through his head in quick succession. A kind of a blowfly maybe, that had buried a colony of eggs underneath her skin. A hard lump of undigested food that had somehow penetrated the stomach lining and that her body was trying to repel.

But the reality of it was even more horrible than Paul's imagination. For as Jennifer screamed and the paramedics pounded at the door, the bulge on her stomach stretched out until the skin that covered it was almost transparent, and then the dark, twitching object inside bit right through it and bright-red blood splattered out—all over her wrap, all over her thighs—and a flat, eel-like head appeared, silvery and streaked with blood, with a staring and expressionless eye. The head waggled and turned and Paul could do nothing but stare at it in fear and disgust. He was so shocked that he had forgotten Jennifer was still screaming and he didn't hear the glass breaking as the paramedics forced an entry with a fire ax.

"Paul!" screamed Jennifer. "Oh, Paul! Oh, God!"

Paul snatched wildly at the eel's head. The first time, too scared, he missed it. But the second time he went closer and the eel darted forward and caught the side of his hand in jaws that seared like a red-hot barbecue fork.

Automatically Paul whipped his hand away. The eel clung on and he dragged the whole length of it, four feet, out of the hole in Jennifer's stomach. Jennifer fell back onto the floor. Paul heard her head thump but all he could think about was the eel that had fastened itself to his finger and wouldn't let go.

He lashed the eel against the wall but still it kept its grip. He lashed again in rising panic, but however hard he hit it, the eel refused to let go. He was so confused, so frightened, that when two paramedics suddenly appeared in the kitchen, all he could do was to hold up the eel like a fishing trophy.

"Snake!" one of the paramedics shouted and unhitched a large knife from the back of his belt. "You see to the woman. I'll deal with this."

He came forward, feinted, lunged, and then gingerly grasped the eel by the middle of its body. The eel thrashed and struggled but he managed to hook it over the kitchen table and keep it pressed down against the butcher block.

"You want to look away?" he asked Paul. He had a young, serious face with large brown eyes and a bushy brown mustache. Paul swallowed, closed his eyes and said in a voice that didn't sound like his, "Just do what you have to, okay? But quick. It hurts like hell."

The paramedic placed the edge of the blade close to the eel's head. Meanwhile the other paramedic, who was kneeling over Jennifer, said in awe, "Jesus, Tony, this woman's got a hole in her stomach you could drive a truck through."

Tony said, "Okay, Levi, just wait one moment," and sliced through the eel's body with one swift movement, as if he were skilled at filleting fish. The eel, however, was no ordinary eel. As the paramedic severed its head, its jaw muscles went into a spasm and bit off Paul's little finger, as well as most of the knuckle, and a diagonal piece from the side of his hand. Paul opened his eyes and lifted his hand in disbelief; blood was spraying out of it like a garden fountain.

"God Almighty," said Tony.

Levi turned around and exclaimed, "What the hell—"

Paul tried to clutch his wrist in the confused hope that he might be able to stop the bleeding by pressing on the artery, but then he stumbled forward and collapsed on the floor. Blood pumped crimson graffiti all over the tiles, Jennifer's shuddering legs and Tony's green-and-white shoes. Both paramedics knelt down beside Paul.

"The woman's dead," said Levi tightly. "Severe trauma to the abdominal area, presumably caused by snake attack. Shock, loss of blood through catastrophic internal hemorrhage, cardiac failure, fractured skull."

Tony opened his medical case in silence and began to apply a tourniquet to Paul's wrist. Then he cleaned and dressed the devastated finger joint and gave Paul an injection of anti-tetanus toxoid along with benzathine penicillin. He tried to prize open the eel's jaws to release Paul's bitten-off finger but the eel's muscles remained firmly locked. He packed the head and finger in ice chips and said, "I'll get this guy to the hospital. There's a chance we can save his finger. Meanwhile you'd better call the coroner."

Paul was beginning to recover consciousness. He opened his eyes, stared at Tony and Levi and asked, "Jennie . . . is Jennie all right?"

Tony hunkered down beside him. "Don't you worry, sir. Jennie's going to be fine. Right now the most important thing is getting you straight off to the hospital."

Outside, the sun was shining brightly. Tony drove Paul off toward Hollywood West Hospital on La Brea just as a police patrol car was arriving. Tony gave the cops a brief salute and then turned on his siren, howling his way east with Paul lying semiconscious in the back of the ambulance and his finger lying on the front seat in a plastic bag of ice, still trapped inside the eel's jaws.

Levi had just finished calling the medical examiner when two policemen stepped into the blood-spattered kitchen and warily looked around. Levi hung up the phone and said, "How're you doing?"

"Okay, I guess," said one of the cops. "What happened here?"

"Snake attack," replied Levi. "One dead, one missing his right-hand pinkie."

"*Snake* attack?" said the other cop, wrinkling up his nose. "Are you kidding?"

Levi pointed out the eel's decapitated body lying curled up on the tiles. "That's the snake, at least what's left of it. My partner had to take the rest of it to the hospital with him."

The first cop hunkered down beside the eel's body and prodded it with the tip of his finger. "This ain't no snake," he said.

Levi stared at him, looked away, then put his hand on his hip.

The cop stood up. "I'm telling you, man," he repeated, "this sure as hell ain't no snake."

"It isn't a snake?" said Levi. "What is it then if it isn't a snake? A necktie maybe? Something that fell off the back of somebody's Davy Crockett hat?"

"That's an eel," said the cop. He pushed his thumbs into his belt and gave one of those puckered, defiant looks most cops adopt as soon as they begin to suspect their authority is questioned.

Levi, however, knew from experience how to cope with cops. He whistled softly in admiration and said, "An eel, huh? I never would have guessed an eel. Right out here, so far from the ocean?"

"Still an eel," the cop insisted.

"Well, uh . . . how come you know that?" asked Levi. "How come you're so sure?"

"Fishing," said the cop.

His partner, taking off his cap and waving it in the air as an aid to explanation, said, "Josh here fishes anything. Tuna, snapper, you name it. He was Santa Monica champion three successive years."

Levi looked toward Jennifer's body, draped now in a green sheet. "It seems like it bit her. The eel, I mean."

"Well, eels can be vicious, some of them," the cop

called Josh remarked. He kept on looking around, his neck bulging first from one side of his collar, then the other. He had one of those bland, pugnacious faces that always reminded Levi of Marlon Brando when he could have been a contender.

"In your kitchen?" asked Levi.

"I beg your pardon?" Josh retorted. Polite words spoken with menace.

"Eels can be vicious in your kitchen?"

"Sure eels can be vicious in your kitchen. Eels can be vicious anyplace. Friend of mine flushed an eel down the john; next thing he knew, it came straight back up again and bit his wife in the ass." Josh obviously thought this was hilarious because he suddenly shouted, *"Ha!"* and slapped his thigh.

Then he looked around again and jerked his head toward the body under the green sheet. "Where'd it bite her?"

"Stomach," said Levi. "Just to the right of the navel. Bad bite too. You could have driven a truck through it."

"What do you think happened?" asked the cop's partner. "I mean, do you have any idea of how the eel got in here?"

Josh said, "What kind of a question is that, William? An eel lives in the water, right? And an eel this size is an ocean-going eel, right?"

William nodded doubtfully.

"So how do you think it got in here? It didn't walk, did it? It didn't hitch a ride from the beach on the back of some wetback's pickup? It must of been brought here, either by the deceased because she wanted to cook it and eat it or by the deceased's husband because he'd been out fishing and was stupid enough to bring the fucking thing home."

Levi stared down at the eel's body distastefully. "Some-body would want to eat *that?*"

"Sure they would," Josh told him. "Smoked, stewed, jellied, you can eat eel any way you like. Maybe the deceased was trying out that Chinese recipe where you throw the live eels into a boiling pot and then hold the lid down until they stop struggling."

"Chao shanhu," said William. Josh turned his head and stared at him fixedly. William shrugged and looked vaguely embarrassed.

"This guy doesn't eat nothing except Chinese," Josh explained.

Levi checked his watch. "The medical examiner should be here soon. How about your people?"

"Don't ask me," said Josh, wiping his nose with the back of his hand. "They had a serious shooting down at the Burger King on Highland."

They stood around with their arms folded, trying not to step in the patterns of blood that looped over Jennifer's kitchen tiles. Josh said after a while, "Some accident, huh? You're just about to eat your supper and your supper eats you."

William smirked because he was supposed to and glanced down at Jennifer's green-sheeted body. He frowned, took a second look and then nudged Levi's arm and pointed.

"Look there," he said. "She's moving."

Josh turned around. "Moving!" he exclaimed with morbid amusement. "You don't mean to tell me she's still *alive?* Boy . . . are you going to get it if she's still alive. Some paramedic, huh? Leaves the badly injured victim of a serious domestic-eel accident lying on the cold, tiled floor of her kitchen for ten minutes solid while he passes the time of day with two police officers. Demotion at best. Dismissal more likely."

Levi could see that William was right. The green sheet was humping up and down and moving from side to side as if Jennifer were trying to raise her body off the floor.

"Riboyne Shel O'lem!" Levi cried and quickly crossed the kitchen and picked up the sheet, dropping to one knee as he did.

The eels swarmed out everywhere. Levi shouted—a coarse, terrified shout—and one of the eels jumped at his face and clung to the side of his jaw. Another bit at his ankle and a third went for his calf muscle. There were nine or ten of the creatures and they slithered their way blindly around the kitchen floor, their tails making patterns in the spilled blood.

Levi screamed with pain. He staggered backward, the eel waving from his face. Josh yanked open kitchen drawers, scattering cheese graters, egg slicers and clean tea towels until he at last found a drawerful of knives. He snatched out a poultry knife and dodged his way around Levi while William banged away at the other eels with his nightstick.

"Don't cut it!" Levi shouted. "Don't cut it, for God's sake! It'll bite my face off!"

"Hold still!" Josh yelled at him. "Hold still, will you?"

Levi tried to stay where he was, trembling with pain, while Josh slowly approached him, glancing quickly down now and then to make sure there were no eels around his feet and kicking them aside when they were too close. Levi stared at him, his eyes wide, the long, silvery eel swinging from the right side of his jaw, its teeth fastened in his flesh. Every time Levi spoke, the eel swung, causing him acute agony. But he had to speak.

"The guy . . . who was here before . . . my buddy . . . cut the eel's head off . . . and it bit the guy's finger clean through. The jaw muscles . . . closed . . . instead of opening."

"All right," Josh said softly. "If that's the way they play the game, this is the way *we're* going to play it."

He beckoned to his partner and indicated that he should hold Levi from behind, under his arms, to support him and keep him comparatively still. Then, coming closer, he grasped the eel's swinging tail, touching it with all the expertise and care of an experienced fisherman, and gradually slid his hand up until he was holding it just behind the head. The eel's eye stared, the eye of a creature without feelings, a creature that lives only to sustain itself.

Josh lifted the poultry knife and slid its long, thin blade between the eel's partly open jaws, the sharp edge facing toward him.

"You see what I'm going to do?" he asked Levi. "I'm going to hold onto the eel's body and then I'm going to slice toward myself so the knife separates the eel's jaw muscles. He won't get a chance to bite you, believe me."

Levi nodded. The pain was too much now for him to want to speak. The eels on his ankle and calf were causing him even more agony. His right trouser leg was stained dark with blood.

Josh grasped the eel's body carefully, stroking it so its nervous system would grow accustomed to the sensation of being held and not recognize it as a threat. "All right now," he said. "I'm going to count to ten and when I say ten, brace yourself because that's when I'm going to cut this bastard's head wide open. You got me?"

Levi grunted to show that he did.

"One," said Josh. Levi's eyes widened.

"Two," said Josh, not noticing another eel that had slithered close to his shoe.

"Three." The eel beside his shoe raised its head, its bright, maniacal eye glistening yellow in the sunlight crisscrossing the kitchen floor.

"Four." The eel nudged aside Josh's trouser cuff and began to lift its head up past his sock.

"Five. You ready there, my friend? This is where we do it."

"Six." The eel poured up inside his trouser leg.

"Seven—what?—*ahhhh!* Shit! Shit, get out of there! *Gaahh,* you bastard!" Josh violently kicked his leg and dropped the knife to grapple with the eel inside his trousers. He spun and pirouetted; he slammed his leg against the side of the breakfast bench again and again. But the tough, slippery eel slid up as far as his thigh, and even when Josh realized what it was after and clutched himself tightly with cupped hands, the eel forced its narrow head underneath his hands and bit him.

Josh roared like a madman and fell backward onto the floor, jerking, convulsing and kicking his legs. He wrestled his belt open and dragged down his trousers. His shorts were stained with blood. The eel's silvery body protruded from the side of them, coiled tightly around his thigh like one of the classical serpents of Laocöon. "The knife!" he roared, his face crimson. "Give me the fucking knife!"

William scrabbled on the floor for the poultry knife. Levi, in desperation, tried to tug away the eel suspended from his jaw. Its teeth snapped audibly and it bit away a chunk of Levi's face, down to the bone. Levi shouted in pain and horror and fell to the other side of the kitchen, leaving a foot-wide smear of blood down the side of Jennifer's oak-fronted cabinets.

William found the poultry knife and handed it with trembling fingers to his buddy. Josh's face was strange and grim. He was biting the flesh inside his mouth to keep from screaming, and blood ran freely down each side of his chin. He lifted his buttocks, bit by bit, and gradually edged down his shorts. The eel had swallowed his penis almost up to the root and although its teeth had penetrated the skin, it had not yet closed its jaws. Its eyes stared up at Josh with predatory calm.

"I can't . . ." Josh said bloodily, "I can't get the knife between its jaws."

His partner inspected the eel in fear and disbelief. "What are you going to do?" he asked in a voice as pale as milk.

Josh bit even harder at the flesh inside his mouth and his eyes filled with tears.

"You're going to have to . . . take hold of its jaws. See if you can keep them open . . . long enough to pull it off me."

"These are real powerful, these bastards," William said worriedly. "Suppose I can't hold its jaws open long enough?"

"Well, what the fuck *else* am I going to do?" Josh hissed at him, his lips bubbling blood. There was a scream from the other side of the kitchen. It was Levi, tearing off another eel and another chunk of flesh. But the cops took no notice.

"Listen, listen," said William. "That paramedic, he's bound to have some sedative, right? Some real powerful sedative. Supposing I can inject that bastard eel with enough sedative to send it to sleep? Then it will drop off, right? Fall asleep and drop off . . . and you won't . . . well—"

Josh was turning gray with shock. "Yes," he said thickly. "Try it. Maybe it'll work. Ask him to get it ready for you."

William loped across to the other side of the kitchen and hurriedly spoke to Levi. The paramedic was in shock himself. He had torn off all three eels and now he was lying next to his medical box, dressing his terrible injuries and preparing to inject himself with anti-tetanus toxoid. He could barely understand what William was saying but at last he nodded his head and with trembling, blood-smeared hands made up a hypodermic of thiopentone sodium. "This should . . . send a whale to sleep, okay?"

William loped back, holding up the hypodermic. "He said to inject it right behind the head."

Josh nodded, his chin running with blood. William looked at him and said, "You're sure you want me to do this?"

"For Christ's sake, just do it," Josh urged between clenched teeth.

With infinite care William raised the hypodermic and positioned the point of the needle behind the eel's gleaming head. He licked his lips, sniffed and then lowered the needle until the point was actually indenting the eel's skin.

The two cops stared at each other. They had been through three years of service together, over a thousand days of violence, tedium, danger and injury. This, however, was something different. This was the day they had unwittingly come face-to-face with the Devil himself.

Josh nodded. William stuck the needle into the eel's body with a faint pop of punctured skin. The eel showed no sign that it had felt the prick of the needle, nor did it move when William gradually depressed the slide and filled its nervous system with anesthetic.

The cops waited nervously. The sun came out from behind a cloud and the kitchen suddenly brightened. They looked around. The rest of the eels had disappeared, leaving the body of the woman who had borne them lying bloody and ravaged. Levi had injected himself with an analgesic and was propped against a cabinet with his head drooping between his shoulders, too shocked and dopey to do anything but hold on until Tony returned.

Josh looked down at the eel. "What do you think?" he asked. "Do you think it looks like it's sleepy?"

William peered at it closely. "Do they have eyelids?" he asked. "I mean, when they go to sleep, do they close their eyes?"

Five minutes passed. Josh was beginning to tremble with fatigue. "The damn thing must be asleep now," he said in a hoarse voice.

"You want me to try to take it off?" William asked.

Josh nodded but before William could take hold of the eel, he raised his hand. "Wait," he said. He carefully reached down to his holster, unbuttoned it and eased out his .38 revolver.

"What's that for?" William asked, scared.

"In case," Josh told him. He cocked the gun and held it up so the muzzle was touching his right temple.

"Josh—" William protested but Josh snapped, "Do it!"

William reached up until his hands were positioned on either side of the eel's jaws. His idea was to grip each jaw between finger and thumb and to keep the jaws stretched apart while he removed the creature from his buddy's body. He prayed on his mother's life that the anesthetic had worked and that the eel's reflexes were now dead; there was no way of telling whether they were or not. The creature's body remained coiled around Josh's thigh, its eyes wide open.

"This is it," he said, more to himself than to anybody else. He took hold of the eel's jaws, feeling their bone structure through the slippery skin, and slowly lifted the sharp teeth out of the skin of Josh's penis. He paused for a moment, sweating, holding his breath. The eel's eyes stared at him coldly, mockingly. The jaw muscles were stronger than William had expected and it was all he could do to keep them apart.

Josh breathed, "Take it off, William. Slowly now, slowly, but for Christ's sake, take it off."

William swallowed. He had just begun to ease the eel downward, however, when the broken kitchen door banged open and two detectives walked in.

"What the hell's this?" one of them demanded. "What the hell's going on here?"

William glanced up and as he did, his fingers slipped.

Josh shouted as the eel's teeth punctured his skin yet again, and he tried in panic to wrench the creature loose.

The eel's jaw muscles snapped shut with a gristly crunch.

Josh roared like a kamikaze and pulled the trigger of his .38. With a thunderous report, his head emptied itself all over the kitchen.

He fell sideways and as he did, the eel unwound itself, quick and silvery, and slithered away to the other side of the room and disappeared. William wasn't watching it anyway. He was kneeling in front of Josh, his face spattered with blood, his hands still held up helplessly, the way they had been when he had lost his grip on the eel's jaws.

The detectives had whipped out their guns when Josh had fired and now they were crouched on the far side of the kitchen in wary perplexity.

"You want to tell us what's happening here?" one of them asked, reholstering his gun and distastefully making his way between splashes of blood.

William shrugged. "I tried," he said, his voice choked. "I tried my level best."

Outside, two sirens cried in the sunshine. Levi tried to raise his head to see what was happening.

Nine eels, meanwhile, had slithered out of the house, seeking places to hide. Three of them buried themselves in the dry, sun-baked soil in Jennifer's garden next to her rose bushes. Another coiled itself up in the darkness at the back of the shed that housed the swimming-pool pump. Two more managed to find a way through to the neighbor's yard, where one of them slid into a squirrel hole and the other found a niche for itself in an abandoned outhouse. Two poured like liquid mercury down a nearby sewer grate and would gestate in an archway regularly flooded with raw sewage. The last tried to cross Paseo del Serra just as the local road-sweeping truck was crawling past and was whipped up by the brushes and carried, still alive, to the garbage dump, where it was buried under tons of newspapers, gravel, Coke cans, dried yucca leaves and excrement.

It lay there, its eyes staring, its gills slowly opening and closing, waiting to grow.

19

It had been seven weeks now and the Night Warriors had found no trace of Yaomauitl. After they had failed to destroy the Devil in the clockwork city, they had gone out night after night, crisscrossing the darkened landscape of Southern California in search of the slightest heartbeat that would tell them Yaomauitl was concealed close by. They had penetrated dream after dream. Dreams of carnivals, of love affairs, of drownings. But though they had glimpsed many demons and many dark anxieties, though they had felt the furtive scuttling of many guilty figures and heard the whispering of many evil names, they had failed to find the Devil they sought.

"Maybe we've scared him off," Tebulot had suggested one night as they had sailed by moonlight over the Sepulveda Dam Recreation Area.

Kasyx had looked grim. "I don't want to scare him off. I want to get him back in that box in San Hipolito where he belongs."

After the third week they had agreed to split their nightly patrols so only two of them went out at once. Although their mortal bodies had remained peacefully sleeping in their beds, their minds had been growing weary from nights of searching. After the fifth week they had given up patrolling every night and instead had flown out twice a week, spreading their search as far as San Luis Obispo in the north and Palm Springs in the east. Kasyx had felt it was unlikely that Yaomauitl had returned to Mexico.

These days they scarcely saw Springer. Occasionally she was there when they went to the house on Camino del Mar, but she was quiet and uncommunicative and her clothing was growing increasingly lavish and decorative, as if to show them that every day the Devil remained free, the world grew a little more decadent.

The Night Warriors still met each other during the day. Henry's cottage had become something of a casual heaquarters where they came and went as they felt the need to talk. Lloyd stayed over a couple of nights despite protests from his mother, and Gil was a regular visitor. Occasionally Susan dropped by too when she came down to the beach to swim, and they would all sit out on Henry's veranda and drink lime-flavored Kool-Aid and talk about the battle they had fought on the plain of ashes and what they would do the next time they came face-to-face with Yaomauitl.

They had nobody else with whom they could talk about their adventures as Night Warriors; they had nobody else in whom they could confide their fears. They had been terrified there in the clockwork city but who were they going to tell?

"If I said anything to my analyst about it, he'd have me bouncing around in a padded cell before sundown," Henry had remarked.

Henry was finding it increasingly difficult to resist the vodka bottle. As each night ended without a trace of Yaomauitl, his sense of failure and frustration began to irritate his nerve endings and how he longed to anesthetize those nerve endings in Smirnoff. He went to the liquor cabinet two or three times a day, opened it and stared at the half-filled bottle of vodka that stood there, then closed the cabinet again. He felt that he had entered into a solemn agreement with the other Night Warriors not to drink. After all, they were young, and their lives depended on him.

But as each night went by and the Deadly Enemy remained hidden, Henry's craving grew stronger. One drink, he thought. Just one. Just to give me that glow, just to give me that extra confidence. Just to relax this whirling, overheated brain of mine and to give me some peace.

His equilibrium had not been helped by the matter of Salvador's death. Although the police had eventually been satisfied that the presence of Henry, Gil and Lloyd at the Scripps Institute had not been contributory to Lieutenant Ortega's accident—mainly due to evidence given by Andrea—the Institute itself was considering a prosecution for unlawful trespass and damage to property, and the police made a point of calling Henry at all times of day as if checking up on him.

And whether the police were satisfied or not, Henry, Gil and Lloyd knew that while they had probably saved Andrea, they had certainly been largely responsible for what had happened to Salvador. It was no good making excuses about "casualties of war." Henry had gone to see Salvador's widow, taking a bunch of flowers for her and a Fisher-Price windup Ferris wheel for her children. The children had sat on the green nylon rug and the windup Ferris wheel had played "In the Good Old Summertime" and afterward Henry had slumped in the passenger seat of Gil's Mustang with tears running down his cheeks.

Daffy, Susan's friend, kept complaining that Susan was "eons away" and that she just wasn't any fun anymore. Susan apologized as often as Daffy complained but there was nothing she could do to explain how she felt. Even if she could have told Daffy about the day the Devil had kept her captive, and even if Daffy had believed it, Daffy wouldn't have understood. Not even Henry or Gil or Lloyd could understand. Because even though Susan had been alone, she had been frightened that day beyond any fear she had ever known. That day she had understood exactly what she was—an assemblage of bones, skin and convulsing muscle—and she had understood that the difference between life and death was nothing more than a fragile spasm.

That understanding had brought her closer to her grandparents; these days she could even tolerate her grandfather's corny ribbing. But it had taken her farther away from her own generation, to whom death remained comfortably unthought-of.

Daffy was right. She was no fun anymore. But she was

far more caring and far more sympathetic than she had ever been, and she knew that when they had defeated Yaomauitl at last, her sense of fun would return. If only she could have told Daffy how hard it was to laugh during a war.

Gil's experiences had divided him from his friend too, and from his parents. Apart from the matter of the borrowed gun, which had cost him two weeks' allowance and a month of working mornings in the store, he found that he was completely unable to confide in his father and mother the way he used to. Phil Miller tried to talk to him several times to find out what was wrong. "You're not sick, are you? You're not in love?" But Gil found it impossible to give his father an explanation that would have described how he felt, even remotely. He felt like Tebulot and how could he tell his father that? He felt strong, philosophical, aggressive, moral and dedicated. He felt a need to fulfill his destiny as a Night Warrior by finding and destroying Yaomauitl, the Deadly Enemy. How could he put any of that into words his father could accept—his father, whom he loved dearly but whose horizons were bounded by pepper salamis and boxes of Cap'n Crunch?

The changes that had occurred in Lloyd's life were more oblique. He had always been thoughtful and deeply involved in everything he did, whether it was schoolwork, athletics or developing a friendship. His father was a serious man, a man of such honesty of spirit that in his own small way he was almost a saint. Lloyd had inherited that honesty, combined with the passionate enthusiasm of his mother, and so when he had started to close himself away from the rest of the family to think over his experiences as a Night Warrior, nobody had noticed anything particularly unusual.

Lately, however, Lloyd had begun to feel that there was a great fulfillment awaiting him. Not just the fulfillment of winning a five-hundred-meter track race, not just the fulfillment of scoring top marks in English, not just the fulfillment of being black and doing well in a white man's world. Lloyd had begun to smell greatness in the wind, the sharp aroma that stirred up ordinary men and made them heroes.

One evening in the sixth week of looking for Yaomauitl, Lloyd's father had come into his bedroom and stood there for a long time, his glasses in one hand and a folded copy of the evening paper in the other, and at last had said, "Lloyd, I want you to tell me the truth."

"Daddy?"

"Lloyd, are you sniffing anything? You tell me the truth now."

Lloyd had actually smiled. "No, Daddy," he had told his father quietly, his face half-shadowed by the light from his desk lamp. "No, I'm not sniffing anything."

On the third morning of the seventh week the skies along the Southern California coast were gray and hazy but the early weather forecast predicted that the sun would burn through the haze before ten o'clock. After the weather forecast came the local news and Henry was sitting in the kitchen eating a bowlful of *muesli* when it was announced that the body of a young woman had been discovered in a house on Prospect Street, La Jolla, with massive abdominal injuries.

The newscaster said, "Police were reluctant to say last night whether the slaying was the work of a ritual killer or whether the girl's death resulted from some kind of bizarre accident."

Henry slowly put down his spoon. Massive abdominal injuries. He wondered whether at last he had found the key to Yaomauitl's long silence. Leaving his breakfast, he went through to the living room and leafed through the telephone directory until he found the listing for the San Diego coroner's office. He punched out the number, running his hand repeatedly through his untidy hair while waiting for an answer.

"Mr. John Belli," he said when he was eventually connected.

John Belli sounded tired and unhappy. "Who is this?" he demanded, clearing his throat.

"Mr. Belli, this is Henry Watkins, Professor Henry Watkins. I was one of the three people who originally discovered the body of Sylvia Stoner."

"Yes?" John Belli asked suspiciously.

"Well, sir, I'm sorry to bother you but I heard on the news this morning that another girl had been found dead. On Prospect Street in La Jolla."

"Yes." Flatly this time. Cautiously.

"May I ask you just one question about her?"

"You can ask. I can't guarantee I'll give you an answer."

"Well," Henry said, "you don't have to say yes if what I'm going to ask you is true. But if it isn't true, I'd be obliged if you would say no."

There was a pause. Then John Belli said, "Go ahead, ask."

"The question is, does the evidence indicate that the girl found at La Jolla was killed in the same way as Sylvia Stoner?"

There was another pause. Then John Belli hung up.

Henry held the receiver in his hand for a moment, listening to the burring of the dial tone. Then he slowly cradled it and stood up. So that was it. Yaomauitl had been waiting for his new offspring to be hatched. A girl at La Jolla had died, and who knew how many more women had been impregnated by a Devil who could disguise himself as anything and anyone he chose? There could be hundreds of eels greedily eating their way out of the wombs of scores of women. And even though they were not yet grown—even though they were only embryos—they could begin to dream, and once they could begin to dream, they could join their father and master, Yaomauitl, as reinforcements.

Yaomauitl was preparing to annihilate the Night Warriors and carry his invasion through the dreams of every American. He might not be able to exert his influence during the day, when men were rational, wakeful and alert, and skeptical of Devils. But at night, as they slept, his evil influence could coax them, tempt them and turn their minds. His shadows would rise up in their nightmares and preach intolerance, cruelty and self-indulgence; and all the achievements of religious civilization—those achievements that had been won by hundreds of years of war, anguish and human suffering—would be toppled and swept away. Out of a nation's nightmares a new Dark Age would begin to flood, staining the map of the world like ink.

Henry called Gil. "Gil? This is Henry. Did you hear the news this morning?"

"I was slicing corned beef."

"Listen, Gil, it's happened again. They've found a girl in La Jolla, dead, with her stomach eaten open. No eels—at least the news didn't mention any—so presumably they managed to get away and bury themselves."

Gil said, "What does this mean? I'm not sure I understand."

"The way I interpret it," Henry said, "is that Yaomauitl has been waiting for the birth of new embryo Devils so he can outnumber us and then wipe us out."

"When? Where? Any ideas?"

"Not yet. But I think we ought to go out tonight, all of us, and see if we can pick up his scent."

"All right, you're on. Eleven?"

"Eleven it is."

Henry called Susan and Lloyd. Lloyd was out but his suspicious mother took a message. Susan sounded grave on the phone and asked Henry if he thought this was the showdown.

"Showdown? You make it sound like *High Noon*," Henry joked.

"He wants to kill us though, doesn't he?" asked Susan, still grave.

Henry hesitated and then said, "Yes, he does."

"And if he kills us, when we're Night Warriors?"

Henry reached down and rubbed the leg that had been

bruised during their battle in the depths of the clockwork city. "You know what Springer said. If he kills us as Night Warriors, our physical bodies will never wake up."

"Eleven o'clock?"

"You don't have to come if you don't want to."

"You need me. How are you going to find Yaomauitl without Samena's sixth sense?"

"You still don't have to come. We'll find him somehow."

Susan said, "Henry, the very worst that can happen is that I get to rejoin my parents."

Henry didn't know how to reply to that. It was both mature and mystical, a statement of adult resignation and childlike faith. He said with a thickness in his throat, "All right then. Eleven o'clock. I'll look forward to seeing you."

The day seemed to take an eternity to pass. Henry went to the liquor cabinet even more frequently than usual, and once he even went as far as unscrewing the cap of the vodka bottle. He sniffed it and let the fumes of it rise up into his nostrils. One drink, just to focus his mind. One single, solitary drink, just to prepare him for the battle he knew the night would bring him.

He screwed the cap up tight again, put the bottle back and went outside for a short walk along the promenade, breathing in the breeze from the ocean. He had thought he was over the worst of his desire for alcohol, especially after seven weeks without it. Surely his system must have dried out by now. But the craving seemed to be worse than ever and he wondered if he would ever be rid of it. His mind was already spinning out ready-made excuses: *You've been teetotaling for seven weeks, you deserve a drink. One won't hurt you; you'll be able to prove to yourself that you're not an alcoholic after all if you have just one. If you have one, you'll be drinking like normal people do. You'll be cured. After all, how can you say you're cured if you're still not drinking any alcohol at all? Staying completely on the wagon is like admitting you're still sick.*

He met by accident an old friend of his, John Lund, a

hoary old history professor who wore fraying Panama hats and linen coats that looked as if they had previously done service as mail sacks. John was short, bespectacled and voluble, and he didn't drink, so Henry suggested they have lunch together. They linked arms and went to a vegetarian restaurant farther along the strip called Brother Bread, and Henry managed to pacify his desire for vodka with a cool bowl of home-cultured yogurt and a plate of fresh-sliced melon. While he ate, he listened to John's latest interpretation of the War of Independence, which had something to do with the English not wanting to win it anyway.

While John spoke, a man sitting opposite, eating alone, opened his copy of *The Los Angeles Times*. Henry only glanced at the headlines at first, out of the corner of his eye, but then he peered at them narrowly and read them with a rising sense of fright: "Killer Eels Slay Wife, Attack Husband and Cops. Officer, emasculated, shoots self. Medic and husband suffer multiple bites."

"And after Valley Forge . . ." John was saying earnestly as he cut his melon into small pieces.

"John, excuse me," Henry said and went across to the man with the paper. "Could I borrow your front page for just a minute?" he asked. The man shrugged and peeled it off for him.

John Lund watched Henry through the lenses of his smeary glasses as Henry quickly read about the eels that had attacked a middle-aged couple as well as paramedics and police on Paseo del Serra in Hollywood. The wife's body, the report said, "had been very severely mutilated . . . with stomach wounds that Sergeant Garcia described as 'worse than anything Jack the Ripper ever perpetrated.'" Only a detailed examination of the body would reveal exactly what had happened.

"What is it?" asked John. "You look worried."

Henry said, "I am worried. Actually I'm more than worried, I'm scared stiff."

"You? Scared? What on earth does a professor of philosophy have to be scared of?"

Henry handed the newspaper back to the man at the opposite table. Then he said to John, his hands clasped in front of him, "Supposing you were told you had to fight one of those Japanese sumo wrestlers?"

John guffawed. "I'd lose," he said. "No question about it."

"Supposing you were told that if you lost, the whole of the human race would die out?"

John said with a frown, "What is this, one of your peculiar oriental riddles?"

Henry shook his head. "What would you do? How would you feel? Would you fight or would you forget it?"

John slowly stirred his coffee and then helped himself to another spoonful of brown sugar. "I'd fight," he said, "but I'd be scared."

"Exactly," said Henry.

"You mean that you—?" asked John, unable to come to grips with what Henry was telling him.

"Me," said Henry. "Me and the sumo wrestler and the whole human race. Only it's not a sumo wrestler."

"May I ask what it is?" John asked, mystified. He had heard Henry talk sober nonsense and he had heard Henry talk drunk sense, but he had never heard Henry talk like this before.

Henry leaned forward and grasped the coarse linen shoulder of John's coat. "It's the Devil," he whispered, and of course John smiled, sat back, shook his head, smugly crossed his legs . . . and didn't believe him for a moment.

They had all arrived well before eleven, serious and eager. Springer was there too, a man this time, dressed in a strange suit of gray and black that rustled like tissue paper when he walked. He touched the hands of each of them and looked into their faces, one after the other, his eyes like slanted windows into outer space, eyes that told of absolute emptiness, distant stars and meanings that could only be dreamed about.

"I knew you would be here tonight," he said. "You have interpreted Yaomauitl's maneuvers well."

Kasyx lifted a crimson gauntlet and slowly parted his fingers. Sparkling blue electricity jumped from one fingertip to the next. He had never before absorbed so much of Ashapola's energy and he knew that one accidental discharge would be catastrophic. But tonight, if they were to encounter Yaomauitl yet again, they would need all the power they could muster.

Springer said, "Tonight will be your greatest adventure. Tonight you will know the true power of Night Warriors. In the name of Ashapola and the sacred Warriors of ancient times, may you be protected from evil, and may your light cleave the darkness for the liberation of the world of men."

These were plainly words Springer had repeated time and again in years gone by, words from the greatest days of the Night Warriors, when scores of Devils had walked the earth and those who had fought them in dreams and nightmares could be counted in their thousands. A dark company, who had brought the virtues of peace and understanding to every corner of the world, no matter how uneasy that peace and understanding may have been.

The Night Warriors rose up into the evening air. Because Springer had alerted Samena that he had felt cold vibrations somewhere to the east, they glided over the golf courses and condominiums around the Fairbanks ranch and headed up into the hills, where the night air was pungent with the aroma of eucalyptus and lights sparkled from expensive Spanish-style homes hidden among the lemon groves and yucca.

"Any feelings?" Kasyx asked Samena as they sailed silently over Rancho Santa Fe, where lights from the windows of the white-painted inn cast bright-green patterns across the croquet pitches that surrounded it. Then they were back in darkness again, searching the hills for the least warning that Yaomauitl was close.

Xaxxa said, "Maybe we were wrong, man. Maybe he isn't ready to fight yet."

"He's ready," Kasyx affirmed. "He wouldn't have allowed those embryos to have been born so publicly if he wasn't ready to fight. He knows we know about it, and he knows we're out here looking for him."

"Well, anytime, man, anytime," said Xaxxa.

Tebulot said nothing. He was too deep in thought about the problems he was having with his parents and about the dangers the Night Warriors would face tonight. He hadn't lost his nerve. Far from it. But he wanted the fighting to start and to start soon so he could be given some respite from his endless, wrangling anxieties. He loved his father and mother; he didn't want to be alienated from them. But until the Warriors had found and vanquished Yaomauitl, there was nothing he could say to his parents that would truly reunite him with them.

They were almost ready to turn back toward the coast when Samena said quietly, "He's here. He's close by. I can feel him."

The other three moved in closer to her, gliding together in ghostly formation between the hills. They followed every turn and dip she made, like an aerobatic team coming in to land in total darkness.

"Right a little, right," Samena said, and they banked toward the right until at last they were rustling through a thick grove of fan palms and into the grounds of a large, ocher-painted house that stood by itself on a bend in the highway.

"This is it, he's here," said Samena, and without hesitation she penetrated the clay-tiled roof and entered one of the bedrooms.

An oriental-looking man lay asleep with his wife on a wide brass bed covered with a black-satin sheet. The rug was white, the furniture was white, and there was a large stylized painting by Sotaro Yasui on the wall. The Night Warriors stood at the foot of the bed and looked at the sleepers with caution.

"Which one is it, the man or the woman?" Tebulot asked.

"The man," Samena replied. "The feeling is really strong, stronger than it's ever been."

"Are we ready for this?" asked Kasyx.

They nodded. Kasyx lifted his hands and drew the octagon. When he divided the night air between it, he saw whiteness, and falling snow.

"Looks like this is going to be a cold one," he said, but without hesitation he raised the octagon over their heads. As it slowly descended around them, he gripped the hands of each of them in turn, giving them encouragement and extra strength. "We're going to win this time," he assured them. "This time we're going to bring Yaomauitl back to Mexico, and on a permanent basis too."

When the octagon reached the floor, and they were immediately engulfed in utter silence, a silence so complete that none of them moved, none of them spoke. They simply lifted their heads and listened.

They were knee-deep in the softest of snow, and snow was falling thickly, without a whisper. There was no wind blowing and the air was surprisingly warm. They looked around but as far as they could see in every direction, there was nothing but snow.

Tebulot came wading over to Kasyx, his machine slung over his shoulder. "I never saw snow like this," he remarked, his eyes darting uneasily from one side to the other.

"Maybe it's Japanese snow," Kasyx said. "Samena? Do you have any idea of where our Devil might be?"

Samena cupped her hands over her face and was silent for almost a minute. The snow dropped silently onto the feathers of her hat, turning them white. Xaxxa meanwhile was walking around in circles, holding out his hands and watching the snowflakes melt in his palms. "Do you know something?" he grinned. "I never saw snow before this in my whole life, not ever. Isn't it weird?"

Samena at last pointed vaguely to the right. "Over there, I think. It's difficult to tell. I can feel something but the feeling doesn't seem quite right."

"All the same, we'd better give it a try," said Kasyx, and they began to trudge in the direction Samena had indicated, leaving wide, deep tracks in the fluffy white surface.

"I wonder if this is a nightmare or a dream," Tebulot said, still looking around suspiciously.

"It feels like a nightmare," said Samena. "There's something not quite balanced about it, like it's peaceful but that's only a sham. I keep picking up the idea that somebody's died and there's a funeral nearby."

"For many Orientals, white is a color of mourning," said Kasyx. "Maybe this whole dream is some kind of funeral."

They continued to push their way through the snow. Where the ground dipped, it had drifted and they found themselves buried almost up to their waists. But the soil beneath the snow seemed firm and hard-packed and so they managed to make good progress.

"Do you think we're making a mistake?" asked Tebulot as they paused for a rest.

Samena shook her head. "There's no mistake. He's here someplace. But he's probably trying to disorient us and tire us out."

"He's not making a bad job of it either," said Tebulot.

Xaxxa said, "It's going to take more than snow to put me off, man."

Kasyx placed his hand over his forehead and examined their surroundings with infrared to see if there were any traces of heat, Devilish or human. But all he could register were the glowing yellow-and-blue bodies of Tebulot, Samena and Xaxxa and the golden pulsing of Tebulot's highly charged machine.

"You still think we're heading in the right direction?" he asked Samena.

"As far as I can tell," she said. "The feeling is stronger than it was but it keeps breaking up and dividing and it's hard to say exactly where it is."

Kasyx said, "All right. We'll keep on going for another couple of miles. If we haven't located anything by then, we'll leave this dream and see if we can't find Yaomauitl someplace else."

Samena told him, "He's here, Kasyx, I promise you."

"Come on," Kasyx said, and they began to march slowly through the drifts once more, four small figures in a huge, whirling landscape of white. As he marched, it struck Tebulot as amazing that this entire world could exist inside one man's sleeping mind and that this one man would have only to turn over in bed to start dreaming about another world altogether, a world quite different but just as vast. This was one thing his experience as a Night Warrior had taught him: that inner space was as infinite as outer space but far more complicated because it obeyed none of the laws of the material world. In inner space, a building could float in the sky, an animal could talk, a dead husband could come to life again. In inner space, snow could fall in the hottest month of the summer and Devils could hide like Arctic wolves.

It was then that they heard a sudden clashing sound. The snow shuddered as it fell and began to spin around in wild eddies. They heard whoops, cries and the shaking of dozens of small bells, and out of the snowstorm a huge sled appeared, drawn by over a hundred harnessed polar bears. It passed them only fifty feet away, its wooden runners hissing over the snow. It was constructed entirely of yew and articulated in the middle so it could turn quickly. The front section was three stories high and heaped with animal furs. The rear section was crowded with masked soldiers in breastplates and winged helmets that reminded the Night Warriors of the hordes of Genghis Khan, and each soldier carried a strange, wide-barreled rifle. At the very back of the sled there was a wooden tower, sixty feet high, whose sides were clustered with silver bells and ribbons as well as the carcasses of dead wolves, snowshoe rabbits and the flowing black scalps of human beings.

At the top the of tower, in midnight-black armor that resembled a beetle's carapace, stood a being whose eyes gleamed yellow and malevolent: the lord of all darkness, Yaomauitl.

Tebulot yelled, "Hit the deck!" and the Night Warriors plunged facedown into the snow. The jangling sled wheeled around them in a wide circle and they could hear the Tartar soldiers screeching through the snowstorm like voracious crows. Kasyx lifted his head and immediately the snow around them exploded into hundreds of powdery white plumes. He ducked down again, glanced across at Samena and said, "I think we take it all back. You found him all right."

Tebulot eased back the T-bar of his machine. "If I can hit Yaomauitl himself, maybe we can get this over with."

They heard the terrible sled sliding closer. The paws of a hundred bears shook the snow as if an earthquake were impending. Tebulot made a confident circle of finger and thumb and gave Kasyx a wink from behind his face mask. "Here goes nothing," he said and lifted himself out of the snow.

Instantly there was an ear-splitting barrage of fire from the soldiers at the rear of the sled. Each shot made a sharp breathy shriek like a bicycle pump drawing in air. As the sled thundered past, towering high above their hiding place, Kasyx saw three soldiers lean over the side of it and fire at them, and then he realized what the whistling was.

The Tartar's rifles, instead of firing a projectile, *sucked in* whatever they were aimed at. When they missed and struck the ground instead, a thin bullet of snow would be plucked up and zapped backward into the gun's barrel. It took only a little imagination to picture what would happen if they managed to aim straight at a human being.

With the sled scarcely past them, Tebulot rolled onto his back and fired a dazzling blast of concentrated energy at the wooden tower. The energy bolt screamed in through one of the tower's windows and for a moment nothing happened. Then the tower blew up in a tumbling shower of shattered wood and scorched wolf carcasses, and a ball of orange fire rose up over the sled and vanished.

Two rear runners collapsed and the giant sled ground to a halt in a spray of ice. Immediately the Tartar soldiers swarmed down the sides and dropped into the snow so the Night Warriors would find them more difficult to hit. One of the Tartars ran around and cut loose the bears, waving a bright-red flare at them to frighten them away. Samena watched this particular Tartar for a while and then unhooked an arrowhead from her belt. She crossed her arms and fired the energy arrow along the side of the sled, where it pierced the soldier's hand so that he dropped his flare. Immediately two of the bears turned around and shuffled toward him, snarling. The Tartar cried out and began to run but the bears were faster. They came up behind him and knocked him down in a spray of blood. One of them went for his head, and from two hundred feet away, the Night Warriors could hear his skull crunch.

The flare, meanwhile, had dropped among the furs and the front of the sled began to burn. Within three or four minutes it was ablaze from end to end.

Kasyx kept a lookout for Yaomauitl but there was no sign of him. He said to Xaxxa, "How about making a quick pass overhead? Do you think you can do that without getting hit? I want to see where Yaomauitl's hiding."

Xaxxa said, "You got it," and lay flat on his back in the snow. Then he covered his face with his mirrorlike mask, double-somersaulted backwards and streaked up into the snowy sky on a slide of shining gold.

For a moment Xaxxa disappeared completely and they waited anxiously for his return. The wooden sled crackled and popped and there was a thick, nauseating odor of burning fur. The Tartars kept their heads well down, especially since Tebulot was ready for them with his machine fully cocked.

Samena asked, "You don't think he's lost, do you?"

But before Kasyx could reply, they heard that familiar jet-plane whistle and Xaxxa came flashing across the snow only two feet above the ground, crouched on his shining slide like the greatest surfer that ever was.

One of the Tartars lifted himself out of the snow and aimed at Xaxxa with his wide-barreled rifle. But Xaxxa weaved and ducked in midair and kicked the Tartar in the jaw with a two-footed dropkick that carried an impact velocity of three hundred miles an hour. The Tartar was flung across the snow and his rifle dropped and fired at one of his comrades who had been crouched next to him. It was then that the Night Warriors saw what the weapons could do. A six-inch plug of living flesh was snapped out of the soldier's thigh and sucked bloodily into the rifle's open barrel. The soldier screeched and dropped to the snow, clutching his leg.

Xaxxa made another flying pass and then circled around and rejoined the Night Warriors.

"Terrific kick," Kasyx complimented him. Then, "Any sign of Yaomauitl?"

"I don't think that creature we saw was Yaomauitl himself," Xaxxa panted. "I saw its armor lying empty in the snow and something lying next to it that looked like that Devil we burned at the Scripps Institute, only smaller and redder. Whatever it was, it was dead meat."

"One of Yaomauitl's new offspring," Kasyx breathed. "While they dream, they can take on his adult appearance, but when you destroy them in their dream, they revert to what they really are: embryos, undeveloped demons. What did Springer call them? Joeys."

Samena asked, "How about the rest of the soldiers? Do you think we can manage to beat them?"

"I'm not so sure," Xaxxa said. "They've dug themselves in pretty good. It's going to take a lot of energy to shift them."

"Energy is one thing I don't want to waste," said Kasyx. But then Tebulot lifted his hand and said brightly, "I've got an idea, listen! I read it in a cowboy book once. It's something the Cheyenne Indians did to distract their enemies."

"You realize the Cheyenne Indians got beaten in the end," Xaxxa said.

"Well, come on, it's only an adaptation of what the Cheyennes did," Tebulot explained. "What we could do is this: pick up that Tartar soldier, the one who's been wounded in the leg, and fly him down the whole length of the Tartar lines, spraying them in blood. Then we round up the rest of those bears and drive them back here. As soon as they smell that blood . . . well, they're going to go crazy, aren't they?"

"When you say *we*, you mean *me*, if I understand you right?" Xaxxa asked. "I mean, seeing as how I'm the only one here who can fly."

Tebulot said, "We'll be covering you."

Xaxxa looked at Kasyx, who said, "It's a good idea but you don't have to do it if you don't want to."

"No, I'll do it," Xaxxa said. "I just wanted to make sure nobody here was taking me for granted."

"Are you kidding?" smiled Samena.

Without further delay, Xaxxa flashed off through the falling snow and vanished once more. When he came back, he was traveling so fast they didn't see him until he reached down out of the blizzard and snatched up the wounded Tartar like a buzzard picking up an injured gopher. The other Tartars lifted their weapons and fired a sharp, shrieking salvo at him but he managed to fly the length of the Tartar lines, his victim hanging bleeding from his arms.

He dropped the hapless Tartar into a deep snowdrift and then climbed away into the sky to round up the polar bears.

Kasyx waited impatiently as minutes passed. The snow was still falling thickly, covering his crimson armor like white wool. Samena sat beside him, her face calm, turning around now and then to make sure the Tartars hadn't yet decided to attack. Tebulot kept his weapon ready and humming but he knew there was nothing he could do at the moment.

Samena said, "I hope Xaxxa isn't lost. He doesn't have the same directional senses I have. Not in this kind of weather anyway."

"He'll be all right," Kasyx said, although he wasn't completely convinced of it. Xaxxa was a little too fast and a little too flamboyant. If he had accidentally run into another of those articulated sleds, he could have been killed without their knowing it.

Ten minutes passed. Then Samena said, "They're advancing. Look."

Kasyx raised his head and changed his sight to telescopic. Samena was right. The Tartars were rising up from the snow, their winged helmets black against the blizzard. A shot screeched past Kasyx's head—not a bullet but a thin column of air, sucked back into the rifle at twice the speed of sound. He dropped down and said, "There must be thirty of them at least. Do you think you two can hit them all?"

"We'll try," Tebulot said. "We hit ten times that number of corpses when we fought them on the plain."

"Sure you did," said Kasyx. "But those corpses weren't armed with suck guns the way these jokers are."

Samena said quietly, "We have to take the risk, Kasyx. Xaxxa took the risk."

"Well, I know," Kasyx replied. "It's just that you're . . ."

"Young?" smiled Samena. "Yes, we are. But Warriors have always been young. That's what makes their sacrifice so special."

Tebulot lifted his head. The Tartar soldiers had fanned out and were making their way across the snow toward them in a wide pincer movement, dark and sinister, their rifles held high. Tebulot aimed his machine and fired three bright energy bolts that burst into jagged "shrapnel," uncontrolled electrical charges that could tear their way through armor plate. With a crackling sound, seven Tartars dropped to the ground and smoke drifted through the falling snow.

Samena dropped two more Tartars with wire-flailing arrowheads, immaculate shots that killed them with a minimum of energy. But then the remaining soldiers began to fire at them from three sides and they had to drop back into the snow.

"Where the hell is Xaxxa?" Tebulot demanded, more to himself than to anyone else.

Tebulot needn't have worried for suddenly the shrieking of suck guns died away and the three Night Warriors heard confused shouting, and then screams. Cautiously they peered out of the snow and there was Xaxxa twenty feet up in the air, floating toward them, his arms outspread, his mirrored face inscrutable and terrifying, even to them.

Ahead of him, roaring and rumbling, jogged sixty or seventy fully grown bears, the remains of the sled's harness team. At first they had run this way because Xaxxa had frightened them, looping from side to side in shining figures-of-eight. But now they could smell the fresh blood he had spattered over the Tartar soldiers and their hunger drove their legs like superheated steam-driven pistons.

Kasyx rose to his feet, as did Samena and Tebulot. The sight was extraordinary. Each of the bears must have weighed close to a ton, yet they all shambled forward at nearly twenty miles an hour, their teeth bared, their black lips curled back, their yellow eyes staring with mindless hunger. The Tartars opened fire on them. Bloody strings of flesh were snatched from the flanks of four of them and three collapsed onto the snow, but the others began to canter forward faster, their breath smoking, their claws scratching on the ice crust. The Tartars wavered and then dropped their rifles and ran.

With a last rush, the bears brought down the soldiers in showers of bloody fury. The Night Warriors watched with a mixture of horror and relief as their enemies were overtaken one by one and clawed down onto the snow, where their bodies were ripped, their helmets scattered and their entrails dragged blue-gray and steaming across the snow.

A little way off, almost hidden by the thickly falling snow, the sled had been burned down to a trough of ashes, and now a wind arose that blew away the sparks.

The Night Warriors cautiously retreated from the scene of the battle so they wouldn't disturb the bears. Following Samena's instincts, they trudged off through the snowstorm again and within minutes, when they looked back, all trace of the sled, the bears and the bodies of the Tartars had vanished.

For over an hour they walked blindly through the snow. Kasyx asked Samena several times if she was sure Yao-mauitl was near, and each time she assured him he was. "I feel it, Kasyx. He's here. He wants to fight us to the bitter end this time. He won't run away."

"I wouldn't even mind if he ran to meet us," Xaxxa complained. "He might save us a walk."

Strangely—though it reduced visibility to little more than a few feet—the snow was neither wet nor particularly cold. It was more like thickly falling feathers, the way snow ought to be in dreams. Xaxxa's and Samena's costumes were brief but neither of them were affected by the blizzard. Their body temperature, in fact, was the same as that of the dreamer himself as he lay in his black-satin bed.

After a while the Night Warriors found that they were descending into a wide valley and that the snow was beginning to clear. The sky, however, remained deep red, almost maroon, and the clouds that moved through it, stately and slow, were tinged with pink. As the snow dissipated altogether, they looked up and saw that flamingos were flying around in the clouds, their wings beating lazily on unseen air currents, and that on some of the clouds there were colonies of untidy nests.

The snow beneath their feet began to clear away too, and soon they found themselves walking through bracken interspersed with wild flowers, and then the sun began to shine. Below them the valley spread out wide, with a silvery river looping its way through sparkling water meadows and willows sadly washing their hair from grassy banks.

It was difficult to decide where this place actually was, whether it was in the West, in the Orient, or somewhere else altogether. They knew the dreamer was Japanese, or half-Japanese, but this landscape was nothing like Japan. Nor was it anything like California either. It was still and warm and regretful, a landscape of memories and lost loves, but there was also a vaguely threatening quality about it, an indefinable instability.

The Night Warriors reached the river and slowly forded it. The water glittered in the sunlight and ran thick with fish. They climbed the muddy bank on the other side and sat down beside one of the rustling willows to rest briefly and to look around at this extraordinary world in which they found themselves.

"Isn't this the most peaceful place you've ever been?" Samena asked.

Xaxxa was lying on his back in the grass, chewing the stem of a wild flower, his hands laced behind his head. "If this wasn't somebody else's dream, I tell you I'd stay here."

Tebulot put down his machine, eased off his helmet and ran his hand through his hair. "I think Yaomauitl's taken a powder, if he was ever even here. There's nothing Devilish going on in *this* neighborhood, believe me."

But Kasyx felt uneasy. He sniffed the fresh water in the wind and the bright fragrance of the flowers, and he plucked a blade of grass and began to twist it around his finger, but still he sensed trouble. Not in the way Samena sensed the presence of Yaomauitl and his offspring, through disturbed emotions and subtle currents of fear, but through plain analytic logic. Yaomauitl needed to eliminate the Night Warriors before he continued his invasion of America's dreams, both as a matter of practicality and as a matter of pride. It was hard for Kasyx to believe that he wouldn't try to destroy them at the earliest possible opportunity. The longer your enemy lives, the stronger he becomes.

"Where do we go from here?" he asked Samena.

She shaded her eyes against the sun. "I suppose we could try walking along to the far end of the valley."

"You mean you don't know?"

Samena said, "I'm not sure. I seem to have lost the scent."

Kasyx stood up. He was worried now. Xaxxa watched him from where he was lying in the grass twiddling a flower stem between his teeth. "What's the matter, man? You look like something's under your skin."

"I don't know, I don't know. This is all wrong," Kasyx said. "Listen, I vote we get out of this dream now we've lost the trail. Let's go back and try again from the beginning. We've managed to kill off one of Yaomauitl's offspring; let's chalk that up for tonight and leave the rest until tomorrow."

Tebulot was down by the edge of the river trying to scoop up one of the fish. "I think we ought to stay here for a while and enjoy it. Come on, Kasyx, enjoy! How often do we get into a dream like this? This is paradise."

Kasyx said anxiously, "Please, let's go. There's definitely something wrong here. I can feel it."

"If you can feel it, how come Samena can't?" Tebulot wanted to know.

But Kasyx didn't answer. He was staring out at the wide reflecting surface of the river. Something had disturbed the surface of the water and caused it to furrow. Then something else: a small triangular point rising out of the water, and another, and another. No, not points but spears.

Silently, with dreadful majesty, an entire army rose from the water, a black-armored army mounted on black steeds that looked like horses but had the skin of reptiles. The soldiers wore huge helmets with horns on top of them, and breastplates that rose up on either side of their heads like the wings of vultures. Their eyes glowed venomously yellow and they carried long spears that began to hum on a deep vibrating note. The soldiers themselves started to hum too, deeply and discordantly, a triumphant hum of victory and death.

The river crept away from the horses' clawed hoofs. The grass shriveled up with a sound like crinkling cellophane and turned white. The willows shed their leaves and their trunks wrinkled with premature age. Behind the soldiers, the sky turned from red to threatening black and lightning scuttled along the spines of the distant hilltops, cracking rocks and incinerating trees.

The leader of the army nudged his horse forward and approached the Night Warriors like a mounted nightmare. He glared down at them without speaking and then he addressed them in words they could hear only inside their minds.

"You have been warned before not to interfere in my affairs. You have caused me great grief and for this, you shall die. You will see no more mornings, Night Warriors. Look around this dream, for this is where you will meet your end and this is where I shall bury you forever."

A cold wind began to blow, snatching the dead leaves from the trees and drying the last of the river, where the fish now flapped and gasped. It lifted Yaomauitl's cloak and shook it so it sounded like thunder. The Devil's eyes flared and his steed roared and clawed at the air.

Kasyx stood forward. "In the dark and holy name of the Night Warriors, we shall see you chained up forever!" he shouted.

Tebulot rolled away sideways, yanked back the T-bar of his weapon and let fly half a dozen energy bolts. Four of them struck the black shields Yaomauitl's soldiers carried and were deflected in a spray of incandescent sparks, but two of them zapped through to their targets and two soldiers exploded like bursting boilers, toppling from their steeds with unspent energy snaking over their armor.

Xaxxa shot away, out over the valley, with a shower of humming spears flying after him. He dodged and twisted but as he circled around to fly back toward the soldiers, he suddenly looked over his shoulder and saw that the humming spears were still following him with the deadly tenacity of heat-seeking missiles.

He climbed steeply, his feet sliding up the vertical strip of glowing energy as if they were on rails. The spears climbed after him. He looped the loop and still the spears pursued him, edging their way ever nearer.

He climbed again, as high as he dared, then paused and rolled over sideways in the air and dove straight for the ground. Even Yaomauitl's soldiers turned in their saddles to watch as he plummeted out of the thundery sky, a golden meteor. He disappeared behind the hills and the humming spears flashed after him.

Kasyx feinted first to one side, then to the other, and then he grabbed Samena's arm and began to run. There was nothing else for it. With Xaxxa lost, they stood no chance of fighting Yaomauitl and his army of offspring in the same way they had fought the army of corpses. Tebulot gave them a brilliant horizontal spray of covering fire that knocked two more of Yaomauitl's soldiers from their steeds; then he came running after them.

A flight of humming spears pursued them but Kasyx whipped up his arm and stopped them with a sizzling burst of energy that sent them bounding away. Two or three more spears followed but when Kasyx knocked those away too, Yaomauitl uttered a harsh order that clutched coldly at Kasyx's heart; although it was spoken in an unknown language, he knew intuitively what it meant. He heard scythes being drawn out of metal scabbards with a steely, ringing sound and the cries of the Devil's soldiers urging their steeds to run faster. He heard jingling harnesses, clattering armor, and clawed hoofs tearing at the ground.

Kasyx, Samena and Tebulot scrambled away as fast as they could but the gradient of the hillside grew steeper and they knew they didn't have the strength to outrun Yaomauitl's reptile horses for more than a few seconds longer.

Kasyx stopped running and then Samena stopped too, and finally Tebulot came to a halt, doubled over, gasping for breath. The soldiers encircled them, as black and threatening as shadows, their steeds fretting and sidestepping, their scythes gleaming in the storm light, their eyes as frightening as the fires of hell glimpsed through a secret grating.

Yaomauitl came forward again and dismounted. He was unbelievably tall; he seemed to stretch above them the way a shadow stretches as it falls across a cemetery at sunset. He exuded an extraordinary and repellent odor, like goats, musk and decaying chickens. It was more than the odor of death, it was the odor of complete physical and moral corruption.

"You will kneel before me, minions of Ashapola, and you will kiss my feet and then you will die. For hundreds of years I was imprisoned by your forefathers, and you thought you could take up their weapons and imprison me again. Well, it was not to be and never will be, world without end, amen."

Yaomauitl reached down and lifted his engulfing cloak. He revealed beneath his armor the shaggy legs and cloven hoofs of Pan, the hair matted with grease and filth, and crusty with droppings.

"Kneel!" he commanded. "The pure before the impure! The good before the evil! Kneel and kiss my feet!"

Kasyx said to Tebulot under his breath, "We have only one chance."

Tebulot turned and stared at him.

"That's right," Kasyx said. "I can discharge all of my energy at once and we can blow the whole damned lot of them to kingdom come."

"Can you really do that?" asked Samena, her eyes wide.

"*Kneel!*" roared Yaomauitl, and together the three of them knelt.

"I can do it, sure," said Kasyx. "The only trouble is, it'll probably wipe us out too. And even if it doesn't, we won't have enough energy left to get out of this dream. Yaomauitl was right. This is where we're going to meet our end."

"Do it," said Tebulot decisively.

"Samena?" Kasyx asked softly.

"Do it," she whispered without hesitation.

Yaomauitl's offspring had climbed down from their steeds now and gathered around the Night Warriors to witness this final humiliation. Their robes swished in the rising wind like the curtains of confessionals in blasphemous cathedrals. Thunder grumbled in the distance, and hawks with the faces of men wheeled and turned over the naked trees.

Kasyx lifted his head and said to Yaomauitl, "I will not kiss your feet."

"Then I shall have your head cut off and your dead lips shall kiss my rump," Yaomauitl replied in the coarsest of voices.

"No, you misunderstand me," said Kasyx. "I recognize now that you are greater than Ashapola and that I have been mistaken all this time. I wish to do more than kiss your feet. I wish to embrace you. I wish to hold you close and feel that you and I are one."

Yaomauitl was suspiciously silent for a while. Then he said to Kasyx, "Stand."

Kasyx got to his feet again and stood in front of the Deadly Enemy face-to-face.

"Can I believe you?" Yaomauitl asked.

"What harm could I possibly do you?" asked Kasyx. "You have defeated me now. I am your thrall."

Slowly snow began to fall once more, the snow that had followed Yaomauitl's coldness from the Arctic regions where the Night Warriors had first penetrated the dream. Thunder, lightning and softly falling snow. It was the climate of madness.

Yaomauitl suddenly laughed. The snow seemed to have given him glittering new confidence. He could crystallize the very air in the middle of an electric storm. He could do anything! He could ride through the dreams of men like a whirling avenger, creating anarchy and havoc wherever he went. He had defeated the Night Warriors that Ashapola had sent against him. More than that, he had defeated their spirit too, so that they now knelt before him and acknowledged that he was the master of darkness and Ashapola was nothing more than the dust of twenty million unopened Bibles!

"Embrace me, then!" he roared to Kasyx, and Kasyx opened his arms wide and advanced into the huge, black shadow of Yaomauitl's cloak.

For a fraction of a second Kasyx thought he had done it, that he was going to hug Yaomauitl as tight as he could and then release every ounce of energy stored up inside himself. Yaomauitl would be exploded into atoms beyond any resurrection. Even though he and his fellow Night Warriors would die in this haunted dream, unable to return to the waking world, at least they would have done their duty.

But then one of Yaomauitl's offspring suddenly stepped forward and stood between Kasyx and Yaomauitl.

"You have shown no love of my father until now," he grated, his voice echoing inside Kasyx's head. "Prove that you are sincere in your change of affections. Embrace me first."

Kasyx tried to sidestep the embryo Devil but the half-born creature grabbed his arm. Kasyx repelled him with a sharp burst of power. The Devil screamed and Kasyx pushed him aside and lunged at Yaomauitl, triggering the mental formula that would discharge all his energy.

Yaomauitl, however, was too quick. He whirled his cloak around and knocked Kasyx away, sending him flying into the thick of his own offspring.

"*Kasyx!*" screamed Tebulot. There was a mind-splitting explosion that turned the world into dazzling white and cracked the atoms in the air. When Tebulot could open his eyes again, Kasyx was standing with his arms straight up over his head, his hands glowing electric blue while quivering curtains of pure energy flickered around him and snaked across the ground.

Samena saw Yaomauitl transfixed, his huge cloak raised to shield his eyes. She unhooked an explosive arrowhead from her belt, fitted it onto her finger and took aim at him. But at the very second she fired, Yaomauitl's cloak collapsed to the ground, empty, and Yaomauitl was gone. Her arrowhead zipped away through the darkening sky and vanished without exploding.

The wild bursts of energy gradually died away. Tebulot and Samena slowly approached Kasyx, who was standing on the hillside surrounded by the abandoned armor of his enemies and the dead bodies of fifty embryo Devils. They were curled up, glistening and red like baby birds who had fallen out of their nests. Blowflies began to buzz around them even though it was still snowing.

"Kasyx?" asked Tebulot gently.

Kasyx lowered his arms and looked at his hands. "I'm all right," he said at last. "I've used up all my energy but I'm all right."

Samena put her arms around him and held him close. "Kasyx," she said in a voice so soft he could hardly hear it.

"I'm sorry this was the only way," Kasyx said, looking around at the carnage.

"Yaomauitl escaped," said Samena. "I tried to shoot him but he disappeared."

"Back to the waking world," said Kasyx. He didn't have to add that they would never return there, that their lives would last only as long as this dream lasted and that this dream would be the last thing they would ever see.

"You're totally out of power?" Tebulot asked.

"Flat," said Kasyx with a wry smile. "I'm not exactly the Duracell of Night Warriors, am I?"

"I still have *some* energy left," said Tebulot. He lifted his weapon to show that the charge scale was still glowing.

"I have some too," said Samena.

Kasyx slowly shook his head. "I shouldn't think it will be enough, even between both of you. But here, let's try anyway." He beckoned them to stand on either side of him and place their hands on his shoulders. He closed his eyes and felt their small reserves of energy drain back into his system.

"Well?" asked Tebulot anxiously.

Kasyx touched his fingers to his forehead. Then he said, "I'm sorry. A little more perhaps and we could risk it. But I won't even be able to draw the octagon with this amount."

Tebulot dropped his machine on the ground. "Well," he said, "nice try."

It was at that moment, however, that they heard a yell. A wild, high yell as if somebody were whooping with glee. They turned and looked up, and there, streaking across the floor of the valley, came Xaxxa, his fists held high in the air, triumphantly. He landed beside them, shook each by the hand and then admired the devastation that lay around them.

"Man, how did you *do* this?"

"More important," Kasyx asked, "how did you get away from those spears?"

"World War One fighter-pilot trick," explained Xaxxa. "I saw it in that George Peppard movie, *The Blue Max*. If somebody's chasing you, you dive straight for the ground, right? But you pull up at the last moment and he can't."

"But what took you so long?" asked Tebulot.

"In *The Blue Max* they didn't misjudge it and halfway concuss themselves, that's what took me so long."

Kasyx said, "Xaxxa, how much energy do you have left?"

"I don't know. Why?" asked Xaxxa, frowning.

"Give it to me," Kasyx told him.

Xaxxa gave Kasyx a strange, perplexed look but placed his hand on Kasyx's shoulder without asking questions. Kasyx felt the energy stream into his body, adding to the small store that Tebulot and Samena had given him.

"Well?" asked Tebulot anxiously.

The ground was beginning to rise and fall beneath their feet. They recognized the rhythm; it was the dreamer's breathing as he slowly began to wake up. As the world started to tilt, they knew that if they were unable to escape from this dream, they would soon dwindle into nothingness, forgotten by all humanity as if they had never existed.

"I'm not sure," said Kasyx. "I'm not at all sure."

"Well, try," Tebulot urged. "You have to try."

"Very well," Kasyx agreed and held up his hands. He drew the octagon in the air, only a faint and glimmering octagon but strong enough for them to see it. They clasped hands and Kasyx directed the octagon to rise up over their heads.

"I pray we make it," Samena said. The ground trembled beneath them and as the dimly flickering octagon slowly descended, they said as one, "Amen."

20

John Lund was slowly strolling along the promenade past Henry's cottage when he saw an unfamiliar-looking young man in a gray turtleneck sweater and gray slacks obviously trying to force open the front door. John stood and watched him for a minute and then he approached, lifted his Panama hat and said, "Excuse me, but I don't think this is your house."

The young man snapped around and stared at him. John was startled, for the man's eyes were blazing yellow like a panther's or a demon's and his mouth was drawn back from his teeth in the most terrifying snarl John had ever seen.

"I, er . . . I . . . seem to have made a mistake," John said weakly and replaced his Panama hat and started to back away.

Instead of running off or continuing to force open the door of Henry's cottage, the young man followed John down the path to the promenade and took his arm. He was strong; his hand felt like an iron claw gripping John's arm. He said softly, "You know who lives here, old fellow?"

John swallowed, his stringy Adam's apple bobbing up and down in his soft cotton shirt collar. "Yes, sir. I know who lives here."

"Then come with me. I'm paying him a visit."

"Young man, I don't think I—"

"Come along," the young man urged. He leaned so close that John could smell his breath. It was foul as if he had been drinking, or chewing cloves of garlic. "Your friend won't mind if you pay him a visit, will he?"

"It's kind of early," John protested as the young man almost frog-marched him up the path.

"It's nearly seven-thirty. That's not early. And besides,

some people like to be awakened by their friends, don't they?"

John didn't know what to say. All he could do was to stand by helplessly while the young man eased open the front door with the blade of a long screwdriver and then kicked the door sharply to break the mountings that held the security chain.

"There we are. Old Kasyx must have been expecting us," the young man smiled.

"Old who?" frowned John. "You must have the wrong place. The man who lives here is named Henry Watkins. He's a professor of philosophy at the University of California."

The young man hissed with laughter. "Henry Watkins! Now that's a romantic name, isn't it? Well, he may be Henry Watkins to you but he's Kasyx to me, and this house stinks of Kasyx!"

John said, "You're not thinking of stealing anything, are you?"

The young man's eyes gleamed yellow. "I don't think there's anything worth stealing, do you? A few books, a few sentimental photographs, a couple of bottles of liquor. A microwave oven. No, I don't think I'm going to steal anything."

He beckoned John to follow him across the living room to the corridor that led to the bedroom. John reluctantly did as the young man wanted and even more reluctantly looked into the bedroom itself, where he could glimpse Henry lying asleep.

"I don't know what you're up to," he said hoarsely, "but I think you'd better leave now before you get yourself into real trouble."

The young man hissed again. "Real trouble? Surely you're joking. Only one person is in real trouble, and that's Kasyx. He's asleep, you see; his mind is away somewhere else, dreaming. But just supposing his mind came back and found it no longer had a body to go to?"

"Are you a student of his?" John demanded. "I don't understand any of this but it sounds like nonsense to me, and dangerous nonsense at that. If I were you, young man, I'd leave, because if you don't leave, I'm going to call the police and then you'll *have* to leave."

Without warning the young man produced a surgical scalpel out of his pocket and held the blade up so the point of it almost touched the tip of John's nose.

"Have you ever wondered what it's like to be one of those unfortunate people who are gravely disfigured?" he asked. "One of those unfortunate people who can never go out in public without people staring at them because their faces are so distorted? No nose perhaps, or a terrible cleft in the upper lip, or a cheek that is nothing more than gristle?"

John squinted down at the point of the scalpel and said almost inaudibly, "It's okay. I won't call the police, if it's all the same to you."

"You are a man of great intelligence," the young man smiled. "Now, come into the bedroom and let us see what fun we can have with your friend Henry Watkins here, the man *I* call Kasyx."

"You're not going to hurt him?" John whispered anxiously.

"Oh, no," the young man replied. "I'm not going to hurt him. You can't hurt somebody who isn't here, can you? And Henry Watkins isn't here, at least not yet. This is nothing but his physical body. His real personality is far away from here, farther than you, old man, could even conceive possible."

John said in a hopeless voice, "I pray to you, young man, don't hurt him. Please. He's a very old friend of mine, and a very good man."

"Good by *your* lights. But to my way of thinking, he is the worst of all possible pests. He is meddlesome, pompous and sanctimonious. He deserves to die for his hypocrisy alone."

"I pray to you, please," John repeated, but the young

man turned on him and lifted the scalpel, and there was no need for him to warn John again. John was a brave man in his way, but a fatalist too, and he knew exactly what would happen if he tried to play the hero. No nose perhaps, or a terrible cleft in the upper lip. Or even death.

The young man approached the bed and leaned over Henry with a satisfied, foul-breathed grin. He touched Henry's face and turned to John with a smirk when there was no response. Then he tugged down the covers and bared Henry's chest, exposing its wiry gray hair and its slightly paunchy nipples, and he prodded Henry's skin with the point of his scalpel as if he couldn't decide where to start his first incision.

He stood back. "I want his heart, you see," he told John. "I want to cut his heart out and hold it pumping in my hand. That will satisfy justice. A single heart for my children. Nobody can complain about that."

"You're crazy," John said. "You can't cut his heart out."

"You don't think so?" the young man grinned. "But you're going to watch me do it! You're going to witness it in person. Come over here, come closer. I want some of the blood to pump out on you so everybody will know for sure that you actually stood here and watched it happen!"

He snatched at John's arm but John screamed, "Let me go! You're crazy! Let me go!"

The young man twisted John's arm behind his back in an agonizing half nelson and held the scalpel against his withered throat. "I could end it all now," he breathed in John's ear. "I could cut your throat right through to your vertebrae and then we could see who was crazy!"

"Please, I apologize. Let me go," John begged.

The young man considered the apology for a moment and then released him. "I'll have to think about you," he told him. "Having your heart cut out, that's too dramatic for you. Too heroic. Only Warriors have their heart cut out. It shows that somebody respects them enough to want to put an end to them altogether. But you, you deserve something more insulting. You deserve to have your foot cut off and thrust down your throat."

John was backing away from the young man and his bloodthirsty threats, back toward the bed. So it was he alone who saw Henry open his eyes, look up at the young man's back and quietly raise his head from the pillow.

The young man said, "Maybe I'll cut both your feet off and—"

He stopped in mid-sentence. His eyes had caught the sideways glance John had made toward Henry. He froze where he was, yellow eyes shining, and then he suddenly jumped around so he was facing Henry, his scalpel lifted.

But Henry was sitting up in bed now, and in his fist he grasped the bag of nine seals the priest had given him in San Hipolito.

"Yaomauitl," he said, managing a smile, "you know what these are?"

The young man stared at the bag and began to breathe slowly and deeply. His face lost its color and his forehead broke out into beads of sweat.

"Who gave you those?" he asked in his harsh, deep voice.

"The people of San Hipolito. The people who believe that you belong there, not just now but for all time."

"You are a fool. You cannot send me back. You have already seen my power."

Henry climbed off the bed and stood in front of the young man, holding the bag of seals up in front of his face. "I've seen your power, yes. But I've also seen the power of Ashapola, and I've seen the power of simple human faith. You haven't been defeated by corpses or robots or battle-scarred veterans. You've been defeated by young people who know that they're capable of great deeds of heroism and great acts of personal sacrifice."

Henry loosened the drawstring on the bag, brought the seals out one by one and brandished them in the young man's face.

"You think this superstitious nonsense can scare me?" the young man mocked him. "You think these relics can make me cringe? Let me ask you this, old fellow: What do you think those relics really are? Humbug, that's what they are. Faked-up souvenirs of the son of God. And who was the son of God, old fellow? Do *you* believe in the son of God? Do you believe he actually walked this earth all those years ago and that his disciples left these pitiful fragments?"

Henry glanced at the seals and smiled. "You're quite right, of course," he admitted. "These are ridiculous, aren't they? But the funny thing is, I *do* believe in them. I *do* believe that the son of God walked on this earth, and I *do* believe that these relics came from his disciples. There are times, you know, when even a professional skeptic like me has to take some articles of faith for granted."

He paused and then said, "There are some things, you see, that can be proved only by the feeling in your heart."

In front of Henry's eyes the young man's face began to shift and change. His hair darkened, his features altered, and in a matter of a few seconds he had turned into Salvador Ortega. Henry thought to himself: The Devil certainly knows where to find a man's weakest and guiltiest thoughts.

John whispered, "My God, he's somebody else. Look at him! He's somebody else!"

"Don't worry, John," Henry said. "He just looks like somebody else. He's doing it on purpose to upset me."

Salvador said, "Henry? Listen to me, Henry."

Henry replied, "You're not Salvador. Don't even pretend you are."

"Henry, you're making a mistake," Salvador persisted. "You know what I felt about my religion, about Jesus and the Holy Virgin. But I've seen heaven for myself now, Henry. I've seen it with my own eyes and it's nothing like the priests told me it was going to be. It's wonderful, Henry, you shouldn't feel guilty. But there's no God there, no Jesus, no angels, no Holy Mother. It's a place where you can do and think and be whatever you want. It's freedom, Henry, that's what heaven is. It's total freedom. Throw down those pieces of trash, Henry, and I'll show you. Come on now, throw them down."

Henry shook his head. "I'm holding onto these seals, you bastard, because they're going to put you away where you belong. John, I'm pleased that you're here. I want you to look on my desk. You'll find a telephone number there on top of my notepad. It's a Baja number. Call it now and ask to speak to the priest. When you get through to him, say you're calling for Henry Watkins and that he should send up the elmwood box. Tell him to send it as quickly as he can."

"Elmwood box," John repeated, mystified. "Elmwood box. All right, Henry."

Now Henry stood alone with Yaomauitl. They faced each other in silence. Henry could feel the coldness of sheer evil pour from Yaomauitl like the vapor from liquid oxygen.

"Perhaps I can tempt you," Yaomauitl suggested in a throaty voice.

He twisted his hand and produced, like a stage magician, a tall glass of chilled vodka with an olive in it. "Only one, Henry. Just to prove that you're cured. You deserve it after all, now that you've defeated the great Yaomauitl."

Henry stared at the drink for a long time. Then he looked back at the Devil. It was a curious thing but after last night's battle, his craving for alcohol seemed to have subsided, and being so blatantly tempted now with his principal weakness somehow helped him overcome it even more completely. He was a man; he was a Night Warrior. There was nothing that could deflect him from his power and his principles, especially not liquor.

Yaomauitl twisted his hand and the glass of vodka vanished. "Women, perhaps?" he suggested, and for a second, Henry glimpsed voluptuous bare breasts, curving thighs and provocative lips. "You *do* like women?" Yaomauitl smiled.

Henry said, "You can try anything you like, Yaomauitl.

But you're going back to San Hipolito and they're going to shut you up in that elmwood box and that's where you're going to stay till hell freezes over, I promise."

Yaomauitl glared at him with yellow eyes and began to hiss. Then, incredibly, his head seemed slowly to explode like a speeded-up movie of a growing cauliflower. His cheeks grew pitted and scabrous, his forehead bulged and horns pushed out of his hair. His chest grew too, and his hands turned into hairy claws with long, curved nails that looked as if they could rip a man's heart out with one swipe. His legs thickened and grew shaggy with hair, and his feet narrowed into cloven hoofs. This was the true shape of Yaomauitl. This was the legendary Devil whose appearance had been described again and again by witches and warlocks and frightened priests down through the centuries. But this Devil was real, and he stank of death, and he stood in Henry's bedroom.

"Now," Yaomauitl roared harshly. "Now I am going to slay you, old fellow. Now you are going to experience hell!"

He lashed at the air and his claws made a sound like a thunderclap. Henry held up the seals and shouted, "In the name of Ashapola! In the name of God!" But the Devil gripped him in both hands, his nails piercing Henry's pajamas and digging into his flesh, and lifted him off the floor.

For a second Henry was staring at eyes that blazed like blowtorches and double layers of teeth that could have bitten out his Adam's apple in one ferocious snap. But then he screamed: "I believe in God! I believe in the Father! I believe in the Son! I believe in the Holy Spirit! I believe in the Holy Virgin! And in the resurrection! And in the life to come! And I repudiate you, Yaomauitl! I deny you! I have defeated you!"

The Devil shook Henry until he could feel his brain thumping against the inside of his skull and the beast's claws digging through his flesh, scraping against his ribs.

"Oh, God!" he cried out and lifted the nine seals of the disciples and waved them in agony before Yaomauitl's face.

Yaomauitl screeched, dropped Henry onto the floor and covered his eyes with his hands, shuddering as if he were having a fit. Henry, bruised and bleeding, tried to crawl away. Even the floor was trembling, and a picture dropped off the wall.

Then Yaomauitl fell, but his falling was soft and silent, and when Henry at last managed to heave himself around and to prop himself against the side of the bed, all he could see was a huddled figure like a dead dog's, shaggy and misshapen. Yaomauitl twitched and then lay still.

John appeared in the doorway, his face the color of his linen jacket. "I've called the priest," he said in a papery voice. "He seemed to know what it was all about. He said he'll be here as quickly as possible."

When he saw the stains of blood on Henry's pajamas, he came into the bedroom and knelt beside him. "You're hurt," he said. "I'd better call for an ambulance too."

"No, no," said Henry. "I don't think the paramedics would quite understand. Just go to the bathroom and bring me some bandages. And then go to the liquor cabinet and bring me a bottle of vodka."

Slowly, painfully, Henry eased himself out of his pajamas. The wounds Yaomauitl had inflicted in his sides were deep but comparatively narrow. He dabbed them with his rolled-up pajama top. Then when John came in with bandages and the bottle, he splashed them with Smirnoff to sterilize them. He winced and clenched his teeth as the liquor burned into his skin, but the stinging soon faded and he was able to bind his sides with the bandages.

John said, "I suppose you can't possibly explain any of this?"

Henry nodded toward the huddled figure of Yaomauitl. "I told you I had to fight the Devil. You didn't believe me, but there he is. And what's more, I've won."

"But why *you*, Henry? Why did *you* have to fight the Devil?"

"I don't know," Henry said philosophically. "I suppose one day everybody has to."

— EPILOGUE —

It was evening when six Mexican laborers slowly lowered the huge elmwood box back into the tomb in the floor of the church of San Hipolito. The tiled lid was lowered over the top and the priest sprinkled a crucifix of holy water over it. Henry, Gil, Susan and Lloyd stood a little distance away, watching the ceremony with a strange mixture of pride and regret.

"O Lord, keep this Devil securely entombed until the Day of Judgment shall dawn, when he shall be required to bow down before You and acknowledge Your holy supremacy. And protect all those who have incurred this Devil's wrath, and all those innocent instruments who may be used in the commission of his revenge, and may the world of men be kept free of his stain for ever and ever."

"Amen," said Henry.

"Amen," said Gil and Susan and Lloyd.

They went out into the sunlit porch, shook hands with the priest and gave money and cigarettes to the laborers. The laborers crossed themselves and then hurried off to get home before the sun went down. One of them muttered, *"Yaomauitl,"* and spat into the dirt.

The priest said, "You have saved the lives of many, my friends. You deserve our thanks."

Henry rubbed the back of his neck tiredly. "We deserve some sleep, I can tell you that much."

They left San Hipolito and drove down the dusty roadway. As they drove north, Gil asked, "What do we do now? Are we still Night Warriors or what?"

Henry glanced at him. "We're always going to be Night Warriors, you know that."

"But all the Devils are safely locked up now."

"That doesn't stop us from being Night Warriors."

Gil dropped Susan and Lloyd at home and then he and Henry went to Henry's cottage for a cup of coffee.

"Are you going to start drinking again?" Gil asked.

Henry came out of the kitchen wiping his hands on a tea towel. "I don't think so. I don't think I need it anymore."

They stayed up until two o'clock in the morning. At last Gil said, "I'd better get home. I have to work in the store tomorrow morning."

Henry looked at the empty coffee cups and nodded.

"You look tired," said Gil.

"I am," Henry agreed. "I just don't want to go to bed, that's all."

Gil said nothing but he knew what Henry was feeling. Henry said, "To tell you the truth, I'm afraid to dream."

GRAHAM MASTERTON

THE BEST IN HORROR